About the Authors

Marion Lennox is a country girl, born on an Australian dairy farm. She moved on, because the cows just weren't interested in her stories! Married to a 'very special doctor', she has also written under the name Trisha David. She's now stepped back from her 'other' career teaching statistics. Finally, she's figured what's important and discovered the joys of baths, romance and chocolate. Preferably all at the same time! Marion is an international award-winning author.

Helen Lacey grew up reading *Black Beauty*, *Anne of Green Gables* and *Little House on The Prairie*. These childhood classics inspired her to write her first book when she was seven years old, a story about a girl and her horse. She continued to write with the dream of one day being a published author and writing for Mills & Boon is the realisation of that dream. She loves creating stories about cowboys and horses and heroines who get their happily ever after.

Previously a teacher, pig farmer, and builder (among other things), **Meredith Webber** turned to writing medical romances when she decided she needed a new challenge. Once committed to giving it a 'real' go she joined writers' groups, attended conferences and read every book on writing she could find. Teaching a romance writing course helped her to analyse what she does, and she believes it has made her a better writer. Readers can email Meredith at: mem@onthenet.com.au

Australian Nights

December 2020
Longing for Summer

January 2021
Her Outback Fling

February 2021
Heat of the Night

March 2021
The Marriage Conquest

April 2021
Sun. Sea. Seduction.

May 2021
Waves of Desire

Australian Nights: Waves of Desire

MARION LENNOX

HELEN LACEY

MEREDITH WEBBER

MILLS & BOON

First Published in Great Britain 2021
by Mills & Boon, an imprint of HarperCollins*Publishers* Ltd,
1 London Bridge Street, London, SE1 9GF

www.harpercollins.co.uk

HarperCollins*Publishers*
1st Floor, Watermarque Building,
Ringsend Road, Dublin 4, Ireland

AUSTRALIAN NIGHTS: WAVES OF DESIRE © 2021
Harlequin Books S.A.

Waves of Temptation © 2014 Marion Lennox
Claiming His Brother's Baby © 2015 Helen Lacey
The One Man to Heal Her © 2015 Meredith Webber

ISBN: 978-0-263-30030-7

MIX
Paper from
responsible sources
FSC
www.fsc.org
FSC™ C007454

WAVES OF TEMPTATION

MARION LENNOX

For Marion

PROLOGUE

SHE WAS HUDDLED as far from the receptionist in the funeral parlour as she could get. Curled into one of the reception area's plush chairs, she looked tiny, almost in a foetal position.

Her dirty, surf-blonded hair was matted and in desperate need of a cut. Her cut-off-at-the-thigh jeans were frayed, her too-big windcheater looked like something out of a charity bin and her bare feet were filthy. Her huge grey eyes were ringed with great dark shadows.

In ordinary circumstances, Matt Eveldene would have cast her a glance of sympathy. He might even have tossed her a few coins to get a decent meal.

Not now. Not this girl.

He knew as much about her as he'd ever want to know. Her name was Kelly Myers. No. Kelly Eveldene. She was seventeen years old and she was his brother's widow.

She rose as she saw him. She must know what he'd been doing—identifying for himself that the body lying in the funeral home's back room was indeed his brother's.

'I...I'm sorry,' she faltered, but she didn't approach him. Maybe his face stopped her. It was impossible to conceal his anger. The white-hot rage.

The waste...

He'd just seen Jessie. His beloved big brother. Jess,

who'd laughed with him, teased him, protected him from the worst of their father's bullying.

Jessie, who was now dead, aged all of twenty-four. Jessie, who for some crazy, unfathomable reason had married this girl two weeks before he'd died.

'How can you be married to him?' he snapped. It was a dumb thing to ask, maybe even cruel, but it was all he could think of. He knew so little of what Jessie had been doing for the last few years. No one did. 'You're only seventeen.'

'He wanted to marry me,' she said, almost as a ghost might talk. As if her voice was coming from a long way away. 'He insisted. He even found my father and made him give permission. I guess…my father's still my guardian, even if—' She broke off and sat down again, hard, as if all the strength had gone out of her.

But Matt had no room left in his head for pity. Not now. He'd loved his big brother. Jess had been wild, free, bordering on manic, but he'd lit their lives. Or he'd lit Matt's. In the big old mansion overlooking Sydney's famous Bondi Beach, with its air of repressed elegance and propriety, and its walls echoing with his father's displeasure, it had always been Jess who'd brought in life.

But that life had been more and more out of control. The last time Matt had seen him he'd been in a rehabilitation ward in West Sydney. Jess had been twenty-two. Matt had been eighteen, confused and desperately frightened at the state of his big brother.

'I can't go back home, Matt,' Jess had told him. 'I know what Dad thinks of me and it always makes it worse. The black dog…depression…well, when you're older maybe you'll understand what it is. When I get out of here I'm heading overseas. Following the surf. The surf gets me out of my head like nothing else can. If I'm to stay off the drugs, that's what I need.'

What had followed then had been two years of intermittent postcards, the occasional press clipping of minor success in surf competitions, and demands that his parents didn't try and contact him until he'd 'found' himself.

Had he found himself now, on a slab in a Hawaiian mortuary? Jess... He thought back to the last time he'd seen his brother, as a recovering addict. Recovery had been for nothing, and now he was facing this girl who was calling herself Jessie's wife.

His anger was almost uncontrollable. He wanted to haul up her sleeves to expose the tracks of the inevitable drug use, and then hurl her as far as he could throw her.

Somehow he held himself still. He daren't unleash his fury.

'He wanted to be cremated,' the girl whispered. 'He wants his ashes scattered off Diamond Head, when the surf's at its best. At sunset. He has friends...'

Matt bet he did. More like this girl. This...

No. He wasn't going to say it. He wasn't going to think it.

Married! His father was right—he needed to pay the money and get rid of her, fast. If his mother knew of her existence, she might even want to bring her home, and then the whole sad round would start again. *'Please go to rehab... Please get help. Please...'*

He was too young to face this. He was twenty years old but he felt barely more than a child. His father should be here, to vent his anger, to do what he'd ordered Matt to do. Matt felt sick and weary and helpless.

'Can you afford cremation?' he demanded. The girl—Kelly—shook her head. Her grey eyes were direct and honest, surprising him with their candour.

'No,' she replied, her voice as bleak as the death that surrounded them. 'I hoped... I hope you might help me.'

In what universe could he help a woman who'd watched his brother self-destruct? Even if she looked…

No, he told himself. Don't think about how she looks. Just get this over and get out of here.

'I'm taking my brother home,' he told her. 'My parents will bury him in Sydney.'

'Please—'

'No.' The sight of his brother's body was so recent and so raw he could barely speak. Dear God, Jess… He needed to be alone. He felt like the world was closing in on him, suffocating. How could his father demand this of him? This was killing him.

Maybe his father was punishing him, too. Punishing him for loving his big brother?

Enough. He had to leave. He hauled a chequebook from his jacket and started writing.

The girl sank back down into her chair, tucking her feet back under her, assuming once again that position of defence. Her eyes became blank.

The cheque written, he handed it to her. Or tried to. She didn't put out her hand and he was forced to drop it onto her grubby knee.

'My father had an insurance policy in my brother's name,' he said, struggling to hold back his distress. 'Even though we doubt the validity of your marriage, my father acknowledges that you may have a claim on it. This pre-empts that claim. This is the total value of the insurance policy, given to you on the condition that you make no contact with my parents, that you never attempt to tell my mother that Jess was married, that you keep yourself out of our lives, now and for ever. Is that clear?'

She didn't pick up the cheque. 'I would like to write to your mother,' she whispered.

'I can think of a hundred reasons why you shouldn't contact my mother,' he said grimly. 'The top one being she has had heartbreak enough and doesn't need to be lumbered with the mess you've made of your life as well. My father has decided not to tell her about the marriage and I understand why.'

She closed her eyes as if he'd struck her, and he found his fury fading.

This was unfair, he conceded. This girl was a mess, but, then, Jessie's life had been a mess, too. He didn't need to vent his grief solely on her—but he had to get out of there.

'Use the cheque,' he said. 'Get a life.'

'I don't want your cheque.'

'It's your cheque,' he said, anger surging again. 'It's nothing to do with me. All I want is for you—his *widow*—' and he gave the word his father's inflection, the inflection it deserved '—to sign the release for his body. Let me take him home.'

'He wouldn't have wanted—'

'He's dead,' he said flatly. 'We need to bury him. Surely my mother has rights, too.'

Her fingers had been clenched on her knees. Slowly they unclenched, but then, suddenly, she bent forward, holding her stomach, and her face lost any trace of remaining colour.

Shocked, he stooped, ready to catch her if she slumped, concerned despite himself, but in seconds she had herself under control again. And when she unbent and stared straight at him, she was controlled. Her eyes, barely twelve inches from his, were suddenly icy.

'Take him home, then. Give him to his mother.'

'Thank you.'

'I don't want your thanks. I want you to go away.'

Which fitted exactly with how he was feeling.

'Then we never need to see each other again. I wish you luck, Miss Myers,' he said stiffly. Dear God, he sounded like his father. He no longer felt like a child. He felt a hundred.

'I'm Kelly Eveldene.' It was a flash of unexpected fire and venom. 'I'm Mrs Eveldene to you. I'm Mrs Eveldene to the world."

'But not to my parents.'

'No,' she said, and she subsided again into misery. 'Jess wouldn't have wanted his mother hurt more than she has been. If you don't want to tell her, then don't.' Her face crumpled and he fought a crazy, irrational impulse to take her into his arms, to hold her, to comfort her as one might comfort a wounded child.

But this was no child. This girl was part of the group that had destroyed his brother. Drugs, surf, drugs, surf… It had been that way since Matt could remember.

Get out of here fast, he told himself. This girl has nothing to do with you. The cheque absolves you from all responsibility.

Wasn't that what his father had said?

'Sign the papers,' he told her roughly, rising to his feet with deliberation. 'And don't shoot the entire value of that cheque up your arm.'

She met his eyes again at that, and once again he saw fire.

'Go back to Australia,' she said flatly. 'I can see why Jessie ran.'

'It's nothing to do—'

'I'm not listening,' she snapped. 'I'll sign your papers. Go.'

Kelly sat where she was for a long time after Matt had left. The receptionist would like her gone. She could understand that, but she was the widow of the deceased. The funeral home would be repatriating the body to Australia. It'd be a nice little earner. It behoved the receptionist to be courteous, even if Kelly was messing with the décor.

She needed a wash. She conceded that, too. More, she needed a change of clothes, a feed and a sleep. About a month's sleep.

She was so tired she could scarcely move.

So tired...

The last few days had been appalling. She'd known Jess's depression had deepened but not this much, never this much. Still, when he'd disappeared she'd feared the worst, and the confirmation had been a nightmare. And now... She'd sat in this place waiting for so long...

Not for him, though. For his father. She hadn't expected a man who was scarcely older than she was.

Matt Eveldene. What sort of a name was Eveldene anyway?

A new one. She stared at the bright new ring on her finger, put there by Jess only weeks ago. 'You'll be safe now,' he'd told her. 'It's all I can do, but it should protect you.'

She'd known he was ill. She shouldn't have married him, but she'd been terrified, and he'd held her and she'd clung. But she hadn't been able to cling hard enough, and here she was, in this nightmare of a place.

She'd been here for almost twenty-four hours, waiting for whoever came as the representative of Jess's family. She knew they'd have to come here.

She had to ask.

'If ever something happens, will you scatter my ashes out to sea, babe?' Jess had asked her. Had that only been a week ago? It seemed like a year.

She'd failed at that, too. Matt had simply overridden her.

Like father, like son? Jess had told her of his bully of a father. She'd been gearing herself up to face Henry Eveldene, but Matt's arrival in his father's stead had thrown her.

She'd failed.

'I'm sorry,' she said to the closed door behind which Jessie's body lay. 'I'm so sorry, Jess.'

There was nothing more she could do.

She rose and took a deep breath, trying to figure how to find the strength to walk outside, catch a bus, get away from this place of death. Nausea swept over her again but she shoved it away. She didn't have the energy to be sick.

'Mrs Eveldene?' The receptionist's voice made her pause.

'Yes?' It was so hard to make her voice work.

'You've dropped your cheque,' the girl said. She walked out from behind her desk, stooped to retrieve it and handed it to her. As she did, she checked it, and her eyes widened.

'Wow,' she said. 'You wouldn't want to lose this, would you?'

Matt stood outside the funeral parlour, dug his hands deep into his pockets and stood absolutely still, waiting for the waves of shock and grief to subside. The image of Jess was burned on his retinas. His beautiful, adored big brother. His Jess, wasted, cold and dead on a mortuary slab.

He felt sick to the core. The anger inside him was building and building, but he knew deep down that it was only a way to deflect grief.

If he let his anger take hold he'd walk right back in there, pick up that piece of flotsam and shake her till her teeth rattled, but it would do no good at all. For that was all she was, a piece of detritus picked up somewhere along Jessie's useless mess of a life.

What a sickening waste.

But suddenly he found himself thinking of the girl inside, of those huge, desperate eyes. Another life heading for nothing.

But those eyes…that flash of anger…

That was more than waste, he thought. There was something that Jess had loved, even a kind of beauty, and, underneath the anger, part of him could see it.

He could turn around and try and help.

Yeah, like he'd tried to help with Jess. Useless, useless, useless.

He'd given her money to survive. 'Don't waste it all,' he found himself saying out loud, to no one, to the girl inside, to the bright Hawaiian sun. But it was a forlorn hope, as his hopes for Jessie had always been forlorn.

Enough. It was time to move forward. It was time to forget the waif-like beauty of the girl inside this nightmare of a place. It was time to accompany his brother's body home for burial.

It was time to get on with the rest of his life.

CHAPTER ONE

SHE HAD THE best job in the world—except right now.

Dr Kelly Eveldene was the physician in charge of the International Surf Pro-Tour. For the last four years she'd been head of the medical team that travelled with the world's top surfers. She was competent, she was popular, she understood the lingo, and she knew so many of the oldtimer surfers that the job suited her exactly.

There were a couple of downsides. This year the pro tournament had moved to Australia for the world championships. She wasn't happy about coming to Australia, but Australia was big. The other Eveldenes lived in Sydney and the surf championship was to be held on the Gold Coast in Queensland. Her chances of running into...anybody were minuscule.

She'd done the research now. Henry Eveldene—her ex-father-in-law—was a business tycoon, rich beyond belief, and Eveldene was an uncommon name. Still, surely the presence in the country of a couple of inconspicuous people with similar names wouldn't come to his attention.

Her other quibble was that Jess was competing this year, his first time out of juniors. He was seventeen years old, surf mad and as skilled as his father before him. She couldn't hold him back and she didn't want to try. Her son was awesome. But now, at this level, with the surf so big and Jess trying so hard, she had qualms.

She had qualms right now.

She was in the judging tent on the headland, as she always was during competition. There were paramedics on jet skis close to the beach, ready for anything that happened in the surf. In the event of an accident she'd be on the beach in seconds, ready to take charge as soon as casualties were brought in. If it looked like a head or spinal injury—and after long experience with the surf she could pretty much tell from seeing the impact what to expect—she'd be out there with the paramedics, organising spinal boards from the jet ski, binding open wounds so they didn't bleed out in the water, even doing resuscitation if it was needed.

The job had its grim moments, but at this professional level she was seldom needed for high drama. What she dealt with mostly were cuts, bruises, rashes and sunburn, plus the chance to combine her medicine with the surfing she loved. It was a great job.

But now Jess was competing and her heart was in her mouth.

He had thirty minutes to show the judges what he could do. The first wave he'd caught had shown promise but had failed to deliver. It hadn't given him a chance to show his skills. He'd be marked down and he knew it. He hit the shallows, flagged down an official jet ski and was towed straight out again.

Then there was an interminable ten minutes when the swell refused to co-operate, when nothing happened, when he lay on his board in the sun while the clock ticked down, down. Then, finally, magically, a long, low swell built from the north-east, building fast, and Kelly saw her son's body tense in anticipation.

Please…

She should be impartial. She was an official, for heaven's sake.

But she wasn't impartial. She wasn't a judge. For this moment she wasn't even Dr Eveldene. She was Jessie's mother and nothing else mattered.

He'd caught it. The wave was building behind him, swelling with a force that promised a long, cresting ride. The perfect wave? He rode to the lip and crested down, swooped, spun, climbed high again.

But...but...

There was another wave cresting in from the south-east. The surfers called this type of wave a rogue, a swell that cut across the magic wave that had seemed perfect for the best of the rides.

Jess wouldn't be able to see it, Kelly thought in dismay, but maybe it wouldn't matter. Maybe his wave would peak and subside before it was interfered with. And even the waves crashed together, surely he'd done enough now to progress through to the next stage.

But then...

Someone else was on the rogue wave.

The surf had been cleared for the competition. No one had the right to cut across a competitor's wave. Only the competitors themselves were in the catching zone—everyone else was excluded. But a pod of enthusiastic juniors had set themselves up south of the exclusion zone, lying far out, hoping to get a better view of the surfer pros. This must be one of those kids, finding a huge swell behind him, unable to resist catching it, too much of a rookie—a grommet—to see that it would take him straight into a competition wave.

Uh-oh. Uh-oh, uh-oh, uh-oh.

The judges were on their feet. 'Swing off. Get off,' the judge beside Kelly roared. His voice went straight into the loudspeaker and out over the beach but the surfers were too far out, too intent on their waves…

Jess was in the green room, the perfect turquoise curve of water. He'd be flying, Kelly knew, awed that he'd caught such a perfect wave at such a time, intent on showing every ounce of skill he possessed. He'd be totally unaware that right behind…

No. Not right behind. The waves thumped into each other with a mighty crest of white foam. The grommet's surfboard flew as high as his leg rope allowed, straight up and then crashing down.

She couldn't see Jess. *She couldn't see Jess.*

That impact, at that speed…

'Kelly, go,' the judge beside her yelled, and she went, but not with professional speed. Faster.

This was no doctor heading out into the waves to see what two surfers had done to themselves.

This was Jessie's mother and she was terrified.

'Matt, you're needed in Emergency, stat. Leg fracture, limited, intermittent blood supply. If we're to save the leg we need to move fast.'

It was the end of a lazy Tuesday afternoon. Matt Eveldene, Gold Coast Central Hospital's orthopaedic surgeon, had had an extraordinarily slack day. The weather was fabulous, the sea was glistening and some of the best surfers in the world were surfing their hearts out three blocks from the hospital.

Matt had strolled across to the esplanade at lunchtime. He'd watched for a little while, admiring their skill but wondering how many of these youngsters were putting their futures at risk while they pushed themselves to their limits. No one else seemed to be thinking that. They were all just entranced with the surfers.

Even his patients seemed to have put their ills on hold

today. He'd done a full theatre list this morning, but almost half his afternoon's outpatient list had cancelled. He'd been considering going home early.

Not now. Beth, the admitting officer in Accident and Emergency, didn't call him unless there was genuine need. She met him as the lift opened.

'Two boys,' Beth told him, falling in beside him, walking fast, using this time to get him up to speed. 'They're surfers who hit each other mid-ride. The youngest is a local, fourteen years old, concussion and query broken arm. It's the other I'm worrying about. Seventeen, American, part of the competition. Compound fracture of the femoral shaft, and I suspect a compromised blood supply. I've called Caroline—she's on her way.'

Caroline Isram was their vascular surgeon but Matt knew she was still in Theatre.

'He'll need both your skills if we're going to save the leg,' Beth said. 'Oh, and, Matt?'

'Yeah?'

'Coincidence or not? His surname's Eveldene.'

'Coincidence. I don't know any seventeen-year-old surfer.'

Kelly was seated by the bed in Cubicle Five, holding Jess's hand. It said a lot for how badly he was hurt that he let her.

He had enough painkillers on board to be making him drowsy but he was still hurting. She was holding his hand tightly, willing him to stay still. The colour of his leg was waxing and waning. She'd done everything she could to align his leg but the blood supply was compromised.

Dear God, let there be skilled surgeons in this hospital. Dear God, hurry.

'They say the orthopaedic surgeon's on his way,' she whispered. 'The emergency doctor, Beth, says he's the best in Australia. He'll set your leg and you'll be good as new.' *Please.*

'But I'll miss the championships,' Jess moaned, refusing to be comforted.

The championships were the least of their problems, Kelly thought grimly. There was a real risk he'd lose a lot more. Please, let this guy be good.

And then the curtains opened and her appalling day got even worse.

The last time Matt had seen his brother alive Jess had been in drug rehab. He'd looked thin, frightened and totally washed out.

The kid on the trolley when Matt hauled back the curtain was...Jess.

For a moment he couldn't move. He stared down at the bed and Jessie's eyes gazed back at him. The kid's damp hair, sun-bleached, blond and tangled, was spreadeagled on the pillow around him. His green eyes were wide with pain. His nose and his lips showed traces of white zinc, but the freckles underneath were all Jessie's.

It was all Matt could do not to buckle.

Ghosts didn't exist.

They must. This was Jessie.

'This is Mr Eveldene, our chief orthopaedic surgeon,' Beth was telling the kid brightly. The situation was urgent, they all knew it, but Beth was taking a moment to reassure and to settle the teenager. 'Matt, this is Jessie Eveldene. He has the same surname as yours, isn't that a coincidence? Jess is from Hawaii, part of the pro-surf circuit, and he's seventeen. And this is his mum, Kelly. Kelly's not your normal spectator mum. She was Jessie's treating doctor on the beach. She's established circulation, she's put the leg in a long leg splint and she's given initial pain relief.'

He was having trouble hearing. His head was reeling.

What were the odds of a kid called Jessie Eveldene turning up in his hospital? What were the odds such a kid would look like Jess?

Sure, this kid was a surfer and all surfers had similar characteristics. Bleached hair. Zinc on their faces. But… but…

The kid's green eyes were Jessie's eyes, and they were looking at him as Jess's had looked that last time.

Make the pain go away.

Focus on medicine, he told himself harshly. This wasn't his older brother. This was a kid with a compromised blood supply. He flipped the sheet over the leg cradle and it was all he could do not to wince. The undamaged foot was colourless. He touched the ankle, searching for a pulse. Intermittent. Dangerously weak.

'We took X-rays on the way in,' Beth told him. 'Comminuted fracture. That means there's more than one break across the leg,' she said, for Jessie's benefit. 'Matt, he needs your skill.'

He did. The leg was a mess. The compound fracture had been roughly splinted into position but he could see how it had shattered. Splinters of bone were protruding from the broken skin.

'Blood flow was compromised on impact,' Beth said softly. 'Luckily Jess has one awesome mum. It seems Kelly was on duty as surf doctor. She went out on a jet ski and got Jess's leg aligned almost before they reached the shore. The time completely without blood couldn't have been more than a few minutes.'

So it was possible he'd keep his leg. Thanks to this woman.

He glanced at her again.

Kelly?

It was impossible to reconcile this woman with the

Kelly he'd met so briefly all those years ago. This couldn't possibly be her.

But then her eyes met his. Behind her eyes he saw pain and distress, but also…a hint of steel.

Kelly. A woman he'd blamed…

'Well done,' he said briefly, because that was all he could think of to say. Then he turned back to the boy. If they had a chance of keeping this leg, he had to move fast. 'Beth, we need an ultrasound, right away. Tell Caroline this is priority. This blood flow seems fragile. Jess…' He had to force himself to say the name. 'Jess, you've made a dog's breakfast of this leg.'

'Dog's breakfast?' Jess queried cautiously.

'Dog's breakfast,' Matt repeated, and summoned a grin. 'Sorry, I forgot you were a foreigner.' Gruesome humour often helped when treating teens, and he needed it now. The anaesthetist needed Jess settled—and he needed to settle himself. 'It's slang. A working dog's breakfast is usually a mess of leftovers. That's what this looks like.'

'Ugh,' Jess said, and Matt firmed his grin.

'Exactly. We need to pin it back together and make sure enough blood gets through to your toes. That means surgery, straight away.'

The kid's sense of humour had been caught despite the pain. 'Cool…cool description,' he said bravely. 'Do you reckon someone could take a picture so I can put it on Facebook? My mates will think "dog's breakfast" is sick.'

'Sure,' Beth said easily. She'd stepped back to snap orders into her phone but she resurfaced to smile. Beth had teenage boys of her own. Priority one, Facebook. Priority two, fixing a leg. She waved her phone. 'I'll snap it now if that's okay with your mum. But then it's Theatre to make you beautiful again.'

'If your mother agrees,' Matt said.

Jess's mother. Kelly. Doctor in charge at the world surf championships.

Kelly Eveldene. The undernourished waif curled up in a funeral director's parlour eighteen years ago?

The images didn't mesh and Matt didn't have time to get his head around it. The boy's leg was dreadfully fractured, the blood supply had already been compromised and any minute a sliver of bone could compromise it again. Or shift and slice into an artery.

'You have my permission,' Kelly said, her voice not quite steady. 'If it's okay with you, Jessie?'

What kind of mother referred to her kid for such a decision? But Kelly really was deferring. She had hold of her son's hand, waiting for his decision.

Jessie. This was doing his head in.

Maybe he should pull away; haul in a colleague. Could he be impersonal?

Of course he could. He had to be. To refer to another surgeon would mean a two-hour transfer to Brisbane.

No. Once he was in Theatre this would be an intricate jigsaw of shattered bone and nothing else would matter. He could ignore personal confusion. He could be professional.

'Matt, Jessie's mother is Dr Kelly Eveldene,' Beth was saying. 'She's an emergency physician trained in Hawaii.'

'Mr Eveldene and I have met before,' the woman said, and Matt's world grew even more confused.

'So it's not a coincidence?' Beth said. 'Matt…'

Enough. Talking had to stop. History had to take a back seat. These toes were too cool.

'Jess, we need to get you to surgery now,' he told the boy. There was no way to sugar-coat this. 'Your leg's kinking at an angle that's threatening to cut off blood supply. Caroline Isram is our vascular surgeon and she's on her way. Together we have every chance of fixing this. Do we have your permission to operate? And your mother's?'

Finally, he turned to face her.

Kelly Eveldene had been a half-starved drug addict who'd been with his brother when he'd died. This was not Kelly Eveldene. This was a competent-looking woman, five feet six or seven tall, clear, grey eyes, clear skin, shiny chestnut curls caught back in a casual wispy knot, quality jeans, crisp white T-shirt and an official surf tour lanyard on a cord round her neck saying, 'Dr Kelly Eveldene. Pro Surf Medical Director.'

Mr Eveldene and I have met before.

'Are you a long-lost relative?' Jess asked, almost shyly. 'I mean, Eveldene's not that common a name.'

'I think I must be,' Matt said, purposely not meeting Kelly's eyes. 'But we can figure that out after the operation. If you agree to the procedure.'

'Dr Beth says you're good.'

'I'm good.' No place here for false modesty.

'And you'll fix my leg so I can keep surfing?'

Something wrenched in him at that. Suddenly he heard Jess, long ago, yelling at his father over the breakfast table. 'All I want to do is surf. Don't you understand?' And then saw Jessie arriving home from school that night, and finding his board in the backyard, hacked into a thousand pieces.

But now wasn't the time for remembering. Now wasn't the time to be even a fraction as judgmental as his father had been.

'I'll do my best,' he said, holding Jessie's gaze even though it felt like it was tearing him apart to do so. 'Jess, I won't lie to you—this is a really bad break, but if you let us operate now I think you'll have every chance of hanging ten or whatever you do for as long as you want.'

'Thank you,' Jess said simply, and squeezed his mother's hand. 'Go for it. But take a picture for Facebook first.'

* * *

She'd been a doctor now for nine years, but she'd never sat on this side of the theatre doors. She'd never known how hard the waiting would be. Her Jess was on the operating table, his future in the hands of one Matt Eveldene.

Kelly had trained in emergency medicine but surfing had been her childhood, so when she'd qualified, she'd returned. Her surfing friends were those who'd supported her when she'd needed them most, so it was natural that she be drawn back to their world. She'd seen enough wipe-outs to know how much a doctor at the scene could help. Even before she'd qualified she'd been pushing to have a permanent doctor at the professional championships, and aiming for that position after qualification had seemed a natural fit.

But she'd spent time in hospitals in training, and she'd assisted time and time again when bad things had happened to surfers. She knew first-hand that doctors weren't miracle workers.

So now she was staring at the doors, willing them to open. It had been more than three hours. Surely soon…

How would Jess cope if he was left with residual weakness? Or with losing his leg entirely? It didn't bear thinking about. Surfing wasn't his whole life but it was enough. It'd break his heart.

And Matt Eveldene was operating. What bad fairy was responsible for him being orthopaedic surgeon at the very place Jess had had his accident? Wasn't he supposed to still be in Sydney with his appalling family? If she'd known he was here she would never have come.

Had she broken her promise by being here?

You keep yourself out of our lives, now and for ever.

She'd cashed the cheque and that had meant acceptance of his terms. The cheque had been Jessie's insurance, though. Her husband's insurance. Surely a promise couldn't negate that.

The cheque had saved her life. No, she thought savagely. Her Jess had saved her life. Her husband. Her lovely, sunbleached surfer who'd picked her up when she'd been at rock bottom, who'd held her, who'd made her feel safe for the first time. Who'd had demons of his own but who'd faced them with courage and with honour.

'We'll get through this together, babe,' he'd told her. 'The crap hand you've been dealt…my black dog… We'll face them both down.'

But the black dog had been too big, too savage, and in the end she hadn't been able to love him enough to keep it at bay. The night he'd died…

Enough. Don't go there. In a few minutes she'd have to face his brother, and maybe she would have to go there again, but only briefly, only as long as it took to explain that she hadn't broken her promise deliberately. She and Jess would move out of his life as soon as possible, and they'd never return.

It took the combined skill of Matt Eveldene, a vascular surgeon, an anaesthetist and a team of four skilled nurses to save Jessie's leg.

'Whoever treated it on the beach knew what they were doing,' Caroline muttered. Gold Coast Central's vascular surgeon was in her late fifties, grim and dour at the best of times. Praise was not lightly given. 'This artery's been so badly damaged I have no idea how blood was getting through.'

She went back to doing what she was doing, arterial grafting, slow, meticulous work that meant all the difference between the leg functioning again or not. Matt was working as her assistant right now, removing shattered slivers of bone, waiting until the blood supply was fully established before he moved in to restore the leg's strength and function.

If Caroline got it right, if he could managed to fuse the leg to give it the right length, if there'd not been too much tissue damage, then the kid might...

Not the kid. Jessie.

The thought did his head in.

'I think we're fine here,' Caroline growled. 'Decent colour. Decent pulse. He's all yours, Matt.'

But as Matt moved in to take control he knew it was no such thing.

This kid wasn't his at all.

The doors swung open and Matt Eveldene was in front of her. He looked professional, a surgeon in theatre scrubs, hauling down his mask, pushing his cap wearily from his thatch of thick, black hair. How did he have black hair when Jessie's had been almost blond? Kelly wondered absent-mindedly. He was bigger than Jess, too. Stronger boned, somehow...harsher, but she could still see the resemblance. As she could see the resemblance to her son.

This man was Jessie's uncle. Family?

No. Her family was her son. No one else in the world qualified.

'It went well,' he said curtly from the door, and she felt her blood rush away from her face. She'd half risen but now she sat again, hard. He looked at her for a moment and then came across to sit beside her. Doctor deciding to treat her as a mother? Okay, she thought. She could deal with this, and surely it was better than last time. Better than brother treating her as a drug-addicted whore.

The operation had gone well. She should ask more. She couldn't.

There was only silence.

There was no one else in the small theatre waiting room. Only this man and her.

There were so many emotions running rampant in her mind that she didn't have a clue what to do with them.

'Define...define "well",' she managed, and was inordinately proud of herself that she'd managed that.

'Caroline had to graft to repair the artery,' he told her. 'But she's happy with the result. We have steady pulse, normal flow. Then I've used a titanium rod. You know about intramedullary nailing? There wasn't enough bone structure left to repair any other way. But the breaks were above the knee and below the hip—well clear—so we've been able to use just the one rod and no plates. He has a couple of nasty gashes—well, you saw them. Because the bone fragments broke the skin we need to be extra-cautious about infection. Also Caroline's wary of clotting. He'll spend maybe a week in hospital until we're sure the blood flow stays steady. After that, rest and rehabilitation in a controlled environment where we know he can't do further damage. You know this'll be a long haul.'

'It'll break his heart,' Kelly whispered. 'It's going to be six months before he's back on a surfboard.'

'Six months is hardly a lifetime,' Matt said, maybe more harshly than he should have. 'He'll have some interesting scars but long term nothing a surfer won't brag about. Depending on his growth—at seventeen there may or may not be growth to come—we may need to organise an extension down the track but the rod itself can be extended. Unless he grows a foot he should be fine.'

So he'd still be able to surf. She hadn't realised quite how frightened she'd been. She felt her body sag. Matt made a move as if to put a hand on her shoulder—and then he pulled away.

He would have touched her if she'd been a normal parent, she thought. He would have offered comfort.

Not to her.

It didn't matter. He'd done what she'd most needed him to do and that was enough.

She made to rise, but his hand did come out then, did touch her shoulder, but it wasn't comfort he was giving. He was pressing her down. Insisting she stay.

'We need to talk,' he said. 'I believe I deserve an explanation.'

She stilled. Deserve. *Deserve*!

'In what universe could you possibly deserve anything from me?' she managed.

'Jessie has a son!'

'So?'

'So my brother has fathered a child. My parents are grandparents. Don't you think we deserved to know?'

'I'm remembering a conversation,' she snapped, and the lethargy and shock of the last few hours were suddenly on the back burner. Words thrown at her over eighteen years ago were still vividly remembered. 'How could I not remember? Make no contact with your parents. Do not write. Never tell your mother Jess and I were married. Keep myself out of your lives, now and for ever. You said there were a hundred reasons why I should never contact you. You didn't give me one exception.'

'If you'd told me you were pregnant—'

'As I recall,' she managed, and it hurt to get the words out, 'you didn't want to know one single thing about me. Everything about me repelled you—I could see it on your face.'

'You were a drug addict.'

She took a deep breath, fighting for control. 'Really?' she asked, managing to keep her voice steady. 'Is that right? A drug addict? You figured that out all by yourself. On what evidence?'

He paused, raking his long, surgeon's fingers through

his thatch of wavy, black hair. The gesture bought him some time and it made Kelly pause. Her anger faded, just a little.

The present flooded back. This man had saved her son's leg. Maybe she needed to cut him some slack.

But it seemed slack wasn't necessary. He'd gone past some personal boundary and was drawing back.

'No,' he said. 'I made…I made assumptions when Jess died. I know now that at least some of them were wrong.'

Her anger had faded to bitterness. 'You got the autopsy report, huh?'

'You need to realise the last time I saw Jessie alive he was in drug rehab.'

'That was years before he died.'

'He told you about it?'

'Jess was my husband,' she snapped. 'Of course he told me.'

'You were seventeen!'

'And needy. Jess was twenty-four and needy. We clung to each other.' She shook her head. 'Sorry, but I don't have to listen to this. You never wanted to know about me before, and you don't now. Thank you very much for saving my son's leg. I guess I'll see you over the next few days while he's in hospital but I'll steer clear as much as I can. I need to go back to our hotel and get Jess's things, but I want to see him first. Is he awake?'

'Give him a while. We put him pretty deeply under.' He raked his hair again, looking as if he was searching for something to say. Anything. And finally it came.

'You weren't on drugs?'

'You know,' she said, quite mildly, 'years ago I wanted to hit you. I was too exhausted to hit you then, too emotionally overwrought, too wrecked. Now I'm finding I want to hit you all over again. If it wasn't for what you've just done for Jess, I would.'

'You looked—'

'I looked like my husband had just died.' Her voice grew softer, dangerously so. 'I was seventeen. I was twelve weeks pregnant and I'd sat by Jess's bedside for twenty-four hours while he lost his fight to live. Then I'd sat in the waiting room at the funeral home, waiting for you, hour upon endless hour, because I thought that it'd be his father who'd come to get him and I didn't think a message to contact me would work. I couldn't risk missing him. And then you walked in instead, and I thought, yes, Matt's come in his father's stead and it'll be okay, because Jess had told me how much he loved you. All I asked was for what Jess wanted, but you walked all over me, as if I was a piece of pond scum. And now...now you're still telling me I looked like a drug addict?'

There was a long silence. She didn't know where to go with this. She'd bottled up these emotions for years and she'd never thought she'd get a chance to say them.

Somewhere in Sydney, in a family vault, lay Jess's ashes. She'd failed the only thing Jess had ever asked of her. She hadn't stood up to his family.

She should hate this man. Maybe she did, but he was looking shocked and sick, and she felt...she felt...

Like she couldn't afford to feel.

'I'll grab Jess's things and bring them back,' she said, deciding brisk and efficient was the way to go. 'It's only ten minutes' walk to the hotel. I should be back before he's properly awake. The rest of the surfers will be worried, too. There are a lot of people who love my Jess—practically family. Thank you for your help this afternoon, Matt Eveldene, but goodbye. I don't think there's single thing left that we need to talk about.'

There was. She knew there was. She walked down the hill from the hospital to the string of beachside hotels where most of the surfers were staying and she knew this wouldn't end here.

Why did Jess look so much like his father? Why had she called him Jess?

Why had she kept her husband's name?

'Because it was all I had of him,' she said out loud, and in truth she loved it that her son was called Jessie, she loved that he loved surfing, she loved that when she looked at him she could see his father.

But not if it meant…loss?

Her husband had told her about his family, his father in particular. 'He controls everything, Kelly. It's his way or no way. He loathed my surfing. He loathed everything that gave me pleasure, and when I got sick he labelled me a weakling. Depression? Snap out of it, he told me, over and over. Pull yourself together. I couldn't cope. That's why I hit the drugs that first time.'

She knew as much as she ever wanted to know about Jessie's father—but he'd also told her about his brother, Matt.

'He's the only good thing about my family, Kell. If anything ever happens to me, go to him. He'll help you.'

Well, he had helped her, Kelly thought grimly. She thought of the insurance cheque. It had been tossed at her in anger but she owed everything to it.

'So Jess might have been wrong about him being a nice guy, but he's had his uses,' she told herself. 'Now forget about him. You have enough to worry about without past history. For instance, the surf tour's moving on. You'll need to take leave. You'll need a place to stay, and you'll need to figure a way to stop Jess's heart from breaking when he learns that he's no longer part of the surf circuit.'

He felt like he'd been hit with a sledgehammer.

Matt walked up to the hospital rooftop, to the cafeteria

area that looked out over the ocean. He leant on the rail overlooking the amazing view, trying to let the enormity of what had just happened sink in.

Jessie had a son. Somehow, his brother wasn't dead.

Okay, that was a crazy thing to think but right now that was how it seemed. He knew if he phoned his mother— 'You have a grandson. He's named Jess and he looks just like our Jessie'—his mother would be on the next plane. She'd broken her heart when Jess had died, and she'd never got over it. Always a doormat to her bully of a husband, she'd faded into silent misery. Matt worried about her, but not enough to stay in Sydney, not enough to stay near his father.

Should he tell his mother? He must. But if he told his mother, his father would know, too. There was the rub. Could you fight for custody of a seventeen-year-old boy? No, Matt thought, but knowing his father, he'd try. Or, worse, he'd let loose the anger he still carried toward his older son and unleash it on Kelly and his grandson.

The thought of his father bullying Kelly...

As he'd bullied her...

He thought back to the appalling funeral parlour scene and he felt ill.

He'd been a kid himself, a student. The call had come late at night; Jess had had a fall and died. Yes, it seemed to be suicide. His body was at a Hawaiian funeral home and a woman calling herself his wife was making the arrangements.

His father had exploded with grief and rage. 'Stupid, idiotic, surfer hop-head. You needn't think I'm heading off to that place to see him. You do it, boy. Go and get him, bring him home so his mother can bury him and there's an end to it.'

'They say he's married?'

'He's been off his head for years. If there's a marriage

get it annulled. We have more than enough evidence to say he was mentally incapable. And don't tell your mother. Just fix it.'

But Jess had never been mentally incapable. The depression that had dogged him since adolescence had been an illness, the same way cancer was an illness. Underneath the depression and, yes, the drugs when he'd been using, he'd still been Jess, the gentle, soft-spoken big brother Matt had loved.

He might have known he'd have married a woman of spirit.

But a seventeen-year-old?

He'd judged her back then because of her appearance and obvious desperation, but things were making horrible sense now.

All apart from the age. Surely seventeen was under-age for marriage in Hawaii? They'd have needed special permission.

Had they done it because Kelly had been pregnant?

These were questions Matt should have asked years ago, not now.

The questions had been there, though. He'd flown home with Jessie's body and the questions had rested unanswered in the back of his mind. The image of a girl curled in utter misery, of a cheque floating to the floor, of a desperation he'd done nothing to assuage, these images had stayed with him. The questions had nagged while he'd qualified as a doctor, while he'd got himself away from his domineering father, while he'd attempted his own marriage... While he'd come to terms with life, as Jessie never had. Just as Kelly had obviously come to terms with her life.

He remembered his relief when he'd found the cheque had been cashed. Now I don't need to feel guilty, he'd told himself. But the questions had stayed.

They had been answered now—almost. She'd used the cheque, but to what purpose?

To train herself in medicine?

To raise another surfer like Jess?

If his father found out... To have a grandson addicted to surfing...

Better not to tell him. Better to leave things as they were, just get this kid well and on his way.

But he looked so much like Jess...

So? He'd be in hospital for a week or so and then an outpatient for longer with rehab. He'd see him a lot. He had to get used to it.

And his mother?

Her image haunted him. In truth, her image had haunted him for years and now there was this new image juxtapositioned on the old.

Should the new image make the haunting go away?

A surf doctor. What sort of doctor was that?

What sort of woman was that?

A woman with spirit.

How could he know that?

He just...knew. There was that about her, an indefinable strength. A beauty that was far more than skin deep.

Beauty? He raked his hair again, thinking he wasn't making sense. He was too tired, too shocked to take it in. He needed to go home.

At the thought of his home he felt his tension ease. Home, the place he'd built with effort and with love. Home with his dogs and his books.

His house was the only place where he was at peace. His home mattered. He'd learned early and learned hard; people only complicated that peace.

He needed to go home now and put this woman and her son out of his head.

He needed to be alone.

CHAPTER TWO

THE SURF CHAMPIONSHIPS lasted for two more days and Kelly worked for both of them. There were gaps in the day when she could visit Jess, but she had to work for as long as she could. She needed the money.

The surfing community looked after its own, but there wasn't a lot they could do to help. They'd need to employ another doctor for the next round of the championships in New Zealand. As soon as Jess was well enough for Kelly to rejoin the tour, the position was hers again, but pro-surfing ran on the smell of a surf-waxed rag, and they couldn't afford to pay her for time off.

And she would not use the trust fund.

She needed to move from the hotel. One of the locals offered her a basic surfer's squat and she accepted with relief. She'd find a decent apartment when Jess was released from hospital but until then she'd live in her surf squat and focus on Jess's recovery.

From Jessie's charts and from information she drew from junior doctors, she could track Jessie's progress. There was therefore no need to talk to Matt Eveldene. The advantage of Matt being head of the orthopaedic ward was that where Matt went, students followed. She could always hear him coming so she could give Jess a quick hug and disappear.

'Here come the medical cavalry. It's time to make myself scarce.'

'He looks at me funny,' Jess said sleepily on the second day, and she hugged him again, feeling defensive about leaving him.

'Surgeons are a law unto themselves,' she said. 'If he only looks at you funny, you're getting off lightly. These guys spend their days looking inside people, not practising social skills.'

The surf tour moved on. She spent a couple of hours of her first free day moving into her dreary little apartment. Back at the hospital she found Jess awake and bored, so she spent an hour going over the results of the championship he'd missed out on, talking future tactics, as if those tactics might be useful next week instead of in six months.

Finally he went to sleep. What to do now? She knew how long rehabilitation would take. She had weeks and weeks of wondering what to do.

Okay, do what came next. Lunch. She slipped out to find some—and Matt was at the nurses' station.

Was he waiting for her? It looked like it. His hands were deep in the pockets of his gorgeous suit, he was talking to a nurse but he was watching Jess's door. As soon as he saw her, he broke off the conversation.

'Sorry, Jan,' he said to the nurse, 'but I need to speak to Mrs Eveldene.'

'That's Dr Eveldene,' she said as he approached, because her professional title suddenly seemed important. She needed a barrier between them, any barrier at all, and putting things on a professional level seemed the sensible way to achieve it. 'Do you need to discuss Jessie's treatment?'

'I want lunch,' he growled. 'There's a quiet place on the roof. We can buy sandwiches at the cafeteria. Come with me.'

'Say "please",' she said, weirdly belligerent, and he stared at her as if she was something from outer space.

But: 'Please,' he said at last, and she gave him a courteous nod. This man was in charge of her son's treatment. She did need to be...spoken to.

They bought their lunches, paid for separately at her insistence. He offered but she was brusque in her refusal. She followed him to a secluded corner of the rooftop, with chairs, tables and umbrellas for shade. She spent time unwrapping her sandwich—why was she so nervous?—but finally there was nothing left to do but face the conversation.

He spoke first, and it was nothing to do with her son's treatment. It was as if the words had to be dragged out of him.

'First, I need to apologise,' he said. As she frowned and made to speak, he held up his hands as if to ward off her words. 'Hear me out. Heaven knows, this needs to be said. Kelly, eighteen years ago I treated you as no human should ever treat another, especially, unforgivably, as you were my brother's wife. I accused you of all sorts of things that day. My only defence was that I was a kid myself. I was devastated by my brother's death but my assumptions about him—and about you—were not only cruel, they were wrong.'

'As in you assumed Jess was back using drugs,' she whispered. 'As you assumed I was the same. An addict.'

'I figured it out almost as soon as I got back to Australia,' he said, even more heavily. 'The autopsy results revealed not so much as an aspirin. I should have contacted you again, but by then I was back at university and it felt...' He shook his head. 'No. I don't know how it felt. I was stuck in a vortex of grief I didn't know how to deal with. Somehow it was easier to shove the autopsy results away as wrong. Somehow it seemed easier to blame drugs rather than—'

'Unhappiness?'

'Yes.'

'Jess was clinically depressed,' she said. 'You're a doctor. You know it's different. He wasn't just unhappy; he was ill.'

'No antidepressants showed up either.'

'He wouldn't touch antidepressants,' she said, not sure where this was going, not sure that she wanted to go with him. 'He'd fallen into addiction once and it terrified him. In all the time I knew him, he took nothing.'

'How long did you know him?'

She shouldn't say. She didn't owe this man an explanation, and her story hurt. But it was also Jessie's story. It hadn't been told and maybe…maybe Jess would want his brother to know.

'Get in touch with Matt if anything happens to me,' he'd said to her, more than once. *'He'll look after you.'*

If anything happens to me… He'd obviously been thinking suicide. It still played in her mind, and it was still unbearable. So many questions… The questions surrounded her, nightmares still.

But maybe she had to expose a little of that pain. Matt was waiting for her to speak, and after all these years his gaze was non-judgmental. He wanted to know.

Eighteen years ago he hadn't asked, and she'd hated him. But then he'd been young and shocked and grieving, she conceded, and shock could be forgiven.

Almost. There was still a part of her that was that cringing seventeen-year-old, remembering this man's fury.

'I met Jess when I was sixteen,' she said, forcing herself to sound like the grown-up that she was. 'And I was a mess. But not because of drugs. I was just…neglected. My father was interested in surf and booze and nothing else. My mother disappeared when I was four—at least, I think it was my mother; my father never seemed sure. It didn't matter. It was just the way things were. I was dragged up in the surfing community. There were good people who looked out for me, but they were itinerant and there were lots who weren't so good. But all of them came and went. I stayed.'

'It must have been a tough upbringing,' he said quietly, and she nodded.

'You could say that. And then, of course, I reached my teenage years. I matured late, thanks be, but finally at sixteen I became…female, instead of just a kid. Then things got harder. Unprotected and often homeless, camping as we often did, I became a target and my father was little use. I was a little wildcat, doing my best to defend myself, but it couldn't last. Then Jess arrived. He set up on the outskirts of the camp, seemingly intent on surfing and nothing else. I didn't think he'd even noticed us but there was an ugly scene one night when someone offered my father money. I remember someone grabbing me as if he owned me.'

'You were so alone.'

'I… Yes.'

'With no one?'

'No one who cared.'

'Kelly—'

'It was a long time ago,' she said, and she even smiled a little. 'You know, when you spoke then, you sounded just like Jess. Just as angry on my behalf. That night he appeared out of the dark, out of nowhere, and he was furious. I hit out—and Jess moved in before the guy could retaliate. He just…took over.'

'Jess was always bringing home strays,' Matt said. His instinctive anger seemed to have settled and his tone gentled. *Strays.* The word drifted in her mind. She knew no offence had been meant and none had been taken, because

that's exactly what she'd been. A stray. Living in temporary surf camps. Going to school when the surf camp had
been close enough or when her father had been capable
of taking her. Living hand to mouth, the only constant
being the surf.

But then there'd been Jess.

'He was the best surfer,' she said, pain fading as she
remembered the way he'd transformed her life. 'He'd only
just arrived but everyone there respected him. He was
also…large.' She eyed Matt's strongly built frame, his
height—six three or so—his instinctive anger on her behalf—and she remembered Jess. For some reason it made
her want to reach out and touch this man, comfort him,
take away the pain behind his eyes.

She could do no such thing.

'He told me he hadn't seen his family for years,' she
went on, trying to ignore the urge to comfort Matt. 'By the
time you saw his body the depression had left its mark. He
hadn't been eating for weeks. But imagine him as I first
saw him. He lived and breathed surfing. He was beautiful.
He was built like a tank. No one stood up to him—and yet
he stood up for me.'

'You became his lover?'

There was a moment's pause. She really didn't want to
go there, but she needed to tell it like it was. For Jessie's
sake. He'd been her hero, not some low-life who'd picked
up teenage girls.

'No,' she said at last. 'Believe it or not, I was sixteen
and that was how Jess treated me. Dad and I were living
in a rough beach shanty, but Dad left soon after Jess arrived, looking for better surf on the other side of the island. He came back every so often, but Jess built a lean-to
on the side of our hut and we stayed put. Jess said it was
to protect me and that's what he did. He surfed with me,
but it wasn't all fun. He pushed me to go to school. I'd

been going intermittently but Jess insisted I go every day. He gave me money for clothes. He stopped Dad...well, he kept me safe. He was my gorgeous big brother. But then the black dog got too much for him.'

'The depression.'

'He called it his black dog. He said that's what Winston Churchill called it and that's what it felt like. A great black dog, always shadowing him. He said it'd been shadowing him since he was a kid, something he was born with. He told me how his dad hated it, thought he was weak because of it. He told me about how'd he'd tried to escape with drugs when he was in his late teens, and what a mess that had been. I think that was a way of warning me, because drugs were everywhere in our scene. But Jess wouldn't touch them. Never again, he said, even near the end when the depression was so bad and I pleaded with him to get help. "They'll only give me pills," he said, "and I'm not going down that road again."'

'If I'd known...'

'Jess said you didn't want to know,' Kelly said gently. 'Jess said you and he were close, but after rehab... He knew that shocked you. After he got his life together and the surfing was helping, he said he sent you the airfare to come and have a holiday together during your university holidays, but you wouldn't come.'

Matt closed his eyes and she saw the pain wash over him. No. It was more than pain. Self-loathing.

'He'd come out of rehab and gone straight back to surfing,' Matt managed. 'I thought—'

'You know, surfing and drugs don't really mix,' she said gently. 'There are always the fringe dwellers, people like my dad who surf a bit but who love the sun-bleached lifestyle more than the skill itself. But to be a real surfer you're up at dawn, day after day. The sea demands absolute attention, absolute fitness. You need to work as Jess did—he did casual bricklaying to pay bills—but he surfed at dawn and then he was back at dusk to surf every night, falling into bed with every single part of him exhausted. Jess used the surf to drive away his demons and it mostly worked. He had no time for drugs. I swear he wasn't taking them. I swear.'

'I believe you,' Matt said heavily. 'Now. But back then… I'd just found out my brother had killed himself and, what's more, that he'd married a seventeen-year-old just before he'd died. What was I to think? And then…pregnant?'

'That was my fault,' she said evenly, but he shook his head.

'Seventeen was hardly old enough to consent.'

'In those last months Jess wasn't fit enough to think of age differences,' she said evenly. 'The depression was so bad he just…went away. Physically he left for a couple of weeks and when he returned to camp he looked gutted. I was terrified. He was limp, unable to make any decisions. He didn't want to surf. He didn't want to do anything. If I told you all he'd done for me… Well, I was so grateful, I loved him so much, and the state he was in, I was terrified. Anyway, I did everything, anything I could think of to pull him out of it, and in the end I just lay down and held him. I held him all I could, every way I could, and when he finally took me I was happy because I thought he was coming out of it. I thought…he must be.'

'Oh, Kelly…'

'And I'd bought condoms—of course I had—and we used them, but that first time, well, I had the experience of a newt and I guess I was doing the seducing and I didn't do it right and then I was pregnant.'

'You told him?'

'He guessed. And for a while that woke him up. We had this first morning when we knew… I'd woken up sick and he waited until I was better and we took the boards out beyond the surf break to watch the dawn. And we lay there talking about our baby like it might really exist, about this new life that was so exciting. Life for both of us had been crap but this new life...we planned for it. And Jess told me I'd be an awesome mother and he'd try, he'd really try. But that was the last time...'

Her voice trailed off. 'The last time. We came back to shore and Jess found my dad and forced him to sign consent. We married but the dog was back, and with such force that Jess couldn't fight it. He...he went away. I searched and searched but then the police came to find me. And the rest you know.'

The rest he knew?

The rest he guessed.

He'd left a pregnant kid, his brother's widow, to fend for herself.

He'd left her with money. At least he'd done that.

But that had been the least he could do, and it had been her money anyway.

He should have brought her home.

To what? He'd still been a medical student; he'd had no income himself. He'd been sent by his parents to bring his brother's body home, not his brother's widow. If he'd arrived back with Kelly...his father could have destroyed her.

She was twisting a curl round and round her finger. It was a nervous gesture, showing she was tense. He suddenly wanted to reach out and take her hand in his. Hold her still. Take away the pain he'd helped inflict.

He didn't. He couldn't.

'Don't beat up on yourself,' Kelly said gently. 'Matt, it was eighteen years ago. We've moved on.'

'How did you manage?'

'You left me a cheque, remember? I stood outside that day, staring at this obscene amount on a slip of paper, and

I wanted to rip it up. And then I thought, this wasn't my money, it was Jess's, and I was carrying his baby. And I kept thinking of what Jess said to me over and over— "Babe, you're awesome, you can do anything." I thought of the biggest, best way I could keep his baby safe. "Go back to school." Jess had said it and said it. So I got a room with some surfing friends close to the high school and I went back.'

'And had a baby.'

'I had to stop for six months when Jessie was born,' she told him. 'But friends helped me out. I got choosy and I got stronger. My home was where my friends were, and I've made some good friends. It wasn't the easiest existence but finally I qualified and we were safe. Then, just after I got my first job in ER, a kid was hurt in an appalling surf accident. The surf pro-tour was in town and the kid had been hit in the neck by a stray board. He was moving after the accident, but he'd fractured C3. The bones shifted as he was being moved and he died almost as he reached us. The pro-tour organisers were so appalled they decided to fund a full-time medic. Career-wise it was my best fit, so here we are.'

'And what about Jess? Doesn't he go to school?'

'When we're in Hawaii. Otherwise he studies online. He's okay.'

'Online? That cheque was enough for a home,' Matt said roughly. 'It was enough to set you up for life.'

'I told you,' she said, and her voice wasn't rough but it was as determined as Matt's. 'My home's where my friends are. Jess and I have never needed bricks and mortar. Besides, that money is for Jess. Yes, I used some of it to become a doctor but I'm paying it back. By the time Jess turns twenty-one, his father's fund will be intact. He'll have an inheritance.'

'But what sort of career? Once my parents know—'

'Why would I want your parents to know?' She met his gaze, strong, sure, defiant, and he wondered how to answer that.

If his parents knew...

For his mother it'd be the most amazing gift. But his father...

Matt considered his bully of a father, and faltered.

He looked across the table at this amazing woman, and he thought...he thought...

'Tell me about Jess's leg,' Kelly said.

And he thought, yes. Medicine, that was easiest. Retreat to what he knew.

'It's looking okay,' he said. 'The open wounds are healing. We want him on IV antibiotics for another few days. The risks of bone infection after a compound fracture are too great to do otherwise. Caroline's positive about the arterial graft. The physiotherapists are already working with him—you'll have seen that. We're thinking minimal weight bearing in a couple more days, and then a slow rehab. Another few days in hospital until Caroline's happy and then six weeks as an outpatient.'

'I'd like to take him back to Hawaii.'

'You know the dangers of blood clots and swelling. Caroline will concur. Six weeks minimum before he flies.'

She'd known it. It was just hard hearing it. She'd have to get a decent apartment and it'd cost a bomb. She bit her lip, trying to hide her emotions.

There were always glitches. From the time she'd been born she'd been faced with glitches. Everybody faced them, she told herself. It was just that some of her glitches were a bit more major than others.

'Kelly—'

'My name is Dr Eveldene,' she snapped, and then flinched. She had to be polite. 'Sorry. This is not your business. You fix Jess, I'll do the rest.'

'I'd like to help.'

'You already did,' she said brusquely. 'You helped save Jess's leg and more. Eighteen years ago you threw me a cheque. It took me through medical school and it gave Jess and me a life. That's enough. I don't need more from your family.'

'It was,' he said slowly, 'your money.'

'You gave it to me.'

'I threw it at you, yes, but whatever I said at the time it was legally yours. My father made out insurance policies the day we were born—he values his assets, does our father, and he insures them all. But the policy was in Jess's name, which meant once Jess was married it was legally yours. If Dad had imagined that Jess intended marriage he'd have changed the policy in an instant, but you can't change the policy after death. Jess's marriage meant you inherited.' He hesitated. 'Jess knew about the policy. He must have known...'

'That I'd be safe,' Kelly whispered. 'Maybe that was even why... Oh, Jess...' She closed her eyes but then she opened them, moving on with a Herculean effort. 'All that's in the past,' she said. 'I need to look forward. I need to figure what to do for Jess.'

'You're broke?' he asked, and she flinched.

'I have money if I'm desperate, but I don't want to use it.' And then she took a deep breath, recovered, and fixed her gaze on his. 'I told you. I used Jess's insurance to put me through medical school, to get us a future, but I used as little as possible and I treated it as a loan. That money's sitting there waiting for Jess to need it as I needed it.'

'When he finally realises he can't spend his life surfing?'

Whoa. Where had that come from? Shades of his father?

'What are you saying?'

'He can't surf all his life.'

'That's his business.'

She was on her feet, backing away. 'Matt, if I hear you slight my son's lifestyle to him then, medical need or not, he's out of here. Your brother told me your father cares about possessions and power, and that's all. When he was ill, I suggested he might go home and you know what he said? "My father's home is where his things are. Home is where he can gloat over what he's achieved." But home for Jess and me is where my friends are. Our friends and the sea. And that's what we need now. We don't need your money or your judgement, Matt Eveldene. Leave us alone.'

CHAPTER THREE

He SPENT A day letting her words sink in.

He spent a day feeling like a king-sized rat.

He also spent a day being proud of her. That she'd pulled herself up from where she'd been… That she was repaying her legacy… That she had the strength to stand up to him…

He was deeply ashamed of himself, but he was awed by Kelly.

'Jess married some woman!'

He was talking to himself while he walked on the beach near his house. His home was on a headland north of the town, surrounded by bushland and ocean. It hadn't rained for weeks. The country was parched but the scent of the eucalypts and the salt of the sea were balm to any man's soul.

And right now he needed balm.

His two dogs were by his side. Bess was a black Labrador, teenage-silly, joyfully chasing gulls, racing in and out of the waves as she tore along the beach. Spike was a fox terrier, a battered little dog from the lost dogs' home, and he went where Matt did. Spike put up with Bess's company when Matt was at work but when he was at home Spike belonged solely to Matt.

Spike was a dog a man could talk to.

'But why's she letting the kid go down the same road as his father?' Matt asked, stooping to scratch an ear Spike was having trouble reaching. He'd hurt Kelly. He knew he had and he hated it, but still he worried. 'All he seems to know is surfing. The first couple of days he was in hospital there were kids clamouring to visit. Now the tour's moved on, he's watching hour upon hour of surf videos. That's all he does. He's as fixated as Jess was.'

But the kid *was* Jess. The duplication of his brother's name was doing his head in. The likeness was doing his head in.

Kelly was doing his head in.

He'd noted her change of address on Jessie's medical records and he was appalled. Yesterday she'd moved into some kind of apartment at the back of an ancient Queenslander, a big old house up an enormously steep hill from the hospital. On his 'accidental' drive-by he'd decided it looked like it could blow down at any minute. It looked a dump.

She was spending most of her days with her son, but Jess was either sleeping or watching videos or playing video games. What sort of life was that for her? She had a couple of months of the same in front of her.

Dreary months.

It wasn't his business. She'd said that clearly. Back away.

How could he back away?

But to get involved…

See, there was the problem. Kelly had been right when she'd said his family cared for things rather than people. He did, too, but not for his father's reasons. His father accumulated possessions and gloated over them. Matt simply valued his home.

When he'd been a kid, Matt's older brother had been the centre of his world, and he'd been forced to watch as he'd slowly disappeared into his tortured illness. In defence Matt, too, had disappeared, surrounding himself now with his medicine and his home—a real home as opposed to the mausoleum his parents occupied.

His home, though, was solitary. For many, home meant family but it didn't for Matt. One failed marriage had shown him that.

Jenny had been a year younger than him, a colleague, ambitious and clever, warm and fun. His father had been critical but his father was always critical. His mother had approved.

'She's lovely and she's loving, Matt. You make sure you love her right back.'

He'd thought he had. They'd married. They'd bought a beautiful apartment overlooking Sydney Harbour and brought in an interior designer with the brief: 'We want it to be warm. We want it to be a home.'

They'd filled the house with gorgeous furniture and hundreds of books. They'd had separate studies, separate careers, but every night they'd slept together and Matt had felt like he had it all.

When Jenny had pulled the plug he'd been stunned.

'Matt, you love me but it's like I'm your imitation fireplace,' she'd told him. 'For decoration only. I want to keep you warm, but you have your own form of central heating. You're self-contained. You don't need me. I've tried to fit in with your beautiful life but I can't. Now I've met a farmer from west of nowhere. I'm off to be a country doctor, and raise sheep and kids, and have a very messy life and be happy. Good luck, Matt. I'll always love you a little bit. I'm just sorry that you couldn't love me a lot.'

That had been six years ago. He still didn't fully understand but after this time he conceded that maybe Jenny had been right. He wasn't husband material.

He'd moved to Queensland. He'd built a house he was immensely proud of and his career had taken over the gap that Jenny had left until he couldn't quite see where she'd fitted.

His parents' marriage was a disaster. He'd lost his brother and then he'd lost Jenny. There was no need to go down that emotional roller-coaster again. He was obviously a loner—except right now he wasn't. He kept thinking of a kid called Jess.

And he kept thinking of a woman called Kelly. A woman who twisted her curls around her fingers when she was tense. A woman he wanted to touch...

No. That was a road he wasn't going down. He needed to focus on practicalities.

And the foremost practicality? She was living in a dump because of some noble idea of saving her son's inheritance.

So what to do? Offer to pay for somewhere better? He thought of Kelly, of the fire in her eyes, of the hundred reasons she had to hate him, and he knew she'd refuse.

What, then?

He turned to stare up the cliff at his house.

Invite them to stay?

His house had a self-contained apartment, built so his mother could visit now and in the future. Wheelchair access. A veranda overlooking the surf. Its own television and internet access. Everything a disabled kid needed.

What was he thinking? Did he want them here?

Even if he offered, Kelly would refuse.

But if she didn't...

If she didn't then a kid called Jessie would be living in his house. Six weeks of Jess/Jess. Jess, his big brother. Jess, his nephew.

His nephew. His family.

He had to offer.

But when Jenny had accused him of self-containment, she'd been right. He didn't want to feel...the way he was feeling about Jess. Then there was Kelly. She was a woman he couldn't look at without feeling racked with guilt.

And then there was the way he felt when she twisted her curls...

The situation was doing his head in. He walked and walked, and when his cell phone rang and Beth was on the line, saying there'd been a car crash and he was needed, he was almost grateful.

Work, dogs, home, he told himself. They were all that mattered.

Except something else mattered. Someone else. Two someones.

He just needed space to get his head around it.

The car accident had been avoidable, appalling and tragic. One kid had a fractured pelvis but was so drunk it'd be morning before Matt could operate safely. He immobilised his damaged joint but that was all he could do for now. One kid had broken ribs and lacerations to his face. The broken ribs weren't life-threatening. The plastic surgeons would need to take over with this one.

The final casualty—the boy Beth had called him for because his spine was shattered—died just as he arrived.

So in the end there was little for him to do. Matt headed for the door, skirting the cluster of shattered parents, thanking heaven counselling wasn't his role.

Then he paused.

It was nine o'clock. Visiting hours ended at eight. He might be able to drop in and check on Jess without Kelly being present. Without being surrounded by students.

He might be able to talk to Jess by himself.

Why would he want to?

Because... Because...

There was no because. He had no reason, but almost before he thought it, he was in the orthopaedic ward, greeting the nurse in charge, shaking his head as she rose to accompany him, heading down the corridor alone to Jessie's room.

The nurse looked interested and he knew this visit wouldn't go unreported. The hospital grapevine was notorious. Having a kid in here who looked like him *and* shared his name had sent the rumour mill flying.

So what? Rumours didn't affect him and it was normal to visit patients after hours. Even a kid who looked like his…son?

But he was his nephew. Kelly had told Jess who he was. She'd obviously not told him the bleakest parts of their history, though, because the kid always greeted him with friendly interest. It was as he found it intriguing to have an uncle.

Uncle. The idea unnerved him.

Jessie's door was slightly open. He knocked lightly, not enough to wake him if he was sleeping, and pushed it further.

Jess was asleep, but he wasn't alone. Kelly was sitting by the bed, and even by the dim nightlight she looked ill.

'Kelly?' He said her name before he could stop himself. She wanted to be called Dr Eveldene. He'd tried to remember it. But now… What was wrong?

'Kelly,' he repeated, heading for the bedside, looking down at Jess, expecting something dire.

But Jess was deeply asleep. He had a good colour and his breathing was deep and even. Matt flicked back the bedclothes at the end of the cradle and checked the lower leg, using the small torch he often used for evening rounds. Good circulation. No problem.

He glanced again at Kelly. Problem.

She was wearing jeans and a light windcheater. Her curls were hauled back in a ponytail. Her eyes were deeply shadowed, as if she hadn't slept.

A row of welts ran from her chin down her neck and underneath the cover of her windcheater.

The doctor in him went straight into diagnosis mode. Shingles?

He tried to look more closely but she put her hands up to cover her neck. Defensively.

'Yes?' she said, and it was a dismissal in itself. *Yes, what do you want, how soon can you get out of here?*

'What's wrong?'

'Why are you here?'

'Nightly ward round,' he said as if he always did an evening round. He often did, he conceded. Just not to patients who were recovering nicely.

'You don't come in at night.'

'I do when I'm needed.' He relented. 'Car accident. Alcohol. Stupid. There was a death. An eighteen-year-old. Fractured spine, and he died before I could get here. I thought…'

And she softened, just like that.

'Oh, Matt,' she said, her tone suddenly understanding. 'I do that, too. See a kid's death, hug another kid. After I had Jess, that's where I'd be after trauma. Hugging. Jess always knows when I've had a bad day when the hugs are too tight. But…'

'But I have no right to hug Jess?'

'You don't,' she said flatly, but then she relented again. 'Kids killing themselves is the hardest thing.'

'Yet you let him surf.'

There was a moment's silence and when she finally spoke he could hear in her voice that he'd gone over that line again. 'You want me to pack him in cotton wool?'

'I… No. But he should have something other than surfing.'

'Butt out, Matt,' she said ominously, and he should. But right now he was facing a woman with an obvious problem.

Even if her name hadn't been Kelly Eveldene, he couldn't walk away. There was something...

'You want to tell me what's wrong?'

'No,' she said, but he moved before she could react, caught her hands and dragged them down from her neck.

Down the left side of her throat were red weals, clumping in groups of three, some so large they were running into each other. The mass was expanding as it disappeared under her windcheater. Heaven knew what sort of a mess was under her clothes.

'What's this?' He ignored her jerk of protest and concentrating on the welts. It looked like shingles, and yet not. These were angry clumps rather than the mass of irregular swelling that shingles caused.

She looked so unwell...

'Kelly, what did this?' he said gently. 'Can I help?'

'No.'

'Now, that's dumb,' he told her. 'If it's shingles we need to get antivirals on board right away. The sooner it's treated, the shorter the period of discomfort.'

'I know that,' she snapped. 'But it's not shingles.'

'Then what?'

'Bed bugs,' she said, goaded. 'I was dumb. You'd think I'd suspect. Haven't I lived in enough rough places in my time?' She wrenched away from him in sudden anger but the anger seemed to be self-directed. 'Leave it. I'm treating my room. These'll fade.'

'These'll give you hell,' he said, looking at the dark pools around her eyes. 'Did you get any sleep last night?'

'No, I—'

'They must be driving you crazy. Come down to Pharmacy and I'll get you antihistamines. I'll also get you an anaesthetic cream to give you immediate relief.'

'I don't need—'

'You do need,' he told her, and without waiting for

agreement he took her hand and tugged her to her feet. 'Suffering's for those who have no choice and you have a choice. Jessie's asleep. He doesn't need you to look after him now, Kelly. You, however, do need to look after yourself.'

How long had it been since things were taken out of her hands?

They hadn't been. Ever. She looked out for herself. Apart from that one blessed time around her briefest of marriages, she'd been alone.

Even when she'd been tiny, when she'd been sick she'd coped herself, and she was coping now. She'd woken in the small hours covered with bed-bug sores. She'd spent hours trying to rid her dump of an apartment of the creatures, knowing how hard it was to eradicate them from ancient crevices. She should find another place to stay but the thought of paying any more for accommodation when Jess was still in hospital horrified her. The insurance was Jessie's money, college money, and it had to stay intact.

But the thought of going back there tonight made her feel nauseous. Or maybe she felt nauseous because she'd had so many bites. All she knew was that Matt Eveldene suddenly had her by the hand and was tugging her through the hospital toward his goal, the pharmacy. So, on top of nauseous, she felt helpless as well.

She wasn't stupid. She'd taken an antihistamine that morning. She managed to tell him.

'What strength? Do you have them in your purse? Show me.'

'Matt, I'm a doctor.'

'Show me,' he growled again, and it was too much trouble to argue. She just did.

'You took one of these this morning?' He looked at the packet with contempt. 'One?'

'I had stuff to do. I couldn't afford to be sleepy.'

'Yeah, you might go to sleep. What a disaster. This stuff won't even touch the sides. You can take much stronger medicine now, and stronger still when you're home in bed. But not in that bed.'

'I've sprayed.'

'It's a dump.'

'What business is that of yours?'

'You're my sister-in-law,' he growled. 'Family.'

'You are not my family!'

'Try telling that to every member of staff in this hospital.' She had to shut up then, while he threw orders to the woman in charge of Pharmacy. But even as he did, Kelly had to concede that he was right. She'd been aware of sideways glances and there'd even been straight-out questions. Now the pharmacist was filling Matt's scripts but she was looking from Matt to Kelly and back again, as if she could see family ties in the flesh.

Family? No way. She wasn't about to play happy families with an arrogant surgeon.

'Thank you,' she said stiffly, as the pharmacist handed over pills and cream. 'I'll pay—'

'I'm paying,' Matt snapped. 'And we need to get some of that cream on fast. I'll take you down to Emergency and we'll find a cubicle...'

'To do what?'

'Those welts are on your back. You can't reach them.'

'You're not putting cream on my back!'

'Don't be ridiculous. I'm a doctor.'

The pharmacist was watching them with interest, clearly enjoying herself. Clearly enjoying the sparks flying.

'I'll manage,' Kelly said stiffly.

'That's pig-headed.'

'You're not touching me.' She took the pills and cream from Matt's hands and backed out the pharmacy door. Matt followed, and she forced herself to stay still, to wait until the pharmacy door closed. She wanted to head straight for the exit but she had to be polite. This guy was Jessie's surgeon and he'd helped her. There was no need for her hackles to rise.

'Sorry,' she managed as the door closed behind them. 'I'm…I'm a bit of a private person.'

'How are you going to get that cream on your back?'

'I've been putting sunburn cream on my back for years. I'm a surfer, remember?'

He remembered. She could see it in the way his face closed down. And from the past…

My family hates my surfing.' She could still hear Jess, her Jess, whispering to her all those years ago when he'd been in the throes of blackness. *'Don't they understand? When I'm surfing, I'm free.'*

She'd studied depression now; of course she had. When she'd first met Jess she'd had no clue, but she had enough knowledge now to know that he'd been treated the wrong way. Depression was an illness. If his surfing had been time out it should have been encouraged, not rejected. If he'd been encouraged to surf when he'd been a teenager, he might be alive now.

And now…

'Don't you dare judge,' she snapped, and Matt blinked and took a step back.

'I'm not judging.'

'Yes, you are. I can see it in your eyes. Surfing's a waste of space for you and your family.'

'It's a great sport,' he shot back. 'I surf myself. But you can't spend your life surfing.'

'You can if it's the only option,' she snapped. 'If your parents hadn't been so blind they'd have seen…they could have a kid who surfed or no kid at all. They gambled with their son's life and they lost.'

'Is that why you're letting Jessie surf?'

'You think that's why anyone wants to surf? Because they're ill? Butt out.'

'Kelly…'

'You know nothing.'

'I know plenty.' He raked his hair.

And she thought suddenly, he looks tired. Stressed.

Of course he did. He'd coped with road trauma tonight—a dead kid, grieving parents. And now she was laying ancient history at his door.

It wasn't his fault Jess had died. He'd been younger than Jess. The damage had been done by others, not by him.

'Kelly, I want you to come and stay with me,' he said, and her thoughts cut off dead right there.

Stay. With him?

'No.' It was an instinctive rejection; a gut reaction.

'Why not?'

'Because you're Jessie's doctor, nothing more. Because my problems are nothing to do with you.'

'We both know that's not true,' he said wearily. 'Kelly, my big brother loved you. I loved him. I wasn't there for you eighteen years ago and I should have been. There's not much I can do for you now, but I do have a large house with an invalid-friendly self-contained guest apartment. My mother comes to stay sometimes but it's free now. My housekeeper keeps the kitchen stocked and I have two dogs who need walks and company. There's a spare Jeep you can use, as long as you're comfortable driving on the left side of the road. It's a straight ten-minute drive to the hospital. I'm out most of the day. We'd hardly see each other. And best of all, last time I looked I didn't have a single bed bug.'

'No,' she said again, but she didn't sound as sure. She didn't feel as sure.

It was a great offer. Why say no?

Instinct, she thought. Pure animal instinct. There was something about this man that seemed…dangerous.

'Besides,' he said gently, 'I'd really like the opportunity to get to know your Jessie. I'm his uncle. I know he's had no one in the past…'

'He's had me. He's had the surfing community.'

'Don't you think he should be given the chance to have more?'

'Not if it messes with his head,' she said bluntly. 'Not if it means one trace of judgement.'

'There won't be judgement.'

'There already is. You're judging me for letting him surf.'

'I won't judge him.'

'No,' she said again, but she was faltering.

Her son was an Eveldene. Her son was this man's nephew.

Somewhere there was a bully of a grandfather, a man she never wanted to meet, but Jess had loved Matt—and his mother.

Her son had a grandmother, too.

Family was such an alien concept. She'd never had so much as a cousin.

Actually, probably she had. It was just that by the time she'd been old enough to know them her father had driven them away.

As Matt's father had driven his son away?

My mother comes to stay sometimes. That's what he'd said. Nothing about a father there.

But maybe there were similarities between Matt and his father. There were definitely similarities between Matt and his brother. Maybe that was why she was looking at him now and feeling…feeling…

She didn't know how she was feeling.

Matt looked like her husband, like her son. Maybe that

was it—but she knew it wasn't. It was the way he looked at her, as if he was as confused as she was. As vulnerable?

That was a nonsense. He was a chief orthopaedic surgeon, successful, gorgeous and at the top of his game. Vulnerable? Ha!

And he really was gorgeous. Long, lean and ripped. He looked...

Um, no. This wasn't what she should be thinking right now. Or thinking ever. Move on, she told herself. The hormonal rush she was feeling must be her emotions flaring up at his similarities to her long-dead husband, surely. Surely it had nothing to do with Matt.

Concentrate. She'd just been thrown an offer. If she accepted she wouldn't have to go back to her dump of an apartment tonight.

She shouldn't be so pig stubborn about the trust money, she told herself, not for the first time, but there was still the remembrance of that cheque, thrown at her in anger. Her initial urge to rip it in half was still with her. Only the thought of the baby inside her had stopped her. And now... She didn't want to use Eveldene money. She didn't want Eveldene hospitality.

She was also just a little bit scared of how this man made her feel.

'Come home,' Matt said, quite gently, and she realised he'd been waiting patiently for her to come to a decision.

'Home is where Jess is,' she said, too fast, and he grinned.

'There's not a lot of room in his hospital bed,' he said. 'You sound like you've had a lot of temporary homes. What's wrong with making one of them with me?'

'Matt...'

'I know, every part of me repels you,' he said ruefully. 'And I understand that. But for now, what I'm offering is sensible. Let's go find an all-night supermarket and buy you what you need.'

'I can collect my stuff.'

'It'll have to be fumigated before we transfer it.'

'How do you know?'

'I'm a dog owner,' he said. 'I'm used to fumigating.'

'You want to fumigate me?'

'A shower and a washing machine might do the job.'

A shower and a washing machine...

Of all the seductive things Matt could have said to her, that was the one most likely to succeed. A shower and a washing machine...

She knew her gear would be infected by bed bugs. She'd thought of doing a massive laundromat clean today but the thought of taking bedding by taxi had seemed too hard. She'd wanted to be with Jess, and she'd felt ill.

'You have a washing machine?' she said weakly.

'A really big one,' he said, like it was a siren lure, and it was. He smiled and his smile was suddenly tender, as if he'd realised she'd reached the end of her protests. 'Enticement by washing machine,' he said, echoing her thoughts. 'Come home with me, Kelly Eveldene, and see your washing go round and round and round.' He reached out and touched her then, tracing a long, strong finger down her cheekbone. It was a feather-light touch, a touch that meant nothing, but for some reason it made her want to sink against him. Dissolve...

'Give in, Kelly,' he said softly. 'I'm not threatening your independence. I'm not threatening anything. But I am offering you respite, a clean bed and a machine with six wash cycles. Let me take you home.'

And what was a girl to say to that? She looked up at him and tried to speak but for some reason she was close to tears and she couldn't.

It didn't matter. Matt took her shoulders and turned her round and steered her out the back to the hospital car park.

And took her home.

CHAPTER FOUR

THE LAST TIME Kelly Eveldene had felt completely out of control had been the night she'd had Jess. She felt out of control again now.

She was sitting in Matt Eveldene's gorgeous Aston Martin, heading out of town towards who knew where? On the back seat was a parcel of stuff bought at the late-night supermarket, an oversized T-shirt and knickers, toothbrush, toothpaste, a hairbrush. In the trunk was her duffel bag, carefully sealed in two layers of plastic.

The antihistamine was kicking in. She didn't feel quite as itchy but she felt...dirty.

She still wanted to scratch but she wasn't going to scratch in this man's car. Imagine if she dropped a bed-bug egg into the leather?

'If you scratch, you risk infection,' he said, and she glanced across and realised he'd been watching her hands clench and unclench on her lap.

'I won't scratch,' she muttered.

'Good girl.'

'I don't think an Aston Martin with bed bugs would suit your image.'

'I'm thinking you'll have showered this morning and given those clothes a good shake before you put them on. My risk is minimal.'

'Yet still you took it,' she muttered. 'Jess always said you were hero material.'

'Did he?' he said, and she saw his hands grip hard on the steering-wheel.

'He said you stood up to your father.' She might as well say it. It took her mind off the itching—or some of it.

'Jess couldn't,' Matt said grimly. 'Or rather when he tried it didn't work. It wasn't that I was a hero. It was just that when Dad hit me I refused to fall over. I figured from the time I was tiny that showing hurt made me more vulnerable. I just...dissociated myself. Jess, on the other hand, didn't have it in him to dissociate himself. Every punch, it was like it was killing him inside.'

'Your father punched?'

'Yes,' he said curtly.

'Do you still see him?'

'Seldom.'

'But you still see your mother?'

'When Dad's overseas. But she's never had the courage to leave him. I sometimes think she would have, but after Jess died any shred of self-worth she had died with him. She's just...shrivelled. Dad doesn't hit her. He hasn't needed to. Sometimes I think there are worse ways of controlling than physical violence.'

'And that's why Jess...'

'Got sick? Who knows with mental illness? But if I had to take a punt I'd say it certainly didn't help matters. And I hardly supported him either.' There was anger behind his words, impotent fury, and his knuckles on the steering-wheel showed white. But then he seemed to make an effort to recover, forcibly relaxing his hold, forcibly relaxing the muscles around his mouth. 'Sorry. Ancient history.'

'You blame yourself? You were four years younger. But your father—'

'I said it was ancient history,' he snapped again.

'If your mother's still with him then it's current affairs.'

'Current affairs I can't do anything about. Except protect you from him.'

'Why would I need protecting?'

'You might,' he said grimly, 'if he knew he had a grandson…'

'You won't tell him?'

'No.'

'Thank you,' she said in a small voice. She was feeling more and more out of control.

They were heading into what looked like dense bushland. Where was he taking her?

The car swung off the main road onto what looked like a private driveway, but this was no manicured garden. It was still bushland but solar lights nestled among the trees on either side of the track, some glowing brightly, some just faint traces of light, depending, she guessed, on how much sun they'd received during the day. The effect was strangely beautiful.

Isolated and beautiful.

She was heading into nowhere with a man called Matt Eveldene. If she had been back in her surfing days all her senses would be telling her to get out of the car now. But she wasn't a kid and she was no longer defenceless—she hoped.

But still…

'You're quite safe,' he said, guessing her thoughts, and she flushed.

'I never thought…'

'You'd have been foolish not to have thought. This looks like the end of the earth, but in the morning you'll wake up and look over the ocean and you'll almost see Hawaii. Almost home.'

Almost home.

Home… There was a word to give her pause.

A home was what Jess needed now, for a while. But apart from their shoebox studio apartment back in Hawaii, where was home?

Home was work. Home was childcare when Jess had been little, school, university, libraries where she'd studied, with Jess reading or drawing pictures beside her, public playgrounds, beaches, friends' houses. Home was the surf, dawn and dusk. Home was where Jess was.

'Hawaii's hardly home any more,' she said, thinking aloud.

'Where is it, then?'

'Wherever Jess is. Wherever the surf is.'

'No roots?'

'I don't believe in them,' she said, and then for some reason she continued, revealing stuff she didn't normally reveal. 'As a kid I had a stuffed rabbit. Wherever Bugs was, that was home. Then when I was about eight one of my Dad's mates used Bugs to stoke a campfire. Home's never been anywhere since.'

'Hell, Kelly...' And there it was, that retrospective anger on her behalf. Jessie had reacted to stories of her past with fury. But who'd been angry on her behalf since?

No one. But it didn't matter, she told herself. And this man's concern shouldn't make her feel... She wasn't sure how she was feeling.

Push past it, she told herself. She didn't need this man feeling sorry for her. She didn't need this man looking at her with concern.

'It's no use worrying about what's in the past,' she managed. 'And what good did your fancy home do you or Jess? You need people. You don't need homes.' She meant it, too—but then they rounded the last bend in the driveway.

'This is home,' Matt said in a voice she hadn't heard before. 'I'm thinking this home almost equates to Bugs.'

Maybe it did. Sort of.

The house was long and low, nestled into the surrounding bushland almost as if it was part of it. It was built of sand-coloured stone, with wide verandas and a low-pitched roof, with tiny solar lights all around the veranda. Two dogs stood on the top step like two sentinels. A couple of battered surfboards leaned on the rail and a kayak lay near the steps. It looked like the perfect seaside homestead. It was picture-postcard perfect, though in postcards the dogs might have matched. These two were polar opposite, one a boof-headed Labrador, one a pint-sized fox terrier.

The dogs stood perfectly still until the car came to a halt, and then they whirled down the steps like a firecracker had exploded behind them. They raced round and round the car like crazy things until Matt opened his car door. The Labrador kept on whirling but the little dog timed it perfectly. Her circuit ended in a flying leap, straight onto Matt's knee. She gave an adoring yip, and then ceased all movement and gazed enquiringly at Kelly.

She had to laugh. What the little dog meant couldn't have been plainer if she'd been able to speak.

Matt, I'm really, really pleased to see you, but who is this? I need an introduction before we proceed.

'Spike, this is Dr Eveldene,' Matt said gravely, and to Kelly's delight Spike raised a paw and waited, just as gravely, for it to be shaken.

'Call me Kelly,' Kelly said, and Matt grinned.

'Does that go for me, too?'

'I…' She sighed. 'Of course. Sorry.' And then she couldn't say anything else because the Labrador was now in the car, welcoming them both home with far less refinement and far more exuberance than Spike had shown.

Matt grabbed her gear. He dumped her plastic-shrouded duffel bag on the veranda—'That'll wait until morning'—then escorted her, with Spike leading the way, to his guest quarters.

He opened the door, flicked on the lights and she gasped in delight.

It was a self-contained apartment, furnished simply but beautifully. Polished wooden floors were softened with Persian rugs. The furniture looked comfortable and even a little faded, as if the curtains were left wide every day and the sun was left to do its worst. There were two bedrooms leading off the small sitting room. Matt led the way into the first, and flung open wide French windows while Kelly looked longingly at the truly sumptuous bed.

'All this for your mother?'

'Friends come here from Sydney, too,' he said briefly. 'I like them to be self-contained and I like my independence. You'll need to have breakfast with me tomorrow because I didn't think to get supplies, but from then on you can do your own thing. Leave the windows wide for a while—it's a bit musty in here. Would you like a drink? Anything?'

But she was still looking longingly at the bed, and through the door to the bathroom. A long, cool shower to get the heat out of the bites...

'Make sure the water's no hotter than body temperature or you'll make it worse,' Matt said, following her gaze. He dumped her stuff on a luggage stand and put the pharmacy items on the dresser. 'Are you sure you can put this cream on after your shower?'

'I... Yes.'

'I'll leave you to it, then,' he said. 'Goodnight, Kelly. Come on, guys, let's leave the lady to sleep.'

And he clicked his fingers and he was gone. The dogs went with him and he closed the door behind him.

Good. Excellent. She had all the privacy a girl could ask for.

Shower. Bed.

Home?

She didn't do home; she never had. To invest in a permanent base would have meant spending all the money she'd had, and it had seemed wrong. The money had never seemed hers. It was her son's, and it would stay intact for him.

So she'd rented places that would do. On the surf circuit, as part of her job, they'd stayed in decent hotels, but nowhere as good as this.

This was pure comfort. She could sink into bed right now, if she didn't feel so dirty.

She flicked off the lights, stripped naked and tossed her clothes out onto the veranda. She'd cope with them in the morning. Then she headed for the shower. No tiny bed-bug egg was going to get into this place—it'd be a travesty.

Still, there was a niggle. Matt had given her this. She'd be beholden to him, and she didn't want to be any more beholden than she already was.

But... 'I don't owe Matt,' she told herself. 'The insurance was Jessie's. He's done nothing for me but hand me what was rightfully mine.'

He'd saved her son's leg. She'd studied the X-rays. She'd even—heaven forgive her for her lack of trust—scanned them and sent them to a guy she'd trained with who'd gone on to specialise in orthopaedics in the US. The response had come back, loud and clear.

'These before-and-after X-rays are truly impressive, Kelly. That's one hell of a break. Whoever did the repair has saved Jess a lifetime of limping.'

So, yes, she was grateful and here she was, in his home. She was in his bathroom, to be precise, because she'd wasted less than ten seconds getting from naked to under the water.

Matt was right through the wall. Jess's brother.

Was that what was doing her head in? The similarity between Matt and her husband?

It must be, she thought. There was no other explanation, because she was feeling…strange.

Out of control?

It was the bed bugs, she told herself, and the weariness, and the shock of the last few days. Even so, sitting by Matt in the car, following him as he'd strode through the supermarket, figuring out what she needed, knowing that he was…caring…

He didn't care. He was simply doing the right thing for once.

But the concept of caring was insidious. If he did…

He did. He'd been angry on her behalf. And he'd looked at her in such a way…

'Oh, stop it,' she told herself, lathering her hair for the second time with the gorgeous shampoo provided. She must have soap in her eyes. She was getting teary, and she didn't get teary. For some reason the thought of someone caring was almost overwhelming in its sweetness.

She coped alone. She'd always coped and she'd cope again. But for now…for now it was enough to stand under Matt's wonderful shower and then fall into Matt's wonderful bed…

Um…

Another image. Not a wise one. A totally stupid one, in fact. One started by his concern and moving to something else.

Matt was Jessie's brother. You did *not* have fantasies about your husband's brother.

Jess had been dead for eighteen years.

There'd been the occasional fling since—of course there had. Kelly was no black-clad widow, mourning her husband for ever. In fact, sometimes it seemed to her that Jess had been less her husband and more a wonderful, loving friend, someone who'd taken her out of a bad place but who'd been in a dreadful place himself. They'd been two kids fighting demons and Jess had lost.

She'd mourned him but she'd got on with her life, and occasionally a guy had turned up in her orbit. Never seriously, though. She was too busy, too preoccupied, not interested enough.

But Matt...

'Stop it,' she said out loud, and lathered her hair for a third time for good measure. 'Of all the times to indulge in fantasies... Inappropriate, inappropriate, inappropriate. Get yourself dry and into bed.

'Yes, Doctor,' she told herself, and managed a grin. Ooh, that bed...

As if on cue, one of the bites on her back stabbed with pain. Ouch. She turned the water colder and winced.

She had Matt's cream. Dry yourself off and get it on, she told herself. Bed's waiting.

Matt took the dogs for a fast walk out to the headland and then headed back to the house. For some reason he needed to be near. He'd told Kelly she could be independent but...but...

It didn't quite work. He'd like to be making her supper, making sure her bites were coated, making sure she was safely in bed.

Bed. His mind went all by itself to the memory of Kelly looking longingly at the bed.

A bed built for more than one.

Was he out of his mind? He was not interested in her like that. Not!

She was Jessie's wife. If he thought of her as his sister-in-law...

Logically it should help.

It didn't.

He headed back up the veranda and saw her open windows. Her clothes were heaped outside. He grinned. Very wise. He gathered them gingerly and took them to the laundry where he'd dumped her duffel bag.

Did bedbugs escape from laundries?

On impulse he tossed the clothes into the washing machine then unzipped her bag. Clothes only, he told himself; he wasn't looking at anything else.

He could do this. Confirmed bachelors—or confirmed divorcés—were good at laundry.

Most of her stuff was coloured. It all went into the machine. Her delicates—cute delicates, he noticed, before admonishing himself once again—went into the tub to soak. Then he found a can of insecticide, sprayed the room to within an inch of its life and carefully closed all the doors. No sucker would get out of there alive.

Job done. He should go to bed himself. He had an early start in the morning.

Instead, he found himself out on the veranda again, glancing along, seeing Kelly's windows were still open.

Her light was still on.

Why? She was dead on her feet. She should be in bed by now.

When she went to bed was her business—or maybe she slept with the light on.

Maybe there were shadows in her past that demanded nightlights.

Yeah, that didn't bear thinking of. Her past didn't bear thinking of. Thank God Jess had been able to help her.

And suddenly something lightened just a little inside him. His grief for his older brother had stayed raw, even after all this time. What a waste. The mantra had played over and over in his head—the thought that because his father had rejected his illness, Jess had died alone. Jess had had no one.

But he hadn't died alone. He'd had Kelly. She'd held him

and loved him and she'd told him she was bearing his child. And Jess had known of the insurance. No matter how ill he'd been, Jess would have known Kelly would be provided for. He'd have known she and her child would be safe.

And in that moment the gaping bleakness of Jessie's loss lessened, faded. It shifted to a corner of his mind where he knew it could stay in peace for the rest of his life. What a gift! And Kelly, this slip of a girl who'd turned into a woman of such strength, had given it to him.

Kelly, whose light was still on. Because of demons? Because...?

He heard himself call out before he knew he intended to. 'Kelly? Are you all right? Is there anything you need?'

There was a moment's silence. The dogs by his side seemed to prick up their ears, as if they, too, were listening for a response. And finally...

'I'm not as clever as I thought,' she said, sounding exasperated. She was just through the window.

'You want to expand on that?' he asked cautiously.

'Fine,' she said, goaded. 'I've always been able to put sunburn cream on myself. All over. But some time over the last few years, being with Jess rather than alone, I must have lost the knack. "Do my back," I'll say, and Jess does. There are bites on my back that are driving me nuts and I can't reach them.'

'You want help?'

There was a moment's silence. Then: 'I've only got a T-shirt and knickers on.'

'And if I'm to help you'll need to get rid of the T-shirt. Kelly, I'm a doctor.'

'Yes, but—'

'I'll do it with my eyes closed,' he told her, and she snorted.

'Right.'

'You want help or not?'

Another silence. Another moment's hesitation. Then, finally, the French windows were thrust wider and Kelly appeared in the light.

This was a Kelly he hadn't seen before. Her curls were damp and tangled. She was wearing her oversized man's T-shirt. Underneath she'd be wearing the cheap knickers the supermarket stocked, but that was all.

The T-shirt material was cheap and thin. A bit too thin. The shower had been cold...

'You said you wouldn't look,' she said coldly, and he shut his eyes.

More silence.

'Matt?'

'Yes?' he said cautiously. She was sounding...even more goaded.

'I'm a patient,' she said. 'I'm going to lie face down on the bed and pull up the T-shirt and you're required to apply medication.'

'It'd be better if you took the T-shirt off altogether.'

'Better for who?'

'I'm a doctor,' he reassured her. 'And you know I'm right. The night's warm. You're better sleeping with nothing on at all.'

'I might,' she conceded. 'After you leave.'

'After the doctor has done what he needs to do,' he agreed. 'Kelly...'

'Yes?'

'Go lie on the bed and we'll get this over with.'

She stripped off her T-shirt with her back to him—asking him to leave the room again would have seemed... prissy. Then she lay face down on the crisp, clean sheets and waited for him to do his worst.

His best? Surely his best. She needed help. All he had to do was take the cream from the bedside table and rub it in.

She heard him lift the tube, imagined him squeezing the cream onto those gorgeous surgeon's hands…

What was she doing, thinking of those hands?

She was actually thinking of more than his hands.

You're a sad case, Kelly, she told herself. One good-looking guy wanders into your orbit and your body reacts like…

Her body certainly did react. The moment his fingers touched her skin, she felt every sense respond. It was like her body lit up from within, as if the place on her back where he touched was suddenly the centre of her entire being, and all of her wanted to be there.

What the…? Could she have an orgasm because someone was touching her?

This was crazy. She was feeling super-sensitive because of the bites. She'd been without sex for far too long.

Surely this had nothing to do with the fact that it was Matt Eveldene who was doing the touching. Surely if an elderly woman with body odour was applying the cream she'd be feeling the same.

Liar, liar, pants on fire. She was face down in her pillow, muffling thoughts, muffling everything, but all she could see was Matt, with his gorgeous dark hair and his long, sensitive fingers doing indescribable things to her, making sure every last part of her back was covered with the anaesthetic cream. Suddenly, dumbly, she found herself wishing she hadn't worn knickers to bed last night and the bites had gone lower.

Uh-oh. She needed to get a grip fast. She was a mature woman, the mother of a seventeen-year-old son, a competent doctor. She did not grip her pillow and stifle groans because some strange man was applying cream to her.

His fingers stopped and to her horror she heard a whimper of protest. Surely that wasn't her?

It was. Was she out of her mind?

But luckily, thankfully, he misinterpreted it. 'These are bad,' he said. 'Kelly, stay still, I'm going to find some ice. I've made them warm again, putting the cream on. We need to get all the heat out of them so you can get some sleep.'

We. Plural. The word was seductive all by itself.

There wasn't a we. There had been never a we.

Matt left and for some stupid reason she found herself thinking of the night Jess had been born. She'd been staying with friends on the far side of the island. They'd promised to be with her for the birth but Jess had come two weeks early. They'd gone out and she'd had no car.

She'd taken the local bus, an hour's bumpy ride in the dark. She'd walked four blocks to the hospital and she'd delivered her baby with no one but too-busy hospital staff in attendance.

Why think of that now?

We. It was the word; it penetrated her deepest thoughts. The only *we* she knew was herself and her son.

And then Matt was back. She hadn't moved. Her world seemed to be doing weird, hazy things. Maybe it was the antihistamines—how much had Matt given her? Or maybe it was the toxic effect of so many bites. No matter, she couldn't have moved if she'd tried. She didn't speak, just lay absolutely still while Matt applied ice packs wrapped in soft cloth to her inflamed skin.

The feeling was incredible. She no longer felt like whimpering. She felt incredibly, amazingly peaceful, like this was right, like this was where she ought to be.

Like this was home.

There was a dumb thought. Home. For her, the concept didn't exist.

'You know, if you rolled over I could ice your front,' Matt said conversationally, and she finally managed to rouse herself.

'In your dreams, Matt Eveldene,' she managed. 'I can ice my front all by myself. Thank you very much. I'll go to sleep now.'

'Are you sure? I can give you—'

'If you give me anything else I'll never wake up. I'm medicated to my eyeballs. Thank you, Matt, and goodnight.'

'Goodnight, Kelly,' he said softly, but he didn't go. For a long moment he simply stood by her bed.

She wanted to roll over. She wanted, quite desperately, to look up at him.

She was naked from the waist up. A girl had to have some sense.

And it seemed Matt had sense, too.

'Goodnight,' he said again, and then, before she knew what he intended—how could she ever have guessed?— he stooped and kissed her lightly on the head.

'You're the bravest woman I've ever met,' he told her. 'Thank you for loving Jessie. It's the greatest gift you could ever have given me.'

'Is that why you kissed me?' she managed, and what sort of question was that? Dumb, she thought, but equally... important.

'No,' he said at last. 'It's not. But it needs to be.'

She was his sister-in-law. Jessie's wife. He had no business thinking of her...as he was thinking.

Why had he kissed her?

It had been a feather kiss, the kiss one might give a child to say goodnight.

It had meant nothing.

Wrong. It had meant...more.

She hadn't felt like Jessie's wife and she hadn't felt like a child. She'd felt—and looked—every inch a woman.

He left the house and walked down to the beach again,

to watch the moon sending its slivers of silver ribbon over the waves. The dogs were silent by his side, as if they knew how important it was that he be given time to think.

There was nothing to think about.

There was everything to think about. A woman called Kelly, a woman lying half-naked in his guest room, a woman responding to his touch...

She had responded. That hadn't been a doctor/patient treatment. The whole room had crackled with sexuality. With need.

His need?

'It's because I'm guilty and grateful,' he said out loud, but he knew it was much, much more.

It couldn't be more. This situation was complicated enough. It didn't need testosterone as well.

'Back off,' he told himself harshly. 'There's so much to be sorted before you can...

'Before you can what?'

Before you can nothing. He raked his hand through his hair and felt weariness envelop him. The family ramifications were enormous. How to let his parents know?

It'd be easier if he didn't. He'd promised Kelly...

But...but...

'Stop it,' he told himself. 'One step at a time. They're both safe now and that's all that matters. She's asleep and you need to take a cold shower.' He was still talking aloud and the dogs were paying attention. Like what he was saying was important.

He looked down at them and gave a rueful chuckle.

'Okay. With the amount of drugs Kelly has on board, she'll sleep until morning, and I need to, too. So go to bed,' he told himself. 'You have a full list in the morning. You have more to think about than Kelly.'

Kelly. Not Jessie's wife. Kelly. It suddenly seemed important to differentiate the two.

The dogs were getting restless. His unease was communicating itself to them. Bess put a tentative paw on his knee and whined.

'Right,' he said, hauling himself together. He picked up a piece of driftwood and hurled it up the track toward the house. Bess bounded after it. Spike looked towards Bess and back toward Matt and whined.

Both dogs were worrying about him.

'Okay, I'm discombobulated,' he told Spike. 'Do you know what that means? No? Well, maybe I don't know either. Maybe all I know is that I need to get on with my life. Home, bed, hospital, medicine. Get your priorities back in line, Eveldene, starting now.'

CHAPTER FIVE

WHEN SHE WOKE, sunshine was pouring in through the open windows. She could hear the waves crashing on the beach below the house.

Two dogs' noses were on her bed.

Bess was so big the dog's nose was practically beside hers. Spike was standing on his haunches, his nose just reaching the top of the mattress.

Both their tails were going like helicopter blades. *Look what we've found—a person! A person in our house!*

She grinned and stretched and it was enough. Spike was up on the bed with her, as if her stretching had been a command. Bess, obviously trained for restraint, stayed where she was. She was sitting and waiting but her tail was still going a mile a minute.

She felt…

She felt…

She glanced at the bedside clock and felt stunned.

Ten o'clock? She'd slept for almost twelve hours!

Visiting hours started at the hospital at ten. She should be there. Jess would be expecting her.

Actually, Jess wouldn't be expecting her. He'd started gentle physio yesterday. She'd supplied him with a week's worth of surfing videos. Talking to his mother would come far down his list of the morning's priorities.

She therefore had nothing to do but lie in this gorgeous bedroom and be sociable to these very nice dogs.

Where was Matt? There was the question and it was a biggie.

It was Monday morning, she told herself. He'd be back in the hospital, where he belonged.

She had his house to herself.

Cautiously she tossed back the covers, apologising to Spike as she did so. 'Sorry, little one. I should have woken earlier and given you more cuddle time.'

But Spike just wiggled and hopped off and headed out the French windows, as if his job had been done. They'd said good morning and now both dogs were off to enjoy the day.

She followed, but only to where the curtains fluttered in the warm breeze. She wasn't exactly respectable. Actually, she wasn't respectable at all. She did a quick rethink and a bit of sheet-wrapping and then dared to explore further.

The dogs were on the veranda.

The view took her breath away.

Wow. Wow, wow and wow. The Pacific Ocean stretched away as far as she could see. The house was nestled in a valley, and the valley broadened out, sweeping down and spreading to a wide, golden beach. Promontories at either end of the beach reached far out to the sea, forming what Kelly thought looked like perfect surf breaks.

The beach looked deserted but civilisation must lie close by, for there were surfers at each headland, drifting on the sun-washed sea, waiting for the right wave.

An ancient cane settee lay along the end of the veranda, covered with saggy cushions and dog hair. Kelly looked at it and thought that of all the perfect places for Jess to convalesce, this was the best.

She'd have to hide the surfboards, though.

Um…what was she thinking? She shouldn't stay here for his whole convalescence.

Why not? Matt was Jessie's uncle. Family. He owed her.

No. He didn't owe her, she reminded herself. He'd been a kid when his brother had died and he'd been shocked and sick. The words he'd flung at her should have been forgiven long ago.

Maybe they had been.

But still she couldn't suppress a grin. If a bit of guilt made it possible for Jess to stay in this place…

Don't try and manipulate. Not Matt.

Involuntarily she tightened her grip on her sheet. What she'd felt last night…

It was only because she'd been exhausted, she told herself, and the mass of bites had been making her feel nauseous. And the antihistamines had been messing with her head.

It was a wonder she hadn't jumped him.

Good grief. She peered cautiously under her sheet, just checking, and saw the welts had subsided. The angry red had faded.

She was still a bit itchy, but it was manageable.

What she needed, though, was coffee. Her apartment might be gorgeous but it didn't have coffee.

Matt must have a kitchen. Matt must be at work.

Matt must have coffee.

The three together were a deal-breaker. Off she went, wearing her sheet. A couple of steps down the veranda she changed her mind, went back and donned the too-thin T-shirt, wound the sheet around her a bit tighter and tried again.

She needn't have bothered. She found Matt's kitchen and it, too, was deserted.

A note lay on the kitchen bench.

Help yourself to anything you need. The keys to the Jeep in the driveway are on top of the fridge. Assuming you have an international driving licence, feel free to use it. Don't forget to drive on the left. The pills in the yellow packet are daytime antihistamines. They won't make you sleepy. Take two. My housekeeper, Mrs Huckle, will be here at ten. I've phoned her and she'll cream your back. I've washed your clothes and they're out in the sun. In this breeze they'll be dry by lunchtime. Take it easy until then. M.

She'd stayed in lots of friends' houses. She'd been left lots of notes. What was it about this one that made her tear up?

He'd done her laundry?

'You must be Kelly.'

She whirled and found a wiry little woman beaming across the room at her. The housekeeper?

'I'm Sally Huckle.' She was in her fifties or early sixties, skinny, sun-worn, wearing skin-tight jeans and a shirt with too much cleavage showing. The woman took her hand and shook it like it might come off.

'A woman on her own,' she said, still beaming. 'Excellent. Too many dratted couples stay here. Only his mother comes by herself and what use is that? He needs a single friend. You're American? And Matt says you have bites. Where's the cream? Matt says you'll need help to put it on and he's told me to apply ice packs as well. Talk about orders. And if you weren't awake I wasn't to wake you but when you did could I please make you pancakes for breakfast.'

She beamed, and her beam was widely enquiring. 'I'm not Matt's friend,' Kelly said stiffly, before the woman could keep going. 'I'm his sister-in-law.'

'His sister-in-law?'

If Jess was coming here to stay, why not say it? 'Yes. My son's had an accident on the Gold Coast. He's still in hospital but he's coming back here to convalesce.'

'Your son? You're Matt's sister-in-law?' The woman sounded incredulous. 'You're Jessie's wife?'

'I… Yes.'

'Your son is Jessie's son?'

'Yes.' Where was she landing herself?

'Does his father know about you?'

'No.'

'Then God help you when he finds out,' she said bluntly. 'Are you sure it's a good idea to stay here?'

'Matt doesn't seem to have given me much choice.' She hesitated. 'But what's wrong with his father knowing?'

'Do you know about your father-in-law?'

'Not much.'

'Then take a look,' the woman said, and crossed to an alcove holding a desktop computer. 'I'm just the hired help but everyone in Australia knows about the Eveldenes.' She hit the browser and in seconds Henry Eveldene's face filled the screen.

'This was written as a Sunday papers feature a couple of years back,' Sally said. 'As far as I can figure, it's accurate. Take a read while I make pancakes. The man makes my hair stand on end. I've never met him but Matt's mother comes here while he's overseas and that's enough. Downtrodden's too big a word for it. Sit. Read.'

'I don't need pancakes.'

'Matt might not be as scary as his father,' Sally said, 'but he's my boss. He's still an Eveldene and what he says goes. Sit. Read. Pancakes.'

Two hours later Kelly was driving cautiously—why didn't the whole world drive on the right?—trying to take in everything she'd learned about Matt's family.

Jessie's family, she reminded herself. Henry Eveldene was Jessie's grandfather.

He was also a giant of industry, owning and operating a huge consortium of paper mills.

He was also a greedy, avaricious bully.

The page Sally had found for her to read had pulled no punches. It spoke of a man to whom money was second only to power. He operated on a knife edge between legal and illegal. He coerced, bullied, blackmailed, and his competitors had gone under one by one.

The article hadn't stopped at his dubious business practices, though. It had talked of the beautiful, wealthy girl he'd married, and how she'd faded from sight and was now practically a recluse.

The article was careful. Kelly could see litigation concerns all over it, but the implications were everywhere. It described two sons, the expectation that they'd move into the family dynasty and take orders from their father, the older son's breakdown and suicide, the younger son's decision to move into medicine, and the subsequent estrangement.

The picture emerged of a solitary megalomaniac who tried to destroy everyone who opposed him.

What would he do if he discovered he had a grandson?

She shivered and went back to concentrating on the road. Stupid left-hand drivers.

But this was a cool little Jeep, fitted with roll bars to

make it into a dune buggy. She could have fun with this machine.

She scolded herself. It wasn't hers.

Hey, but it was, for the time she was staying with Matt. She had visions of putting Jess in the back seat and heading out to explore the local coast. There were places she'd read about around here where they could drive on the beach. They could look for surf spots where they could return once his leg was healed.

Jess's convalescence was looking a lot brighter because of Matt.

Matt… An enigma. Matt, who caused her stomach to clench and she couldn't figure out why.

Matt, who'd done her laundry. Matt, who'd put cream on her back last night, who'd kissed her hair and who'd made her feel…

Enough. She didn't feel like that. She was solid, sensible Dr Kelly Eveldene and if only she could avoid the odd oncoming car she was off to visit her recuperating son and live happily ever after.

Matt's theatre list took him all morning and into the afternoon. He finished at two, rid himself of his theatre scrubs, figured he needed to do a ward round but first he'd grab a sandwich. Maybe he'd take it up to Jessie's ward to eat.

Was it wise to get any closer to Jess? Maybe it wasn't but the decision had been taken out of his hands the moment he'd offered accommodation to Kelly. Besides, he had a nephew. The thought was unnerving but it wasn't something that'd go away.

The minute he'd seen him he'd known this was Jessie's son. Now, come hell or high water, he'd look out for him.

And if he was to look out for him then he needed to get to know him.

As an uncle.

As a friend to his mother?

He'd look out for Kelly, too, but it wasn't just because Jess had married her. It seemed more.

Except he couldn't define more.

He pushed open Jess's door, balancing sandwiches and coffee. Two faces turned to him. Jess and Kelly.

Jess was so like his father that it made Matt's heart twist.

Kelly was so like…Kelly that for some stupid reason his heart twisted even further.

'Hi,' Jess said shyly. 'Come in.'

'I'm not here on business,' he told them. 'No poking and prodding, unless there are any problems?'

'No problems,' Jess said. 'But thank you for looking after my mom.'

That took his breath away. So someone else was looking out for Kelly.

'I told her yesterday she had to get out of that crappy apartment,' Jess said. 'Thanks for picking her up and forcing her.'

'Do you need to pick her up and force her often?' Matt asked, and Jess grinned.

'If you only knew. She's stubborn as a brick, my mom. Immovable. And stupid about money. She has some dumb idea—'

'Jess!' Kelly intervened. 'Let's not be telling Dr Eveldene our family business.'

'Yeah, but Dr Eveldene *is* our family,' Jess said, shy again. 'Isn't that right, sir?'

'I… Yes. But not so much of the "sir".'

'Uncle Matt?'

'Matt.' The uncle bit did his head in.

'Take a seat,' Jess said, relaxing. 'We're watching the next leg of the surf circuit in New Zealand. This guy coming up next is pretty good. He's getting a bit old, though. I reckon his knees might start crumbling soon.'

'How old is a bit old?' Matt asked, perching on the spare visitor's chair.

'Twenty-eight,' Jess said, and Matt choked on his coffee and grinned and looked across at Kelly and found she was grinning as well.

'Yep, you and I are well and truly on the scrap heap,' she said. 'It's a wonder we can still see our knees.'

'Speak for yourself. I do push-ups,' Matt told her. 'Every morning. I reckon I'll be able to see my knees until I'm at least fifty.'

'Dream on,' Kelly said, grinning back. 'Knees don't exist when you're fifty.'

'Especially old knees in neoprene,' Jess said, and shuddered. 'Old guys in wetsuits...ugh.'

'Thank you,' Kelly said with asperity. 'Shall we talk about something else? Like when Dr Eveldene will let you out of hospital?'

'Call me Matt,' Matt said sharply.

'Matt,' Kelly said, as if making a concession, but then she smiled and he thought...he thought...

Concentrate on Jess, he told himself. Concentrate on what mattered. Jess was his family. Kelly wasn't.

'The vascular surgeon and I concur, a week in hospital,' Matt managed. 'And we talked yesterday about surfing. You know it'll be six months before you can safely surf again. Have you had any thoughts about what you might do while you convalesce?'

This was a conversation he often had with patients. As an orthopaedic surgeon, he often treated people with passions—paragliders, trail bike riders, skiers, people who pushed their bodies to extremes.

Not fronting that question—What will you do while your body recovers?—was an invitation to depression, and with Jessie's family background there was no way Matt was ignoring the risk.

'I'll sulk,' Jess said, with an attempt at lightness that didn't quite come off. He saw Kelly glance at her son sharply and then look away. So she was worried, too.

'When did you leave school?' Matt asked. 'If you're interested, you might be able to go back for a bit. A couple of subjects might hold you in good stead if you decide you need a career when your knees go.'

There was silence in the room. His suggestion had been presumptuous, Matt knew, but, then…his big brother had had nothing but surfing. To see this kid go the same way…

'I've done with schooling for a while,' Jess said, turning back to the surfing on television. 'Mom and I made a deal. No more study.'

What sort of deal was that—letting your son do nothing but surf? But he'd pushed the boundaries as far as he could. Mother and son both suddenly seemed tense and there was no way he could take it further.

'I might learn to play snakes and ladders,' Jess said, attempting lightness but his words weren't light at all.

'I'll buy you a set,' Matt told him. 'No,' he said, as his offer was met by silence. He put up his hands as if to ward off protests. 'I insist. As an uncle it's the only appropriate thing to do.'

Jess chuckled and went back to watching what the surfer was doing on television. Kelly cast him a look of relief and Matt unwrapped his sandwich and wondered where to go next. What was the role of an uncle?

And then his phone went.

Of course. This was part of his job. How many times had meals been interrupted by his phone? At least this was just a sandwich.

He tossed Kelly an apologetic glance—no need to

send one to Jess, who was engrossed again in his surfing world—and answered.

Trouble.

He tossed his sandwich in the bin and headed for the door.

'What?' Kelly demanded.

'Work.'

'Yeah, but it's a biggie,' she said. 'I'm a doctor, too, remember? I know the drill. If you get a minor call, you rewrap your sandwich. You ditched your sandwich so I'm figuring it's major. I shouldn't ask but—'

'Bus crash,' he said curtly. 'A self-drive bus of tourists mucking about off road in the sand dunes. They copped a head-on with a council grader on the far side of a crest. Deaths and multiple casualties. We'll be pushing to get staff to cover it. See you tomorrow, Jess.'

'Matt, can I help?' Kelly asked sharply.

'I don't see how.' He had the door open; he needed to leave.

'Matt, as surf-pro physician I have provisional registration to work in almost every country we visit,' she said, talking fast. 'In emergencies I can stay hands on. In hospitals I require overall supervision from local medics, but I'm a doctor, I'm another pair of hands and I'm available. Do you need me?'

Matt hesitated. An unknown doctor, overseas trained…

But this accident involved twenty or more tourists, Beth had said, and she'd sounded desperate. They were evacuating some to Brisbane but there was only one chopper and most were coming by road. This was the first and only place that casualties could be stabilised.

He steadied. He did know her. He trusted her. He needed to check, though, for the sake of the patients she'd be treating.

'Can you prove your registration?'

'My paperwork's in my travel wallet with my gear at your place,' she told him, as if she'd expected the question. She hauled a card from her purse. 'But you can ring this number. Quote my name and my registration number. They'll confirm fast.'

She'd done this before, he thought. She'd acted as a doctor in a foreign setting. Then, he thought, *of course she had*. Kelly—or the organisation she worked for—would have set up temporary registration from the moment she entered the country, so in an emergency, if there weren't enough medics on hand, she could act as a doctor without repercussions.

'Phone while we hit the lift,' she said.

'Thank you.' There was nothing else to say.

They left Jess to his surfing and headed for Emergency. They didn't speak on the way down. He'd phoned and was listening to someone in officialdom telling him Kelly was fine.

A small army seemed to be waiting for them, but they were mostly nurses. Matt glanced around and saw only three qualified doctors, Beth, Frieda and Emma. Beth and Frieda were good but Emma had only passed her final exams last month. She wasn't confident at the best of times, and now she was looking terrified.

'I'm trying to get more hands here,' Beth told him as she saw his visual sweep of the room and guessed his thoughts. 'But everyone seems to be in the middle of something urgent. Brisbane's on standby. We're pulling in another chopper, but for now it's down to us.'

'Kelly's offered to help. She's an emergency physician accredited for work here under supervision. I've done the checks.'

'Excellent,' Beth said with relief. 'Matt, can you do a fast tour, show her what's needed and find her some scrubs. Kelly, can I put you on triage with Rachel, our senior nurse? Direct the straightforward ones to Emma, the harder ones to the rest of us.'

Kelly nodded. Matt saw her assessing the teams of nurses, checking the doctors, then glancing at Emma, who looked like she was about to faint.

'Maybe Emma and I could work together,' Kelly suggested. 'With Rachel's help, we could do triage and urgent stabilisation as a team. I'm supposed to work under supervision if Australian doctors are present so it'd cover all the bases.' Then, as Emma visibly relaxed at the thought of not working alone, Kelly moved on. 'Do you have an anaesthetist?'

'That's Frieda,' Matt told her, signalling to a grey-haired woman currently tossing orders to nurses on the other side of the room. 'If we need 'em, intubation and tracheotomies are her specialty.'

'I can do trachies in my sleep.' Frieda threw her a friendly grin. 'We're always short-staffed, but this is looking crazy hard. Glad to have another Eveldene on board.' She gave a brief smile.

'I hope you don't need me,' Kelly told her, but then the scream of an ambulance outside announced the first arrival and there was room for no more talk.

They needed Kelly. They needed everyone.

This was war-zone stuff.

Kelly had trained as an emergency physician. She'd done mock-ups of this type of scenario but she'd never been in one. Nevertheless, her drilled-in training kicked in, making her reactions instinctive. By her side the very junior Emma was visibly shaking. Emma supervising Kelly? Ha!

The first arrival, a girl of about sixteen, had a deep gash running from under her arm to the small of her back.

Her blood pressure was dangerously low—the drip wasn't going fast enough. The other casualty coming through was a spinal injury with breathing difficulties. Matt and Frieda took that case, while Beth headed out to greet whoever was coming next.

That was almost the last time Kelly had time to see what everyone else was doing. She focused only on the kid under her hands.

She reached for the adrenaline, showed Rachel—thankfully capable—where to apply pressure, and snapped orders to Emma. 'Get another line in. We need as much fluid as we can.'

Emma's hands shook as she tried to do as ordered.

'Stop,' Kelly said, grabbed the young woman's hands and held for one harsh moment. 'Deep breath. Emma, you will not mess this up. You can't. The only wrong way is not at all. You know how to do this. Move to automatic pilot. Don't think of the consequences. You've had years of training. This is what you're here for, Emma. Do it.'

And Emma met her gaze, took a deep breath and visibly steadied. She picked up the syringe and inserted it into the back of the girl's hand. It went exactly where it was supposed to go and she didn't even pause for breath before turning to grab bags of plasma.

From fifteen feet away, where Matt and Frieda were working on a woman who probably wouldn't make it but had to be given every chance, Matt saw and felt a jab of relief. Yeah, he'd watched. He had too much on his plate, but he'd assured Beth that Kelly was qualified. Lives were in her hands and it would have been negligent not do a fast visual check.

Two minutes in he was completely reassured. Not only did she work like an efficient machine but she'd settled Emma, so instead of one terrified novice, they had a team of two steady, intent doctors.

'It has to be cervical spine fracture,' Frieda barked. 'Get her straight through to Imaging.'

And then the woman's shallow breathing ceased. Kelly was forgotten, everything was forgotten as they fought to get her back—and lost.

And when they surfaced from defeat there were more casualties waiting. A couple more doctors arrived. The department looked even more like a war zone.

He lost sight of Kelly. He lost sight of everything except trying to save lives.

CHAPTER SIX

BY NINE THAT night there was nothing left for Kelly to do. Patients had been transferred, to Theatre, to wards, to other hospitals at need. A couple were in the morgue.

That was a gut wrenching she could never get used to. In emergency situations Kelly worked on the front line, but eventually surgeons, anaesthetists, paediatricians, neurologists, even grief counsellors, moved in and took over.

But sometimes Kelly thought she needed counselling herself. She felt like that now, but she'd done what she'd needed to do. When the last patient was wheeled out, Beth thanked her and told her to go home.

'We wouldn't have had the outcome we did without you,' she told her. 'And the way you hauled Emma together...your help today meant we had five doctors instead of three.'

'Emma's a good doctor,' Kelly said, wishing, stupidly, that Matt was still here, but Matt was an orthopaedic surgeon, one of those who kept working after emergency imperatives had been met. He'd probably be operating until morning.

'She's good *now*,' Beth told her. 'Thanks to you, she worked well, and she'll never be as terrified again. And as for you, if you'd like part-time work while you and Jessie are stuck here, just say the word. It'd be a huge pleasure to have two Eveldenes working in this hospital.'

Two Eveldenes… That was a weird concept.

She and Matt.

Something was twisting inside her. What?

Today she'd been part of Matt's team. Matt had vouched for her and she'd worked in his hospital. Beth was referring to them as the two Eveldenes.

Strangely it felt like she had family, and the feeling was weird.

She found herself wishing she could go home with Matt now. She'd seen him as they'd wheeled the last patient out of Emergency to Theatre. He was facing multiple fractures. He'd be working all night.

And he'd looked haggard already.

He was nothing to do with her.

Wrong. He was an Eveldene.

Family?

Needing to ground herself, she headed back to Jessie's room. Jess was deeply asleep. She sat by his bed, just watching him. Settling herself in her son's presence.

After a while the nurse in charge of the ward popped in. 'I've been sent to take care of you,' she said, efficiency overlaid with kindness. 'Would you like tea and a sandwich? Or something hot? The whole hospital knows what you've done today and we're grateful. We can heat you some soup if you like. Anything.'

'Thank you, no.' She rose, feeling bone weary. There was no point in staying here. 'I need to go home.'

'And you're staying with Matt. You're his sister-in-law, the wife of his brother who died. That's awfully sad.'

'It was a long time ago,' Kelly said repressively, but knowing hospital grapevines were the same the world over. She had as much chance of hiding her history as flying.

'But still…' The woman glanced at Jess. 'They say he's

just like his dad, and you've brought him up in America but finally you've brought him home.'

'This isn't home.'

'You just said it was,' the woman said gently. 'And we all think you're wonderful already. If Jess needs an uncle and you need roots, why not stay? Heaven knows, Matt needs a family.'

'Matt has a family.' She was sounding curt to the point of rudeness now but the woman wasn't noticing. What was it about the medical world that made its inhabitants think they could intrude into their colleagues' lives? It happened the world over and here was obviously no exception.

'One failed marriage, one wimp of a mother and one bully of a father,' the nurse said softly, thoughtfully. 'The whole hospital's been trying to get our Matt paired off for ever. We'd practically given up.'

'I'm his sister-in-law, not a potential girlfriend,' Kelly snapped, and the nurse grinned.

'Of course you are,' she agreed. 'But as you said yourself, all that was a long time ago. And our Dr Matt is gorgeous.'

Our Dr Matt is gorgeous.

The problem was that he was.

Kelly drove home in the dark. She normally needed all her attention to stay on the left, but the road was quiet and there was a fraction of her mind free to stray.

She'd been acutely aware of Matt today. Beth was in charge of Emergency but she'd almost unconsciously deferred to Matt. He'd worked like two men, one part working to salvage mangled limbs, the other watching what was going on in the rest of the room. He'd snapped curt orders, not just for the patient he was treating but for others as well. He didn't interfere with any other doctor's treatment, but he was covering the room, making sure equipment, plasma, saline, everything needed was on hand.

Supply should have been a full-time role but there hadn't been enough medical hands on deck to cover it. Matt had done it seamlessly, as well as ensuring at least two people didn't need amputation. As well as reassuring frightened patients. As well as fielding a call from the overseas parents of the girl who'd died under his hands. The hospital counsellors had moved in to take most of the calls but for that one the counsellor had approached him.

'They know their daughter didn't die instantly. They have visions of her dying in agony. Matt, if you could...'

Matt could. He'd stepped to a corner of the room near where Kelly had been working and she'd heard him speaking, quietly, gently, as if he'd had all the time in the world.

'With the blow to the head as well as the spinal injury she'd have been instantly unconscious and not frightened or in any pain. Apparently they were having a wonderful time in the bus. It started slipping on the dunes and everyone thought it was fun. The passengers thought it was supposed to happen, so there was no terror. Yes, she was alive when she was brought into hospital but the paramedics assure me she was deeply unconscious from the moment of impact.'

And then... 'No. I'm so sorry but even if we'd been able to save her, her brain damage would have been massive and the spinal injury would have meant total paralysis. Of course I'm available to answer any questions you might have in the future, and certainly if you decide to come to Australia to take your girl home, I'll talk to you then. Or before. That goes for any of our staff. The paramedics who brought her in, the counsellors, any one of the men and women who've cared for her, we're all here for you.'

Kelly hadn't been able to hear the other end of the conversation but she'd listened to Matt's reassurances and she'd thought somewhere on the other side of the world devastated parents would put down the phone knowing everything that could have been done for their girl had been done.

She'd been in caring hands.

Caring…

She thought of the Matt she'd met eighteen years ago. Caring was the last word she'd have thought to apply to him.

That had been a long time ago. So…what?

Her thoughts were drifting and she wasn't sure where. Or maybe she did know but it scared her. She needed to think of someone…of something else.

She'd been offered a job. That was a good thought. If she could work and earn, maybe she wouldn't have to stay in Matt's house.

But Jess would love staying in Matt's house, and Matt was Jessie's uncle. Did she have the right to refuse to let them get to know each other? A week ago she'd have said yes. After tonight, seeing Matt's skill, seeing Matt's inherent kindness, she thought: possibly not.

But where did that leave her? The way she was feeling… Matt's skill and kindness was doing her head in.

Was that down to his likeness to her husband?

Possibly not, she thought. She'd been widowed for eighteen years and her memories of her husband had been obscured by time. He was a loving ghost at her shoulder, but he wasn't one who reminded her to mourn. Neither was he one who claimed ownership.

He'd be troubled that she'd never had another serious relationship, she thought, and she struggled to conjure him up. What would his advice be?

Do what's right for today, Kell, he'd say. *Don't let tomorrow's monsters scare you. Tomorrow they'll look like minnows. You can kick them away with the pleasure you gain from today. Especially from today's surf.*

Maybe she needed a surf.

Now? In the dark?

Maybe not.

What she needed now was bed. What she needed now was to make the confusion in her head go away.

'You'll all be minnows tomorrow,' she told her doubts, but the image of Matt on the telephone superimposed itself.

There was no way Matt Eveldene would ever be a minnow.

Matt slept badly. He always did after tragedy. While he'd trained he'd thought eventually he'd get used to it but he never had. The anger at the waste of life, because one unskilled driver had thought it would be fun to gun a busload of kids over cresting sand dunes... The grief it caused... The grief that would go on and on...

Like the grief he felt for his brother.

He thought of the woman presumably sleeping just through the wall from him and the grief she'd endured. He could have helped her.

There was yet more grief.

He found himself thinking of his mother in that appalling mausoleum of a house, afraid to walk away from her husband, afraid of her own shadow. But maybe she wasn't afraid, he thought. Maybe she couldn't escape grief wherever she went, so why try? He brought her here when his father was away but she was totally passive. She sat on the veranda and stared out to sea, and as soon as her husband was due home, she packed and left.

He'd tried to persuade her to seek help. He'd made appointments for her with psychologists, but no one had been able to break through.

Could Kelly?

Could Jessie?

There was another worry keeping him awake. If he let his mother know of Jessie's existence, it'd bring joy, but it'd also set loose the full force of his father. Kelly was one strong woman but no one could face down his father.

He slept fitfully, and finally it was dawn. He dropped a hand to greet the dogs at the side of his bed—and found nothing.

Traitors, he thought, remembering they hadn't bounded out to greet him last night either. They'd be with Kelly.

They'd be just through the wall. By her bed.

This was driving him crazy. He'd head down to the beach before work, he decided. At least the waves might clear the fog.

He grabbed his swimmers, headed out to the veranda and paused.

Someone was surfing just below the house. His dogs were on the beach, standing guard as they did when he surfed.

He gazed along the veranda to where two surfboards usually lay, one short and light for when he wanted to push himself, the other a long board, stable and easy to paddle, for times when he wanted to lie behind the breakers and catch the occasional wave with ease.

The small one was gone. It took skill...

She had skill.

He stood and watched in the soft dawn light. A rolling breaker was coming in. The sea was silk smooth, glimmering in the sun's early rays. The breaker was a dark shadow, moving swiftly, building height as it neared the shallows.

She caught its force at just the right time, at just the right angle. In one smooth movement she was on her feet, sleek and light, her feet at one with the board, working it like a lover.

She wasn't content to simply ride the wave to shore. She

crested to the lip and swooped, she flipped a turn, then cruised under the breaking foam. Finally she dropped full length, dipping her head so the wave wouldn't push her backwards, and started paddling, easily and smoothly, out to catch the next wave.

She was wearing a simple black costume. Her hair was a tangle of dripping curls. She looked…she looked…

No. There were a hundred reasons why he shouldn't think how she was looking.

He thought of how she'd been when Jess had found her. Seventeen. She'd been a wild creature, he thought. Maybe she still was.

Why would he prefer to see her as a wild creature? Someone who could never fit into a life like this?

Still, she shouldn't be surfing alone.

He glanced across at the headlands and was almost disappointed to see other surfers in the water. It was an unwritten rule that surfers looked out for others when they could see them. She wasn't actually alone.

But now she'd seen him. He must be obvious, standing on the veranda, watching.

He didn't want to intrude but she waved as if she was including him in her morning—and then the next wave rolled in and she went back to concentrating on the surf.

How could he resist? He couldn't. He had two hours before he needed to leave for work and Kelly was surfing on his beach. Even his dogs were waiting.

Putting away the hundred reasons why he shouldn't, he grabbed his long board and went to join her.

For Kelly, surfing was as natural as breathing. It was her release, her escape. She surfed with friends, she surfed with Jess, but their presence didn't matter.

It was also okay to surf with Matt, for he understood silence.

She'd met chatty surfers and they drove her crazy. It was okay to lie out behind the waves and solve the problems of the world after a long morning's surf, but to choose to talk rather than surf…

Matt didn't. He simply paddled out to her, raised a hand in greeting and concentrated on the next wave.

He caught it with ease, rose, steadied, then manoeuvred the big board with skill and rode it until the wave shrank into the shallows.

A surfing surgeon.

He wasn't as skilled as a pro, but he was more than competent. He was riding a big old board, because she had his good one. He looked good on it. No, he looked great. She'd thought he was married to his medicine but his body was tanned and ripped and he couldn't be as good as this without practice.

A wave swelled and swept past—and she'd missed it. It was a beauty. Matt caught it and in seconds he was in the green room, that gorgeous sapphire tube of perfectly looped water.

If he'd had his good board he could have stayed in there for the length of the ride. As it was, he emerged and glanced back at her and said, 'If you're going to waste waves like that, I want my board back.'

She chuckled and glanced behind and caught the next one, and somehow things had changed between them again.

Something had settled.

This was her husband's brother, she told herself as the morning grew brighter, as they caught wave after wave, as the silence deepened and strengthened between them. He was Jess's uncle.

But she knew, at some deep level, he was becoming much, much more.

It should scare her, but it didn't. She rode her waves and Matt rode behind, before or beside her, and it didn't matter.

Something had changed. Somehow, for this moment, she felt peace.

The morning had to end. Matt had patients waiting. 'Stay if you want,' Matt told her, but she shook her head. In truth, she wasn't as fit as she used to be. Two hours' surfing was enough.

'Do you want to leave the boards in the dunes?' Matt said. 'The surfers at the headlands never come this far. No one comes along here but us. You...*we* could surf tomorrow.'

There was a promise. She managed a wavery smile in return.

'The short one's yours tomorrow.'

'No way. My skills don't match yours. Right now I can blame the board and that's the way I like it.'

She chuckled and they headed up to the house.

If I was a teenager I might reach out and take his hand, Kelly thought, and then hauled herself back under control.

Yeah, but you're not a teenager. You have a whole lot more hormones—and Matt needs to go to work.

Matt.

But...but...

'You're smiling because...?' Matt asked, and she found herself blushing from the toes up.

'Yeah,' Matt said. 'Me, too.'

Me, too? Really? *Really*?

'Not appropriate,' she managed.

'No.'

Okay. That was decided.

'Not when I have a theatre list in forty minutes.'

Hmm. There was enough promise in that statement to take a woman's breath away. 'You get first shower,' she told him, feeling suddenly breathless. 'Unless there's enough water pressure for two showers.'

'There's not," he said.

"Go. I'll make breakfast.'

'I'll grab a coffee at the hospital.'

'You can't surf for hours and then operate on an empty stomach. Surgeon fainting mid-list? Not a good look.'

'Toast, then,' he said, and she nodded.

'Toast. Go.'

'Kelly?'

But his nearness was doing things to her. He was too big, too broad, too almost naked. His chest was still wet. Water was still dripping from his hair. He looked...

'Toast,' she said, and if she sounded desperate, who could blame her? 'But shower, now. Go!'

He ran his shower cold. Really cold. If he could have added ice it would have been a sensible option. He dressed with care, thinking it'd be better if he was consulting rather than operating this morning because then he could dress formally in suit. He could always take his jacket off later, but for some reason it seemed imperative that he be completely, carefully dressed when he saw Kelly again. If he didn't have a suit jacket and tie on it would be so easy to...

No. Any minute now it'd be another cold shower.

Breakfast. Toast. He headed for his kitchen, thinking he should have made it clear to Kelly that he'd eat on his side and she could do whatever she wanted on her side, but he hadn't made it clear and he copped the smell of eggs and bacon before he got there. *In his kitchen.*

Kelly was frying bacon. She had a beach towel wrapped round her like a sarong. Her feet were still sandy. Her curls were tangled damply around her shoulders.

Every part of him froze.

Every part of him wanted.

No. A man had to work!

Sensibly, though, a man also had to have breakfast. Treat this as ordinary, he pleaded with himself. He walked in and she turned and smiled at him and handed him a loaded plate of eggs, bacon, fried tomato and toast.

'A boy's fantasies are all coming together right here,' he managed. He had the plate in his hands. That helped. He couldn't reach out and touch her. But she was still too close and that towel was tucked simply into itself right at her breast and he knew underneath was that simple slip of black Lycra...

'Seduction by bacon,' she said demurely. 'Things your mother never taught you.'

'No.' He hesitated, trying to figure how to get this electric charge out of the room. History, he thought. Remember bleakness. 'Your mother never taught you much by the sound of it,' he tried.

'No,' she said, and the smile slipped a little. 'But I've been around enough surf camps in my life to know a great feed after surfing is a sure way to a man's heart. You'll still have forgotten me by lunchtime, though. You'll see. The lady in the cafeteria will smile at you as she hands you your turkey sandwich and you'll change allegiances, just like that.'

He thought of Tilda in the hospital canteen, fair, fat and fifty. He looked again at Kelly's bare toes and the sand in her cleavage and the way one curl was just trailing downward...

'I think you just won,' he said, and he couldn't keep his voice steady.

'Love's more fickle than you think,' Kelly said serenely, turning back to cook her own breakfast.

'You mean no one ever fell for you after Jessie?' He tried to keep the question casual—and failed.

'Sure they did,' she said. 'I've cooked so many breakfasts I couldn't possibly count.'

'Kelly...'

She turned. The bacon sizzled in the pan behind her. She looked at him.

'I don't do light stuff,' she said in a voice that was anything but light. 'My dad was promiscuous, living with woman after woman after woman. I'm Jessie's mother. That comes first. It always has and it always will.'

'Jess is growing up.'

'And he still needs to respect his mom.'

'How can he not respect you?'

'Eat your breakfast,' she told him, and deliberately turned away. She finished cooking hers, served it out and then sat on the opposite side of the table. They ate in silence. Things were happening between them, and he didn't have a clue what.

I don't do light stuff. It was a warning to back off.

He didn't—necessarily—want to back off, but the complications of falling for this woman were immense.

Was he falling for her?

Had he already fallen?

He'd only known her a few days. She was his brother's wife.

'I need to go,' he managed, thinking he needed space, and, thank heaven, medicine could supply it. 'I'm doing Gloria Matterson's hip replacement this morning. She's been waiting for two years in the public queue and she doesn't need to wait longer.'

'Of course you do. And this... Maybe this morning wasn't a good idea,' Kelly told him.

And he thought, she needs space, too.

What was happening between them? Exactly nothing. They hadn't even kissed.

He rose and carted his plate to the sink. He'd have coffee on the way to work. There was a drive-through...

He turned and Kelly had risen with her plate and she was just...there. Right in front of him.

She looked adorable.

He took the plate from her grasp and put it in the sink behind him. He did it without turning. For some reason it seemed imperative that he didn't break their locked gazes.

I don't do light stuff.

This wasn't light. This was a force he'd never felt before, a sensual pull stronger than any he'd ever known. He wanted to take the beach towel and tug it to the floor. He wanted to run his hands over the curve of her beautiful hips. He wanted...

He'd just have to want. Gloria Matterson wanted, too, and she'd have been given pre-op drugs already.

'I need to go,' he said hoarsely.

'Of course you do.'

'Kelly...'

'Just go.'

'I will,' he said, and if it sounded like a vow, maybe it was. Then, because he couldn't help himself, because there was no way he could stop himself, he took her shoulders in his hands, drew her to him and kissed her.

She should not be kissing Matt Eveldene. Not!

For eighteen years she'd hated this man. She'd hated his family, she'd hated everything he represented. She'd sworn never to have anything to do with him or his ghastly family ever in her lifetime. And now she was in his arms, her mouth was on his, and she was being soundly, solidly kissed.

No. Not soundly. Not solidly. There was nothing about those two words that came near to describing what was happening to her right now.

She was being…subsumed.

Was that the word? Actually, who cared? His mouth was warm on hers, his hands were hugging her close, her breasts were moulding against him and the kiss…oh, the kiss…

It felt like fire. It felt like pure, hot fusion. She could taste him, feel him, melt into him.

He was large and strong and sure. The soft wool of his gorgeous suit was whispering against the bare skin of her shoulders. His hands were in the small of her back, pressing her closer. His strong, angular face was hard against hers.

Her hands rose seemingly of their own accord and ran through his thick, black hair to tug him closer, close enough so she felt their mouths were welded together, a fusion growing stronger by the moment.

As was the heat building through her body. She was on fire.

She wanted this man, right here, right now, but he was already putting her away because Gloria Matterson was waiting and there were medical imperatives and this was… this was…

Crazy.

Her towel slipped. It lay in a puddle on the floor and she thought of what might have happened if there had been no surgical list waiting. She could…

She couldn't. Somehow she managed a deep breath. Yes, that's what she had to do. Recover, think things through and get on with…what she had to get on with.

'Uh-oh,' she managed, but she didn't quite recognise the husky whisper that came out. 'I knew my cooking was good but not that good.'

'There's a lot about you that's good.'

'You…don't know me.'

'There is that. We should have started this as online dating. I'd know your star sign then.'

'So what's yours?' She wasn't making sense, even to herself.

'Libra.'

'Uh-oh. I'm Aries. I'll walk all over you. Favourite music?'

'Wagner.'

'Really?' She choked.

'Um, no.' He grinned, lightening the room with his devastating smile. 'Assuming this is online dating data, I threw that in to scare away the hip-hops. But classical, yes.'

'But mine *is* hip-hop,' she said mournfully, trying to smile back, carefully retrieving her towel and rewrapping it. 'So we're doomed from the start. Take this no further, Dr Eveldene. Go to work.'

'Until tonight?'

'I should move out,' she said worriedly. 'I don't think—'

'Don't move out.'

'Because?'

'Because I don't want you to.' His smile faded. He cupped her chin in his hand and kissed her again, hard and fast. 'You're right, we don't know each other. We have baggage that is certain to get in the way. Hip-hop, classic—problem, but there are always earphones. Kelly...my home is special and I wish to share it with you. Please stay.'

'I'll stay,' she said, and he had to go. She stood and watched as he headed out the door, into his car and out of sight. Her hand stayed on her lips as if she could keep the taste of him just by holding it there.

He disappeared and reality set in. But not regret.

She'd just kissed her husband's brother. For years she'd regarded him as the enemy. Kissing him should have seemed like a betrayal and yet...it hadn't. It had felt right.

More, it felt like the bitterness that had stayed with her

for all those years had melted in that kiss. Ultimate forgiveness? Ultimate moving on?

But what had he said? *My home is special.* It was an odd line for a guy to use. Seduction by interior design?

She glanced about her at his stunning home. She glanced into the living room at the great rock mantelpiece, the exquisite rugs, the floor-to-ceiling windows framing the ocean beyond.

My home is special.

'I'd have stayed anyway,' she whispered, still touching her lips. 'The way you kissed me seems to have wiped away the awfulness of the past. And in such a kiss, I might not have noticed your home.'

She hardly noticed places. No, that wasn't true. She could certainly appreciate that Matt's house was beautiful. It was just that she saw houses—homes—as transient.

My home is special...

It was such an odd statement that she found herself thinking again of the inherent, basic differences between them. Classic, hip-hop. Aries, Libra. Nomad, house-loving. Internet dating wouldn't have stood a chance.

My home is special...

She thought back eighteen years, to her beloved Jess, trying to explain about his family.

'All my dad ever thinks about is things. His home. His possessions.'

Jess had rejected those things and so had she.

'Dad controls people with his possessions,' Jess had told her. *'We don't need them.'*

She still didn't. She'd been fiercely independent all her life, and nothing was changing now. Just because one man had kissed her...

Oh, for heaven's sake. Stop worrying, she told herself crossly. She should take a shower and then head to the hospital. She had a son to visit. Beth had promised to talk to her about a job. She had enough to do today without thinking of possessions controlling her. She had enough to do without thinking of the incompatibility between the two Drs Eveldene.

And in any gaps in her day, qualms or not, she had a kiss to remember.

CHAPTER SEVEN

'How about triage in Emergency?' To say Beth was enthusiastic about employing her was an understatement. 'The local surf competitions come straight after the world tour so we're overrun with surfing casualties. Plus, it's school holidays, which always sees us busy. Could you work mornings from eight to one? That's when most surf casualties come in. Your provisional registration means you're supposed to be supervised, but with your skills I'm happy to supervise from half a hospital away. From what I gather, you can cope with most surf injuries in your sleep.'

So it was settled. Excellent. Wasn't it?

How had her life changed so dramatically? She was living in Matt's house. She was working in Matt's hospital.

She'd been kissing in Matt's kitchen.

Giving in to temptation...

Um, temptation wasn't exactly what she needed to be considering, when the woman in front of her was offering her a job.

'I coped with a kid impaled on a surfboard once,' Kelly told her, trying hard to feel and sound professional. 'A grommit—a learner surfer—thought it'd be a great idea to make his surfboard stand out. He drew the eyes and the razor teeth of a swordfish and whittled the snout to a sharp point. He came off, his leg rope jerked him onto the point and the whole thing went through his thigh. He came into ER with fibreglass still attached.'

'Yikes,' Beth said. 'Happy ending?'

'A textbook surfboard-ectomy.' Kelly grinned, relaxing into the medicine she loved. 'He lived to surf another day.'

Beth grinned back. 'A woman who performs surfboard-ectomies is my kind of doctor. So, do you want the job?'

'Surely you need to check up on me.'

'Matt already did. He phoned your previous bosses this morning. You have glowing credentials from everyone.'

'How did he know who to ask?' Kelly gasped.

'Your son, of course. Apparently Jess thinks it's cool that you'll be working here.'

'Matt asked Jess?'

'He's his uncle, isn't he?'

There was a statement to make her catch her breath. It suggested that Matt had a relationship with Jess that had nothing to do with her. Maybe he did, but…

My home is special and I wish to share it with you.

She couldn't get rid of that stupid statement. Why did the words keep coming back and why did they make her feel edgy? Like the walls were closing in?

She was being paranoid, she decided. She and Jess were accepting Matt's kindness while Jess recuperated. That was all. And it was fine that Jess had told Matt where she'd trained.

And the kiss?

The kiss had been an aberration, she told herself—a momentary temptation and weakness. So why had it felt like a beginning?

'So, do you want the job?' Beth asked brightly again. 'There's a heap of forms to complete if you do. You can take them with you and fill them in while Jess watches his surf videos.'

'How do you know Jess watches surf videos?'

'Matt told me. He took him some sci-fi movies and Jess politely declined. Matt thinks he's a bit obsessed.'

'He told you he thinks Jessie's obsessed?'

'Hey,' Beth said, and held up her hands as if in surrender. 'I'm a mother of three teenagers. I understand obsession. Matt doesn't.'

'But he told you. It's none of his business.'

'Maybe he wants it to be his business,' Beth said mildly. 'But as for me, I'm butting out, right now.'

'So Matt's been lending you sci-fi movies?'

Kelly had made herself wait a whole half-hour before casually asking the question, and Jess didn't look up from the television when she did.

'Yeah. They were dumb. He didn't mind, though, when I refused. It's not like he bought them or anything—they're borrowed. I told him I had more surfing stuff than I could handle but he didn't seem interested. Do you know if he can surf?'

'He can. He's not bad.'

'I guess with Dad for a brother he must know how. A surfing surgeon. That's pretty cool. He was telling me about Dad when he was a kid. Mom, they're saying I can go home tomorrow as long as I come in every morning for physiotherapy. Matt says there's loads of room at his place and he has dogs and I can see the surf. And Beth... she's the doctor in Emergency and she's cool...she has a son who's fourteen and a surf nut but he's teaching himself from videos. She asked if I might have time to talk him through them. She'll bring him out to Matt's.'

Right. All organised. This was good. So why did it feel like the ground was sliding away from under her? Why was she feeling like she was more out of control that she'd ever been?

'That's great,' she managed. 'And I have a job.'

'I know that, too,' Jess said. 'Or I knew they were going to offer. Everyone knows everything around here, even the janitor.' He looked up at her then, with that shy, warm smile that was so like his father's it still did her head in. 'If I had to wipe out, it was pretty lucky I wiped out here. It almost feels like home.'

Home. There was that word again.

She shook off her unease and checked the colour of Jess's toes, not because she needed to—she was sure even a minuscule change wouldn't have escaped Matt's attention. But she needed to be doing something.

She wished she could start work this morning instead of in two days' time when the forms had been cleared. She wished...

She wished she was doing something that wasn't controlled by Matt Eveldene and his hospital and his home.

She wished she wasn't tempted.

There was no way Kelly was raiding Matt's refrigerator again. She and Jess would be independent. So after leaving the hospital she headed to the supermarket Matt had taken her to that first night he'd taken her to his place.

After stocking up on provisions, she made for home. No, she corrected herself, she made for *Matt's place*. Why the differentiation was important she didn't know, but it was. She did Jess's washing then, looking for something else to do, she took the dogs for a walk on the beach.

She wished Jess wasn't so fiercely independent. If he was younger and less fierce about his boundaries she could go back to the hospital and talk to him or read, or even help while he did his physio.

If Matt offered, would Jess let him help?

'The kid needs a father.' Various people had said that to her over the years, or variations on the theme. 'How does he cope without a father figure?'

He'd coped fine. She was proud of him.

So why was she stalking along the beach like she was angry? Was she angry?

If the Eveldenes had been supportive all those years ago, if they'd offered a home and family to her and her son, would she have wanted it?

Did she want it now?

She wasn't making sense, even to herself.

Disconcerted, she headed back to the house. She felt aimless, totally disoriented.

She could surf, but for once there was no one surfing at the far headlands and one of her rules was not surfing without other surfers in sight. She'd made that rule up for Jess. As a kid she'd surfed whenever she'd wanted, but becoming a mother had changed the ground rules. Tempting as it was, if she surfed alone then Jess would, too.

She needed to ask Matt not to, she decided. There was already a hint of change of allegiance in Jess's attitude. She could hear him in her imagination.

'If Matt surfs alone, I don't see why you're worried.'

Oh, for heaven's sake, get over yourself, she told herself. She was worrying about shadows. She turned her back on the ocean and headed for her little kitchen. What to do? What to do?

Bake?

She never baked. She didn't even cook much. In their shoebox of an apartment in Hawaii she had a two-ring burner and a microwave.

'If this place is "home" then I might as well pretend it really is,' she told herself. 'And what do normal people do at home? Bake.'

So she would. She'd make a welcome-home cake for Jess. How hard could it be?

'I'll need a pinafore,' she told the dogs, egging herself

into the role of cook-extraordinaire. 'And maybe some fluffy slippers and hair curlers.'

The dogs wagged their tails, bemused, as well they might be. Kelly cooking? Kelly was a bit bemused herself.

Matt climbed out of the car, taking a breath of the sea air to ground himself—and smelled burning. Smoke was wafting from the windows at the end of the house. He ran, grabbing his phone so he could call emergency services, imagining the worst.

It wasn't the worst. Kelly was at her kitchen bench, surrounded by smoke, staring mournfully at something that looked like a withered, black pyramid.

She looked totally, absolutely crestfallen.

The pyramid was oozing the smoke. It smelled of burned citrus. It was surrounded by flour, eggshells, milk cartons, cream cartons, splattered...mess. The dogs were cruising, obviously hoovering up a week's worth of treats in one hit. Bess was doing better than Spike because she could reach higher. Whatever had splattered had hit walls as well as floor.

'I think I know what the problem is,' Kelly said mournfully, not taking her eyes from the pyramid. 'I should have put the orange syrup on after it was cooked, not before. It sort of spilled over the sides and the bottom of the oven started to smoke. And then flame. And it cooked so fast...'

She had mixture on her face, through her hair, on her jeans and T-shirt. She looked...

Delicious.

'Argument with the mixer?' he ventured, trying desperately not to laugh, and she glared at the offending object as if it was totally to blame.

'I wanted to check if it was thick enough. I lifted the beaters for a second. And your oven's faulty. The recipe said three-fifty degrees for three-quarters of an hour and your oven only goes to two hundred and eighty. But look what it did after fifteen minutes?'

He couldn't help it. His mouth twitched.

'Don't you dare laugh.'

'No,' he said, and walked—or rather squelched—to the bench. She had her laptop sitting on the fruit bowl, where it had, luckily, been shielded from the mixer by fruit.

He read the screen. Yep, the instructions read three-fifty degrees for forty minutes. But this was an American site. An American recipe.

'You ever heard of Celsius versus Fahrenheit?' he asked.

She stared at him, her eyes widening in dawning horror. 'Celsius…'

'And we drive on the left side of the road, too,' he said apologetically. 'Whoops.'

'Celsius! That'd be…' She did a quick calculation in her head. 'A hundred and seventy. Oh, my… Why didn't they say?'

'Because *they're* American.'

'That's crazy.'

'Americans *are* crazy. Almost the whole world—apart from Americans—uses Celsius.'

'Now you're insulting my country as well as my cooking.'

He grinned, took a dollop of goop from the bench and tasted. 'I'm not insulting your cooking. This is good. Ganache?'

She peered suspiciously at the recipe and checked. 'Yes,' she conceded.

'Did you try and layer it into the cake before you cooked it?'

She glowered. 'I'm not completely dumb. It's still in the bowl. Or at least,' she corrected, 'most of it's still in the bowl.'

'So…' He went back to the recipe, fascinated. 'We have

Grand Marnier ganache, some of it still in the bowl, plus chocolate orange cake, slightly singed.'

'Stupid recipe,' she muttered. 'If I can track neural pathways and get high distinctions for forensic pathology, I should be able to follow basic instructions. But no. And now you're making things worse by being supercilious. Go away. Do something useful, like look up cake shop addresses online.'

'You want a welcome-home cake for Jess?'

'That's the idea.'

'I can cook.'

'Right.'

'Honest.' He folded his arms and surveyed cook and kitchen with glinting amusement. She was cute, he thought. She was really cute. And with ganache on her nose he had a strong desire to...

Um...his thoughts had better change direction fast.

'We still have heaps of ganache,' he said. 'We could try again.'

'Again? Are you out of your mind? Your oven needs a jackhammer. I might need to buy you another one.'

He opened the oven. Orange syrup, baked on hard...

He rolled up his sleeves. 'This is men's work,' he said, feeling the need to beat his chest a little. 'Nothing to it.'

'You're lying.'

'I'll prove it. You scrub the walls, I'll scrub the oven.'

'I'd rather fence off the whole area and let it moulder.'

'What would you do if you did this at home?' he demanded, startled.

'Move. We only ever rent.'

He looked at her with incredulity. 'I can't imagine how you get references.'

'I'm a good tenant,' she said with dignity. 'I just don't rent ovens. Apartments with ovens cost more and now I see why. They're lethal.'

'They're fun.'

'Says the man who's offering to scrub one? Matt, it's okay. I made this mess. I'll clean it up.'

'You won't,' he said, suddenly serious. 'I've left you to face enough messes on your own. The least I can do is help you with this one.'

He wouldn't take no for an answer. He changed into jeans and T-shirt and locked the dogs outside, then for half an hour they scrubbed and cleaned. She grew more and more mortified. Then, the last wall wiped, the last pot cleaned, he hauled ingredients and pots and bowls out again and she forgot about being embarrassed, regarding him with horror.

'Matt, this recipe is lethal.'

'This recipe looks great.'

'It could have killed me. I could be a smouldering pile of ash on top of what remains of your glorious home right now.'

'Let's not get carried away.'

'It has it in for me.'

'You just lack the necessary qualification. Did I tell you I'm a surgeon? Precision is my byword. You want to be second in command?'

'No,' she said. 'Think of me as the janitor. Washing up's my forte.'

'I need an assistant,' he said. 'As of now you're employed by Gold Coast Central. As senior surgeon I have the right to tell junior staff what to do. I want two fifty grams of plain flour measured out into a bowl. The scales are in metric. Don't you dare think about conversion. Get to it now, Dr Eveldene. Flour. Weigh. Stat!'

And there was nothing else for a woman to do. Flour. Weigh. Stat.

* * *

This man was a surgeon and that was how he approached his cooking. He treated it as a tricky piece of surgery, like reconstructing a child's knee, with meticulous attention given to detail at every stage.

He insisted on scrupulous cleanliness. Measurements had to be correct almost to the closest gram. Tins were to be lined with perfect circles of baking paper—when her circles were a bit wobbly he made her cut more. Instructions were read aloud by his 'assistant' then checked by Matt, then rechecked as soon as the procedure was complete. There was not a sliver of room for error. And pity any recipe writer who got it wrong, because Kelly could hardly imagine what Matt's reaction would be if he didn't get it right first time.

But, of course, he did. An hour and a half later they were sitting at the kitchen table, admiring a cake that looked better than the picture on the internet. All they had to do when Jess arrived was slice it and insert the ganache.

'And I'll do that,' Matt said sternly.

'You're the surgeon,' she admitted. They were eating toasted sandwiches, which Matt had kindly allowed her to make—under supervision. She grinned. 'There's no need to keep looking at it. I can only cope with so much smugness before I crack and put the ganache where it really oughtn't to be put.'

'It's hard not to be smug about perfection.' He looked even more smug and she lifted the ganache bowl. He grinned back at her and held his hands up in surrender. 'Hey, I'm not being smug about *my* work. I'm being smug about *our* work.'

'Very generous. When did you learn to cook?'

'When I was a kid. We had a cook-housekeeper. Mrs Marsh. Jess used to escape to the surf, but while I was too young to go with him, the kitchen was my refuge.'

'Your childhood was tough, huh?'

'Poor little rich kids,' he said dryly. 'It was better for me than for Jess. He was the elder so he was expected to take over the business. The pressure on him was enormous but I learned to stay out of the way.' He hesitated. 'When I was really young I'd try and intervene. I remember screaming at my father, "*Leave my Jess alone.*" I was belted for my pains and Jess told me he'd do the same to me if I ever tried to interfere again. Not that he would. But I learned...the only way was to disappear.'

'It's a wonder you're still in Australia.'

'Once I got my medical degree I had some form of protection.' He hesitated. 'Even that was down to Jess, though. When I was due to start university my father was so angry with Jess he hardly noticed what I was doing. Jess was the oldest, Jess had to pull himself together and take over what was expected of him. While I was at university he thought I was still under control. I put my head down and kept out of his way. That feels bad now. I should have deflected more of his anger.'

'I think there's been enough guilt,' Kelly told him. 'Jess would have hated you to carry more.'

'He would have wanted me to care for you.'

'I didn't need to be cared for,' she said with some asperity. 'Or maybe I did, but Jess did enough. He married me, he settled my future and he knew I had the strength to take his legacy forward.'

'He knew how strong you were,' Matt said, and lifted his hand and touched her face, a whisper of a touch, tracing her cheekbones and sending all sorts of weird currents through her body, and not one of them bad. 'His independent Kelly.'

If he kept touching her... If she just leaned forward...

'I feel like a surf,' she said, pushing her plate away, striving desperately to push away the longings this man was starting to engender. 'We have an hour before dark. Would you like…?'

'I would like,' he said gravely, and his eyes didn't leave hers. 'I would like very much.'

There was only so much temptation a woman could resist.

They surfed as they'd surfed that morning, but things had changed. They lay out on the sunset-tinged waves, waiting for the next wave to carry them in, but tonight, by unspoken mutual consent, they caught the same waves. And there was no fancy surfing from Kelly. Even though she had the zippy short board, even though her board would have let her run rings around Matt, she was content to ride the force into the shallows beside Matt.

Over and over they caught the waves, but there was no speaking. There seemed no need. It seemed all the talking had been done, everything they needed to know had been discovered, and what was before them now was predestined.

The sun sank low over the hills, sending fire out over the waves. The moon rose over the sea, hanging low, promising ribbons of silver when the sun's rays stopped competing for air play.

Night. The rays would come in to feed. Visibility was dropping by the second. It was time to leave.

They rode the last wave to the beach, tugged the boards up past the high-water mark and left them there. Matt took her hand and led her up to the house and still no words needed to be spoken.

This is right, Kelly thought, a great wash of peace settling over her as her body tingled with anticipation of what was to come.

That was a dumb thought. It was a thought that had to be shelved, and it was, because how could she think of anything but Matt as he led her into the shower off his bedroom? Matt, as he stepped into the shower with her...?

She couldn't think past his body. The rippling muscles of his chest, the traces of sand in the hollows at his shoulders, the way the water ran from his smile right down to his feet. She could see every long, gorgeous inch of him. The water from the shower ran over them, and for this night, for now, every single thing in the world could be forgotten except that this was Matt and he was here, now, and for tonight he was hers.

Nothing else could matter.

'You know this is not a one-night stand,' he muttered thickly into her hair as they stood under the warm water, as somehow their costumes disappeared, as somehow their bodies seemed to be merging into each other.

Not a one-night stand. What was he saying?

It didn't matter, though, because she wasn't thinking past right now, this minute, as Matt flicked off the shower, grabbed towels and started, deliciously, to dry her. This minute, as Matt hung the towels—okay, she did allow herself a moment to be distracted here and think that even now the man was house-proud—but she didn't allow herself to be distracted for more than a millisecond.

Because Matt was lifting her, holding her hard and tight against his body, skin against skin, and it was the most erotic sensation in the world.

And Matt was carrying her back to the bedroom, setting her down on crisp, cool sheets, gazing down at her, taking in every inch of her as she was doing right back to him.

And finally he came down to her. Finally he gathered her into his arms and he made her feel as she'd never felt in her life before.

He made her feel as if she'd found her home.

CHAPTER EIGHT

MATT TOOK A couple of hours off work the next day so he could help bring Jess home. Jess lay with his leg stretched out in the back seat of Matt's car and he signalled his approval as soon as they turned into the main gates.

'Neat place.'

His approval grew even stronger when he saw his room, the veranda—and Matt's indulgent, toys-for-boys media room.

'Can we stay here for ever?' he demanded, and Matt quirked a brow at Kelly and Kelly blushed from the toes up. Why? What was wrong with her?

She knew exactly what was wrong with her.

She'd been tempted and she'd caved right in.

Matt had organised decent crutches, which made Jess pretty much independent. The bathroom in their apartment had obviously been built with Matt's mother in mind. Its easy access and built-in seat catered for the needs of an elderly woman now and in the future, so it was perfect for Jess. Jess checked it out and was obliged to use his approval rating's highest score.

'Über-neat. Now I don't need anyone fussing.'

'Certainly not me,' Kelly agreed, and went and made them all sandwiches. She could at least make sandwiches, she thought ruefully. She wasn't completely useless.

But, then…last night's cake disaster had turned into a success.

Define success?

Success was a highly edible, orange ganache gateau, she told herself, carrying the amazing creation out to the veranda where they'd settled. Nothing else.

'Wow,' Jess said, eyes wide. 'Where did that come from?'

'Your mother made it,' Matt said with aplomb, and Jess looked at him as if he'd lost his mind.

'Not in a million years. Mom struggles with hamburgers.'

'I do not,' Kelly said hotly. 'Or at least, not very much.'

Both guys grinned. Identical smiles.

It did something to her heart. It made her feel…

'You cut,' Matt said, handing her the knife, and she shook her head.

'You're the surgeon.'

'And you're the mother,' Matt said softly. 'You're the mother welcoming her kid home.'

Matt went back to work. Jess went to sleep. Kelly took a book and she and the dogs headed for the beach.

She couldn't read. She walked the dogs but it didn't help. Even a swim couldn't clear her head.

What was happening was some strange, sweet siren song. Temptation plus. Come home… Come home…

What was wrong with it? Why was she so nervous?

Matt was gorgeous. She was pretty sure he wasn't making love to her out of pity or some weird misguided attachment to his long-dead brother. She was pretty sure he'd stopped seeing her as Jess's widow, as she'd stopped looking at him as Jess's brother. He was just…Matt. The past was forgotten, or maybe not forgotten but so far in the past that it was simply a shadow that could be tucked away and left to lie in peace.

Last night had been awesome, and today... The way he'd kissed her before he'd left for the hospital this morning... The way he'd looked at her as she and Jess had laughed over their cake... There was the promise of more. Much, much more.

Home.

See, that was the problem. That was what was making her nervous.

Home.

Matt had outpatients all afternoon. This was the day of the week he liked best. It was his day when patients came for their final check-up after major surgery.

He saw sixty-year-old Lily Devett who'd fallen over her cat and broken her arm. Yes, it had been a nasty fracture but the bones hadn't splintered or broken the skin. Pinning the bones together had been relatively easy.

She brought in chocolate cookies, a bottle of truly excellent whisky and gave him a hug that almost squeezed the breath out of him. 'I can't believe how good it is. When I broke it I thought that's it, it's a downhill road to the nursing home, but it's as good as new. I can even carry my cat again.'

'Just don't fall over it again.' He smiled, and moved on to see Doug Lamworth.

Doug was fifty-two and had tripped while playing a tricky golf shot. The ball had landed on the other side of a creek, the ground was rough and unstable but Doug had refused to play a drop shot. He'd fallen and ended up with an appalling hip injury. It had taken Matt tense, difficult hours in surgery to ensure Doug wouldn't walk with a limp for the rest of his life, but his gratitude wasn't forthcoming.

'It still aches,' Doug snapped. 'After six weeks you'd

think it'd be right. I don't know what you fellas did in there but you've mucked me round worse than the fall. The bruises…hell. And now your blasted registrar won't give me any more of that codeine stuff. I need it. I tell you, I've just about had enough.'

He left without a script for more of the highly addictive drug, complaining he didn't have time for the physiotherapy Matt told him would work much better than painkillers. He left promising he'd sue the pants off Matt if he wasn't better by the time he and his mates left for their Thailand holiday, and telling him that, by the way, he needed a certificate to try and get a compassionate upgrade to business class.

He left and Matt found himself grinning. He thought he'd enjoy telling Kelly about it tonight.

Telling Kelly… There was a thought. Going home tonight and finding Kelly waiting for him.

And suddenly he found himself thinking of his ex-wife. He'd loved coming home and finding her there. He'd loved the concept of wife and family. It was just that Jenny hadn't wanted to fit in. She'd wanted another sort of life and he'd never really understood what.

Was this his second chance?

Things were better. Things had changed since Jenny.

He knew now that things would never have worked out between him and Jenny. They'd been incompatible, and the thought gave him pause. How could things be different with Kelly? One night's passion wouldn't make a long-term commitment.

But the way she'd felt… The way her body had responded to his… It had felt more than right. It had felt as if he'd been waiting all his life to find her.

His next patient was Herman Briggs, who had a list of complaints a mile long. Apparently his knee replacement should have cured all his ills. At Matt's insistence he'd lost weight before the operation but he'd put it back on with interest. Now his hip was playing up, he had a sore back and his other knee was hurting. What was Matt going to do about it?

Matt organised X-rays, sent him back to the dietician and looked forward to going home to Kelly.

She wasn't sure of the rules.

'Why are you pacing?' Jess demanded. He'd abandoned his video game, distracted by his mother's distraction. 'Is there a problem?'

'I'm not pacing.'

'You look like you're pacing.'

'I'm waiting for Matt.'

'Why?'

The question brought her up short. She turned from the window and stared at her son.

Jess was stretched out on the settee. His gaming console was linked to the television. He'd been using a remote to control cartoon characters doing surf stunts. He looked content.

Jess. Her lovely, placid Jess who took what came, who'd been her life for so long.

Why was she pacing?

There'd been illnesses and injuries before, of course there had. This might be an upmarket place to find themselves in while he recovered but essentially things were the same. Jess got on with his life, she got on with hers, but they were there for each other.

She was his mom. Today was Jess's first day home from hospital. It was well after seven and she hadn't even thought about dinner.

Why? Because she was waiting for Matt?

She was thinking about Matt rather than thinking about her son.

And suddenly she felt like she'd been hit by ice-cold water.

Was she nuts? She'd just met a man again whom she'd thought a toe-rag for years. She'd changed her mind. More than that, she'd fallen in lust for him and now she was mooning about, waiting for him like a lovesick teenager.

Or the little wife. When he got home would she invite him in, cook for all of them, start being a family?

It's a wonder she wasn't standing by the door, slippers in one hand, pipe in the other.

The vision was so ridiculous that she chuckled and Jess looked at her curiously. 'What's the joke?'

'Me being dumb.'

'You're dumb all the time. What makes now something to laugh over?'

She grimaced, grabbed a cushion and tossed it at him. 'Dinner?'

'Yes,' Jess said cautiously. He knew her cooking skills and this seemed a place where take-out seemed unlikely.

'Hamburgers,' she said, and he relaxed.

'Yay.'

She headed for the apartment kitchenette and thought that from tonight she needed to step back. To slow down and think of Jess first.

She needed to close the dividing wall between the apartments until she'd settled her hormones into some sort of sensible, working order.

Matt got home at eight and the apartment side of his house was lit. His side of the house was in darkness.

The dogs came to greet him as he garaged the car but they weren't there instantly, as they normally were. He stooped to pat them and their coats were warm, as if they'd just emerged from somewhere cosy.

He looked at the apartment windows, and then looked at his.

Separate houses?

Kelly emerged onto the veranda and walked along to meet him.

'Hey,' he said, and reached for her. She let him hug her, she responded to his kiss, sinking into him, but only briefly and the kiss was less than quarter baked before she tugged away.

'Um…Matt, no.'

'No?'

'Jess's home.'

'Right.' He wasn't sure how to take that. 'So that means…'

'It means we need to step back,' she said, slightly unevenly, as if the kiss had unsettled her—as well it might. It had sure unsettled him. He had an urgent desire to lift her up and carry her into his den, caveman style. He wanted, quite desperately, to have his wicked way with her—and let her have her wicked way with him.

But there was no humour in her eyes, and the passion of the morning had been subdued.

'Jess has known you less than a week,' she told him. 'He hardly knows you.'

'Is that another way of saying you hardly know me?'

'I guess it is,' she whispered. 'Matt, you're my husband's brother. I don't know why I'm responding to you like I am and I need time to figure it out.'

'You don't want to figure it out together?'

'But where does that leave Jess?' she asked. 'He's smart. He has eyes in the back of his head where I'm concerned. He knows I'm conflicted about seeing you again, even though he knows very little about our history. So now he needs to get to know you—as his uncle. I'm not throwing his mother's lover into the equation.'

'Kelly…'

'It won't hurt,' she said, but he knew it did. Her voice wobbled a bit and he thought that for all her planning she was still unsure. Still tempted. 'It can't hurt to step back a bit.'

Wrong. It hurt a lot. The hunger inside him was primitive. He wanted this woman and he wanted her now, but she was making sense.

She was right. His brother's son was just through the wall. There were complications.

And in the middle of these complications…one man and one woman who wanted each other.

'Give us time, Matt,' Kelly pleaded. 'Let things settle. Let Jess get to know you—as his uncle.'

He didn't want it to make sense, but it did.

'Not…after he goes to bed?' he said without much hope, and she snorted.

'Um…we're talking seventeen-year-old with friends on the other side of the world,' she said. 'Teenage sleeping habits. You want me to try tucking him into bed at nine and sending him to sleep with a bedtime story?'

'A really boring bedtime story?' he suggested without much hope, but at least her smile was back. She chuckled.

'Yeah? Like that'll work. He'll be checking tweets over my sleeping body.'

'That's my plans shot,' he said morosely, and she chuckled.

'Not for ever,' she said lightly. 'We just need to take our time.'

'I'll slope off and take a cold shower, then.'

'Come over and have leftover hamburgers with Jess afterwards.'

'I have the makings of steak and peppercorn sauce.'

'See, there's the divide between us,' she told him. 'Unless you've bought your peppercorn sauce in a bottle, we have a chasm a mile wide.'

'We can bridge it.'

'We might,' she said, and stood on tiptoe and kissed him lightly on the cheek, then stepped back fast before he could respond. 'But it'll take time, and both of us need to be patient.'

He showered. He cooked and ate his steak—with his sauce that didn't come out of a bottle. Then he wandered along the veranda. The French doors of Kelly's apartment were wide open, and he could hear the sound of waves crashing inside.

Waves. Inside. Huh?

He didn't need to knock or call out because the dogs had been by Jessie's side by the settee. They bounded across to him as they sensed his presence.

Kelly was curled in an armchair, reading. Jess was sprawled on the settee, controlling surfers on the television. Waves. Lots of waves.

He put down the remote and grinned. 'Hey, Matt.'

Would it be easier or harder if he was less like his brother? Matt wondered. The way his heart twisted...

'Hey, yourself,' he said, as Kelly looked up and smiled and his heart did a little more twisting. 'You guys look comfortable,' he managed.

'We're good at making transitory places home,' Kelly told him, and he looked at the scattered jumble of teenage detritus, the piles of obviously to-be-read books and comics on the table, the bunch of wildflowers popped randomly into a tall drinking glass, already starting to drop petals.

'You look like you want to tidy us up,' Kelly said, and he caught himself. That was dumb. He'd just been...looking.

'It's your apartment for the duration. You're welcome to do what you want with it.'

'Thank you,' Kelly said, and put her book aside. 'It will be neat when we leave. We were about to have hot chocolate. You want some?'

'I… Thank you.'

'My pleasure.' She headed for the kitchenette while Jess lay back on the settee and regarded him with eyes that were curiously assessing. How much could the kid guess about what had gone on with his mother?

'Neat freak, huh?' he asked, but his tone was friendly.

'I guess I have to be. Non-neat surgeons tend to do things like leave swabs inside people.'

'So no swabs in me?'

'Not a snowball's chance in a bushfire. Can I check your leg?'

They both relaxed at that. Doctor-patient was a relationship they both understood. They knew where they were.

And the examination was even more reassuring. Jess was healing with the resilience of the young. His leg looked better than Matt had hoped, and he set the blanket back over it, feeling good.

'So when's the soonest I can surf again?' Jess asked, and the question oddly threw him. Suddenly he no longer felt good.

Memories of his brother were surfacing. 'When can I surf?' The words had been a constant in his childhood, a desperate plea. Surfing had been an escape for Jess, but for the much younger Matt Jess's surfing had meant long days alone with a seething father and a mother who'd suffered because of his father's anger.

It wasn't surfing's fault. Matt had found his own ways of escape, but for Jess surfing had become an obsession. He looked down at his brother's son, and he saw evidence of the same.

Surfing was an obsession for this kid, too.

'In three months you can cope with gentle surf and no

tricks,' he told him, struggling to rid himself of shadows. 'But you need to wait for six months for the big-boy stuff. If you get hit again before your leg's completely healed, you risk lifetime damage.'

'Six months *is* a lifetime,' Jess groaned.

'You could always do something useful in the meantime.'

There was a sudden stillness in the room. Kelly had been stirring the hot chocolate. The stirring stopped.

'Like what?' Jess said. His face had gone blank.

So had Kelly's.

Step back, Matt told himself. This was none of his business.

But, then, he was this kid's uncle. Who else did this boy have looking out for him except a mother who was clearly surf mad herself?

What better time to present an alternative than when Jess was looking at an enforced six-month break? Did he intend spending the whole six months playing computer games? Staring out the window at distant surfers, aching to join them?

'I did suggest you might go to school here,' he said diffidently. 'Make some friends. Maybe even pick up a few subjects that might be useful for later.'

'Later when?'

'When you're old enough not to want to spend every minute surfing.'

There was another silence, even more loaded this time. Jess suddenly looked mutinous. 'Mom and I have a deal.'

'What sort of deal?'

'I'll surf and she keeps off my back about anything else.'

What sort of a deal was that? 'It seems a bit one-sided to me,' he said mildly.

'Yeah, and Mom says my grandfather hated surfing, too,' Jess snapped.

'I don't hate surfing.'

'You want me to do calculus and history instead?'

'It's not my business.'

'It's not, is it?' Kelly said from the kitchenette, and she set down the mugs she'd been about to carry across to them. 'What Jess and I do is for us to decide. Matt, we're incredibly grateful for the use of this apartment but if you're about to try forcing Jess back to school then the deal's off. We'll manage without.'

'I'm not forcing anyone anywhere.'

'Good,' she snapped. 'Your family's done enough damage as it is.'

What followed was another one of those loaded silences, but it was worse this time. 'I'm not my father,' he said at last, because it was all he could think of to say.

'No,' she said. 'And as far as I know, uncles have no jurisdiction over their nephews.'

'They don't. I'm sorry.'

'Will you be judgmental about Jess's surfing the whole time we're here?'

'Of course not.' He raked his hair in exasperation. How to mess with a relationship in two short minutes.

'I don't need school,' Jess growled. 'I've done enough study.'

The kid was seventeen! 'For ever?'

'This is none of your business,' Kelly snapped. 'Do you want a hot chocolate or not?'

She lifted the chocolate and he wasn't sure where she was offering to send it. As an air-based missile?

'I seem to have put my foot in it.'

'You have,' she said cordially. 'Jess and I do things our way and we don't take kindly to interference from the Eveldenes.'

'My family has hardly interfered.'

'They haven't, have they?'

'You sound like you resent that.'

'I contacted your father when your brother was ill,' she said, and every trace of warmth was suddenly gone. 'You have no idea how hard that was, for a seventeen-year-old to find the courage to phone the great Henry Eveldene. I thought if we had a little money I could persuade Jess to see a psychiatrist. But you know what your father said? "I'm not sending money to that waste of space. Tell him to give up surfing and come home." That's it. And now here you are...'

'I'm not withdrawing help because Jess wants to surf.'

'No,' she said flatly. 'And for that we're grateful. But Jess doesn't need to go to school.'

He was going about this all the wrong way. He raked his hair again, exasperated. They were living in their own little world, these two. Sure, Kelly had been hurt by his family, but did that allow her to be a negligent parent? Encouraging her son not to go to school?

'You hurt your leg,' he told Jess, struggling to keep things on an even keel. 'It seems this time you've been lucky and you'll get back to surfing. But eventually you'll want security, a home.' He gestured around him to the house he'd built with such care, the house that had become his refuge. 'Somewhere like this. You won't earn this from surfing.'

'Does it matter?' Kelly demanded. 'That we don't have a home?'

'Of course it matters. Look at the mess you're in now.'

'We're not in a mess,' she snapped. 'We're independent. We don't need anyone and we can handle our issues ourselves. Our only problem now is that we seem to have a judgmental landlord. That doesn't matter. We've coped with landlords before. If they're bad we move on.'

'Hey, don't threaten that yet,' Jess said, startled. 'Mom,

he's being a stuffed shirt, that doesn't mean we need to move. This place is ace. We can manage a bit of aggro.'

'I'm not being aggressive!'

'Nah,' Jess said thoughtfully. 'But pushy. I'd have thought Dad's brother might be more laid-back. Mom, cut him some slack. Matt, have a drink and move on. I want to stay here.'

'I'd like to stay here, too,' Kelly said. 'But not if Matt's controlling. Not if he intends to bully you.'

'I'm not bullying,' Matt snapped. 'And I'll back off. But I'll have a drink next door, thank you.'

'Are you taking your bat and ball and going home?' she demanded. 'Just because we won't let you be like your father?'

'I am not like my father!' His words were an explosion, and even the dogs responded. Spike even whimpered and headed under Jessie's rug. What a traitor!

'Of course you're not,' Jess said at last, as the echoes died. 'Have a hot chocolate and forget about it.'

'I need to sleep. I have work tomorrow.'

'Bat and ball,' Kelly snapped, and he glared, clicked his fingers at the dogs and headed for the door.

The dogs didn't follow. He reached the veranda and looked back. Every single one of them was looking at him with reproach—even the dogs.

Jess went back to his computer game. Kelly went into her own room, lay on the bed and stared at the ceiling. She'd have liked to walk on the beach but there was no way she was risking meeting Matt again.

They should leave. If Matt intended to even think about controlling Jess... He mustn't.

She'd been so careful, for all her son's life. Her Jess adored surfing. She knew what it meant to him, so she'd worked her life and his around it. She'd had to. She'd seen what denying that passion had done to his father. So far Jess had shown no signs of his father's depression and that was the way it was staying.

Even if it meant walking away from Matt Eveldene?

Even that. Of course that. If he put one more step wrong... If he tried to control...

Even if she wanted him?

'And that's something you need to forget about,' she told the ceiling. 'Temptation is just plain stupid. From now on, you go back to being a mom. You go back to protecting Jess, no matter what the cost.'

CHAPTER NINE

HE WAS THEIR landlord. They were his tenants. From that night on, that was the way things needed to operate. He'd keep out of their lives. What he said or thought was none of their business, and vice versa.

Luckily, things were frantic at work. King tides meant the surf was huge. Every novice surfer in the country seemed to be daring themselves past their limit—and ending up in Gold Coast Central. Almost all the injuries were orthopaedic. Matt was needed full time.

He stopped surfing in the mornings. He walked his dogs at dawn and then left for the hospital before there was any movement next door. He did his paperwork in his office instead of taking it home. Normally he wouldn't—it wasn't fair on the dogs—but the dogs seemed to be having a fine time with Jess. When he did get home they bounded out to meet him, but they were always toasty warm and he knew where they'd been.

'Are you avoiding us?' He got home one night and Jess was on the veranda settee, watching the sunset surfers with fieldglasses.

'Just busy,' he said briefly. 'You have a follow-up appointment in two days. I'll see you then.'

'It seems dumb only to see you at the hospital.'

It did.

'I crossed a line,' he said. 'I thought I should back off.'

'Just don't cross the line again,' Jess said cheerfully. 'You make Mom mad. We have doughnuts. You want to come in and have supper?'

'Does your mother want me to?'

'Mom's got her knickers in a twist about you. She needs to get over it.'

'Well, when she gets over it, I'll join you.'

'She's being weird.'

'Then it's best we leave it,' Matt told him. 'We wouldn't want to upset your mother.'

Only he did want to upset Jess's mother. Or something. It nearly killed him to have things hanging in limbo. Each day that passed it seemed worse, like there was tension hanging over his home and his hospital.

Kelly, on the other hand, seemed remarkably unperturbed.

'She's a great doctor,' Beth told him. 'The best. Kids are brought into Emergency and she manages to get the priorities sorted and reassure everyone at the same time. Kids relax with her. We had a boy come in yesterday with concussion and a broken collar bone. He was in pain and his mother was hysterical. The kid had fallen through a roof he'd been forbidden to climb and his mum was so out of it she was saying, "I'll kill him, I'll kill him." Kelly had them sorted in minutes. "Don't you just hate it when they scare you like this?" she said to the mum. "But no killing, not yet. Let me patch him up and then he's all yours." The woman finally ended up giggling. She got the kid smiling, too. Can we keep her?'

'She's only here until her own kid gets better.'

'Then put on a heavier cast and prescribe twelve months of Australian physiotherapy. Keep her. She's good.'

He had an irrational urge to see for himself. The orthopaedic department was too far from Emergency and for the first time in years he found himself wishing he could change specialties. But he was occasionally needed there. Later that morning Beth called him to assess X-rays of a guy who'd come off a motorbike. He was about to leave when noise at the entrance caught his attention.

Paramedics had brought in a child, barely more than a toddler, and Matt saw at once what the problem was. She had her big toe stuck in a bath outlet. The pipe had been cut and she'd been brought in with the pipe still attached.

The noise was deafening. The little girl was hysterical with fear and pain. Her sobbing mother could hardly be prised away, and her father was shouting random commands at the top of his lungs. 'Elly, keep still. Get the thing off. How much longer? I thought you called yourself a hospital. I'll call the fire department, they'll be more use.'

Kelly had obviously once again been paired with Emma, and Emma was struggling to make herself heard. Kelly was struggling to get past the mother and assess the situation. She was attempting to calm the little one, while Emma was trying to hold the irate father back. 'Please, if you could leave her to us...'

The paramedics weren't helping. The situation was escalating.

Was it time for an orthopaedic surgeon to step in, even if it wasn't his patch?

'What's the child's name?' he asked the closest paramedic.

'Elly Woodman, aged two. They've all been screaming since we reached them but we need to go. We have a coronary call waiting.'

'Her parents' names?'

'Sarah and Ben Woodman. The dad's a lawyer and he's already threatening to sue. Good luck, mate.'

The paramedics left. Kelly glanced up, saw him and sent him a silent plea.

There was nothing for it. Matt took a deep breath and dived right in.

'Mr Woodman.' His deep growl cut across the commotion like a harsh blow. He aimed himself directly at the little girl's father, no one else.

'There are too many people in here,' Matt said, fixing his gaze on the young lawyer. 'We need to settle your daughter so we can give her an anaesthetic, but we need space. Therefore her mother stays and that's all. Dr Kellerman—Emma—will take you to Administration, where you can fill in admission details. Please leave.'

'But I'm supposed to be—' Emma ventured, but Matt cut her off with a placatory glance.

'I'm taking over assisting Dr Eveldene.' He laid a hand on the mother's shoulder. 'Stop crying,' he said, and it was a command, not a plea. 'You're scaring your daughter.'

'I can't...' the woman sobbed.

'Stop crying or leave with your husband. Your daughter needs you to be a sensible woman, not a watering can. Hold Elly's arm, Doctor,' he ordered Kelly, but Kelly was already moving.

Matt's commands had distracted the child enough for Kelly to take hold. She manoeuvred Elly before her mother could hug her close again. Before the little girl had time to react, Matt took her arm and held it.

They worked as a team, almost instinctively. Kelly swabbed fast while Matt held. She lifted the anaesthetic syringe from the tray and administered it. The syringe was out of sight before the child knew what had happened.

Kelly relaxed. A hysterical child was a nightmare. The thrashing had been making her foot swell even more and the metal groove of the plug was digging in deeper. The department had been stretched to the limit, there'd been no nurses available and coping with only the inexperienced Emma had been impossible.

But Matt's intervention had the situation under immediate control. The fast-acting injection of relaxant and painkiller took effect almost instantly. Already the little girl was slumping back in her mother's arms.

Emma had successfully steered the lawyer dad away. There was now only the four of them, and as Elly stopped struggling, her mother relaxed.

'I'm…I'm sorry,' she whispered.

'There's no need to be sorry,' Kelly told her, making her voice deliberately soothing. The time for snapping orders was over. 'But now Elly's nice and sleepy we need to move. How do you suggest we go about this, Dr Eveldene?'

'I'm thinking Elly needs a good sleep while we assess the situation. Sarah, keep cuddling Elly,' Matt told the mum. 'We'll elevate her foot to relieve the swelling but we won't do anything until she's totally relaxed. Meanwhile, we'll cover you with blankets so we can make this as cosy as possible. A bit of storytelling might be called for, all about a bear who gets his toe stuck. You can tell her all about the handsome doctor who slips it off while she's asleep.'

'Handsome?' Kelly queried.

'I like incorporating fact with fiction.' Matt grinned and the young mother gave a wobbly smile and things were suddenly okay.

More than okay.

'You're both Dr Eveldenes?' the young woman asked, looking from Kelly's lanyard to Matt's and back again. She'd relaxed now as Elly snuggled peacefully against her. 'Are you married?'

'Um…no,' said Kelly.

'They just live together.' Beth had come in behind them, obviously wanting to check that things were okay. 'They share a house and a name. They have a kid and two dogs so I don't know why they don't just get married and be done with it.'

Whew.

Despite his shock, Matt understood why Beth had said it. Beth had been in the next cubicle, coping with the guy who'd come off his motorbike. She'd have heard what was happening but not been able to help. Now she was adding her bit, distracting the mother still further. 'There's a spare bed in cubicle five,' she told the young mum. 'It's the quietest. You snuggle down with your little one while these two discuss marriage. There. All problems solved. I do like a happy ending, don't you?'

And she beamed and chuckled and headed off to cope with the next crisis.

Once Elly was deeply asleep things were straightforward.

Elevation and lubrication didn't work but Plan B succeeded. They wound a fine, strong thread down the length of the tiny toe, over and over, with each round of thread placed hard by the next so the toe was enclosed and compressed. Then Kelly managed to manoeuvre an end through the ring. Then they lubricated the thread and gradually started unwinding, using the thread to push the metal forward as they went.

To everyone's relief the toe gradually worked free. Matt gave a grunt of satisfaction—cutting the metal would have been much harder. The thing was done.

Matt patted the kid's head, said his goodbyes and headed back to his work.

It was after her knock-off time. Kelly was free to go.

But not quite. Jess's physio session was running late. The therapist glanced up as Kelly arrived, and waved her away.

'We need an extra half an hour, Dr Eveldene. Jess is doing great.'

Jess was struggling, Kelly could see that, and it was hurting. He was balancing between two standing bars, trying to bear weight.

Kelly knew her son well enough to understand that he wouldn't want her to watch. She waved and left them to it, then headed up to the rooftop cafeteria. She bought a sandwich and headed outdoors to eat it—and Matt was there.

The rooftop was deserted. There was Matt and one table. There were a dozen more tables to choose from.

Don't be pathetic, she told herself, and sat at his.

'If you're about to talk about what sort of flowers you want our bridesmaids to carry, I'm out of here,' Matt said, and she stared at him and then, to her surprise, found herself chuckling.

'Well, it did work,' she conceded. 'It made Sarah focus on gossip instead of what a bad mother she was for letting Elly get her toe stuck. The only problem is it was overheard by half the emergency staff and rumours have probably reached London by now.'

'You need to stop wearing a wedding ring.'

She looked down at the slim band of gold on her finger, very slim, the cheapest wedding ring they had been able to find all those years ago.

'No.'

'You've been faithful to him all these years?'

'You know I haven't,' she said evenly. 'But I still love him.'

'So do I.'

'I think,' she said quietly, hearing his pain, 'that your loss must have been as great or even greater than mine. I was able to mourn him. I was surrounded by people who loved him. More, I've always been able to talk of him with pride, whereas you...'

'I was proud of him.'

Deep breath. 'If you were proud of him you wouldn't be talking to your nephew about wasting his life surfing.'

'I only suggested—'

'It's not your place to suggest.'

'Kelly, he'll have nothing,' he exploded. 'Heaven knows whether he can get that leg strong enough to go back to competitive surfing but even if he can, there'll be more accidents, there'll be the natural aging of his body, there'll be life. How can he possibly earn enough to buy himself a decent home, a decent future.'

'He's able to sort that himself,' she snapped. 'He's a smart kid and he knows what he's doing. But even so...is a decent future predicated on a house like yours?'

'Yes,' he said, sounding goaded. 'It'd be his, something he can control, a sanctuary that can't be taken away from him.'

'Lying on the surfboard at dawn is something that can't be taken away from him as well. Friends, a community, that's something, too.'

'It's not enough. You need a home.'

'We never have.'

'I don't know how you've existed.'

'We've done more than exist. We've been happy.'

'So you're condemning him to a lifetime of being a nomad?'

'Me?' She met his gaze head on. 'You think I should be dictating my son's life? As your father dictated yours?'

'He didn't.'

'I think he did,' she said evenly. 'He drove Jess away and he made you so fearful that you put your home above everything. It's not your retreat, Matt, it's your prison.'

'How can you say that?'

'This hospital is a goldfish bowl.' If he was going to make assumptions about her son, she could throw a few home truths back. 'Everyone talks about everyone. They say you spend more time with your house and your dogs than with your friends—that you don't get close. They say your marriage didn't last because you held yourself aloof. You have a reputation for being a loner, for helping others but never asking for help yourself. You care for your patients but you care for solitude above all else.'

'Is that what everyone says?'

'Yes,' she said evenly. 'And I reject your life plan. My son is a lovely social kid who cares about the world. He's surrounded by his friends. Even though he's a long way away, he has people Skyping him on the computer at all hours. He's not depressed, like his father. He's not obsessed with possessions, like his uncle. Do you think he'd be desolated if he was living in that dreary little apartment I found first? As long as we'd got rid of the bugs he'd hardly notice.'

'He loves my home.'

'Yes, but if you asked him to choose home or his friends, it'd be his friends in a heartbeat. That's how I've raised him, and I'm proud of the man he's turning into. He's healthy and he's happy and I won't have you judging him.'

'We're worlds apart on this one.'

'Yes, we are,' she said, and somehow she managed to keep her voice even, she managed to keep her twisted heart under some sort of control. She'd held this man in her arms. For a short time she'd thought…she'd thought…

Well, enough of thinking. She needed to act on evidence, not emotion.

'We are worlds apart,' she told him sadly. 'I guess it doesn't matter, though. We've lived in separate worlds all our lives. As soon as Jess is better we'll do so again. But, please, until then keep your judgement under control. I'd love Jess to know he has an uncle; a link with the father he never knew. If you can figure some way to relate to him without your prejudices getting in the way, it'd be great, but don't interfere. I won't risk him ending up like you or his father. As for you and me…what was between us must have been only that. Temptation. Sex. A stupid rush of blood to the head. So now we put it aside. I need to keep Jess safe and if I'm to do that, you and I don't take what's between us any further.'

Did she think he was a danger to Jess? Did she think he could pressure the kid into illness? The thought left him cold.

'What's between you and Mom?' Jess asked him. It was a Sunday. He was out on the veranda, watching Kelly walking down on the beach, when Jess thumped his way out to talk to him.

'What do you mean?'

'I mean every time you're near she puts on this weird smiley face and takes the first excuse to escape. I know things have been non-existent between Dad's family since I was born but now Mom's acting as if you're a threat.'

'I can't see that I'm a threat.'

'You did threaten to send me back to school. I'm over that, but Mom still seems scared.'

Scared… Over and over the word echoed.

Eighteen years ago he'd blamed himself when his brother had died. He hadn't done enough.

He should step back now.

'Maybe it's my family,' he offered. 'Your grandfather's a powerful man. He likes control. If he knew you existed he'd want some sort of control.'

'He doesn't control you.'

'It's taken a lot to get away from him.'

'He wouldn't control us, and I don't think Mom's scared of him. I think she's scared of you.'

'She has no reason to be.'

'That's what I told her,' Jess said. 'But, still, whenever you're near she sort of freezes. I don't understand.'

'Neither do I.'

'Then talk to her about it,' Jess said, irritated. 'It's messing with my serenity.'

'Your serenity?' Matt said, startled, and the boy grinned.

'She's cool, my mom,' he said. 'But she's supposed to worry about me, not the other way round. I'd appreciate it if you could fix it.'

He headed back to his video games, leaving Matt to his thoughts.

Fix it. How was he supposed to do that? A chasm seemed to have opened up between them that he didn't have a clue how to cross. Okay, he understood her fears, but how could she not see how important a home, a base, was? Jess was at risk of ending up with nothing.

Matt's career and his home had given him power over his father. For Jess not to have that same power seemed appalling. Kelly was scared, but there was more than one path to disaster.

This was a deep divide and it meant he couldn't do what Jess wanted. It was messing with Jess's serenity, but it was also doing more. It was causing a man and woman to stand apart.

Maybe it was just as well. He'd had one failed marriage and he still didn't fully understand the cause. Maybe he was meant to be a loner. He had his dogs and his home and his career. What more could a man want?

A woman like Kelly?

No.

He went to work, he came home and he avoided Kelly. She was always on the edge of his consciousness but he'd made a decision.

He'd been a loner for ever and it couldn't stop now.

* * *

If it wasn't for Matt Eveldene she might even be enjoying this forced pause in her life, this time dictated by Jess's accident. Her days were full. Every morning she dropped Jess at the hospital rehab unit. He spent the next few hours working with the physios, exercising to keep his muscles from wasting and making friends in the process. Jess enjoyed his mornings and so did she. Her work in Emergency was varied. She was often run off her feet. She felt useful, the staff were friendly, and it was only Matt's occasional presence that caused her unease.

She didn't know how to handle the way he made her feel. When he walked into the ward it was like she had brain freeze. She had no idea why he made her feel like that, but he did and she didn't like it.

She liked the afternoons, when she took Jess home, when they had the house and the beach to themselves and she knew Matt was at work and wouldn't disturb their peace. Jess mostly snoozed and played computer games. She swam and read and felt…like she was home?

It was a great place, she conceded. It was indeed a lovely home. But for Matt to say it was all-important… For Matt to pressure Jess because he might not be able to afford a home like this… It clearly showed the gulf between them—the gulf that had killed Matt's brother?

Things weren't important. Her attitude to Matt was right. She tried to tell herself that. His house—his *home*—was amazing, but it couldn't be put above all else.

Forget it.

But she couldn't relax. Her body didn't know how to. As soon as Matt returned she retreated to her side of the house. He was her landlord; anything else was too threatening.

Until the day of the suicide.

* * *

Mid-morning. Friday. Outside the day was gorgeous. 'I hate not being able to surf,' Jess had grumbled as she'd driven them both to the hospital, and she'd agreed. Today was a perfect day to be outside. A perfect day to live.

But for the boy who was wheeled into Emergency at six minutes past ten the day must have seemed anything but perfect. The ligature marks on his neck were raw and appalling. The paramedics were still working frantically as they wheeled him in, but Kelly took one look and knew they were too late.

Beth did the initial assessment and Kelly, standing behind her, ready to move into resuscitation mode the moment Beth said the word, was relieved that it was Beth who had to shake her head, Beth who had to remove the cardiac patches, close her eyes briefly and say, 'I'm so sorry, guys, but we've lost this one. Thank you for trying.'

The police arrived.

And Matt.

She briefly remembered that Beth had called Matt down to see to an elderly patient's hip fracture. He stood at the inner door to Emergency and took the scene in at a glance. They were wheeling the kid into a private cubicle but everyone still seemed paralysed with horror.

A middle-aged couple came through the outer entrance. They stopped and stood still, as if terrified to enter. The boy's parents? The man was in work overalls and heavy boots, clothes that said he was a builder or similar. The woman was all in white, dressed for lawn bowls. They were holding each other for support but not giving it to each other. They looked bewildered, shocked to the point of collapse.

Kelly took a deep, fast breath. She glanced through to Beth, knew she was caught up with the police, and knew the job of caring for the parents fell to her. She walked towards them, signalling to a nurse to help.

The nurse stepped forward but then stopped, put her hand to her mouth and shook her head wildly. She retreated fast.

Vomiting was what Kelly felt like doing. The angle of the boy's neck…the horror of that ligature…

He was, what? Twenty maybe? Young enough to be the nurse's brother.

Or husband?

Hold it together, she told herself harshly. You're no use if you can't keep emotion in check. If you can't suppress history flooding back.

The older of the paramedics was still there, grim faced and silent. She took his clipboard and searched for what she needed.

Toby Ryan. Aged nineteen. Found by the surf-club manager in the club storeroom half an hour ago.

'Positive ID?' she asked, and the paramedic nodded.

'The surf-club manager knows him. Seems he's been a club member since he was a nipper.'

There was no question, then. She knew what she had to do. She turned back to face the parents.

'Mr and Mrs Ryan?'

It was the woman who found the strength to nod.

'Y-yes.'

What had they been told?

Assume nothing.

'Toby's your son?'

'Yes.' The woman closed her eyes and put her hand up as if to ward off what was coming.

'Come through where we can be private,' she said gently.

They already knew. Someone must have phoned them;

someone from the surf club? The woman's legs were giving way under her.

Kelly moved to catch her before she sagged, but Matt was there before her, catching her under the arm, holding her upright.

'I have her,' he said. 'You help Mr Ryan. This way, sir.'

Together they led them into the counselling room, set up for just this purpose. It held a settee and two big armchairs and a maxi box of tissues. The woman slumped onto the settee, stared at the tissues and moaned. Her husband sat beside her, clasped his hands and stared at the floor.

'I knew it'd come to this,' he whispered. 'We've been dreading this day. Was it…was it quick?'

'Yes,' Kelly said, thinking of the snapped vertebrae. 'Almost instant.'

'Did a good job, then,' the man said heavily.

'Sir…' Matt said, but the man glared at him as if he was the enemy.

'Call me Doug,' he snapped. 'And Lizzie. We're Toby's Mum and Dad. There's no "sir" about it. No bloody formality today. No bureaucrats. No one helped our Toby. No one could.'

'We knew it was coming.' Lizzie was talking to herself. She was a dumpy little woman in crisp bowling whites, and the life seemed to have been sucked out of her. It was as if a ghost was talking.

'He was born with it, we reckon,' she whispered. 'The black dog. It wouldn't let up. Wherever he went, whatever he did, it kept coming back. Black, black, black. We couldn't help him. His sisters, his brother, all our family. We love him so much. We love him and love him and we can't help. We don't know what to do.'

Her segue into the present tense, where her son was still alive, where problems were still here, still now, seemed to catch her, and for Kelly it was too much. Professional detachment be damned. She was down on her knees, gathering the woman into her arms and hugging her close.

'There's nothing more you can do except keep on loving him,' she whispered, as she held and the woman sobbed and the man beside her groaned his anguish. 'You've done everything you could and Toby knows that. You love him and that's all that counts. The disease has killed him, but that's what it was, a disease. It's tearing your heart out, but what stays is your love for your son. You did everything you could. You couldn't defeat it but no matter what's happened, Toby's love will stay with you for ever.'

Matt had an afternoon of consultation booked but he cancelled. His secretary took one look at his face and didn't ask questions. Kelly finished at one, and he was in the car park, waiting for her. Jess was already in the car.

'Disaster of a morning,' he'd told Jess. 'A kid of your father's age when he died was brought in. Suicide. And your mother had to deal with it. We're taking her home. We'll come back later and pick up the Jeep.'

'Mom's tough,' Jess said. 'Stuff doesn't upset her much.'

Yeah? Matt saw his Kelly's face as she emerged from Emergency and he knew Jess was wrong. A cameraman and a reporter were waiting at the door. Toby had been a surf coach, popular and involved in the community. His death would hit the local news. The camera flashed, the reporter pressed forward but she extricated herself, fast.

She was some woman.

'Kelly?' He headed toward her, ignoring the media. She glanced up and saw him and her face relaxed a little.

'I need to fetch Jess.'

'We're both here,' Matt said gently. 'We're taking you home.'

'There's no need.'

'There's every need.'

'Hey, Mom,' Jess said, as she reached the car.

Her face crumpled then. She'd been keeping up a front, he saw. She'd probably been planning to keep on the same coping face she'd used for her son for years, but Jess's concern had slipped behind her defences.

She reached out and hugged him and Jess let himself be hugged.

Then she had herself together, hauling back, swiping her face and giving a shame-faced smile.

'It's okay. It's just…'

'Matt says a guy died just like Dad.'

'I… Yes.'

'I can't imagine how you must feel,' Jess said, and Matt looked at Jess and thought this kid was seventeen but suddenly he sounded like a man.

He wanted to hug them both. A lot.

He couldn't. He was on the outside, looking in.

'I'm playing chauffeur,' he asserted. 'The crutches get to ride up front with me. You guys travel in the back.'

'I can drive,' Kelly said. 'I don't need—'

'You do need,' he said harshly. 'You've needed for eighteen years and I've done nothing. Get in the car, Kelly, and let me help.'

She did. He drove them home, the back way, not past the surf club, where police cars would still be clustered, but through the hills behind town. Jess set up a stream of small talk in the back seat, though actually it wasn't small talk, it was all about his rehabilitation, about what Patsy, the rehab physician, had told him, about how the strengthening exercises were going and what he could reasonably hope for as he healed. Getting such information from a teenager was normally like pulling teeth, so Kelly was forced to listen, forced to respond, and Matt saw a tinge of colour return to her face.

He gave Jess a thumbs-up via the rear-view mirror, and

Jess gave him a return man-to-man nod and went right on distracting his mother.

He was a kid to be proud of, Matt thought. A son to be proud of?

And right there, right then, he realised how much he loved the pair of them. What was he on about, pushing the kid to do what he thought was important? He watched the pair of them and he thought they knew what was important. If they wanted to surf every day of their lives, who was he to judge? Whatever they did, it was okay by him.

And more. Whatever they did, he wanted to join them.

But now wasn't the time for declarations. Now was simply the time for being in the background, giving them space, but he glanced back and saw the way Jess held his mother's hand, saw the way she tried to smile at him, saw the deep concern in the kid's eyes for his mom and he thought...

He thought for the first time in his life, he desperately wanted to share.

CHAPTER TEN

SHE SPENT THE afternoon trying to work things out in her own mind. Matt was nowhere to be seen. She made Jess hamburgers for tea, and then, as he settled in with Matt's dogs and his computer games, she gave him a hug and made her decision.

'I need to go talk to Matt.'

'Of course you do,' Jess said, not taking his eyes from his game. 'He's shattered, too.'

'You think?'

'Yeah,' Jess said. 'When he came to get me in physio he looked like he'd been wiped out and held under for ten minutes. Well, maybe not ten,' he corrected himself, 'but three. Time enough to see his life rolling before his eyes.'

'What do you know about life rolling before your eyes?' Kelly demanded, startled, and Jess grinned.

'Hey, I've lived through a Very Bad Accident. When I felt that board crack against me I thought of all the levels of *Major Mayhem* I had yet to play. It was a sobering experience.'

She gave him a pretend slap to the side of the head and chuckled.

'So you don't mind if I go and see Matt now?'

'Stay the night,' Jess offered. 'I'm a big boy now.'

'Jess!'

'Seriously, Mom,' Jess said, and finally he turned away from his computer game. 'Matt's great and he cares. Don't let me—or Dad—get in the way of something beautiful.'

'Beautiful?' she choked.

He grinned. 'Heart and flowers and violins. Yuck.' But then he sobered. 'Or just real good friends. Go for it, Mom. Think of yourself for once.'

Right.

It was a discombobulating little speech, and she was still feeling discombobulated when she headed out onto the veranda.

Matt was sitting on the settee, holding a beer, staring out at the moonlight.

'Pa Kettle,' she said cautiously. 'You need to make that settee a rocker.'

'I need my dogs,' he said. 'Traitors.'

'Jess has popcorn. No contest.'

He grinned and went to rise.

'Don't get up.' She perched beside him. 'I need to talk.'

'So do I.'

'Me first,' she said, and then she paused because all of a sudden it seemed hard. Matt watched her in the moonlight, then left her and came back with a glass of wine. She took it and swirled it in his gorgeous crystal glass and thought of all the chipped and cracked kitchenware she and Jess had used over the years. And then she thought, it didn't matter. It didn't matter one bit.

People were what was important. This man was important.

Up until now her hurt had all been about herself and her son. Somehow today had made her see that long-ago devastating scene in the funeral parlour in a different light. It made sense of the tie Matt had with things rather than people and it had exposed the knot of hurt and pain this man had carried for years.

Today she'd looked at the shattered parents and she'd known that she couldn't protect Jess, any more than Matt could have protected his brother.

'You know it wasn't your fault,' she said into the stillness, and the words seemed to freeze and hang. 'What happened to Jess… Today I looked at Toby and I saw a kid who had everything. Loving parents. Sisters and brother who adored him. After you left Toby's sister came in and she talked and talked, and I had time to let her. Toby was loved. Whatever he did was fine by them. He had his beloved surf club. He had his whole community behind him, but the depression, the illness wouldn't let go. His family knew this was coming, she said. It was like watching a slow train coming toward them and not being able to get off the track. Doctors, treatments, everything that could be done was done. And yet the depression won.'

'Kelly—'

'No, let me say it,' she said. 'I've been angry. I lost my Jess and then you came and you were the embodiment of all the things I thought had caused Jess to die. Jess used to talk about your house, the Eveldene mansion. He used to talk about all the things he had, all the things your family valued, as if they were the cause. So when you came, I hated you and I hated what you represented. I swore my Jess would never learn your values. Then…what happened between us…somehow it felt like a betrayal, and what you said to Jess made it worse.

'But today, maybe for the first time, I figured out how unfair my anger was. Your suggestion that Jess study was just a suggestion. It was nothing to make a big deal over. And as for eighteen years ago… You were a kid yourself. You were doing what your father should have done, but even that's immaterial. What matters is that today I let go of my anger. Eighteen years and it's finally gone.'

'One kid's death...' he said slowly, but she shook her head.

'No. It's lots of things. How the hospital staff react to you. Your kindness toward your patients. The fact that you care. The way you've treated Jess, and then stepped back when you realised you'd hurt him. And this afternoon I finally figured it out. You've been hurting as much as I have. It's a no-brainer yet finally I've seen it. You loved Jess. You lost him and now you hold on to things instead. Like this house. This place. Your career. Tangible things are important but it's not because you're impersonal. It's anything but. It's because once upon a time you saw your brother on a slab in a mortuary and part of you died.'

And something within him twisted, so hard it was as if things were ripping apart. The pain of the last eighteen years. The way he'd reacted to this woman the first time he'd seen her, with such unforgivable anger. The aching helplessness of knowing his big brother had been self-destructing and there hadn't been a thing he could do about it.

Something changed.

He stood abruptly, knocking the beer at his feet so it spilled its contents. Who cared? He didn't. Where to go from here? So many emotions, coalescing in one morning's tragedy. In one woman's words.

'Kelly, maybe that was what I was going to tell you,' he managed. He was trying to figure it for himself. How to put it into words.

'I did blame myself,' he said. 'I was four years younger than Jess and I ached for him, but every time I tried to do anything I had to retreat. My dad reacted with anger, but Jess himself retreated. I ached because he asked me to come to Hawaii when I finished school. He sent me the plane fare. But I was eighteen. I thought he was on drugs. My father was apoplectic when I even suggested it. It was too hard and I've hated myself for ever because I didn't have the courage to stand up to my father. But today I saw that it wouldn't have made one bit of difference. Nothing I said or did...'

'Nor me,' Kelly said, and she stood beside him and slipped her hand in his. 'We both loved him and somehow we ended up hating each other because of his death. It was dumb. We both ended up rejecting...something that's important.'

He turned to her then, taking her hands so they were locked together in the moonlight.

'You mean...important as making a go of...us?'

'We could give it a try,' she said softly. She ventured a faint smile. 'I might learn to love this house as well.'

'It's a great house.'

Her smile faded. 'Matt...'

'I didn't mean,' he said, 'that this house is as important as people. I didn't mean this house is as important as you.'

'Or happiness?'

'Or happiness.'

'We need to take things slowly.' She bit her lip, looking up at him in the moonlight as if she was trying to read his mind. 'And, Matt...despite what I just said I won't have you lecturing Jess. You need to respect that he's his own person.'

'I will respect that.'

'The truth's in the doing,' she said with a touch of asperity. 'But you're stuck with us for another few weeks. If you let us hang around, I'll see what you're made of.'

'And I'll see what I'm made of, too.'

'No judging?'

'Just loving.'

'It seems,' she said uncertainly, 'that loving's the given. It's fitting everything else in that's the problem.'

'You mean you might love me?'

'I think I might,' she said with all seriousness, and then she gasped as he tugged her close. 'Matt, we have all sorts of stuff we need to work out first.'

'We will work it out. Give us time.' But he spoke thickly because his face was in her hair. He was kissing her, tugging her tightly into him. 'We'll sort it.'

'Matt…' She still sounded worried.

'Let the past go,' he told her, sure of himself now, holding his woman in his arms and knowing nothing else was important. 'There's just us.'

'And Jess and our careers and your dogs and your house…'

'Kelly?'

'Mmm?'

'Is Jess likely to disapprove if I pick you up, cart you to my lair and have my wicked way with you?'

'Jess practically ordered me to submit,' she said. 'And he's just reached the next level in his game. Who's noticing?'

'I'm noticing,' he said, as he swung her into his arms and kissed her, a long, deep kiss that held all the promise of life to come. 'I'm noticing a lot,' he said, as he pushed the door open with his foot. 'I'm noticing and noticing and noticing. But, Dr Kelly Eveldene, all I'm noticing is you.'

'So are we happy-ever-aftering?'

It was the morning after the night before. Kelly was making pancakes on her side of the beige door. She was demurely dressed in her respectable bathrobe. She'd showered, she'd brushed her hair and she was trying hard to look like nothing had changed. She was a mom looking after her kid.

She was different.

'What?' She plated two pancakes for her son. 'What do you mean?'

'I mean you look like the cat that got the canary. Smug R Us. Does Matt look the same?'

'I… He might.' She tried to fight it but she could feel herself blushing from the toes up.

'Excellent,' Jess said. 'He's cool.'

'Didn't he tell you to go back to school?'

'Yeah, but it was only past history that made me react,' he said. 'The way you told me Grandpa treated Dad. I've thought about it. Judging someone because of what happened years ago might be dumb. If we tell him about my—'

'Jess, don't tell him yet,' she said, suddenly urgent.

'Why not?'

'Because if we're to have some sort of future together I want him wanting us, warts and all.'

'Then push him further. You could give up medicine and come surfing. The way he's looking, he might even come, too. I shouldn't say this about my own mother, but you're still hot. He's tempted. Anyone can see it, and you're tempted right back. There's waves of temptation all over the place. Why resist, people? Go for it.'

'Oh, Jess.' Where had this funny, wise, grown-up kid come from?

'So what are you going to do about it?' Jess demanded.

'Maybe I could invite him in for pancakes,' she conceded.

'Why not?' Jess said amiably. 'But don't stop there. Why not knock a hole in the wall and be done with it?'

He had everything he wanted, here, now. Kelly was living in his house. She was part of his life. It was like he'd been missing a part of himself and the part had fitted back together, making him complete.

'Jess says I look like the cat that got the canary,' she told him, lying in his arms on Sunday morning. 'I think you do, too.'

'You're an extraordinarily beautiful canary.'

'I'm a happy canary,' she said, and snuggled down against him. 'Did you know you have the most beautiful body I've ever seen? They should freeze you and use you in anatomy lessons. Perfect male specimen. Plastic surgeons, eat your hearts out.'

'They can have me in fifty years.'

'Okay,' she said. 'I expect you'll still be perfect in fifty years. Goodness, though, think of all the things we'll have done in the interim. You might have a few life scars.'

'We both might,' he said, tugging her closer still. 'But they can't make you less than beautiful. They'll be shared scars.'

'I want to visit the Amazon,' she said, running her fingers down his chest in a way that made his whole body feel alive. 'You want to risk a few mosquito bites?'

'The Amazon?'

'One day. It's just…single mom, medicine, there's never been time or money for anything else. You want a few adventures with me?'

'I'm pretty happy where I am, right now,' he said, and she drew away slightly.

'That sounds like the man who loves his house.'

'I'll take you to the Amazon.'

'You'll want to come to the Amazon? It's different.'

'I guess it is.'

'Matt…'

'Mmm?'

'Will we be all right?'

'We'll be all right,' he said, and kissed her and knew he'd do whatever it took to keep this woman in his arms.

For ever.

They loved, they slept, things were perfect, but there was this niggle. This faint unease.

She was slotting into his perfect life. Jess had suggested she throw in medicine and go surfing to test him, but he didn't need testing.

He was her gorgeous Matt, and she'd love him for ever. She'd do whatever it took.

Would he?

It was a tiny niggle. She should put it aside. It was nothing, not when he held her, not when he loved her, not when his loving swept all aside in its wonder.

And then his parents came.

It was late Sunday morning. They'd surfed, dressed, breakfasted, and were sitting on the veranda, feeling smug.

'We need two rockers,' Kelly said, pushing away that stupid, worrying niggle. 'It's not just Pa Kettle. It's Ma and Pa and the whole domestic set-up.'

'Sounds pretty perfect,' Matt said, but then the helicopter hovered into view, and to their mutual astonishment it came down to land on their beach.

'What the...?' Matt said, and rose and stared down the cliff track. And then he swore. 'Dad!'

Dad. Henry Eveldene.

Kelly was wearing shorts, T-shirt and bare feet. Her hair was still damp from their swim.

She wanted to be in hospital whites, she thought. She wanted to be professional, in charge of her world, in a position to face this man on her own terms.

But this was her own terms, she told herself. It had to be.

Jess had limped out of the house with the dogs to see what was happening. She reached behind her and grabbed his hand.

This wasn't threatening, she told herself. This was an elderly couple. How scary could they be?

The woman didn't look scary. She was tiny, seemingly frail, dressed in a plain blue skirt and white shirt, with pearls around her neck, and her white hair caught up into a soft bun with curls escaping. This must be Rose, Jess's mother.

Henry was almost her polar opposite, stout and business-suited. Bald, red faced and already looking angry, he was striding up the path to the house as if he was wielding a battering ram. Rose was struggling behind.

Matt strode down to meet them, heading straight past his father to gather his mother into a hug. 'Mum!'

'Matt,' Rose whispered, and put a hand to his hair as if assuring herself he was real. But she was ignored by her husband. Henry was obviously here on a mission.

'Who the hell is she?' Henry demanded, booming loudly enough to be heard on the next beach. He shaded his eyes and stared up at the house at Kelly. 'Is that her?'

'Is that who?'

'Kelly Eveldene.' He hauled a newspaper clipping from his breast pocket and waved it angrily at Matt. 'You know I have shares in half the country's local papers and I have a notify order if the name Eveldene ever comes up. Dr Kelly Eveldene was named as treating doctor for a kid who suicided. Based in the hospital you're working at. I called the hospital. It took three calls and a bribe and then I found out she was living with you. With you!' He stared up at the veranda again, at Kelly.

And then he saw the boy beside her.

'Jess.'

The word came out as a strangled gasp but it wasn't from Henry. It was from Rose.

Kelly had seen this woman's picture. It had been in Jess's wallet when he'd died. Sometimes she still looked at it, and Rose's face still smiled out.

Rose wasn't smiling now. Her face was bleached white. 'Jess,' she said again, and possibly she would have crumpled if Matt wasn't holding her.

'Mum,' Matt said, and the way he said it was like a caress. 'I was wondering when this should happen, and I'm so glad it finally has. Mum, this is Jessie's son. He's called Jessie, too, and he's your grandson. And this is Kelly. Kelly was Jessie's wife. They're family.'

And he said 'family' so strongly, so surely, that Kelly's world settled. It was an all-encompassing statement, a word that included her for ever.

But it seemed that Henry Eveldene didn't think so. His breath drew in in a hiss of shock and fury. 'What nonsense is this?'

'It's not nonsense,' Matt said evenly. 'Jess married Kelly eighteen years ago. You knew that, Dad.'

'My Jess...married?' Rose gasped, and Matt's grip on her tightened.

'Dad made a decision not to tell you,' Matt said. 'He thought you were shocked enough. It was the wrong decision. We made a lot of wrong decisions back then.'

'Jess's son...' She sounded dazed beyond belief.

'Hey, Grandma.' Jess was a typical teenager, ignoring undercurrents, listening to everything with his typical insouciance. 'I've always wanted a grandma. Cool. And... Grandpa?'

'I am not your grandfather.' It was a roar of rage that made even Jess blink. 'If you're after money...'

'What are you on about?' Jess asked, astounded, and Rose gave a moan of pain.

'No one's after money,' Matt snapped.

'I paid you off,' Henry roared, directing his fury straight at Kelly. 'You cashed that cheque and the deal was that you kept out of our lives for ever.'

'But Jess's insurance policy belonged to his wife.' Still Matt spoke evenly, and Kelly recognised that he'd faced down his father's fury before. Matt went on, his voice stern. 'That money belonged to Kelly, no matter what we decided. We had no right to claim otherwise. We had no right to put conditions on it.'

But Henry wasn't listening. He couldn't hear past his fury. 'So now you've come crawling back, wanting more—'

'That's enough, Dad,' Matt snapped. 'Kelly and Jess want nothing.'

'You're giving them a place to stay.'

'Yes, but—'

'And what does the boy do? Nothing, like his father?'

'He surfs,' Matt said through gritted teeth.

And Kelly thought she should say something and then she thought, No. She could walk away. This fury was between Matt and his father.

'Surfs...' The word came out like the worst of oaths.

'Dad, leave this. You're shocked,' Matt said. 'Don't say anything you might regret. Come up and meet them.'

'You have no right to be here,' the man snapped at Kelly.

'She has every right.'

'And you're calling yourself a doctor,' Henry spat at Kelly. 'You're not even qualified to practise in Australia. I did a fast check before I came. *Dr* Eveldene. Qualified in Hawaii. Do you intend practising in Australia? Ha! I have influence. If you think I can't get you kicked out of this country, you're dead wrong.'

'Dad, what's Kelly ever done to hurt you?' Matt demanded.

'What she's done is immaterial. I have no idea what her game is but I want no part of it. Jess married her when he was a drug-addicted nut case. The marriage should never have been allowed and we owe her nothing. Whatever story she's conned you with, it's to end. She can get out of this country, now.'

But there was another player in this drama. Rose. The elderly woman's eyes hadn't left Jess.

'Henry, stop yelling,' she said, in a strange, wandering voice that somehow cut across her husband's anger. 'Matt, you're saying Jess had a son?'

'This is nothing to do with us,' Henry snapped.

'But it has!' Rose was stumbling over her words. 'Of course it has. My son had a son? Oh, Matt, why didn't you tell us?'

'I didn't know,' Matt said.

'But you knew about Kelly?'

'I… Yes.'

'But you didn't tell us about her either.'

'Dad knew. He thought the truth would break your heart.'

'But my heart had already broken,' Rose whispered. 'When Jess died.'

And Kelly's heart twisted, just like that. Anger was forgotten. No matter what had gone before, this was a woman who'd lost her son.

'Your Jess carried your photograph in his wallet for all the time I knew him,' she said, speaking directly to Rose and ignoring the crimson-faced bully beside her. 'He had it with him when he died. He spoke of you often, with love. I honoured your husband's wishes not to contact you but now it's happened, I'm glad.' She gripped Jess's hand. 'This is your grandson. No matter what's gone on before, surely that's all that matters.'

'It is,' Matt said strongly. 'Dad, our family has treated Kelly appallingly. It's time for it to stop.'

But Henry Eveldene wasn't done. He'd obviously had twenty-four hours knowing who Kelly must be. Twenty-four hours to work himself into a rage. It'd be part guilt induced, Kelly thought, trying hard to be compassionate. He'd rejected his son. To now embrace his son's wife and his grandson would be acknowledging something that was possibly unbearable.

'There's not one reason for it to stop,' he snapped.

'There's a hundred reasons,' Matt snapped back. 'And not one reason why it has to continue. What is it, Dad? Why can't you accept Jess's family?'

'Jess has no family.' The words were a blast that rang over the cliffs and out to the sea beyond. Down on the beach the helicopter pilot stood by his machine, waiting.

Kelly thought idly, I wonder what he thinks of this family reunion?

Not much, probably. After all, it wasn't much of a family.

'You've broken your pledge. I'll drum you out of the country,' Henry snarled.

But still Kelly was calm. How much self-hatred must lie behind his bluster? She was feeling weird, almost analytical. This man had no power to hurt her.

But Rose… She looked at the elderly woman's distressed face and she thought she couldn't distress her further.

'You won't need to drum me out of the country,' she said. 'We're only here because my Jess broke his leg, surfing.'

'Surfing…' Henry spat, as if the word was foul.

'Surfing,' Kelly continued, cutting over his rage. 'We're stuck here for another few weeks. Matt has been kind and we'll always be grateful, but we acknowledge how you feel. I don't want Jess to have any part of your anger. We'll leave as soon as he's healed, and we won't come back.'

'Kelly…' Matt released his mother, and in a few long strides he was on the veranda. 'No!'

'I want no part of this.'

'Yeah, we don't have to cop this,' Jessie said.

'Leave it, Matt,' Kelly said. 'We want no part of a family feud.'

'It's bullshit,' Jess said.

And Matt stood beside these two who had come to mean so much to him, he looked down at his parents, and he thought that's exactly what this was. Bullshit. He might not have used the teenager's expression but right now it seemed to fit.

But there was no way he could stop this viciousness. His father was powerful. He had contacts in every media outlet in the land. If there was anything in Kelly's past to be dragged up, he'd find it.

Kelly had spent her childhood in a strange, unconventional environment. There'd be things his father could use and he would use them. He'd twist them, he'd spit them out in any form that suited him. He could do real damage.

And he looked again at Kelly, at the tilt of her chin, at her defiance, and he thought of all the other ogres she'd had to face beside his father. He'd been one of them.

No more, he thought, right there and then. This woman was no longer alone. His father was attacking her and it was personal. She was family.

She was his family.

His love.

'If Kelly goes, I go,' he said, into the sun-washed day, and the world seemed to pause at his words. 'I'll leave the country to be with her.'

Kelly gasped. She opened her mouth to speak and nothing came out.

Nothing, nothing and nothing.

Inevitably, it Jess who was first to recover. He had teenage resilience. Teenage enthusiasm.

'You want to come back to Hawaii with us? Cool.' Ignoring the tension around them, he launched himself straight into the future. 'I can show you the best surf spots. The Pipeline's awesome but there are even better places. Matt, it'll be great.'

But Kelly was staring at him as if he'd slapped her.

'You can't...you can't be serious?'

But he looked into her eyes and he'd never been so serious in his life. Everything else faded but his need to say it like it was.

By his side, Bess and Spike were standing very still, as if they, too, knew this moment was life-changing. What were the requirements for taking dogs abroad? He'd need to find out. No matter, that was detail. What mattered now was taking that look of disbelief from Kelly's face.

He fought for the right words and he found them, maybe not word perfect but close enough. He said them now, with all the love that shone through the centuries since the vow had first been made.

'"Whither thou goest, I will go,"' he said softly. '"Thy home will be my home and thy people shall be my people."'

'Matt...' She could hardly breathe. 'Matt, you can't.'

'Why can't I?'

'This is your home.' She gestured around, to the house he'd built with such love and such pride. This house that had been so important to him but now seemed nothing compared to what he felt for this woman.

'I think...' he said softly. 'I hope that my home is you.'

'But you love this house,' she breathed.

'I love you more.'

'You can't.'

'I can't think of a single reason why I can't. I can think of a hundred reasons why I can.'

'You and your hundred reasons,' she said, her eyes misting with tears, her voice cracked with emotion. 'I bet you can't.'

'Shall I start? Number one, you make excellent pancakes. And hamburgers. We'll forget about cakes. Two, anyone who sees you in a bathing suit will be in love in an instant. Three, your chuckle does something to my insides that leaves me breathless. Four…'

'This could get boring,' Jess said, grinning.

'Not…it's not boring,' Kelly managed. 'I like it.'

'Are you out of your mind?' The baffled roar from beneath the veranda made them all pause. Henry looked as if he was about to explode. 'What nonsense is this? This woman's leaving.'

'With me,' Matt said evenly, and then, because it seemed the right thing to do, the only thing to do, because Kelly's eyes were still confused, because their whole future seemed to hang on this moment, he did what any sane man would do.

He caught her hands and tugged her round to face him. And he dropped to one knee.

'Kelly Eveldene,' he said, strongly and surely, 'will you marry me?'

'Wow,' Jess whooped. 'Wow and wow and wow. Mom, say yes.'

'If she says yes I won't have a son,' Henry roared.

'If she says yes I'll have my own son,' Matt said evenly, his eyes not leaving Kelly's face. 'If Jess will have me.'

'Only if you increase my allowance,' Jess said, and grinned.

'Done,' Matt said grandly, and then looked a bit uneasy. 'Hang on. By how much?'

'We'll negotiate,' Jess said. 'What do they call it? A marriage settlement.'

'Have your lawyers speak to my lawyers,' Matt said, and he was smiling, but he didn't take his eyes from Kelly. 'Love?'

'You can't,' she whispered, and she knelt to join him. 'To leave everything…your career, your gorgeous house, your place in life…'

'People are what's important,' he said, knowing that

finally he had it. Kelly held everything important to him, in her smile, in her courage, in her life.

A hundred reasons? There must be a thousand, he thought, and more to come. He had a lifetime of learning how to love this woman. A lifetime of being loved in return.

'Kelly, if you can...'

'You mean it?'

'More than anything else in the world.'

'Then of course I can,' she said, caught between laughter and tears. 'Oh, Matt, I love you. I love you and love you and love you. Do I need to make that a hundred times, too?'

'Three will do,' he said grandly. 'We have all the time in the world to make it up to a hundred. Or a thousand or a million or whatever comes next.'

'We're not making sense.'

'I guess we're not. But you will be my wife?'

'Yes.'

'Then that's all the sense I need. Everything else will follow.'

And finally she was being kissed, deeply, soundly, possessively, and she was kissing back with every single emotion returned in full.

How did she love this man?

For a while she'd thought it was to do with her old love, but it wasn't that. When she'd first married she'd been a child. Her husband had been her saviour and her hero. What she felt for this man was far, far different. It was an adult's love and acceptance.

This man was flawed. He'd been hurt, he'd retired to solitude, he'd built walls around himself. She thought of his failed marriage and knew that he'd probably hurt people himself.

He wouldn't now. She knew that with the same surety she knew her love for him wouldn't fail. He'd shed his armour, he'd opened himself to her, and he was hers. He was her gorgeous wounded warrior, as scarred by life as she was, but ready now to step forward. With her.

He loved her and she loved him. All the love in the world was in this kiss. The years ahead stretched gloriously and she thought, I can love, I can love, I can love.

She did love. She was being kissed until her toes curled and nothing else mattered. Nothing, nothing, nothing.

Except…there was the odd spectator or two. Two dogs, Jess, her…parents-in-law? The helicopter pilot down on the beach?

The world.

Somehow they broke apart but not far. Matt's arms still held her. They rose and she looked down at the couple below and felt sad for the pair of them.

'I'm sorry,' she whispered. 'I didn't mean this to happen.'

'Hey, but it's great.' Jess was practically bouncing. 'But I'm not being a pageboy. Think again, people.'

'But I can see you as a ring bearer in pantaloons,' Kelly said. Matt choked and Jess grabbed a cushion from the settee and tossed it at her. But there were still things to be said. Matt fielded the cushion before it reached his beloved and tossed it back. Then he turned to his parents.

'That's it,' he said, in a voice he hadn't known he possessed until now. He'd never known he could feel so sure. 'It's settled so take it or leave it. I'm sorry, Mum,' he said, gentling as he addressed his mother. 'I know this is a huge amount to toss at you in one hit, but Dad's lied to you for years.

'To my shame, I haven't told you about Kelly either. But no more lies. I loved my big brother and I lost him, as you did, but Kelly lost her husband, and her loss matched yours. She was left with a baby to care for on her own. That she's brought him here now, into my life, is a gift beyond price, and that I've fallen in love with her makes things perfect. Kelly and I are family now, and so is Jess. Mum, I still love you, but my way is with Kelly.'

Once more there was silence. But it was okay, Kelly thought, dazed beyond belief.

She wasn't sure what had just happened. She needed space. She needed to go and lock herself in her room and think it all out.

She'd quite like to take Matt to her room with her.

No. Now was not the appropriate time to jump her man. But he *was* her man. Her fiancé. Her soon-to-be husband. Soon she could jump him whenever she wanted—for the rest of her life?

The thought was so overpowering that she felt herself gasp. Matt glanced sharply at her and then he grinned. Could he read her mind? She hoped not, but she met his glinting laughter and she knew…

Happy ever after was right here by her side.

'We're leaving.' Henry's words cut across the intimacy between them. He had no way of hurting them, Kelly thought, but then she glanced at Matt and saw him look at his mother and flinch.

Rose was losing another son.

But maybe not. Henry had grasped Rose's arm, hauling her round to march her down the cliff path, but Rose was balking. Her sensible shoes dug into the track, and when he gave her another, harder tug she wrenched away. She dug her toes in further, as if creating a wedge that would keep her here.

'I have my own money.'

'What are you talking about?' Henry demanded, making to grab her again, but she thrust him off.

'I can do this,' she said. Her faltering words were growing stronger. 'I will. Matt, if you don't mind… If I was to get a little apartment in Hawaii…would you mind if I visited?' She glanced at Jess and her longing was naked for all to see. 'Would it be possible for me to get to know my grandson?'

'What a wonderful idea,' Kelly said, before Matt could answer. Matt was so astounded that he hadn't found his voice. His mother had been a doormat for years, a down-trodden mouse. Suddenly the mouse was squeaking. More, she was laying down ultimatums.

'Don't be ridiculous,' Henry gasped. 'You wouldn't dare.'

'I would dare,' the mouse said, and turned and faced him head on. 'I would dare because Matt and Kelly and Jessie...' Her voice trembled as she said Jessie's name but she made herself continue. 'Matt and Kelly and Jess will be a family, and I want to be part of it.'

CHAPTER ELEVEN

TWO MONTHS LATER they left for Hawaii. Not, in the end, to stay, but to visit. Kelly and Jess needed to pack up their apartment and say their goodbyes, and they had another task to do, too.

They carried an urn with them. Matt stood with Jess and his mother and they watched together as Kelly scattered his brother's ashes into the sea at Diamond Head.

This was where Jess had wanted his ashes scattered. Eighteen years later, his ashes had come home.

But this was no longer home for them. They were here to say farewell to a brother, husband, son and father. They were here to let Rose take her fledgling steps as a grandma. Then they were going back to Australia. They were facing Henry's threats down.

'Four against one,' Jess had said. 'We're a family. What threats can possibly mess with us?'

There might be trouble, Matt conceded, but if it came they'd face it together. And Kelly loved his house. His home.

'Let's try,' she'd said. 'The Gold Coast is a perfect place to live. I'm sure I can get full Australian accreditation. Matt, you love it.'

'Not as much as I love you,' he'd growled, but she'd kissed him and held him and smiled.

'Then let's see if we can put it all together as a package,' she'd said. 'Our careers, your house, your dogs, our family. Us. And the university in Brisbane seems great. Jess is already excited about the courses there. It's worth a try.'

And that had been the next shaking of his foundations. His last judgement call shattered. A week after Henry had thrown them his ultimatum, Jess had woken the house with his whooping. It seemed he'd been studying for years, in Hawaii and online when he and his mother were travelling. His exam results—the International Baccalaureate—were through, and meant almost any university course in the world would now be open to him.

'But not until I've surfed for another eighteen months,' Jess told him. 'That's the deal Mum and I made. If I get decent uni entrance exams, Dad's money will fund me for two years on the international surfing tour. She thinks that's what Dad would have wanted.' He'd looked ruefully at his leg. 'I might not make it back to the top,' he conceded, 'but I'll have fun trying. And then, maybe medicine? Maybe architecture. I'm not sure yet, but I have time to plan.'

It had taken Matt's breath away. The pair of them took his breath away. Jess and Kelly. Two astonishing people.

He never ceased to be astonished. And the most astonishing thing was that Kelly loved him. Kelly wanted to be his wife.

And so it was.

Living the dream was what she was doing right now, Kelly thought as she stood by her brand-new husband's side and heard the words that sealed their union for ever.

'I now pronounce you man and wife.'

They were standing on the beach below Matt's house, but this wedding wasn't all about Matt's place in the world. Her world was here, too. They'd timed the wedding so the surfing circuit was back in town, and to her joy a bunch of surfing and doctor friends had made the trip from Hawaii.

Everyone they loved was here, Kelly thought with deep satisfaction. Everyone important.

Even Matt's ex-wife, Jenny, was here with her husband and four kids. She'd flown to the Gold Coast as soon as she'd heard Matt was engaged, and five minutes after meeting Kelly she was beaming.

'I never thought it would happen,' she told Kelly. 'I found it with my Peter but I've always felt sad for Matt. But now... He's smitten. Anyone can see the transformation. Kelly, you're a wonder woman.'

She wasn't a wonder woman, Kelly thought as she and Matt turned to face their friends, hand in hand, man and wife. She was just Kelly. Doctor. Surfer. Mother of Jess. Wife to Matt.

And one extraordinarily happy woman.

'If my chest swells any further I'll bust my tux,' Matt said, and she smiled and smiled.

'Just as well you have your swimming trunks on underneath.'

'I don't. Do you?' he asked, startled.

'Yep. A white bikini.' She spun and showed him the back of her wedding gown. The gown dipped to below her waist, exposing her beautiful bare back, plus the fine cord of a white bikini top, enticingly tied with a bow.

Their audience was cheering, but for this moment they had eyes for only each other. Man and wife, from this day forward.

'Do you think...?' Matt said longingly, touching the bow.

'I do not think,' she said serenely. 'We have two hours' surfing in front of us and photographs, then dinner, the odd speech, then a bit of dancing. There's a hundred reasons why you can't carry me off to your lair right now.'

'There's a thousand reasons why I should.'

'You have time to tell me,' she said, and she couldn't resist. Her new husband had already kissed her, but she was kissing him again. 'You have a lifetime to tell me.'

'It's not long enough,' Matt growled, kissing her back with a passion that brought gasps and laughter from their friends and family. 'All those reasons…I need to start now.'

* * * * *

CLAIMING HIS BROTHER'S BABY

HELEN LACEY

For Nani
Because big sisters really are the best!

Chapter One

Cassie Duncan placed her four-month-old son in his bed and gently rubbed his belly through the pale blue cotton onesie. Oliver's breathing slowed and she watched his tiny chest rise and fall, marveling at the perfect little person who'd come into her life.

If only your daddy was here...

But Doug was gone. Killed eight months earlier while on tour in the Middle East, he never got to see his son born. Now it was just the two of them, getting through each day. Cassie adored being a mother and loved Oliver more than she'd imagined she could love anyone. But she was sad that Doug would miss seeing his son grow up. He'd had very little family, just a younger brother in South Dakota he rarely saw. And Crystal Point was a long way from there. With a population of eight hundred, the small Australian beachside town sat at the southernmost point of the Great Barrier Reef. It was the perfect place to raise her child—quiet and safe—a place where she fit in, where she led a valuable life.

She grabbed the baby monitor, flicked on the colored shaded night-light and left the nursery. Mouse hunkered down the hall when he saw her. The one-hundred-and-sixty-pound black-and-white Great Dane always stood point at the end of the hall when she was in the nursery with Oliver. The dog pushed his big head against her leg and Cassie rubbed his neck.

"Feel like a snack?" she asked and kept walking.

Mouse followed her through to the kitchen. She gave him a couple of doggy treats and filled up the kettle. Oliver would stay asleep for a few hours, so she had time to make dinner and watch a movie. She rummaged through the pantry and settled on tinned soup and sourdough toast. The dog climbed into his bed by the door and Cassie set about making her meal.

Friday nights always seemed the quietest somehow. In the old days she would have called her best friends, Lauren and Mary-Jayne, to come around and they would have opened a bottle of wine and eaten cheese and crackers and shared stories about their week. But Lauren was recently engaged and making wedding plans with her fiancé. And Mary-Jayne was locked away in her workshop and wouldn't be around for a week.

And I have Oliver.

Having a baby had changed her priorities. Not that Cassie had ever been much of a party girl. She'd dated Doug for three years before his death and although they hadn't seen much of one another in the last eighteen months, she had stood by her commitment to their relationship. Being involved with a career soldier had been difficult. However, the long absences and constant worry for his safety hadn't altered her feelings. She'd loved him, and now she loved their son.

She cranked the lid off the soup tin, poured it into a saucepan and sliced some bread while she waited for the soup to heat up. The baby monitor was quiet and Cassie relaxed when she sat down at the big scrubbed table and ate her dinner. The house was silent, except for its usual creaks and moans. But she loved the house and had lived in it for most of her life.

When her grandfather had fallen ill four years ago and needed full-time care, the house had been sold to an investment buyer to pay for his care and she had become a tenant in her own home. Of course she was grateful to have been able to stay on and lease the property from the new owner.

The new owner had turned out to be Doug and when he briefly returned from his tour and came around to check on the house, they'd quickly fallen for one another. There weren't fireworks or a rush of crazy heat, but they'd shared something more…something lasting. It was grounded in friendship and Cassie would have happily spent her life with him had fate not intervened. But only months after she'd told him she was pregnant Doug was dead, killed by a sniper in a secret operation along with two other soldiers.

She'd been living in the house ever since, paying the rent and utilities, and had begrudgingly started looking for another place to live while waiting for the home she loved to be pulled out from under her and Oliver.

Because the house now belonged to Doug's brother, Tanner McCord. She'd met him twice and on both occasions he'd proven to be the disinterested, brooding loner Doug had described. She knew the tension between the two men went back a long way and whenever she'd asked Doug about it he'd quickly dismissed her questions. Now all she could do was wait until she learned what Tanner planned to do with the house. Eight days earlier she'd received an email. He was coming back to Crystal Point. He wanted to see her. He wanted to talk.

He wants to kick me out of my home...

Cassie shuddered. Damn. She should be better prepared. She should have found somewhere else to live. She should have contacted a lawyer again and ascertained whether Oliver had any rights to Doug's estate. Instead, she'd buried her head in the sand, plastered on her regular happy smile and hoped things would work out. Like a naive fool. As always.

She shook off the unease in her blood and finished her meal. Once she'd eaten and washed up, she left the kitchen, checked the baby, gathered her things and headed for the bathroom. Twenty minutes later she was showered, dried and wearing her comfiest gray sweats. By seven she was in front of the television watching a DVD.

But not even her favorite romantic comedy could hold her attention. She'd had a headache all afternoon, amplified by the increasing funk she'd been in since Tanner's email had arrived. She was nervous. On edge and restless at the idea of facing him without Doug by her side. And she felt...alone. Something she hadn't truly experienced since her parents had died. Or since her grandfather had gone into the nursing home. Even when she didn't see Doug for months at a time she hadn't labored over being alone. This was something else. Something more. Cassie couldn't figure why the feeling was so intense. Since Oliver's birth she hadn't any time to linger over what she had lost, or the life she'd never have with Doug. But tonight the feelings were acute. Tonight she was *lonely.*

When her parents had died in a boating accident Cassie had gone to live with her grandfather Neville Duncan. She'd been eight years old and had grieved the loss of her family for a long time. Lauren's folks had helped, and her granddad had done his best. But it wasn't like having a family, a mother and father, of her own. With Doug she'd hoped that together they would make a family. But that wasn't to be. Still, she was determined to tell her son everything she knew about his father. Doug wouldn't be forgotten.

As for Tanner...she'd deal with whatever happened.

I can make this work.

I have to.

It was dark out and Tanner McCord had been sitting in the car for over half an hour.

Waiting.

And knowing he should have let the lawyers handle it instead of traveling halfway around the world to see her. They were only connected by her child. Doug's son. The son his brother would never see.

Tanner drummed his fingers on the steering wheel. It had been over two years since he'd seen her. And that was only the second time since she'd become involved with Doug. But now Doug was gone. And Tanner was home to fulfill the unspoken promise he'd made to his brother.

He looked toward the house. A silhouette passed by a window. Tanner's stomach lurched and he sucked in a deep breath. His leg ached and he pressed his palm hard into his left thigh. After months of rehab he could finally walk without that damn stick. The pain was worse when he drove for a length of time, and the five-hour haul from Brisbane to Crystal Point after twenty-plus hours in the air crossing the Pacific had taken its toll. He mostly avoided pain meds in favor of massage and physical therapy, but right now needed something to take his mind off the soreness and maintain his focus. Tanner popped a couple of aspirin and waited for the pain to ease as it usually did when he put pressure on the main fracture line.

There was more movement by the window, followed by a light being switched on in the front room. The big, low-set brick-and-tile home was positioned well back from the road and in the fading dusk he'd noticed how overgrown and unkempt the garden was. Tanner could see the flickering light from the television bouncing shadows off the curtains and he wondered if he should wait until morning before disturbing her.

Instead, he got out, pushing past the pain in his leg, and closed the door. Tanner walked across the curb and stalled in the middle of the driveway. Driving for hours had exaggerated his limp and he pulled his leg forward to force a straight stride. When he reached the door he knocked twice and waited. Seconds later he heard the soft sound of feet padding over floorboards before the door opened back on its hinges.

Cassandra.

His stomach rolled again. She was beautiful, as he remembered. Hair the color of treacle, pale blue eyes, porcelain skin and soft, even features. The first time Doug had introduced her to him, Tanner's breath had been sucked from his chest. The second time he was better prepared—he managed a quick visit while Doug was home on leave and had kept his distance from her. And this time...this time he had his head screwed on right. He wasn't in Crystal Point to lust over his dead brother's girlfriend.

History would not repeat itself. Not ever again.

"Tanner?"

She said his name in that soft, breathless way and a familiar jolt of awareness rushed through his blood. He finally drew in some air and spoke. "Hello, Cassandra."

Her gaze narrowed as a huge dog moved around her legs

and sniffed the air. The animal eyed him suspiciously and lifted his ears in alert mode. She certainly looked as though she had all the protection she needed. "You're here…"

"You got my email?"

"Ah…yes…but I wasn't expecting you until next week."

"I got an earlier flight," he explained and pressed down the jolt of pain contracting his thigh. "I'm sorry if I startled you. I probably should have called first."

She looked flustered and a little put out, and guilt twitched Tanner behind his shoulder blades. He should have waited until morning. Or he should have let the lawyers handle it.

"No, it's fine," she said and nodded. "You can come inside."

When she opened the screen and stepped back Tanner moved through the doorway. She closed both doors behind him and suggested they go into the living room. The dog trailed her and Tanner hung back for a moment. He finally followed her down the hall and remained by the doorway when she entered the front room.

Tanner watched her. She looked cautious. On edge. Out of sorts.

Suspicious.

The room had altered a little since the last time he'd been in it. There was some new furniture, new rug, different paintings on the walls. There was a fireplace with one of those fake heaters and a photo on the mantel caught his attention. Doug. In uniform. The face seemed as recognizable as it did unfamiliar. When he was young he'd worshipped Doug.

But things had a way of changing.

"That's quite an animal you have there," he said.

"Mouse," she replied and ushered the dog to sit on a rug

near the fireplace. The animal gave Tanner a wary once-over before curling on the mat.

"Mouse?"

She smiled a little. "The idea was to make him seem less intimidating."

When the dog was settled, Tanner crossed the threshold. "How are you?"

She nodded. "Fine."

"And the—your son?"

"Oliver," she said, as though he didn't know the child's name. "He's asleep."

He took a few steps and noticed how her gaze fell to his uneven gait. She knew about the accident that had laid him up in hospital for over a month. It was the reason he hadn't made it to Doug's funeral.

"And are you well?" he asked and moved behind the heavy sofa.

"I said I was." She looked him over. "More the point, how are *you*?"

Tanner tapped his thigh. "Better. Good as new."

Her brows came up. "Really?"

He shrugged. "Maybe not exactly like new. But I'm getting there."

"I should have called," she said quietly. "But after Doug…you know…and the baby came…and by then I didn't have time to think about anything but Oliver."

He understood. And he hadn't expected her to call. They weren't friends. They weren't anything. She was Doug's woman. The mother of his brother's child. It didn't matter that her blue eyes and soft smile invaded his dreams. Wanting her was pointless. He'd never act on it, never give in to it. Never put himself through the inevitable humiliation of her rejection. Staying in South Dakota and living his life far away from her and Doug had been the sensible option.

"It's okay, Cassandra. You don't have to—"

"Cassie," she said, correcting him. "No one calls me Cassandra."

Tanner lingered over the thought. He'd always called her that. Funny how he'd never picked up that she didn't like it. "All right…Cassie."

She smiled a little and sat on the sofa. "Would you like coffee? Tea?"

"No, thank you."

"You can sit down if you want."

He nodded and moved farther into the room. She watched him intently as he eased into the opposite chair and stretched out his left leg. She couldn't have missed the way he favored the one side when he walked.

"Are you in pain?" she asked.

Tanner shrugged. "It was a long trip."

The suspicion in her gaze didn't abate. "You said in your email that you wanted to talk. So, what did you want to talk about?"

In normal circumstances it might not have sounded like a fraught, loaded question. But nothing about the situation was normal. And they both knew it.

"Don't look so wary, Cassie. I would have been here eight months ago if it hadn't been for the accident. I finally got the all clear to travel and came as soon as I could."

"For what?" she asked quietly, but she was clearly on edge. "Doug's dead. Anything that needs to be sorted could be done through lawyers."

Silence stretched between them like frayed elastic. *She doesn't want me here.* He ignored her mention of lawyers. There was time to get to all of that. "You're right," he said, consciously keeping his voice light. "Doug is gone. But his son is very much alive."

Her pale eyes widened. "You came to see Oliver?"

"Of course."

"Why?"

Tanner sucked in a heavy breath. "Because he's the only family that I have."

Family.

Cassie almost choked out a sob the way he said the word. She longed for Oliver to have a family. But this man was a stranger. Unknown. Someone she'd met a couple of times and who had always managed to unnerve her even though they'd barely spoken. She wasn't sure why, but knew it wasn't simply a reaction to his handsome face. There was something about Tanner...something that almost felt familiar...as if they were connected somehow. It was stupid, of course. There was no connection...no common link other than Doug.

Still...he was extraordinarily handsome—dark brown hair, eyes the color of warm toffee and he possessed a strong, muscular frame. Features that made him impossible to ignore. He was taller than Doug had been, and leaner in the waist and hips and broader through the shoulders. He was the kind of man who'd look good in jeans, chambray shirt and cowboy boots, or a suit and tie.

Tanner McCord was gorgeous, no doubt about it. But she wasn't about to get caught up in his good looks. She took a deep breath and spoke. "I didn't realize family was so important to you."

It was a direct dig and he obviously knew it. "Doug and I had different lives," he said and stretched back against the chair. "Which doesn't mean we didn't care about each other."

"I know how Doug felt about you," she replied carefully. "He told me how he looked after you when your parents died."

Tanner's eyes darkened. "He did, that's right. I was nine years old. Doug was twenty-one. I lived with him for three months before he joined the army."

Cassie frowned. She knew Tanner was about to turn thirty-one and born the same year she was. "I thought Doug went into the army when he was twenty-three?"

There was another stretch of silence, longer this time, as though he was working out how to answer her. "No. Twenty-one."

"And where did you live then?"

"Boarding school," he replied. "He visited when he could."

It wasn't quite the story she'd heard. Doug hadn't mentioned sending his younger brother away to school at such a young age. "Well, of course he would do that, being Doug," she said, and ignored the tiny stab of disapproval tapping in her head. "So, how long are you staying in town?"

"Awhile."

How long was "awhile"? "To see Oliver?"

"If that's okay?"

She wondered how her cheerful, lovable son would take to the man whose eyes were just like his own. *No, they're Doug's eyes.* But she didn't have any reason to refuse his request. "You can see him tomorrow."

"Thank you, Cassie."

She looked at the clock on the mantel. It was nearly eight o'clock. Early. Probably too early to send him on his way. "So, you're staying in Bellandale?"

The town, with its sixty thousand residents, was twenty minutes away from the small beachside community of Crystal Point and had many quality hotels.

"Yeah, I'm sure I'll find a hotel."

Cassie frowned and tried not to think about how his

soft accent seemed to warm her skin. "You didn't book a hotel room?"

He shrugged. "I'll find somewhere. I picked up a rental car at the airport. I was born in Bellandale, remember? I know my way around town."

She did know. In fact they'd been born at the same hospital, barely a week apart. But they had never met until after she'd started dating Doug. "So, about ten tomorrow?"

"Sure," he said and got to his feet.

Cassie noticed the slight wobble and how he pushed down hard on his right leg. He was obviously in pain. She didn't know much about his accident, only that it had been life threatening and something to do with a horse. Now wasn't the time to ask. And really, the less she knew the better. Tanner wasn't part of her life. Nor did she want him to be.

She was just about to say good-night and walk him out when he faltered on his feet and quickly gripped the back of the sofa for support. Cassie rushed forward. "Are you okay?"

"Fine," he said and grimaced. "Damn leg locks up sometimes. It'll pass."

Cassie wasn't so sure. He looked pale and uncomfortable. The long drive to Crystal Point that had followed an even longer flight from South Dakota had clearly caught up with him. "Are you sure you can drive?"

He shrugged fractionally. "I guess I'll find out. Good night, Cassie."

She watched as he took a slow step, then another. He was in tremendous pain and trying not to show it. "Tanner?" His name fell from her lips.

"Yes?"

What am I doing?

"You...you could stay here tonight," she said quietly and

couldn't quite believe the words were coming out. But she didn't want him driving and potentially crashing. He was Doug's brother. Oliver's uncle. Old-fashioned consideration surged through her. "You're not exactly in any condition to drive. And you said you'll be coming back to see Oliver tomorrow anyway. And since you haven't booked into a hotel. I think... I think..."

What? Having him spend the night is a good idea? In what stratosphere?

"You think what?"

She shrugged lightly. Okay, maybe it wasn't a good idea. But he *was* Oliver's uncle. And family, in a way. Plus, technically the house was his. He had every right to stay.

"It was just an idea. You look tired and in pain, that's all. And there are two spare rooms. But if you'd rather go to a—"

"If you're sure," he said, cutting her off.

She wasn't sure about anything. Especially when it came to Tanner McCord. "Of course."

He watched her, rattling her nerves in that way he always seemed to do. "Then I'll stay. And you're right, Cassie, I'm beat. I'd really like a shower and some sleep. Thank you."

So it was settled. He was staying.

"I'll show you to your room," she said quietly and forced some air into her lungs.

"I'll get my bag. Be back in a minute."

She told Mouse to stay put, walked from the room and up the hall and waited while Tanner headed back outside. He returned in a few minutes with a battered duffel draped over one strong shoulder. He wore dark jeans and a long-sleeved black shirt with piping around the pocket and cuffs and, despite the now pronounced effort as he walked, Cassie felt a sharp niggle of awareness way down low. That he could do that to her, despite how much she had loved Doug, always made her resent him just that little bit more than she would have liked.

"This way," she said and walked down the hall. He followed and stood in the doorway once she entered the bedroom. "The sheets are fresh and there are spare towels hanging in the bathroom."

"Thank you," he said as he walked into the room and dropped his bag at the foot of the bed.

"Well, I'll leave you to it. I need to check on Oliver."

Cassie left the room as swiftly as she could and headed for the nursery, and tried not to think about how she suddenly had a man staying in her spare room.

His spare room. His house.

With a heavy heart it occurred to her she was now a visitor in her own home.

Once she'd checked on the baby Cassie made it to the kitchen and turned on the kettle. She heard the shower running and tried to concentrate on making tea. The wall clock read just past eight-thirty and she hoped once Tanner had showered he'd give in to the jet lag and crash out for the night.

But not so.

Fifteen minutes later he appeared in the doorway. He wore low-rise, loose-fitting jeans and a white Henley shirt that did little to disguise the washboard belly and broad shoulders. His hair was damp and flopped over his forehead.

So, he's as sexy as sin.

It wasn't exactly a news flash. The first time she'd met Tanner she'd been aware of his many physical attributes. Doug had joked how his brother had gotten all the looks in the family. Not that he'd been unattractive, but he certainly hadn't possessed the classic handsomeness of the man now hovering in the doorway.

"Tea?" she asked and tried not to think about how the air seemed suddenly thicker.

He shrugged. "Coffee?"

Cassie nodded and grabbed a couple of mugs. "Is instant okay?" she asked. "Or I can put the percolator on for—"

"Instant is fine," he said easily.

She relaxed a little and began making the coffee. "Now that you've showered and changed do you feel human again?"

"Yeah. I don't mind flying, but I always seem to get a chronic case of jet lag."

"Doug loved flying," she said as she poured his coffee and then sugared her tea. She remembered that Tanner liked his coffee with only a little milk. *Funny how some memories stuck.*

"My brother always was the adventurous one."

Cassie didn't quite believe that. While Doug had joined the army and made a career as a soldier, she knew Tanner had traveled the world before settling in South Dakota to work his special kind of magic with horses. He had the swagger and confidence of a man who knew who he was. Now she wondered how much the accident had changed his life and the work he loved.

"Can you still ride?" she asked, figuring there were things that had to be said and she needed time to work up to the hard questions.

"Not yet," he replied and came farther into the room.

Cassie glanced up. "When you called to say you couldn't come to the funeral because you were in hospital I kind of zoned out and didn't ask many questions about what had happened to you. I think I was still in shock at the time."

"Understandable," he said and walked around the table.

He pulled out a chair and sat down. "I was in a bit of shock myself. I guess I always thought Doug was invincible." He tapped his leg in a kind of ironic gesture "Turns out, no one is."

Cassie brought the mugs to the table and sat down. "So, what happened?"

"You mean the accident? I got in the way of a frightened horse and was trampled."

It sounded oversimplified and she raised her brows. "And?"

"A busted leg, broken wrist, four fractured ribs and concussion. Cuts and abrasions. And I lost my spleen."

"A horse did that?" she asked, horrified by the seriousness of his injuries.

He sipped his coffee. "I was at a friend's ranch. His young daughter got between the colt and the fence and I pulled her out of the way. But I wasn't quick enough to make it back through the corral gate. The horse struck me in the chest and once I was down that was it. There was nothing anyone could have done."

Cassie's throat tightened. "You could have been killed."

He shrugged lightly. "I spent a month in hospital and the next six working to get back on my feet."

"It happened only a few days or so before Doug died," she said quietly, thinking of the irony. "It must have been hard for you, being in hospital and getting the news your brother was gone."

He shrugged again, but Cassie wasn't fooled. There was something in his expression that told her losing his brother had been shattering. She'd always thought Tanner to be aloof and insensitive. Doug had called him a free spirit, the kind of man who would never settle down, never lay down roots. But she wasn't so sure. She decided to ask him.

There was no point in being coy. There was too much at stake. "What are you really doing here, Tanner?"

He sat back slowly in his seat and watched her. "I told you."

"To see your nephew?" It seemed too easy. Too simple.

"That's right."

"How long are you staying?"

He pushed the mug aside. "I'm not sure."

Cassie's back stiffened. "Then I have to ask you," she said and pushed her shoulders back. "Are you kicking us out of this house?"

Chapter Two

Tanner had expected the question. He knew she'd want to know about the house. It had to be hard for her. She'd lived in the house since she was a child. When her grandfather's health had declined, the house was put on the market and sold...to Doug. Tanner had no idea why his brother had bought the place. But he knew Cassie had a deep connection to the home she'd once shared with her grandfather.

"Of course not."

She let out a long breath, as though she'd been holding it. He noticed her knuckles were white around the mug. "Oh, okay."

"This is still your home, Cassie."

"But Doug—"

Tanner straightened his spine. "It's still your home," he said again, firmer this time.

"For the moment. And according to Doug's lawyer, the house belongs to you."

"An oversight, obviously."

It wasn't the truth. It wasn't even close to it. But Tanner wouldn't divulge that knowledge. There was no point. Doug was dead. His brother had left a mess behind—one Tanner had to clean up before he returned to South Dakota.

"I don't understand what you mean."

He lied again. "I'm sure Doug had every intention of—"

"I'm not sure what Doug intended," she said, cutting him off.

But Tanner did. Doug had made his thoughts about the house and the child Cassie carried very clear. He drank some coffee and looked at her. She was so effortlessly pretty. His insides stirred and he quickly pushed the thought aside.

"It makes no difference now."

She shook her head. "But the house —"

"It has a mortgage," he said quietly. "Did you know that?"

She shook her head again. "I wasn't sure. Doug never talked about it much when he returned from tour. I've been paying rent and the utilities like I've done since he first bought the place." She stopped and looked at him. "How large a mortgage?"

His stomach tightened as he named the figure.

"Oh...that's...that's a lot."

It *was* a lot. It was a six-figure hole that wouldn't be covered by Doug's insurance policy. Most of the money had gone to repay the balance on three maxed credit cards and a bank loan taken out to purchase the top-of-the-range Ducati stored in the garage.

He pushed down the resentment thickening his blood. Whatever Doug had done, Tanner had come to Crystal Point to fix things...not make matters worse. And definitely not to upset the woman who'd borne his brother's child.

"We'll talk about it tomorrow," he said gently, trying to put her at ease.

"I'd rather—"

"Tomorrow," he said again and stood, scraping the chair back. "I think I should crash before the jet lag really takes hold."

"Okay. Good night."

"'Night, Cassie."

He left the room quickly and ten minutes later he was asleep. Only his dreams were plagued by images of pale blue eyes and soft lips. And memories of the girl he'd met so long ago, but who didn't remember him.

Cassie got up during the night to feed and change the baby and tumbled out of bed at a little after six the following morning. Oliver was awake in his crib, gurgling and pumping his little legs. Cassie scooped him up and inhaled the scent of lotion and baby shampoo. She never got enough of holding him or cuddling him. She gave him a bottle and when that was done she changed him out of pajamas and into a navy-and-white-striped jumpsuit and popped him in his bouncing rocker, which sat secured by two bolts on the big scrubbed table.

Mouse lingered by the back door waiting to be let out and once the dog was outside Cassie filled the coffeepot.

"Good morning."

Tanner.

She wasn't used to having a man in the house. Doug's visits over the past couple of years had been sporadic. When they were together he was charming and familiar and despite how much she had loved him, didn't set her pulse racing at a galloping speed. Not so his brother. Tanner stood in the doorway, dressed in the same jeans he'd worn the night before and a pale blue T-shirt that enhanced his well-cut arms and broad shoulders.

Once again she was struck by a sense of familiarity... of connection...of memory...of something...

"'Morning," she said chirpily, shaking the feeling off. "Coffee's on and I'm just about to make breakfast."

Oliver chuckled and the sound instantly grabbed Tanner's attention. Cassie watched, fascinated as he made his way toward her son and stopped by the table. Oliver's chuckle became a laugh and she saw Tanner smile. He held out his hand and the baby latched on to his finger. It was both a painful and poignant moment for Cassie. Doug never had the chance to see his son and now Tanner was in her kitchen, making the very connection with Oliver she knew belonged to his brother.

"He's cute," Tanner said and looked at her. "He has your eyes."

"They're brown," she said and poured the coffee. "Like yours."

"The shape is all you, though," he replied. "Lucky kid."

Cassie ignored the fluttering in her belly. Being around Tanner had always done it to her. It didn't mean anything. Just a silly awareness of his good looks. Even a rock would notice.

She started on breakfast and listened as he talked softly to Oliver. He had a nice voice, softly accented and a mix of his Australian roots combined with a quiet, Midwestern drawl. Oliver seemed mesmerized and she had just slid some bread into the toaster when Tanner spoke to her.

"Can I hold him?"

She looked up. "Sure. Do you know how?"

Cassie was sure one brow came up. "I know how. My best friend has three kids," Tanner explained. "He lost

his wife in a car wreck when the youngest was a couple
of months old."

"That's so sad."

"Yeah, that was two years ago. I help out if I can. Grady
owns a place up the road from mine so I'm on hand if he
needs a sitter. With three daughters under six he has his
hands full."

Cassie watched as he carefully extracted the baby from
the rocker. His movements seemed natural and effortless,
as if he'd done it a hundred times before. She remembered
her own first stumbling weeks when she'd come home
from the hospital with a newborn. There were days when
she'd never felt more overwhelmed or alone in her life.

Oliver gurgled delightfully and her heart tightened.
Tanner cradled the baby in one arm and easily supported
his head with a strong hand. "He's a big boy," he said and
came toward the countertop. "Clearly a hearty eater?"

Cassie smiled. "He does love his food. He also likes to
puke, so watch out."

Tanner laughed and the rumbling sound made her belly
flip over. For a reason she couldn't quite define Cassie
wished he would stop being so likable. Doug had always
been the charming one. So many times he'd said his younger
brother was moody and serious with little time for anyone
or anything other than his horses and his ranch. The two
occasions they'd met she'd had no reason to question that
description. He'd hardly spoken to her. Oh, he'd been polite,
but there had been almost a cool reserve in his manner.
She hadn't taken it personally because Doug had warned
her that Tanner wasn't exactly warm and friendly. It had
also made the unexpected spark of awareness she'd experienced easier to ignore. But now, watching him hold
Oliver with such open affection suddenly seemed at odds
with Doug's depiction.

"You're good with him," she said, surprising herself as she buttered the toast.

"Thanks," he replied and tucked the baby into the crook of his arm.

Cassie grabbed a couple of plates and took the food to the table. "He hasn't had a lot of interaction with men. Well, except for Gabe."

His expression narrowed fractionally. "Gabe?"

"My best friend's fiancé. Lauren and Gabe got engaged some months back. They're good friends and very supportive. And Lauren's parents insist I take him to see them once a fortnight. They said he's their honorary grandson, which is nice."

"It's hard when you don't have family."

It didn't sound like a question. And she was quick to remember what he'd said about Oliver being the only real family he had. "Sometimes." She smiled "On the good side there are less birthdays to remember."

He didn't smile back straightaway. "How's your grandfather?"

She was surprised to think he remembered she had any relatives and Cassie quickly explained her grandfather's slide into dementia as she brought fruit and then coffee to the table.

"He doesn't know you at all?"

"Not really," she replied. "Sometimes he calls me by my mother's name. I've taken Oliver to see him a few times but he just sits and looks at us. He's always friendly but I miss the man he used to be. He was all I had after my parents died. He's on dialysis now and has numerous other health issues, including a weak heart."

"I'm sorry."

She shrugged and tried not to let her sudden emotion show. It was difficult talking about her only remaining grandparent. "Don't be. I still like to see him even if he doesn't know me. But I know he's ill and probably not going to be around much longer." She motioned to the food on the table. "You can put Oliver back in the rocker if you like."

"I can manage," he assured her as he pulled out a chair and sat down, positioning her delighted son in the curve of his elbow so he could see her from across the table. He rocked Oliver a little. "I like getting to know my nephew."

"I'd like him to know you, too."

It wasn't the truth. Not really. Because she was confused by her feelings for Tanner. And it was difficult imagining her son could have some kind of worthwhile relationship with a man she hardly knew. A man she wasn't sure *she* wanted to know.

And that, she realized, was at the core of her reticence. It wasn't about Oliver.

It was the lingering awareness and unwanted attraction she had for Tanner that made her reluctant and suspicious. *They're my own secret demons.* And she had to get over them. For Oliver's sake.

"And your ranch?" she asked, changing the subject. "That's going well?"

He nodded. "Sure. I've mostly been working with injured or traumatized horses for the last couple of years." He managed a wry smile and glanced down at his leg. "Kind of ironic I guess."

She relaxed fractionally. "Doug said you were some kind of horse whisperer."

He laughed and the sound hit her directly between the ribs. "My brother always did like to make me sound like a crackpot."

"I don't think it sounds like that. And you know what

they say—working with kids or animals is one of the hardest jobs in the world."

"I think that's in the movies, Cassie," he said and smiled. "I just train horses to trust people again."

She nodded, thinking that he'd probably managed to accomplish that as easily as he breathed. "And you're happy there?"

He stilled and looked at her. "Yes, very happy."

Cassie swallowed hard. "So you wouldn't...you wouldn't consider..."

"Consider what?" he asked and rubbed a gentle hand over the back of Oliver's head.

She shrugged. "Moving back... Moving here..."

His brows shot up. "To Crystal Point? No. My life isn't here anymore."

She knew that. But unease still rippled through her veins. Because she knew what it meant. "Are you going to sell the house?"

He stared at her with blistering intensity. "Unfortunately, I'll have to."

Her blood stilled. "I could try and raise the money to..." Cassie stopped and thought about what she was suggesting. She'd never be able to commit to such a large debt. Her minimum wage job and the cost of child care put that option out of reach. She shrugged again. "I thought perhaps the insurance might have covered the mortgage."

"No," he said quietly. "There was some other debt and—"

"The Ducati," she said and sighed. "Doug bought it the last time he was home."

"Yes," he said, still quiet. "I'm sorry about the house, Cassie. I know it was your grandfather's home and means a lot to you."

Heat pinged behind her eyes and she blinked quickly.

She didn't want his sympathy. Or his pity. If the house needed to be sold, then she had no option but to go along with his plans. She wanted to ask him about the "other debt," but didn't. What difference did it make now? Her home was going to be sold and there was nothing she could do about it.

"I'll need some time to arrange things," she said and concentrated her gaze on her smiling son. "Perhaps a month to sort through my—"

"There's no rush."

Tanner saw the emotion in her stare. He didn't want to alarm her or make her life complicated. In fact he wanted the opposite. He'd come to Crystal Point to *right* a wrong. To forgive and find a kind of peace so he could get on with the rest of life.

She stared at him over the rim of her mug. *She really does have the most amazing colored eyes.* Eyes easy to get lost in. Eyes that made it even easier to forget that Doug had loved her. And that she had loved his brother.

"I guess that depends on how long it takes to sell," she murmured.

"I have an appointment with Doug's lawyer on Wednesday," he explained. "We'll know more after that."

"We?" She looked skeptical. "The house belongs to you, Tanner. It's your decision. Your call. I've got nothing to do with it."

You've got everything to do with it...

Guilt pressed between his shoulders. And rage toward his brother that he quickly pushed back down. "On paper, perhaps. However," he said and touched Oliver's cheek, "there's more to this situation than an out-of-date last will and testament. And there's little point in imagining the worse outcome before *we* have all the facts."

"But the mortgage—"

"We'll see what happens. And any money left from the insurance will go into trust for Oliver."

"But that's not what Doug wanted," she replied quickly. "He left everything to you."

Tanner knew it had hurt her. How could it not? She was in a relationship with his brother and Doug had failed to provide for her and her child when she needed it the most.

In typical Doug fashion.

It wasn't the first time his brother had betrayed a woman he'd professed to love.

"He would have changed things," Tanner said, lying through his teeth as he looked down at the baby. "If he'd had the opportunity and the time. But he was in a war zone and on a covert mission, Cassie…and probably not thinking clearly."

She sighed heavily. "I know that. He was…surprised… I mean, when I told him about the baby."

Surprised? Tanner knew that wasn't the half of it. Doug had called him at three in the morning in a rage, ranting about how Cassie had deliberately gotten pregnant and probably planned to trap him into a marriage he didn't want. He played devil's advocate as best he could, insisting that Cassie wouldn't be so manipulative. But Doug was unswayed. He didn't want marriage. Or children. And Tanner knew his brother intended telling Cassie as much, had he lived. He had the proof via several emails Doug had sent before he was killed.

The baby gurgled and he grabbed on to the distraction. He couldn't tell her the truth. He wouldn't. It was better she believed Doug wanted to do the right thing by her and his son.

"This little guy is my nephew and I promised Doug

I'd look out for him," he said softly and touched Oliver's head. "And you."

She visibly stiffened. "I don't need looking out for, Tanner. I can take care of myself and Oliver."

The air crackled and Tanner didn't miss the edge of resentment in her voice. Not that he really blamed her. Cassie Duncan had no real reason to trust him. But he didn't want to be at war with her, either.

"Can you at least meet me halfway, Cassie?" he asked. "I know you've been through a lot these past few months, but I'm not your enemy."

"Then what exactly are you, Tanner? My knight in shining armor?"

"How about your friend?" he suggested and the moment the words came out, he felt like a complete fraud. He could never be friends with Cassie. He'd do what he'd returned to Crystal Point to do and then hightail it back home.

She stared at him. "Friends? Sure..."

But she looked as unconvinced about the idea as he was.

He placed Oliver back in the rocker. "I've got a few errands to run. But I'll come back a little later to see this little guy again and get my bags, if that's okay?"

She nodded. "Okay."

Then he left her alone.

His leg ached, and Tanner pressed down heavily on his heel to help ease the pain as he walked from the house and headed for his rental car. He needed to clear his thoughts for a while. And knew just where to do that.

Five minutes later he turned the car into a familiar driveway. The old farmhouse looked much the same, as did the seventy-five-year-old woman who stood on the porch, waving at him to come inside. Tanner waved back and got out of the rental car.

Ruthie Nevelson had lived just out of Crystal Point for

over sixty years. A widow for more than a quarter century, she'd been a friend and neighbor when his folks were alive and a much needed friend to him once they were gone. From her front gate, in the distance Tanner could see the rooftop of the home he'd lived in as a young boy. It was still a working sugarcane farm and he breathed in a heavy, nostalgic breath. If his parents had lived he would have taken over the farm and been the fourth generation McCord to do so. Instead, the place had been sold to another neighboring farmer three months after their deaths and Tanner was shipped off to boarding school a couple of weeks later. After that, he spent the holidays with Ruthie. Doug was in the army by then and returned whenever he could. But there were times when Tanner didn't see his brother for six or more months.

It was Ruthie who showed him kindness and offered comfort and understanding while he grieved the loss of his parents. Not really a grandmother, but as close to one as Tanner had known. It was she who'd pushed him to pursue his talent with horses and arranged the opportunity for him to work with her brother-in-law, a horse breaker and rancher, in South Dakota. After traveling through Europe for a couple of years, Tanner settled in Cedar Creek ten years ago and finally found a place he could call his own.

He locked the car and headed up the path.

"'Bout time you got here," Ruthie said with a wide grin as he took the narrow steps in two strides and landed on the porch. "I've had the coffee ready for half an hour."

Tanner hugged her close. He hadn't seen Ruthie for two years and she still looked as vibrant and healthy as she did back then. Her hair was still dyed an impossibly bright red, and she still wore moleskins, her favorite cowboy boots, and moved with that straight-backed confidence he'd recognize anywhere. Ruthie Nevelson was the best person he'd ever known, and he'd missed her like crazy.

"Hello, Ruthie," he said, smiling broadly. "It's good to see you, too."

She set herself back to get a better look at him. "That leg still ailing you?"

He nodded. "A little. The long flight didn't help. It'll ease up in a couple of days."

"Good," she said and grabbed his arm. "Now, come inside and eat the cake I made for you."

There had always been something about Ruthie's cooking that could cheer him up, and she knew it well. He followed her inside the house and down the narrow hall. Two small dogs came scurrying to greet them and bounced around his feet for attention.

"Ignore them," she said as she dropped her hat on the cluttered counter and pointed to a seat at the table. "They'll lose interest soon enough."

"They're new," he said and pulled out a chair. "What happened to Bluey?" he asked about her old sheepdog.

"Got sick and died last spring," she replied. "Inherited these two when Stan Jarvis passed away a few months ago."

Stan had been Ruthie's on-again, off-again suitor for over twenty years. "I'm sorry to hear that."

She shrugged and grabbed two mugs. "Everybody dies," she said and gave him a wide smile. "Even this old girl will one day."

"Impossible," Tanner said with a grin, then more seriously. "It's so good to see you."

"You, too." Ruthie poured coffee and brought the mugs to the table. "I was expecting you yesterday. Where'd you stay last night?"

"Cassie's," Tanner said as he sat down and spotted a

large frosted cake in the center of the table. He reached out to steal a fingerful of frosting, giving an approving "Mmm" at the delicious flavor.

Ruthie stared at him. "I see."

"It was late when I got there," he explained. "And since I wanted to see the baby anyway, she offered—"

"You told her about the house?" Ruthie asked in her usual straight-to-the-point way.

Tanner shrugged. "We discussed things."

She shook her head. "Messy situation. Typical of that no-good brother of yours."

Ruthie had never pulled punches when it came to Doug. But Tanner respected her too much to disagree. "I'll have to sell the place."

"I thought as much." Ruthie's expression narrowed. "It's not your fault. Some things even *you* can't fix."

Tanner took the mug she offered. "I can try."

She tutted. "And get your heart broke all over again? I dunno if that makes you a fool or a saint."

"I'm no saint," he said with a half grin. "You know that better than anyone."

"What I know is that you can't keep cleaning up his chaos," Ruthie said, her voice harder than usual. "That girl should be told the truth about him."

The truth about Doug? To the outside world he was charming and likable and there was no doubt he'd been a fine soldier. But he'd had troubles, too. In civilian life he'd been unreliable. The army had sorted him out eventually. But it wasn't a truth that Cassie needed to know.

"I'll tell her enough," he said quietly.

Ruthie looked unconvinced. "And will you tell her that Doug McCord got your eighteen-year-old girlfriend pregnant and then dumped her right before he stole your inheritance?"

Chapter Three

No. Tanner had decided. He wouldn't be telling Cassie anything about the girl who'd cheated on him with his brother and when she'd gotten pregnant how Doug had bailed on his responsibility. Or that his brother had taken the money put in trust for Tanner when he reached twenty-one, and used it to fund his partying and gambling. It had ended badly. For him. For Doug. For everyone. But telling tales wasn't his style. And it had been twelve years ago. There was no point in rehashing old betrayals.

"Still protecting him?"

Ruthie's voice got his attention again. "I just don't want anyone to get hurt unnecessarily."

"Anyone?" Her silvery brows came up. "You mean Cassie Duncan?"

"I mean *anyone*," he emphasized.

"She should be told," Ruthie said, relentless. "Putting

him on a pedestal won't change the truth. You were too quick to forgive and forget."

I haven't forgiven.

Not yet. It was why he'd come back. Why he had to make things right for his nephew.

Losing Leah had hurt. Even though their relationship was new and filled with the usual teenage angst, he'd fallen for her quickly. Four months later she'd announced she was pregnant and in love with his brother. But Doug made it clear he didn't want her or the baby and skipped town, taking Tanner's inheritance with him. Unable to get past such a betrayal, it was all the motivation Tanner needed to pack his bags and leave Crystal Point. He spent close to two years backpacking in Europe before Doug finally tracked him down and by then Leah and the baby she'd tragically miscarried were a distant memory to his brother. Doug returned some of the money, said he was sorry, and Tanner did his best to believe him. But the experience had forever changed their relationship. He came home, stayed with Ruthie for a month and then moved to South Dakota.

And he'd never really looked back.

Until now.

Until Cassie.

But he'd already loved one woman who'd preferred his brother. He wasn't about to do that again. No matter how much her blue eyes haunted his dreams.

Still, he was tired of being angry. Tired of resenting Doug and wishing things were different. Tired of living in the past. For years Tanner had battled the anger he'd felt toward his brother. It had kept him shut off and restrained in relationships with almost everyone he knew. Except for Ruthie and his closest friend, Grady Parker, who knew some of what happened between him and his brother.

Almost losing his life in the accident had shifted his

perspective. Tanner didn't want to be angry anymore. He wanted to live the rest of his life without blame and bitterness. And to do that he had to truly forgive Doug. Only then would he find the peace of mind he craved.

"I know what I'm doing," he assured the old woman sitting opposite.

But he was pretty sure she didn't believe it.

She nodded anyway. "So, you gonna stay there tonight?"

"No," he replied. "I'll check into a hotel in Bellandale."

"Nonsense," she huffed. "You'll stay here."

Tanner grinned. "You know, you're getting bossy in your old age."

"Hah…I've always been bossy." Ruthie's throaty laugh made him smile. "Besides, I've got a new colt that needs breaking."

Tanner tapped his leg. "I'm not quite back in the saddle yet."

"No problem. I just need help mouthing and long reining." Ruthie's brows came up and she grinned. "You still look fit enough for that. As long as you can do it without whining like a girl."

Tanner laughed loudly. Ruthie always cheered him up. He left a short time later and headed back to Cassie's. She was in the front yard when he pulled into the driveway. Oliver's stroller was parked nearby in the shade and Mouse sat by the front wheels. She wore cutoff jeans, a gray T-shirt, trainers and thick gardening gloves. A bougainvillea twisted up and across the paling fence and she was cutting off some of the biting vines as he approached.

He patted the dog and flipped his sunglasses off. "Gardening?" He stood by the stroller. "Looks like fun."

Cassie stepped back and turned. "Well, maybe not fun, but necessary at least. I've neglected the yard since Oliver arrived. My grandfather always took such pride in his garden."

Tanner looked around, hands on hips. "It's a big yard. Perhaps getting someone in would be a better—"

She stiffened. "I can do it."

"I'm sure you can do anything you set your mind to." He smiled at the defiance in her expression. "Would you like some help?"

Cassie nodded and bent to collect the gloves. "If you have time. I could make lunch." She stilled and met his gaze. "Unless you've already eaten?"

"No, I haven't."

She held out the gloves. "Great. I'll take Oliver inside and you see if you have any more luck cutting back that vine. See you back in the house in half an hour."

Tanner grabbed the gloves and clippers and got to work on the overgrown vine. He made short work of it and once the branches were hacked he hauled them into a respectable pile. But the spikes, he discovered, were unforgiving and the razor-sharp thorns bit through his T-shirt. He pulled the shirt off, removed the spikes from the fabric and re-dressed before he headed up the path and toward the house.

He cleaned up in the laundry and Cassie was in the kitchen making sandwiches when he rounded the corner and stalled by the threshold. She looked up instantly and brought plates to the table.

Tanner spotted the stroller by the table. "Is he asleep?"

"Yes. I gave him a small bottle and he went out like a light."

Tanner walked into the room and peered into the stroller. Oliver's little face looked peaceful. It occurred to him that he might be able to help out with the baby. "You don't...you know...feed him yourself?"

Her brows came up slowly. "Do I breast-feed, you mean?"

Tanner tried to ignore the ridiculous heat that crawled up his neck. "Yeah."

She shook her head. "I did for a few weeks. But after that I couldn't." She shrugged and walked back to the countertop. "Sometimes it happens that way. I was unwell and after Doug—"

"It's okay, Cassie," Tanner said quickly. "You don't have to explain." No, because he understood. The man she loved was dead, she had a new baby and she was faced with the knowledge that the home she'd lived in most of her life was about to be pulled from under her feet. It wasn't difficult to figure out why she'd struggle to nurse her son.

She shrugged again and he was sure he saw moisture in her eyes before she blinked and turned toward the refrigerator. Half a minute later she returned to the table and sat down.

"Where'd you go this morning?" she asked and pushed a plate toward him.

"Ruthie's," he explained.

She nodded. "Ruthie Nevelson? She sent me a card when Oliver was born. Doug never visited her much. I guess you're closer to her than he was."

"I guess," he said. "I always spent my summers with Ruthie once school was out. Doug was in the army by then."

Cassie looked up and smiled. "My friend Lauren and I used to swipe oranges from her tree when we were kids. Funny," she said and toyed with her sandwich. "We never saw you there. I mean, Crystal Point is a small town— you'd think we would have crossed paths at some point."

We did.

But Tanner didn't say it. Even though the memory was

etched into his mind. At thirteen they'd met briefly. It was fourteen years later that he met her again. And by then she was Doug's girlfriend and hadn't remembered those few moments on the beach so many years earlier.

"I was usually hanging out with my friends," he said, taking a sandwich and smiling. "No time for girls back then."

"And now?" she asked, grinning slightly. "Is there someone in the picture?"

He shrugged one shoulder. "No one at the moment."

"But there was?"

Another shrug. "For a while. It wasn't all that serious."

In truth, Tanner hadn't ever been completely committed in a relationship. For a time, with Ash, he'd thought they might have a future. But it had faded quickly once they realized they were better as friends than lovers. It had ended over a year ago and he hadn't been inclined to pursue anyone since.

"But you want to settle down eventually?"

"Eventually," he replied and took a bite of the sandwich.

"In South Dakota? I mean, you're settled there?"

He nodded. "Cedar Creek is a good town, with good people."

"Like Crystal Point?" she asked.

"There are similarities," he said. "Small towns tend to breed a certain kind of people."

"I suppose they do." She stared into her plate, and then spoke a little wistfully. "Doug didn't share the same beliefs about small-town life. He never seemed happy here."

"It just wasn't his...*fit*," Tanner said. "The military was his home."

She nodded. "Maybe that's why he found it so hard to come back. Even when he did he was always..." She stopped, paused, clearly thinking and not wanting to say too much. "He was always a little unsettled."

Tanner knew that. And knew why. "He wasn't the settle-down type, I guess."

He quickly picked up the way her eyes shadowed. "That's what he used to say about you."

"I mean, he wasn't the type to settle down to a life as a cane farmer."

"I know what you meant," she said, bristling, and pushed the plate forward. "I'm not completely blind to who he was."

There was pain in her words and he gave himself a mental jab. "He did love you," Tanner said and immediately wished he hadn't.

Her eyes lost their luster, as if she was thinking, remembering. "Not enough to come home." She stood and pushed the chair back. "I shouldn't have said that. Doug's gone. Wishing for him to be different is unfair."

"Cassie, I didn't mean to—"

"I need to run a few errands myself this afternoon," she said through a deep breath. "I shouldn't be too long."

Tanner stood and looked at her half-eaten lunch. "I'll finish in the garden while you're gone if you like. And head off when you get back."

"Fine," she said and within seconds had wheeled the stroller from the room.

"What's he like?"

Cassie raised her gaze toward her best friend Lauren and rocked Oliver in her arms.

He's a gorgeous, sexy cowboy who makes my pulse race.

"He seems nice."

Lauren's brows shot up. "*Seems* nice?"

She shrugged again. "What do you want me to say? I hardly know Tanner."

"Apart from what Doug told you?"

True. Only, everything Doug had said about his brother didn't seem to match the man she'd come to know over the past twenty-four hours.

"Okay, maybe he's not the brooding loner Doug made him out to be. Although I'm not going to make too many judgments after one day."

Lauren nodded. "But he wants to be a part of Oliver's life?"

"That's what he said."

"And he's selling the house?"

Cassie drew in a breath. "That's also what he said. There's a large mortgage."

"I'm sorry," Lauren said after a long pause. "I know it isn't what you'd hoped."

"I knew it might come to this," she said, hurting all over at the thought of losing her home, but determined to put on a brave face. "And it's only a house. I'll make a home for Oliver somewhere else."

"You can stay with us," Lauren offered. "You'll always be welcome."

Cassie blinked back the heat in her eyes. "Thanks, but I'll be fine."

"You don't look fine," Lauren said, clearly concerned. "You look pale and tired."

"It's just a headache," she said and managed a smile.

She *did* have a headache. And a scratchy throat and a quickly growing lethargy. But she didn't admit she was feeling increasingly unwell as the day progressed. Lauren's fiancé was a doctor and her friend would have had her under the stethoscope in a heartbeat if Cassie said she was feeling ill.

"If you're sure," Lauren said, still looking concerned. "Just be careful. I don't want to see you get hurt."

Cassie tapped her own chest. "I'm impervious to hurt," she said with a wry grin. "Tough as nails, you know that."

But she knew her friend didn't believe it.

By the time Cassie bundled Oliver into the car and pulled into the driveway it was well past four o'clock. She noticed immediately how the once out-of-control bougainvillea vine was now three piles of tightly bound cuttings and what remained of the hedge had also been carefully clipped back. Plus, the lawn was mowed and the scent of fresh cut grass lingered in the air.

Tanner had been busy. In a matter of hours the front yard was transformed into a neat and tidy copy of what it had once been—before Doug's death, before the bills had piled up and she'd taken leave from her job and had to watch every penny she spent.

Inside, Cassie headed straight for the kitchen and made up formula for Oliver.

She could hear the shower running and once the baby was fed she carried him to the nursery, laid him on the changing table and stripped off his clothes.

"Hey there."

She stilled and turned. Tanner stood in the doorway— hair damp, wearing washed-out jeans and a black collared T-shirt that looked way too good on his broad-shouldered frame. "Hi."

"Did you have a good afternoon?"

Cassie nodded, trying to ignore the throb at her temple. "I went to see my friend Lauren."

"Ah, the orange thief?" he said with a grin.

Cassie laughed softly. "Yes. Were your ears burning?"

He grinned. "Talking about me, eh?"

"Maybe a little," she replied. "I'm going to give Oliver a bath now."

"Sure."

She took the baby into her arms. "Thanks for doing the yard."

"No problem."

Cassie felt the warmth of his stare through to her bones and tried to disregard the heat coiling up her legs. He really did have the sexy thing down pat. She willed some good sense into her limbs and headed from the room, conscious of how he moved aside to let her pass. She lingered in the nursery with Oliver after his bath and by the time she'd dressed him in a navy romper suit and settled him down to sleep it was dusk outside.

When Cassie returned to the kitchen she found Tanner talking to Mouse, and the dog was staring up at him, listening intently. Again, she was struck by the image of the man Doug had told her he was, and the contrasting man he seemed in reality. Not closed off and moody. Not a brooding, unfriendly loner.

Not anything like the man Doug had described.

He looked up. "Is Oliver settled?"

"For the moment," she replied. "He'll sleep for a couple of hours. His usual routine gives me enough time to have a shower and eat something."

Tanner checked his watch. "Then I should probably go."

Something niggled at her. She couldn't define it. Maybe she didn't want to. She drew in a long breath and frowned.

"Are you okay?" he asked, watching her.

Cassie nodded. "I've had one of those daylong headaches."

He laughed and then must have realized how insensitive it sounded. "Sorry, I was thinking that maybe since I've been here for twenty-four hours there was a connection."

She smiled. "No. Although…"

His brows came up. "Although?"

She shrugged. "Well…you're not…"

"I'm not…?"

Heat crept up her neck and she searched for the words. "It's only that you're not exactly who I thought…" She shrugged again and took a deep breath. "I guess I thought you wouldn't be so…easy to get along with."

Tanner rested against the counter and folded his arms. "Compared to what?"

She hesitated as her gaze shifted to the floor. "To the person I thought you were."

"Who you thought I was," he said quietly. "Or who Doug said I was."

Her shoulders came up for a second and then dropped. "I suppose. He said you were quiet and…"

"And what?" Tanner asked when her words trailed. "Indifferent and unfriendly?"

She looked up. "Words to the effect."

"And what do you think?"

Cassie stepped back. "I think you're confident and sensible. I think you don't waste time trying to charm or manipulate people." She paused and took a breath. "I think you know exactly who you are. And what you want."

His brown eyes darkened. "And do you?" he asked softly. "Do you know what you want, Cassie?"

At that moment she wanted to run. Everything about him reached her on some base, heady level. She was hot all over and she knew why. Tanner McCord made her remember she was a woman. And it scared her to death.

"Ah…what about dinner," she said quickly and took a sharp breath. She pointed to the telephone. "I have the number of a great pizza place on speed dial. I mean, unless you want to leave right away."

He pushed himself off the counter. "Dinner would be good."

Cassie nodded and left the room. After checking on Oliver she took only minutes to collect fresh clothes and lock herself in the bathroom. She showered and dressed in cargo pants and a sensible blue shirt buttoned up to her throat.

By the time she headed back to the kitchen another half hour had passed and she ducked her head around the corner of the nursery to ensure the baby was still asleep. At the kitchen doorway she stilled. Tanner stood by the counter, one elbow in the air and he tugged at the back of his shirt.

"Something wrong?" she asked and stepped across the threshold.

He swiveled around and dropped his arm. "I think I caught a barb this afternoon."

"A what?"

"From the vine," he explained and winced.

Cassie walked toward him. "You're hurt?"

He shrugged. "I'll be fine."

"Do you want me to take a look?"

He took a step back. "I don't think so."

Cassie ignored the sudden heat in her cheeks. If he'd been injured pruning the hedge she needed to be sensible and find out how bad it was. "It could get infected."

"I'm sure it will be—"

"Let's see," she said matter-of-factly. "Where is it?"

He hesitated for a moment before moving one shoulder. "Left side."

Cassie stepped closer. "Okay, turn around."

He did as she asked and she took a second before reaching out. His shirt was soft between her fingers and she tugged it down a fraction. When she couldn't see anything other than one incredibly well-defined shoulder blade, Cassie released the shirt.

"It has to come off."

He turned his head. "What?"

"Your shirt," she explained. "I can't see anything. I'm too short."

"I'm sure it's not—"

She ignored him, moved back around the countertop and grabbed the small first-aid kit from the bottom drawer. "It won't take a minute."

He didn't seem convinced and hesitated before he shrugged again and then pulled the shirt over his head and dropped it on the table.

And of course she couldn't look anywhere but at his bare skin.

Sweet heaven.

He didn't possess the body of a man who spent hours in a gym—but of one who worked outdoors, using and honing muscles every day. His tanned skin looked as smooth as the sheerest silk pulled across pressed steel and the light smatter of hair on his chest was incredibly sexy. He was pure beauty and temptation. And she had to stop thinking about it.

"Turn around please."

His eyes darkened and Cassie was sure she caught a tiny smile tugging at the corner of his mouth. So, maybe she did sound way too polite and incredibly tense. That was her nature...her *way*. He turned and Cassie saw where the bougainvillea thorn had pierced his skin directly below his shoulder blade. The spike was easily an inch long and was lodged deep. Cassie opened up the first-aid kit and took out a needle.

"I see it. This is going to hurt," she said. "You might want to brace yourself against the counter."

"Sure," he said and stepped forward, levering his hands on the countertop.

She sterilized the needle and as she moved closer, Cassie tried not to think about his smooth skin and well-defined muscles. Or the fact she picked up the spicy scent of soap and some kind of citrusy shampoo that somehow amplified the awareness she experienced whenever he was near.

With purposeful intent, Cassie reached out and touched him. She sensed rather than felt the tension coiling up his back as her fingertips connected with his skin. She used the needle quickly and started dislodging the thorn.

"Ouch!"

She pulled back. "Don't be such a baby."

He jerked his head around and scowled. "Don't be such a brute."

Cassie stopped the grin that threatened. "I thought you were a tough cowboy."

"I thought you were sweet and gentle."

She sucked in a shallow breath. His words stilled in the air between them. *Sweet and gentle?* Is that how he saw her? Not lonely and guarded and desperate to keep her distance?

"Is that who Doug said I was?"

He didn't respond immediately. "Yeah, of course he did."

Cassie ignored the stab of guilt, grabbed the tweezers and extracted the barb. "All done," she said and stepped back.

Tanner turned and she was faced with the solid wall of chest. She noticed a long faded scar below his rib cage, but other than that there was nothing imperfect about him. Her belly swayed and she got mad with herself. Being attracted to Tanner was out of the question.

Perhaps one day she'd find someone to share her life— a friend, a lover, a husband. Someone who she could love and who would welcome the role as father to her son. But not yet. She wasn't ready. And she certainly had no intention of paying too much attention to the burgeoning attraction she had for the man in front of her.

Still, it was easy to get drawn into the warm depths of his liquid brown eyes. Easier still to stare at his broad shoulders and satin-smooth skin. Heat crept over her skin. *Maybe I have a fever?* Yes, that had to be it. She was unwell. Out of sorts. It had nothing to do with his brown eyes and broad shoulders.

"Cassie?"

His voice brought her stare upward and she locked his gaze as the air flamed, swirling up as it coiled around them. And suddenly she couldn't pretend it was anything other than raw attraction. *Chemistry.* Undeniable and absolutely unwanted.

And from nowhere, a sudden memory kicked in. She'd felt it once before, long ago. She'd all but forgotten that hot summer when she was thirteen. She recalled the boy who'd captured her attention on the beach one late afternoon. Her first crush. Her first kiss. The fluttering in her belly caused a familiar rush and she quickly pushed the memory away.

"I should check Oliver," she said on a shallow breath.

A car pulled out outside.

"Our pizza," Tanner said and grabbed his shirt off the table. "Thanks for the first aid. I'll be back with our dinner."

He walked from the room and Cassie stared after him. Being around Tanner was a mistake. Maybe the biggest of her life.

Chapter Four

Tanner sensed the change in Cassie's mood the moment she returned to the kitchen. He couldn't miss the tension in her expression as they ate and afterward when she refused his offer to help clean up. Uncomfortable by the sudden awkwardness, he left her alone for a while. The awareness between them was hard to deny and he wondered if she realized he was attracted to her and that's why she seemed so closed off. He headed back to the guest room and packed his bag and dropped it in the hallway. Tanner was in the living room looking at the photographs on the mantel when she came into the room some twenty minutes later.

"Everything all right?" he asked and propped the photo of Doug back on the shelf.

"Fine," she replied and pointed to the photograph. "That was taken years ago. I don't have anything current, in case you wanted a copy."

"I have photos," he said and turned. "But thanks."

She nodded. "I also have Doug's things stored away in the spare room. You're welcome to go through the boxes and see if there's anything you'd like to keep."

"Won't you want those as keepsakes for his son?"

"I've selected a few things already. And I have several videos Doug made while he was on tour. Oliver will know his father."

He heard the dig and wondered why she was so tense. It's not as if she owed him any explanations—about anything. "You know, not every conversation we have has to be a battle."

Her eyes flashed brilliantly. "I don't—"

"You act like I'm the enemy."

She crossed her arms and sighed heavily. "Can you blame me?"

He wasn't sure what she was getting at and shrugged. "Which means?"

"I've been in limbo for months, Tanner. Maybe I did shove my head in the sand when it came to the house and Doug's estate, but that doesn't make me any less shocked that you've turned up and now I'm faced with the prospect of leaving the only home I've known since I was a young girl."

Tanner's insides contracted. "I didn't come here to make things harder for you," he assured her. "On the contrary…"

Her brows came up. "Do you think your being here would make things easier?" She shook her head. "The fact is, you're a walking, talking reminder of exactly how much my life is about to change."

Of course he would be. So the sooner he did what he had come to do and then got back to his own life, the better.

"I have no intention of disrupting your life."

"Do I seem so naive to you, Tanner?" She took a couple

of steps farther into the room and seemed to waver on her feet. "Your very presence is a disruption."

She wanted him gone...that was evident enough. "I'm sorry you feel that way, Cassie. Be assured that as soon as I have the estate sorted I'll be returning to South Dakota. But as I said yesterday, Oliver is my nephew, the only family I have, and I'd like to play some role in his life."

"As what?" she asked quietly. "The absent uncle?"

Tanner pushed back the irritation weaving through his blood. Obstinate, infuriating woman. "I'm here now. And I'd like to stay in contact once I go home. It's what Doug would have wanted."

Her brows came up. "Is it?" She paled and an uneasy silence filled the room. When she spoke again her voice was unusually raspy. "Are you sure about that? You and Doug weren't exactly close."

"Things between us improved these last few years."

There was some truth in his words. His brother had tried, in his way, to mend their broken relationship. And Tanner had cautiously let him back into his life. He'd returned to Crystal Point on two occasions to see Doug and his brother had briefly visited his ranch in Cedar Creek six months before his death.

She raised her chin. "He never did tell me why you were estranged."

Tanner's stomach tightened. "It was a misunderstanding that happened years ago."

"Really?" Her brows came up. "What kind of misunderstanding?"

He shrugged. Tanner had no intention of telling her about Leah or the money or anything else from his past. "It doesn't matter now."

She raised her chin in that stiff, determined way he was getting used to. "So you won't tell me?"

"No."

She laughed, the sound brittle in the room. "Well, Doug did say you had a stubborn, unforgiving streak."

He tensed. Of course his brother would have said that. Doug wasn't one to take responsibility for his actions or his *mistakes*.

Her expression narrowed. "What was your relationship like when you were kids?"

"Good," he replied truthfully. "But with twelve years between us we were never really kids together."

She nodded. "You said Doug joined the army at twenty-one and sent you to boarding school?"

"That's right." He named the school that was about two hundred miles west of Bellandale.

"Were you happy there?"

It seemed an odd question. "I've never really thought about it."

She pushed on. "You'd just lost your parents, correct? Why do you think Doug made the decision to send you away when you were so young?"

"He joined the army," Tanner said. "I guess he did what he thought was the best thing at the time."

Cassie didn't look completely convinced. "But what did *you* think?"

He opened his mouth to speak, then clamped it tightly shut. She stared at him, looking intrigued and a little confused. He drew in a slow breath. "I thought... I suppose I thought I'd been abandoned."

"Did you ever tell him that?"

Silence stretched like elastic for a moment. Finally, he spoke. "I don't think I've ever told anyone that."

"Then thank you," she said. "For not dismissing the question. I suppose I'm trying to understand why Doug would have done such a thing. I mean, you really only had each other."

"What twenty-one-year-old wants to be saddled with a kid? Especially someone like…"

Tanner stopped when he saw her expression shift. He met her gaze and waited for her to speak.

"You mean, someone like Doug?" she asked, her voice a bare whisper. When he didn't respond she spoke again. "You know, don't you?"

Tanner shrugged a little. "I know what?"

"You know Doug wasn't exactly thrilled about the idea of having a baby?"

Wasn't exactly thrilled? His brother had flat-out said kids weren't in his plans—ever.

"I know he had some reservations."

She shrugged and maintained her resilient look. "It was a shock, that's all. We'd never talked about children and when I found out I was pregnant I was surprised at first. When I told Doug, he didn't…well, he wasn't happy about it."

He knew the story. Doug had no intention of ever being a father to his child and Tanner knew his brother would have told Cassie that very thing had he lived.

"I'm sure it was the shock, like you said."

As he said the words and tasted the lie, Tanner knew he had to keep the truth from her. It would hurt her deeply if the truth ever came out.

"I suppose we'll never know," she said, softer still.

Tanner shrugged fractionally. "I should get going."

"Are you heading into Bellandale?" she asked.

"No," he replied. "I'm going to crash at Ruthie's for a few days. But I'd like to drop by tomorrow afternoon to see Oliver if that's okay?"

"Of course."

"Good night, Cassie. I'll see myself out."

She nodded and watched him leave. Tanner grabbed his bag from the hall and headed through the front door and realized that leaving was the last thing he wanted to do.

When Cassie sat up in bed at six the next morning she knew the headache and scratchy throat she'd been harboring for days had finally taken hold. But Oliver's cries made her ignore her pains, push back the covers and roll off the mattress. She changed into jeans and a T-shirt, took a couple of aspirin and worked through her sluggishness. It was well past the half hour by the time she'd fed him and then made herself some soothing peppermint tea.

But Oliver was unsettled for most of the morning and in between doing two loads of washing and putting a casserole in the slow cooker, she took him for a long walk. When she got home it was after three and she gave him a bath and a bottle before putting him to bed for a nap.

And even though her head hurt and her throat ached, she kept thinking about what had transpired over the past forty-eight hours. She thought about Doug. And Tanner.

The brothers clearly had a much more complex relationship than she'd realized and Cassie knew that the undivided faith she'd always held in the man she'd loved—the man who had fathered her child—was unexpectedly under threat. Why would Doug have sent a vulnerable and grieving child to a boarding school so far away from the only home he'd ever known? It seemed incredibly callous and at odds with the man she knew. The man she'd *thought* she knew.

A man she clearly hadn't known.

He'd charmed her with his smile and humor and she'd never really questioned his honesty or integrity.

Until now.

And Tanner? He was very different from the man Doug had described. He wasn't moody and indifferent. In fact, he was the complete opposite. And she was as confused as ever.

With her headache worsening and her whole body slowly succumbing to an unusual lethargy, by four o'clock Cassie grabbed the baby monitor, made tea and then curled up on the sofa in front of the television.

She drifted off to sleep and was plagued by dreams. Of Oliver. Of her parents. Of Doug. And of Tanner. Of his warm brown eyes and sexy smile. When she awoke she discovered a throw had been laid over her bare arms. The monitor was gone from its spot on the coffee table and she sat up quickly. *Oliver.* The headache hadn't abated and she pressed a hand to her temple. It was dark outside and the lamp in the corner gave off a soft glow. Someone was in her house. With the monitor missing, the lamp on and throw draped across her, it was the only explanation. Perhaps Lauren had stopped by? Or M.J.? Both her friends knew where she hid the spare key.

Her legs were heavy as she stood and Cassie rested her knuckles on the side of the sofa for support as she ditched the throw and slipped her shoes back on. She swallowed hard and winced at the stinging pain in her throat. She left the room and headed down the hall toward the nursery. No Oliver. Her heart raced and she rushed down the hallway. And heard voices. Well, one voice. One very familiar, deep and hypnotic voice. She came to a halt in the doorway and listened as Tanner spoke to her son, who he held gently in the crook of one arm while he whisked eggs in a bowl with his free hand.

"—and it won't be a truly superb omelet, of course, without peppers…but it will do. Did you know your daddy was allergic to eggs? I suppose we'll find out if you inherited that from him soon enough. Since you've already had your bottle you might even think about shutting those big eyes of yours and getting some sleep."

"Tanner?"

He stopped talking and whisking and looked toward the door. "Hey there." He turned Oliver around. "Look whose awake, little man. Mommy."

She smiled at her beautiful baby and then looked at the man holding him. "What are you doing here?"

"I said I'd drop by, remember," he reminded her. "And I knocked, around four-thirty. Your door was unlocked."

Cassie felt too unwell to reproach herself for leaving the front door unlocked and then crashing on the sofa. Crystal Point was a safe place...but still...it was irresponsible. Especially with a baby in the house. Although she doubted Mouse would let an intruder in without alerting her. Speaking of which...

"Where's my dog?"

"In the backyard," he explained. "Fed and waiting to be let back in, I'm sure."

Cassie nodded. "You let me sleep."

"You seemed to need it."

She shrugged and tried to ignore the pain in her head. She really was feeling worse with every passing moment. "I guess I did." She looked toward her baby. "He'll need changing before he's put down for the night."

"Done," Tanner said and moved toward her. "I'm somewhat of a dab hand with a diaper these days. I had practice with Grady's kids when they were babies."

Her brows came up. "And you're making dinner?"

"To order," he replied and grinned. "If you don't like omelet."

Cassie thought about her wavering stomach. "Actually, I put a casserole on this afternoon," she said and pointed to the slow cooker on the counter. "But I might just have some soup a little later."

"Soup it is. But first I'll put this little guy to bed."

Normally she would have protested. But the headache and wobble in her knees was getting steadily worse and she didn't quite trust her balance. "That would be great. Thanks."

Once he left the room Cassie sank into a chair and rested her arms on the table. When Tanner returned she was still in that position.

"Everything okay?"

She nodded and sighed heavily. "Just tired I guess. Thank you for watching Oliver."

"My pleasure," he said and came around the table. "He's a good baby. You know, you don't look so great. Are you sure you're all right?"

"I think I'll—"

She stopped as his hand reached out and he rested it against her forehead. "You're burning up."

Cassie's skin tingled from his touch and she pulled away fractionally. "I'm fine."

"You're not fine. You have a fever."

She shook her head and pushed the chair back. "I'll be okay. I only need some rest," she insisted and stood. But her legs wavered and she gripped the edge of the table for support.

"Like hell. You're sick."

And without another word Tanner scooped her up into his arms.

By the time she had the strength to protest he was down the hallway and had shouldered her bedroom door open and placed her gently on the edge of her bed. "Now get some rest."

"You didn't have to pick me up," she protested feebly,

pushing back her embarrassment and trying not to think about how it felt to be held against his broad chest. He was still recovering from an injury and the last thing he needed was to damage his leg again. "I could have walked."

"And fallen over most likely," he said. "You need to take care of yourself, Cassie."

"I will. I *do*. I have a headache, that's all. It'll pass once I get some rest."

"You have a fever," he insisted as he strode toward the bed and pulled the comforter back. "I'll bring you some water. Where do you keep your aspirin?"

She rolled her eyes. "In the pantry, top shelf, but I really think I—"

"Be back in a minute."

She watched him leave the room and then rounded out her shoulders. The man certainly was stubborn. She flipped off her shoes and shimmied farther onto the mattress.

When Tanner returned she pasted on a grateful smile. He passed her a glass of water and a couple of painkillers. "Thank you. I appreciate your concern," she said and looked at him over the rim of the glass. "Even if you are being bossy."

"If it gets you into bed, then I'll do what I have to."

Cassie was sure he didn't mean to sound so suggestive, but once the words were out the air in the room seemed thicker, hotter, as if a seductive wind had blown through the opened doorway. She looked at him, felt the heat rising between them and desperately willed it to go away. But no. It stayed. And grew. And made her mounting awareness of him bloom into a heady, full-blown attraction. *It's because he's handsome and sexy and friendly, that's all.* She'd have to be a rock not to notice, right?

She said his name and waited for several seconds while

he continued to watch her and the heat in Cassie's blood intensified and her cheeks burned. Her skin was on fire and she wondered how much it had to do with her fever, and how much had to do with the man standing beside her bed. She'd never experienced anything quite like it before and despite the headache, sore throat and fever, Cassie knew that whatever she was feeling, he was feeling it, too.

But how? Why? Cassie didn't have any illusions about herself. She wasn't beautiful or glamorous or overly smart. She was pretty at best. The same ordinary girl she'd been all her life. A single mother. *The mother of his brother's child.* The very reason they shouldn't be looking at one another with such scorching desire.

Finally, he spoke. "I should go. Get some rest, Cassie."

"Oliver will—"

"I'll take care of the baby. Just rest."

He left the room quickly and Cassie stared after him. Okay…so they had…*chemistry.*

It didn't have to go anywhere. It wouldn't. It couldn't. She was Oliver's mother. She had a child to think about and fantasizing about a man like Tanner wasn't going to do anyone any good. She dropped back onto the bed and pulled the covers up. Her head hurt, her throat hurt, even her bones ached. Maybe he was right about getting some rest.

I just need to sleep and clear my head.

By tomorrow she'd be over it. And over her attraction for Tanner.

There was no other option.

Around ten the following morning Tanner found Cassie's cell phone and called her friend Lauren. Within an hour she and her doctor fiancé were on the doorstep. Cassie's fever had become progressively worse overnight and by morning she was burning up and clearly unwell. He managed to get her to take some more aspirin and drink a little water just before midnight and she woke again after seven, coughing and shaking from the chills.

"You were right to call us," Lauren said when she came from Cassie's room and met him in the nursery. "Gabe said she has a mild flu. I'll arrange for some medicine to be delivered as soon as possible. That and a few days' rest and she should be fine." She looked at him and smiled. "You don't seem surprised by the diagnosis."

"I'm not," he replied and held Oliver against his chest. He wasn't about to explain he'd spent most of the night alternating between the chair in Cassie's room to make sure he was close by if she needed anything, and the sofa in the living room. If he'd thought it was something more serious than mild influenza he would have bundled her in the car and taken her to hospital. "But I'm pleased she'll be okay."

Lauren gently touched the baby's head. "You stayed last night?"

"Of course."

She nodded slowly. "Well, I'm glad that you're here to look after…things. However, we can take Oliver home with us if you—"

"No," he said quickly. "That's not necessary. I'll stay until Cassie's feeling better. And I'm sure she'd prefer that Oliver remain here."

He thought she might insist, but Lauren only nodded. "You're probably right. Let me know if you need anything. You have my number."

They left a few minutes later and Tanner quickly checked on a restlessly sleeping Cassie before he headed for the kitchen to feed Oliver. He'd become quickly attached to the little guy and was enjoying the time he got to spend with his nephew. Oliver was a placid baby and caring for him made Tanner think about the prospect of having children of his own. One day. He was surprised how much he liked the idea. The ranch could be a lonely place and more so than ever before, he let himself imagine a couple of kids running across the yard to the house and then along the wide verandah. And a woman...a wife. Someone to talk to. Someone with soft skin and warm hands to curl up with at night. Tanner liked that idea, too.

He'd spent so many years pouring all his energy in his horses, building the ranch and trying to live in the present and forget the past he'd somehow ignored the future. But being with Cassie made him think about it.

No, he corrected immediately. It was Oliver who got him thinking. Cassie was just... She was just the girl who'd sparked his interest all those years ago on the beach. Being around her brought back those memories, that's all. He had a handle on his attraction for her. And he'd forget all about it once he went home.

Only, last night he could have sworn he saw something in her eyes...a look...a connection...and it was something he hadn't expected. Because she'd loved Doug.

Which means she can never be mine.

He shook the feeling off. The less he thought about Cassie being his or anyone else's, the better. Tanner put the baby down for a nap and then took a quick shower. He dressed back into his jeans and padded barefoot down the hall toward the spare room. He rummaged around and found some of Doug's clothes hanging in the wardrobe. He pulled out a shirt and slipped it on. It was a little tight in the shoulders and baggy around the waist, but it would do. He stayed in the room for a while and flipped through a few of the boxes. He found his brother's uniforms neatly packed inside one box and another smaller carton held his medals. Tanner sat for a while, looking at the collection of memories. What would Doug make of him being with Cassie and Oliver? Would his brother be angry? Resentful? Would he eventually have come around to the idea of being a father to Oliver?

Tanner didn't think so. Doug liked his freedom. Strange, then, that he'd joined the military. But Tanner understood why. His brother needed the army to give him companionship. And to give him solitude. Within the corridors of discipline and routine he found the family he'd needed. He'd bonded with people who understood him, who were like him, who had his back. Tanner knew his brother had never felt that with his real family. When their parents were killed Doug was already estranged from them. He'd never fit into the life on the farm. He'd never wanted to work the sugarcane and small herd of cattle. Doug had bailed at eighteen and headed for the city, where he worked a succession of transient jobs. After their parents' accident he returned and reclaimed what he believed was his…and promptly sold off Tanner's legacy.

Then came Tanner's years at boarding school. During that time he learned to despise his brother…and yet still love him. He was family. And family was everything. Despite the repeated betrayals. Despite Doug's behavior with Leah. Despite the mishandled inheritance. Despite all of it, a part of him still wanted to believe in the idea of brotherhood.

Tanner ignored the heavy feeling in his chest, folded the box shut and got to his feet. He headed to the kitchen, heated up some soup he found in the pantry and carried a tray into Cassie's room.

She was sleeping and he was pleased that the racking cough that had kept her awake for most of the morning had abated for a while. Tanner slipped the tray onto the bedside table and watched her for a moment. She stirred and let out a soft moan. The soft hum of the humidifier he'd found in the nursery cupboard and set up by the bed was the only other sound in the room. He noticed she'd pushed the blanket aside and moved closer to pull the cover back up. She looked peaceful in sleep and as he watched her a strange sensation knocked behind his ribs. For years he'd put her out of his thoughts and programmed himself to *not* think of her. But when Doug died that changed. He had a blood tie and a responsibility to Oliver. His nephew would never feel what he had when he was a child—alone, abandoned, discarded. He'd always be there for his brother's son regardless of where he was or what he was doing. Oliver was his only family and family was all that mattered.

And Cassie?

She was Oliver's mother and that was all she could ever be.

She'd loved Doug. Wanted Doug. Borne his child. Which meant she was off-limits. Despite how being around her messed with his head, his libido and his heart. His attraction to Cassie would fade once he returned to South Dakota and got back to his regular life. He'd put her from his mind before. He could do it again.

One thing he knew for sure…he wasn't about to fall in love with her.

Not a chance.

Chapter Five

When Cassie awoke it was dark outside. She knew she'd been drifting in and out from sleep and wakefulness for several hours. Or was it days? Her head and throat still hurt but she sensed the fever that had taken hold so quickly had mostly left her body.

She pushed back the covers and eased herself into a sitting position. The bedside lamp was on and she heard the gentle hum of the humidifier from somewhere in the room. The digital clock read 6:45 p.m. but she had no idea what day it was. She looked down and noticed the cotton pajamas she wore. They were pale lemon and had silly-looking cats on them. Cassie didn't remember changing her clothes. Didn't remember much of anything, really. Only a deep voice that had given her an easy comfort as she'd shifted in and out of sleep, and then someone pressing a glass to her lips so she could have some water. Then she remembered another voice, female and familiar. Lauren.

Her friend had been looking after her. Of course, it could only have been Lauren.

Cassie swung her legs off the bed. The house was quiet. Too quiet.

Oliver...

Where was her baby? Panic crept over her skin for a second, and then she realized he must be with her friend. Cassie forced herself to stand, and when her knees wobbled she clutched the bed to get her bearings. Once she had her balance she grabbed her robe from the foot of the bed and pushed her arms into it and tightened the belt. She made a quick bathroom stop and then moved back into the bedroom. The door was open and she made her way across the room as steadily as she could. A light illuminated down the hall and she followed it to the nursery. But the room was empty. The panic returned and quickly seeped deep into her bones. Where were they?

She turned on her bare heels and hurried back down the hall to the kitchen.

Still nothing.

When she reached the living room Cassie came to an abrupt halt in the doorway as relief flooded every pore. Oliver was safe. But he wasn't with her friend. He was lying blissfully asleep against his uncle's strong chest.

Tanner was in the recliner, legs stretched out and crossed at the ankles, both hands cradling her sleeping son. He wore jeans and a white tank shirt and his feet were bare. His eyes were closed and his hair flopped over his forehead a little.

Cassie's belly rolled over as she watched them. In a matter of days she'd witnessed him form a bond with her son that touched her to her very core. It was the bond she'd dreamed Doug would have had with his son. But it wasn't

Doug cradling her child so gently. It wasn't Doug who'd been so kind to her over the past few days.

Doug was gone.

And Tanner was now in her life. Until he left. Until the house sold and Doug's estate was sorted. She needed to remember that he was passing through. He was temporary. And once he was gone her life could return to normal. She'd find somewhere to live, go back to work and raise her son...and forget all about Tanner McCord and his sexy smile and broad shoulders.

She looked at him again. His eyes were now open and he was smiling.

"Hey there," he said softly. "How are you feeling?"

Cassie nodded. Her arms were aching to hold her son, but the thought she might be contagious stopped her from rushing forward. And Oliver looked so peaceful and content resting against Tanner's chest.

"Okay," she replied and stepped a little farther into the room. "Weak. I guess I've been out of it since yesterday?"

"Pretty much," he said and pushed up from the chair effortlessly. Oliver didn't protest, but instead seemed to snuggle closer to his uncle. "He was restless," Tanner explained and gently touched the baby's head. "And he seems to like this."

She smiled warmly. "Thank you for taking care of him."

Tanner met her gaze. "That's what family is for, Cassie."

Her throat tightened. *Family.* It had been so long since she'd thought she had anyone to call family. With her grandfather's slide into dementia and Doug's continued absence from her life even though she'd considered them a couple, Cassie had felt very alone for the past few years. Oliver's arrival had changed that of course, but he was a baby and needed her 24/7. To have someone to rely upon, to *need* someone herself, was a different kind of feeling.

Not that she *needed* Tanner. Not at all. But he'd said they were family…and for the moment, while she was feeling so weak and weary, it made her feel a little less alone.

"How about I put him in his crib and then make you some herbal tea?" Tanner suggested quietly.

Cassie nodded. "That would be good."

Careful not to wake the baby, he slowly got out of the chair and came to stand beside her. Cassie's heart rolled over when she gazed into the face of her sleeping son and she touched Oliver's head gently. Glancing up, she saw Tanner watching her with a kind of blistering intensity and the look made her insides quiver. His eyes were dark and hypnotic and she was quickly drawn into his stare. So close, with only Oliver between them, she was more conscious of him than she had ever been of any man in her life. There was a connection between them…a link that had developed over the past few days. And it wasn't simply about Oliver.

This was something else.

This was physical attraction…pure and simple.

An attraction she'd always been able to ignore. Until now.

"Be back in a minute," Tanner said, breaking the visual connection.

He left the room and Cassie let out a long breath. There was nothing right or reasonable about her feelings. Nothing she could say to herself that would assuage the heaviness in her heart. He was Doug's brother so desiring Tanner was out of the question.

He returned about ten minutes later and Cassie was sitting on the sofa, legs curled up, her chin resting in one hand. He came into the room with a tray and placed it on the small table beside the sofa.

"I heated some soup," he explained and passed her a mug. "You should probably eat something."

Cassie took the mug of warm broth and smiled. "Thank you. You've been very kind."

He shrugged loosely, as though he was embarrassed by her words. "It's nothing."

That wasn't even halfway to the truth. She managed a wry smile. "Ah...how did I get into these pajamas?"

"Lauren," he explained. "She was here this morning."

Cassie nodded a little. "Oh, I don't remember much of today."

"Her fiancé checked you out and she organized the medication you needed. She also suggested taking Oliver home with her for the night, but I thought you'd prefer he stay here."

"I do," she said quickly, hating the idea of being apart from her baby. "And you stayed?"

He shrugged again. "It seemed like the right thing to do. You were in no condition to look after Oliver last night and today."

She was tempted to thank him again but sensed it wasn't what he wanted to hear. Instead she sipped the broth and settled back into the sofa. It was strange, she mused, how comfortable she was being around him. She hadn't expected it. On the two occasions they'd met before she'd always had her guard up, and always felt as though Tanner had, too. But this time was different. There was no one to hide behind. No one to whisper words about how unfriendly and indifferent he was. No one to tell her he was the kind of man who preferred his own company and his horses to having real relationships. Cassie was seeing him without Doug's bias and prejudice for the first time... and she liked him. A lot.

"So, I guess you should stay tonight, too?"

The intense way he was watching her made it impossible to look anywhere but into his eyes.

"Do you want me to stay?"

Cassie took a second and then nodded. "I think Oliver would like it."

So would I...

"All right," he said and watched her over the rim of his coffee mug. "I'll return to Ruthie's tomorrow."

"Thank you."

Silence stretched between them and Cassie waited for discomfiture to crawl across her skin. When it didn't come she knew it was because she'd quickly become accustomed to Tanner's company. Despite how attracted she was to him and despite how much she knew it could never go anywhere, he was easy to be around.

He was, she realized, nothing like the man Doug had so often described.

Instead of being a moody closed-off loner, he was friendly and generous and considerate. And he possessed a laid-back kind of charm she found increasingly difficult to overlook. In the kitchen, the garden or the nursery he did everything with such an easygoing confidence it was impossible to *not* be attracted to him.

Admit it...you're also thinking he'd be good in the bedroom...

Cassie shook the thought away. It was stupid. She still loved Doug. And she was a single mother. A soon-to-be homeless single mother who didn't have time to waste thinking about Tanner in that way. In any way, for that matter. But it had been such a long time since she'd thought about strong arms and a broad chest. And longer still since she'd thought about sex. With anyone.

"Are you sure you're feeling okay now?" he asked softly.

"Positive," she lied and managed a smile. "Soup and

sleep therapy will work a treat tonight and I will be back to my usual self by tomorrow."

He nodded. "It's getting late… You shouldn't wear yourself out."

She was touched by his concern. But a part of her wondered if he wanted to shuffle her off to bed so they wouldn't be alone. He had to know she was attracted to him. And she was pretty sure it was mutual. He obviously thought it a bad idea. Which of course it was.

"So, what are your plans?" she asked. "I mean, once you've finishing saving the day here?"

He grinned. "I didn't realize that's what I'd been doing."

"Sure you did," she said and smiled a little.

He shrugged again. "I have an appointment with Doug's lawyer on Wednesday. After that I'm not sure. We'll have to see what the lawyer says."

We…

As if it was inclusive. As if it had something to do with her. As if…well, almost as if they were a couple.

Cassie silently cursed her foolishness and ignored the flush rising over her collarbones at the thought of the idea. Two days together didn't make them anything. "I know you said there was no hurry for me to start looking for a new place to live, but I can't see the sense in putting it off. I could never afford to take on the mortgage here, so the sooner I accept the inevitable, the better."

Tanner's insides contracted. He hated hearing the disappointment and pain in her voice. This was her home. The home she'd made for her son. The home she'd known as a young girl when she'd moved in with her grandfather after her parents had been killed. It had to hurt her. He knew only too well what it was to lose the one place that had made him feel safe when he was a child. He wanted to make it right. But nothing he said would offer her consolation or comfort.

"Like I said, we'll wait and see what the lawyer has to say."

She shrugged as though it didn't matter, but Tanner knew she was resigned to losing her home. And once again he silently cursed his brother. Doug should have provided for Cassie and his son. He should have ensured they had a place to live and were financially secure.

"I think I'll get some rest," she murmured as she placed the mug down and stood. "Thank you again for everything you've done for Oliver...and for me. I know this probably isn't what you expected to be doing when you made the decision to return to Crystal Point. I'm very grateful for your concern and kindness."

Tanner stared at her and a heavy sensation uncurled in his chest. She had a way of doing that to him. It made him feel weak...almost vulnerable. And it gave her a power over him he was certain she didn't know she possessed.

"Good night, Cassie," he said and got to his feet. "Let me know if you need anything."

What I need is a cold shower...

Even in her silly pajamas and nightgown, with her hair mussed and slippers on her feet, she was beautiful and sexy and warmed his blood. No other woman had ever had quite the same effect on his libido. Sure, he'd dated several women over the years...but Cassie Duncan stirred him like no one else ever had. He'd fought it for years, convincing himself that she loved his brother and his own feelings were of little consequence. But sometimes, like the way her blue eyes watched him when she thought he wasn't looking, Tanner couldn't help wondering if she regarded him as more than Doug's brother. More than Oliver's uncle.

Don't be an ass.

Of course it was stupid. And wrong. She'd borne his brother's child. She was clearly still in love with Doug. She'd made it clear that she didn't really want him in her life.

So get moving and take that cold shower.

"Good night," he said again, firmer this time so he could galvanize himself into action and get away from her. "I'll lock up."

She nodded and left the room. Once he was alone Tanner let out a long breath, flicked off the lights and waited until he heard her bedroom door close before he walked from the room and checked that all the windows and doors were locked around the house. Once he was done he moved down the hallway and headed for the bathroom. He took a shower and turned in around nine, spending the next couple of hours staring at the ceiling in between getting up to check on Oliver. By midnight he'd had enough. He pulled on jeans and a shirt and made his way to the kitchen.

A soft glow illuminated down the hall and when he rounded the doorway he noticed the light above the stovetop was on. Cassie was sitting at the kitchen table, a mug cradled between her hands. She'd changed into gray sweats and her hair was pulled back in a ponytail.

"Hey," he said easily, despite the inexplicable tightness that filled his chest. "Couldn't sleep?"

She shook her head. "No. You?"

Tanner nodded and remained in the doorway. "Lingering jet lag, I guess."

"And with looking after Oliver you haven't exactly had a chance to sleep it off, right?"

He shrugged. "It'll work itself out. You, on the other hand, should be resting."

"I think I've slept enough for both of us," she said through a brittle smile. "I had a shower to freshen up and didn't feel tired, so I thought I'd have some green tea and sit for a while," she said and sighed. "I was thinking about Doug."

Of course she was. Tanner didn't doubt that his brother was on her mind most days and nights. "Then I'll leave you—"

"Do you know the details about what happened?" she asked unexpectedly, cutting him off.

Tanner stilled. "Details?"

"About the incident."

"You mean how he was killed?" he queried.

She nodded. "You're his official next of kin so I figured you had the details. I know he was on some covert mission and that he and two other members of his squad were killed by a sniper...but that's all I know. Since I wasn't listed as family it's been almost impossible to get information. I know you got the army to forward his belongings here, but did you know this house wasn't even listed as his place of residence? Instead it's some post office box I didn't know existed and don't even have a key for. And there's a safety deposit box, too, did you know that? I don't have access to it, of course. But I'm guessing you will."

Tanner didn't respond. He didn't want to say anything about the safety deposit box until he'd had a chance to go through the contents himself. He certainly hadn't suspected that Cassie knew about it. Doug's lawyer had told him about it along with the details of his will.

"I'll see what I can find out," he said vaguely. "There's also the matter of Doug's military pension. I'm sure there'll be some money available for you and—"

She waved a hand and frowned. "I don't want any kind of handout," she said and cut him off again. "And I intend to go back to work when my maternity leave is up."

"And Oliver?" Tanner asked as he walked behind the

kitchen counter and grabbed a mug. "What are your plans for him?"

"Day care," she said. "Which is the option of most working single mothers. There's a good day care center not far from the hospital where I work."

"But if there's money available you could—"

"No," she said, interrupting him once again. "Doug obviously wanted his estate to go to you. I can't and won't challenge his wishes."

Tanner wasn't sure whether she was being altruistic or just foolishly naive. "It's not that simple."

"Yes," she defied. "It is."

He flicked on one of the lights and then rested his hands on the counter. "Oliver is Doug's son. Which makes him the beneficiary of my brother's estate. And also the recipient of any benefit that may come about from the years Doug spent defending this country. I won't argue, Cassie. Not on this issue. You can look at me with those beautiful, big, blue eyes all you want...but I won't change my mind on this."

She stilled suddenly, watching him as a tiny half smile creased the corner of her mouth. "You think I have beautiful eyes?"

Damn...

Tanner ignored the way his heart thundered in his chest and shrugged as casually as he could. "Well, I'm not blind." He stopped, thinking he shouldn't say anything else. But good sense *didn't* prevail. "And you're very...pretty."

She laughed softly and raised both brows. "I've always thought I was kind of average."

Tanner frowned. *Average?* There was nothing average about Cassandra Duncan. "You're not serious?"

"Perfectly," she replied. "Doug said I—"

"Doug was an ass."

She laughed again and the delicate sound echoed around the room. "Really?"

"I meant that he—"

"He did have some *ass-like* qualities I suppose," she said and grinned. "But then, no one is perfect, right?"

Except for you...

Tanner pulled himself back from saying anything stupid. Or rather, something even more stupid. "I shouldn't have said that."

"Are you referring to criticizing Doug or complimenting me?"

Was she being deliberately provocative? Tanner couldn't tell. He knew so little about her. Her moods, her thoughts... they were a mystery to him and he knew it needed to stay that way. "Both."

She sipped the tea and then placed the mug on the table. "Well, what's a little harmless flirting? It doesn't—"

"Is that what we're doing?" he asked quickly, fighting the heat climbing over his skin.

She gave a brittle laugh. "I'm not sure what we're doing. I'm not sure what *you're* doing."

Going slowly out of my mind...that's what.

Tanner straightened. "You know why I'm here."

"I know what you came here to do," she said quietly. "I'm still not sure why."

"Does it matter?" he asked, reluctant to say too much. "For Oliver, like I said."

"And to sort out Doug's estate," she added, watching him closely, as if she was looking for answers in his expression. "When we both know you could have done that through lawyers. The house needs to be sold. There's no money left to speak of other than a possible military pension. So if this is all about Oliver, if my son is the real reason you've come all this way, I want to know why. I want to know why family is so important to you, when it didn't seem to matter one way or another when Doug was alive."

There was strength in her voice and a kind of unexpected determination to get answers. She was annoyed. And she wasn't hiding it.

"Okay," he said on a long breath. "The truth is, I don't want Oliver to feel…abandoned."

Her gaze sharpened. "Like you were, you mean?"

"Exactly."

She nodded a little. "But Oliver has me. He's not alone. And I'm not about to shuffle him off to boarding school when he's of age. And although I do appreciate that you want to have a relationship with your nephew, Tanner, I can't see how it will be sustainable once you're back in South Dakota. A part of me is reluctant to let him get attached to you when I know you'll be leaving soon. I know he's only a baby, but he's already bonded with you and I—"

"I intend to come back and see him when I can," Tanner explained, hating all her relentless logic.

Her brows came up. "Like you saw Doug? Once every couple of years? Tell me, how often did Doug visit you when you were at boarding school?"

"Not often."

She shrugged. "I can't see this being any different."

"I'm not Doug," Tanner said. "And if his son—my nephew—ever needs me, then I'll be there."

She looked into her mug for a moment and then lifted her gaze. "It's a nice idea and I guess only time will tell. But have you considered what will happen when you get married and have a family of your own?" Her eyes were questioning. "You do plan to do that, don't you?"

His insides burned. "At some point."

"Do you really think you'll have the time or inclination to nurture a relationship with Oliver when that happens?"

"I won't abandon him."

"You can't take Doug's place in his life."

Tanner gripped the counter. "It hadn't occurred to me to try."

Her brows came up again. "Are you sure? You seem to have ridden in on your proverbial white horse. I'm not saying that I'm not...grateful. I am. Especially with being sick these past couple of days. But it's not your job to look after us. And frankly, I don't want to take advantage of your...generosity."

"You're not," he assured her. "I'm here because I want to be here. I mean, with Oliver. I made a promise and I intend to stick to it. Doug would want me to make sure his son was provided for."

It wasn't exactly the truth. Since Doug hadn't any plans to claim the child he'd fathered or the woman who'd loved him.

She inhaled heavily. "I hardly saw him, you know... I mean, in the last twelve months before he was killed. He returned for about a week, but he was restless...like he didn't want to be here. Like he was waiting to get back to his other life." She shrugged. "That was the week Oliver was conceived. And it was the last time I saw Doug."

Tanner remembered that visit. Doug had called him, complaining about how Cassie was pushing for commitment and how he wanted out of the relationship. He'd talked his brother out of doing something rash, but three months later Doug called again...and this time he wasn't going to be swayed. Cassie was pregnant. He didn't want commitment. He didn't want fatherhood. He didn't want to be tied down to a life he wasn't suited for. Tragically, by paying the ultimate sacrifice for his country, his brother had gotten the freedom he'd craved.

Tanner wanted to tell her that Doug *would* have come

home to claim his family. He wanted to tell her that she would have had the happy-ever-after she deserved. But he couldn't. Because it wasn't anywhere near the truth. Doug had been a fine soldier, but in his personal life he'd repeatedly left wreckage in his wake.

"I'm sorry it didn't turn out the way you were hoping it would."

She gave a derisive laugh. "He told you, I suppose, that I had brought up the subject of marriage."

Tanner nodded. "Yes."

"He said we'd talk about it when he got back. Only, he never did get back. And we never talked."

"Some people just aren't the marrying kind, I guess."

Her eyes widened. "So you don't think he would have married me and settled down?"

Realizing he might have said too much, Tanner back-pedaled. "It doesn't really matter what I think."

"But Doug talked to you," she persisted. "And he obviously told you how he felt about the baby coming."

"He was surprised," Tanner said too casually. "And in a war zone. I don't imagine he had the chance to absorb much of anything at the time."

"I suppose. I only wish… I wish that he'd met Oliver… that he'd had a chance to know this perfectly beautiful baby and hold him just once. I'm sure if he had he would have…he would have felt like I do."

Tanner wasn't so sure. But he didn't say anything. Because her blue eyes were now glistening brightly and her tremulous voice echoed around the room. She dropped her face into her hands for a moment and sighed heavily. Seeing her sudden anguish, he walked around the counter and moved closer. She looked up to meet his gaze and within seconds there were tears on her cheeks.

Without a word he sat down and reached for her hands,

taking them gently within his own. She didn't protest. She didn't move. The only sound in the room was the faint tick from the clock on the wall and the gentle hum of the refrigerator. And she wept. Not racking, uncontrolled sobs, but quietly, with restraint and a calm kind of dignity.

As he held her hands and felt the connection of her skin against his own, a tide of long-buried feelings rose up and hit him squarely in the solar plexus. He pushed them back, willing them away with all his strength because he knew they were futile.

"I'm sorry... I don't know what's come over me," she said, still crying.

Tanner squeezed her fingers gently. "You're tired, you've been ill *and* you're grieving, Cassie. Don't be so hard on yourself."

Tears trailed down her cheeks and he fought the impulse to wipe them away. He wanted to take her in his arms and console her. But he wouldn't.

"The more time that goes by, the less I feel I knew him," she said shakily. "It's like there's this wall of disconnect that keeps getter wider with each day that passes. Sometimes I'm afraid that I'll forget what he was like and I won't be able to tell Oliver about his father."

"That won't happen," Tanner assured her and gently rubbed her fingers. "We both knew Doug... We can both tell his son the kind of man he was. How he was brave and fought for his country. How he could make people laugh with his lame jokes. How, even when we were mad as hell with him, we couldn't help loving him."

She nodded and looked at their hands. Still linked. Still connected. And making his heart beat faster with each passing second. He met her gaze and sucked in a sharp breath when he noticed her lips part fractionally. He knew it was an unintentional invitation, but it was an invitation all the same and the very notion of her lips against his made his skin burn.

He wanted to kiss her. Just as he had all those years ago. He wanted to hold her, as he'd imagined countless times since.

But this was Cassie…the woman who'd borne his brother's child. She'd loved Doug. Just like Leah. And he wasn't about to let his heart get smashed.

Not ever again.

No matter how much he was tempted.

Chapter Six

Cassie was captivated. There was something about the way Tanner looked at her that defied logic. Defied good sense. Defied every warning bell in her head telling her she was crazy to be so achingly aware of him. His brown eyes searched her face, lingering on her mouth, and there was enough heat in his gaze to combust the air in the room. Something rattled around inside her head. A sense. A feeling. It was both familiar and breathtakingly new. She wondered how he could do that to her. How, even though they barely knew one another, there was a growing energy between them that drew her toward him in a way she hadn't expected. *If* she believed in past lives, *if* she believed that two people could have a connection that belied the depth of their acquaintance, she would have sworn they'd somehow shared a moment of time together.

The feeling lingered and she couldn't have moved if she'd tried. She looked to where his fingers stroked her hand and felt the heat of his touch through to her very core. He had nice hands, big and tanned and just a little calloused on the tips. Hands that were made for schooling the most skittish colt, but hands she'd seen soothe her baby son to sleep as no others had. Cowboy's hands, she mused, forged from hard work and skill.

Her thoughts shifted and she wondered how it would feel if his fingers traveled slightly up her arm. The quiet intimacy of the room amplified her awareness of him and Cassie let out a long, shuddering sigh. He felt it, too; she was sure of it. The intensity in his gaze couldn't be faked and the tenderness of his touch was wholly mesmerizing.

It had been so long since she felt a connection to someone.

And the fact that someone was Tanner McCord scared her to pieces.

He drew her hand to his mouth and softly kissed her knuckles. It should have sent her running. It should have had her jumping up in protest and demanding an explanation. But she didn't move. She didn't break the contact.

He did.

Tanner released her hand and got to his feet, staring at her for a few long seconds. "Good night, Cassie."

By the time he'd left the room she was shaking all over. By the time she finally tumbled into bed ten minutes later she was certain she had to pull herself together.

And fast.

It was past seven when she rolled out of bed the next morning. Tanner was in the kitchen preparing Oliver's bottle and she barely looked in his direction when she entered the room and made a beeline for her baby, who was happily chuckling away in his bouncer. It felt so good to hold her son after a day without having him in her arms.

She took a deep breath and inhaled the sweet baby smell that always gave her such comfort.

"Good morning."

Finally she looked at Tanner. He'd pushed a steaming mug of coffee across the counter and Cassie half smiled. "Ah, thanks."

"This is ready to go," he said and shook the bottle in his hand a little. "You want to feed him?"

"Oh, yes," she replied and moved toward the counter. She took the bottle and quickly settled herself at the table. Oliver latched on immediately and she relaxed when he began to feed.

"You're feeling better this morning?"

She glanced up. Tanner hadn't moved from his spot behind the counter. "Yes, much."

He nodded. "Good. Then I'll get going."

"Tanner, I think—"

"I'll call you after my meeting with the lawyer."

There was a terseness to his voice she hadn't heard before. The easy friendship they'd developed over the past few days seemed to have disappeared. He clearly wanted to leave and she had no intention of stopping him. "Okay, sure."

"Goodbye."

She nodded a little. "Yeah...goodbye."

Then he was gone from the room and Cassie barely drew another steady breath until she heard the front door close and the faint sound of his car pulling out from the driveway.

By the time she'd fed and bathed Oliver it was close to nine o'clock, and after she put him down for a nap Cassie took a shower, tied up her hair, applied a little makeup and changed into jeans and a pale lemon-colored sweater.

Keeping busy stopped her from thinking about Tanner, which was exactly what she wanted.

At ten she'd had an unexpected visitor—her longtime friend Mary-Jayne Preston.

"You're here?" Cassie said once they'd finished hugging in the doorway. "I thought you were neck-deep in orders and holed up in your workshop?"

Her friend shrugged. "I bailed and came to see you instead."

Cassie grinned. "I'm so glad you did. But do you want to tell me why?"

Mary-Jayne, or M.J. as she was affectionately called, tossed her mane of dark curly hair. "Not especially. Today was merely just another boring event in my mundane life."

There was nothing boring or mundane about Mary-Jayne Preston. Her beautiful and talented friend designed jewelry. She was vivacious, fiery and had strong ideals about politics and the environment.

"You're the most *un-boring* person I know," Cassie said and ushered her guest down the hall.

M.J. grinned. "I think I'm just restless."

Cassie raised a brow. "Are you thinking of taking off again?"

M.J. often went on spur-of-the-moment vacations to obscure places. Cassie had always envied her friend's fearlessness and adventurous spirit and sometimes wished she was a little more like her. She'd never traveled. She'd never even been on an airplane. Doug had complained many times that she'd lacked daring and was too set in her ways. She always shrugged it off, but deep down she was hurt by his words.

"Maybe," M.J. replied and sat at the table. "You know how I feel about being trapped by routine. But enough about me... How are you doing?"

"I'm good," she fibbed and smiled.

"Lauren said you've been ill," M.J. said, suddenly serious. "Do you need me to do anything for you? Perhaps help out with Oliver?"

She shook her head. "No, I'm fine. I've had—"

"Help?" M.J. asked with a grin. "Yes, so Lauren told me. I hear a certain cowboy has been here."

"Tanner," Cassie explained, and ignored the heat in her cheeks. "Yes...that's right."

"Is he still gorgeous?"

Cassie allowed herself to smile fractionally. "Oh, yeah."

"Does he still make your knees go weak?"

Cassie colored hotly. "I've never said he does that."

M.J. laughed softly. "Maybe not in so many words."

"You're incorrigible." She grinned. "But the truth is..."

"Yes?" M.J. prompted.

"He's...nice. Much nicer than..."

"Much nicer than Doug ever said he was?" her friend asked bluntly when Cassie's words trailed off.

"I guess so. I mean, I knew they didn't have the closest relationship...but there are things Doug said about Tanner that now seem so far from the truth."

M.J.'s brows rose sharply. "You mean Doug lied?"

She nodded. "I suppose he did. It's almost as though he wanted me to think badly of his brother."

"Perhaps so he could make himself look like the better man?" M.J. suggested.

Cassie's mouth flattened. The idea of that sounded mean and spiteful. It wasn't how she wanted to remember the man who'd fathered her child. "I know you think I was blind to Doug's faults, but I did know he wasn't perfect."

"He never deserved your love, Cassie," M.J. said quietly. "Or your loyalty. The way he reacted when you told him you were pregnant was truly awful. You know that in your heart."

Cassie did know it. And Mary-Jayne, with her tell-it-like-it-is personality, was only saying what Cassie knew herself deep down.

"He would have come around to the idea of being a father," she said, way more animated than she felt. "With time, things would have been better." She sighed and looked at her friend. "I have to believe that. For Oliver's sake."

"I get what you're saying," her friend said gently.

But she knew M.J. didn't really understand. And she didn't want to explain any further. If she didn't remain loyal to Doug's memory, then she'd be forced to question her reasons for loving him. Without that love to hide behind she'd be vulnerable...and with Tanner McCord in town, being vulnerable was out of the question.

When Tanner arrived on Cassie's doorstep on Wednesday afternoon he didn't expect to be greeted by a stunning-looking brunette with wide green eyes, who regarded him with a kind of guarded curiosity.

He stepped back on the porch and forced out a smile. "Is Cassie home?"

The brunette leaned against the door frame and shook her head. "So, you must be *the jerk's* little brother?"

Okay. Now he knew who she was. Doug had told him about Cassie's friend who had always been a very vocal critic of his brother's continued absence from Cassie's life.

"Tanner," he said, ignoring the jerk taunt. "You must be M.J. Doug mentioned you once or twice. Nice to meet you."

M.J. grinned. "I'm watching the baby while Cassie's

out visiting her grandfather. She should be home around four. You can stay and wait if you like."

He glanced at his watch and then politely declined her offer. "Just tell her I stopped by and I'll call her later."

Knowing that Cassie was visiting her grandfather made him think about his own family. And the visit he'd been putting off. Tanner got back in the rental car and took the fifteen-minute drive to the cemetery where his entire family was buried. His parents' dual headstone greeted him as it had so many times in the past. He stared at their names, forcing memories into his head. So much about them had been forgotten. But the feel of his mother's embrace and the deep comfort of his father's voice remained locked inside. So many years had passed. Over two decades of being without them and it struck him how similar his story was to Cassie's. They'd both lost their parents around the same time. His died in a car wreck, hers in a boating accident. Thankfully she'd found a home with her grandfather, which he hoped had lessened her loss just a little.

He took a deep breath and turned his gaze to the right. Doug's headstone was glaringly white beside the faded one of their parents. Tanner's stomach churned and emotion quickly thickened his throat as he read the words.

Douglas Ian McCord. Aged 41. Son. Brother. Soldier. Killed in action. Never forgotten.

He blinked away the heat in his eyes. In that moment the loss of his brother hit home in a way it hadn't since the moment he'd heard Doug had been killed. Tanner pressed a palm to his chest to ease the sharp jab of pain that knocked him with the force of a runaway train.

He experienced a mix of emotions. Hate and love. Betrayal and forgiveness. Relief and anguish. Over the years he'd felt them all in one way or another when it came to his brother. After Leah had told him she was in love with Doug and carrying his brother's child, Tanner had shut down and vowed to never speak to the other man again. At eighteen, his heart had been fueled with rage by the knowledge of Doug's treachery. His inheritance was gone. The girl he'd loved was gone. He'd packed his bags and taken off for Europe, never intending to look back.

Two years had passed before Doug tracked him down and for so long afterward Tanner wondered why his brother had sought him out. For a man who didn't want commitment or anything or anyone tying him down, he'd worked hard to rekindle their broken relationship.

Guilt...

He hated to think that was his brother's sole motivation. But nothing he'd done later in his life made Tanner believe that Doug had changed. Not when he'd bought a house he clearly couldn't afford or wasted money on cars and bikes he'd never use. Not when he'd secured the love of another woman who would go on to bear his son, and then have every intention of casting them aside.

No...his brother hadn't changed.

But he *still* grieved the loss of his only sibling. And he still wanted him back so he could tell him what a damned irresponsible fool he was.

"Tanner?"

A soft voice said his name and he turned. Cassie stood by his parents' headstone, her hands clasped together. In her kitchen he'd almost kissed her beautiful mouth. And he was certain she wouldn't have stopped him. Which meant one thing.

Complicated.

He stepped back, leaning heavily on his uninjured leg

and moved beside her. "I thought I'd come and pay my respects," he said quietly.

She nodded. "I usually stop by on my way back from seeing my grandfather."

"How is he?"

"Granddad?" She stepped closer. "He's had a bad week and didn't know me today."

Tanner saw the pain in her expression. "That must be difficult."

She shrugged. "Yeah...but he's eighty-two and has lived a full life. Not like..."

"Like Doug?" he queried when he noticed her gaze flick to the headstones. "Or my parents? Or your parents?"

"Yes, exactly." She pointed south. "They're down that way."

"Shall we visit?"

She frowned a little and looked at Doug's grave. "You don't want to stay here?"

"I've said my goodbyes."

She lingered for a second and then nodded and, as she turned, the scent of her perfume caught on the breeze. It didn't take long to reach the spot where her parents were and Tanner hung back while she stood at the foot of their graves. She remained there for barely a minute and then turned back to him.

"I've had enough now," she said and started moving away.

"It's hard for you to be here?" he queried as they walked down the path.

She shrugged. "I guess I don't want this place to be how I remember them. No one's life is defined by their headstone."

"You're right," he said and moved in step with her. When they reached their vehicles and she'd flicked the lock mechanism on her sedan he opened her driver's door. "If it's okay with you I'll see you back at the house. I went to the lawyer today and there are some things we need to discuss."

Her small smile faded. "My friend Mary-Jayne is at home looking after Oliver and she always stays for dinner on Wednesday night, so now is probably not a great time."

"I met her," Tanner said and grinned. "I dropped in earlier. Colorful girl."

Her smile returned. "She's a straight shooter. And she never liked Doug much, if that's what you mean."

"She didn't call him anything he didn't deserve," he said drily. "So, how about you play hooky for an hour so we can talk?"

She frowned a little, but then pulled her phone from her bag. "I'll call M.J. and say I'm going to be late. Where would you like to go? Perhaps Ruthie's? Or we could go to the beach and sit on one of the tables near the kiosk."

"The beach," he answered quickly, thinking he didn't want to talk to Cassie beneath Ruthie Nevelson's interested eyes. "We can grab coffee from the kiosk if you like."

"Ah…okay. See you there."

The Crystal Point beach was an idyllic spot where the Bellan River met the sea. There was a surf club near the holiday park and a kiosk that catered to the locals and tourists. It was off-season, so the park was mostly vacant and the kiosk quiet. Tanner parked outside and waited for Cassie to pull up beside him. He got out, locked the car and met her by her door.

Five minutes later he'd bought take-out coffee and they were making their way along the path that led to the beach. They stopped before they reached the sand and took a seat at a concrete picnic table.

"So," she said, getting straight to the point, "what did the lawyer say?"

Tanner took a steady breath. "He confirmed what we already knew. There's a mortgage and some credit card debt. The insurance covered some of the debt but there's still a sizable amount owing."

She wrapped her hands around the foam cup. "And you have to sell the house?"

"Yes."

Her breath came out heavy. "Well, that's not exactly unexpected. I'll start seriously looking for a new place tomorrow."

"It's not that urgent," he said and watched her over the rim of his cup. "The house needs some work done to it before it goes on the market if we're to get the best price."

She sighed. "I know I've let it run down since—"

"It's not your fault. Nor was it *your* responsibility. But I don't want to keep going on about what Doug *should* have done. I'll fix the house up and hopefully it will sell quickly. Whatever money is left from the sale will go into trust for Oliver."

She returned the barest nod and met his gaze. "Will... will I need to get DNA testing done to prove Oliver is Doug's child?"

"You're not serious?"

Color rose in her cheeks. "I thought you might want proof before you handed any money over."

"No," Tanner said gently. "I know whose child he is, Cassie. He has Doug's eyes."

"And yours," she said.

"A family trait," he said and smiled. "He's a beautiful child and I'm glad I've been able to get to know him."

"I'm glad, too." She cradled the cup in her hands. "I know I've been a bit hot and cold about you being part of his life...but I am genuinely pleased that he has an uncle who cares about us."

* * *

She hadn't meant to say "us." But the word slipped out and it was impossible to avoid the query in his gaze. He did care; that was obvious. He was a caring, kind man and she'd been naively deceived by Doug into thinking Tanner was some sort of closed-off, unfriendly loner who didn't need or want any kind of familial relationships. He did want them... The way he'd bonded so effortlessly with Oliver was evidence of that.

"I'll help you get the house ready," she said and smiled. "Some of the rooms need painting and the backyard could do with an overhaul. And perhaps some new light fittings. It shouldn't take long to fix up."

"Sure," he replied. "And don't stress about moving. When the time comes we'll find a place for you both."

"And what about the safety deposit box?" she asked. "Did you find anything important in it?"

He shook his head. "No. It was empty."

It seemed odd, but Cassie didn't press the issue. She nodded and finished her coffee. "I think I'd like to walk for a while."

"Want some company?"

Did she? Being around him was increasingly unsettling. And since the tense moment in the kitchen when he'd comforted her she'd done little else but think about him. She could have sworn he was going to kiss her...and not just on the hand as he'd done. Naive and inexperienced she might be, but there was heat between them and spending time with him only added fuel to the fire.

She should have sent him on his way. *Should have.*

"Okay," she said and got to her feet.

He stood and tossed their empty cups in the trash. "Lead the way."

The beach was deserted and when they reached the

sand she flipped off her sandals and shoved them into her tote. There were gray clouds rolling in from the sea and the wind whipped up around them. "I love it here on days like this," she admitted as they started walking along the sand. "It's got a mysterious mood about it when the clouds rumble and the wind howls."

He laughed. "Cold wind and unswimmable seas...not exactly my idea of a great afternoon at the beach."

"Wimp," she said and laughed back. "Where's your sense of adventure?"

They walked closely together and Tanner quickly steadied her when she lost her footing and tripped.

"Oh, sorry," she said breathlessly, gripping his arm. "I'm something of a klutz."

"I bet you're not. Doug told me you were a dancer when you were young."

She grimaced. "Not exactly. I did ballet with Lauren when I was about ten. But I lasted only a few months."

"Best I not take you to the upcoming Rosemount Rodeo, then," he said and grinned. "There's a cowboy dance being held in the evening. Don't want you stepping on my feet."

She released his arm. "I saw flyers advertising the rodeo when I was in town the other day. It's about half an hour out of Bellandale, isn't it?"

"About that."

She nodded a little. "I've never been to a cowboy dance. I'm not sure I'd know how to move."

"It's easy. You just hang on to one another and sway."

Suddenly the notion of hanging on to him, be it dancing or otherwise, sent another surge of heat coursing through her veins. It had been so long since she felt a man's arms around her. And she missed it. She missed intimacy and closeness and...sex.

Not that she'd had much of a sex life in the past few

years. Doug's visits were so infrequent and brief before she'd fallen pregnant with Oliver she'd begun to question his commitment to her and their relationship. Being involved with a career soldier was one thing…being involved with a man who could leave so easily time and time again, another thing altogether. Doug wasn't tied to Crystal Point. And there were times when she'd wondered if she was little more than a cook and housekeeper for him to come back to every now and then. She'd also wondered what might have happened if Oliver hadn't come along. She knew in her heart there would have to have been some serious changes to the dynamic of their relationship if it was to last.

It certainly wasn't the relationship she'd dreamed of when she was younger. As a teen she'd had her share of romantic fantasies. She'd been quiet and studious and anything she knew about romance and love she'd learned through novels and old movies.

Well, almost everything…

Once, long ago, she'd been swept off her feet. By a boy riding a horse, no less.

She'd been on the beach with Lauren and they'd spotted the lone rider at the edge of the river mouth. Horses were common enough on the beach, so she hadn't taken much notice, until her thirteen-year-old eyes had realized the rider was a boy around her age, and that he looked too gorgeous for words in jeans, plaid shirt and cowboy hat resting low over his eyes. Lauren had pushed her forward when he'd come close and she'd tentatively said hello. He'd done the same and they'd chatted for a couple of minutes. He was on vacation, staying with a relative. She'd explained she lived in the small town permanently. It had been puppy love at first sight for Cassie and she'd agreed to return the following afternoon and he was already riding off on his horse when she'd realized they hadn't exchanged names.

"What are you thinking about?"

She glanced sideways when she realized Tanner was looking at her. "Nothing. You'll think it's silly."

"Try me," he said with a wry grin. "Sometimes we all need a little silly in our lives."

Gosh, he was *so* right. She was tired of being serious all the time. Of worrying. Of overthinking. Of being a grown-up. Some days she longed to be frivolous and just have *fun*.

"All right," she said and took a deep breath. "I was thinking about how right over there," she said and pointed to a crest of sand covered in clumps of grass, "is where I got my very first kiss."

His gaze narrowed. "Really?"

"Yep. I was thirteen and very naive." She laughed and grinned. "Hard to imagine, huh?"

He smiled, as though he'd guessed she was a teenage dork. "And?"

"And he was a boy I met on the beach. He was a cowboy," she said and met his eyes. "Like you, I guess. He had a horse and a hat and a nice smile and he kissed me."

"And that's it?"

She shrugged. "It was enough. It was everything a girl's first kiss should be... It was sweet and soft and his lips tasted like peppermint."

She smiled coyly, embarrassed by how foolish she must seem to him. But Tanner wasn't laughing. He was watching her with such burning intensity she couldn't move. The wind whipped around them and she shivered even though she wasn't cold. Something kindled between them. A look. A memory. Something she couldn't fathom. For the thousandth time she wished she knew him better. And she wished she wasn't scared to death of letting him into her life and then knowing he'd be out of it once he left.

"Anyway," she said, stepping back. "It was a long time ago. And I never saw him again."

"So he just kissed you and took off?" he inquired, continuing to walk. "That's not exactly chivalrous."

Cassie took a few long strides to catch up with him. "Actually, *I* took off. I spooked and ran." She came to a sudden stop and waited for him to halt and turn around. "We should get back. I promised Mary-Jayne I wouldn't be too long."

He crossed his arms, unmoving. "So why did you spook and run?"

"Because that's what I do," she admitted on hollow breath. "When it comes to getting close to someone I guess I spook easily."

He stared at her. "You didn't run from Doug."

"He was never around," she said quickly, hearing her words echo on the breeze. *Did I really say that?*

"But you wanted commitment," he reminded her. "Marriage, family…right?"

"I thought so," she said warily, feeling the intensity of his gaze so acutely it was like a fire racing over her skin. "But maybe…"

"Maybe it was safe to want it from Doug because you knew you'd never get it?"

There was something so elementally powerful about his words she stepped back, stunned by how much truth she heard. Was it possible? Had she set her sights and her dreams on a man she knew would never be able to deliver? Were her expectations and hopes that low?

"I don't know. Perhaps," she murmured, wavering between a sudden rage at Tanner for working her out, and an irrational fear that no one else ever would. "I don't usually psychoanalyze myself."

"You mean you don't dwell on your abandonment issues?"

"I don't have—"

"Sure you do," he said gently. "You lost your parents at a vulnerable age and now you expect everyone else to leave you, too."

"You lost your parents around the same age and you don't have—"

"Of course I do," he said, sounding suddenly impatient as he cut her off. "Anyone who loved Doug ended up as collateral damage in one way or another. I know that from experience. He dumped me into boarding school, remember? Why the hell do you think I'm back here, Cassie? Why do you think it's so important to me that Oliver doesn't grow up thinking that the people who are supposed to protect him didn't bail and take what's rightfully his?"

Chapter Seven

The moment the words were out of his mouth Tanner wanted to snatch them back. He'd said too much. Revealed too much. *Felt too much.* Cassie's eyes were wide and filled with questions. And he couldn't and wouldn't say anything more.

"What does that mean?"

He shook his head and turned. "Nothing. Let's go back."

"No," she said firmly. "I want to know what you mean. We're talking about you, not Oliver. We're talking about something Doug did to you…something he took from *you*. What was it?"

"Nothing," he said again and started walking back toward the kiosk.

Cassie moved up beside him and grasped his arm. "Tanner, stop. I want to know. I *need* to know."

"You don't need to know this," he replied and brushed her hand away.

"Please," she implored. "Tell me. Stop treating me like I'm made of glass. I can handle it...whatever it is."

"Go home, Cassie," Tanner said flatly. "I'll call you about the house in a day or so."

He strode up the beach and waited by their cars until she caught up. When she reached him her cheeks were ablaze and her blue eyes bore into his like icy chips.

"You're a real jerk, McCord, you know that!"

He bit back a grin. She had spunk, that's for sure. And he'd rather see her spirit than her tears. "Talk to you soon."

"So, that's it? You're just going to leave?"

He opened the car door. "I won't be far away."

That didn't seem to give her any comfort. "Go to hell."

He grinned. "Well, I'm not going that far...but I'll be at Ruthie's if you need me."

With that, she gave him one last glare before she got in her car and drove off.

By the time Tanner returned to the Nevelson farm it was past five. He hit the shower, changed into jeans and a T-shirt, and joined Ruthie on the porch for a beer.

"Girl trouble?" she asked with a wide grin.

Tanner bit back a smile. "Don't know what you're talking about."

Ruthie didn't let him off the hook. "You've got the look of a man with a woman on his mind."

He did, but he had no intention of admitting it. "I've got no such thing," he said and drank some beer.

The older woman harrumphed. "Deny it all you like, but I know what I see. Call me sentimental, but I don't wanna see you get hurt."

"I won't," he said quietly. "I know what I'm doing."

Yeah...right.

Ruthie didn't look convinced. "Just make sure you do.

And don't forget you promised to start long reining that ornery new colt tomorrow."

He hadn't forgotten. In fact, he was looking forward to working with the animal. It had been over a week since he'd been near a horse and he missed it as he missed air in his lungs. Plus, he knew working with the colt would take his mind off Doug, Cassie and the letters he'd discovered were in the safety deposit box that afternoon. Letters from Doug. Letters written on old-fashioned paper and with the gold fountain pen that had belonged to their grandfather. Letters to him. To Cassie. Letters his brother had written and sent because he was going into a covert, dangerous mission and wasn't sure if he'd return. They were essentially words written by a man who had predicted his own death. As expected, his brother had begged his forgiveness one final time while insisting none of his past actions were done out of malice. Tanner wanted to believe it. They were Doug's last words to him and should have given closure, and might have if it weren't for the letter he'd written to Cassie. It wasn't sealed and Doug would have to have known he'd read it. Tanner was also sure his brother would know he'd never let her read the words that would break her heart. Perhaps that's what Doug was hoping for? Maybe his brother wanted him to let him off the hook. And he would. But not to protect Doug. Rather to protect a woman who deserved better. Because it was there, in black and white, every possible callous, unfeeling thing a man could say to the woman who was going to have his child. As Tanner had scanned the pages, all the suppressed rage and censure he'd felt toward his brother had risen to the surface and consumed him like a rogue wave.

And he knew one thing.

Cassie would never know the truth.

His brother's legacy wouldn't be that of an unscrupulous

and self-absorbed bastard who didn't care who he hurt. She could spend her life thinking of Doug fondly and without knowing he intended to abandon her and the child she'd borne. Just as he'd done with Leah.

He'd give Cassie a few days to cool off and start work on the house the following week. But he missed Oliver. And he missed her, too, as much as he knew it was foolhardy. He had enough on his mind without wasting time missing her. The house had to be sold and hopefully it would go to contract before he headed back to South Dakota. He'd spoken to a couple of real estate brokers earlier that day and was sure the property would sell quickly once it was painted and the yard tidied up.

As promised, Tanner spent most of the next day long reining Ruthie's colt. He didn't hear from Cassie and figured she was still mad at him for shutting down their conversation at the beach. But he'd said too much. Besides which, he'd been sideswiped by her admitting she'd been kissed there for the first time.

He remembered everything about that day. He'd come to stay at Ruthie's for a couple of weeks during summer vacation and spent most of his time working his horse. When his parents died, Ruthie had agree to keep Rusty, the buckskin gelding he'd owned since he was a small child, at her farm. Vacation time was always spent at the Nevelson farm. That morning he'd been working Rusty along the sand bed. It was low tide and he'd spotted a pair of teenage girls watching him from the crest of a small dune. Boarding at a boys' school meant limited interaction with girls, and naturally curious about the opposite sex, he'd headed across the sand. He'd pulled up in front of the dune and heard their combined giggles.

The girl with pale blue eyes had immediately captured his attention and when she'd smiled Tanner's insides had jumped all over the place. They'd talked for just a moment and then Tanner had dipped his hat lower, clicked Rusty into a trot and headed back over the dune. But with the promise to meet her again the following day.

That's when he'd kissed her. Her first kiss. His, too.

Fourteen years later he met her again. Only this time she was living in Doug's house and sharing his brother's bed. And she didn't remember him. There was no recollection in her eyes. He'd been forgotten. As had their kiss.

Or so he thought.

But he had no intention of telling her that he was the boy she'd kissed. Things were complicated enough already. And he had enough on his mind without dwelling on that teenage kiss.

On Saturday morning, however, she turned up.

Tanner was in the corral and he eased the colt to a smooth halt when he saw her car pull up outside the farmhouse. He watched as Ruthie came down the steps and greeted Cassie by the vehicle. The two women chatted for a moment, and then Cassie pulled Oliver from the backseat. Within seconds the baby was in Ruthie's arms and he heard both women laughing. Something uncurled in his abdomen as he watched them together. Cassie's laughter traveled across the yard and he tried to concentrate on the horse and forget her. Which was impossible. Because while Ruthie took Oliver inside the house, Cassie headed toward the corral. And to him.

She really had no idea what she was doing. Except that she wanted some answers. And fast. She'd been stewing for three days. Getter madder, more confused and more determined than ever to find out what Tanner was really playing at. By the time she reached the round yard she was short on patience and breath.

He stopped what he was doing when she reached the fence.

"Cassie...hello."

He wore dark jeans and a blue shirt that stretched across his shoulders and outlined the strong musculature of his chest. His sleeves were rolled up and he wore a wide-brimmed cowboy hat. He looked, in a word, gorgeous. And he'd been in her thoughts all week.

"We need to talk."

He smiled. Damn. There was a tiny dimple in his cheek. How had she never noticed that before?

His brown eyes caught her gaze. "What about?"

"You know very well," she snapped back. "I may seem like a gullible doormat to you, Tanner, but be assured that I am not."

He actually laughed. "Doormat? I don't think that."

"You must," she said, hands on hips. "Otherwise you wouldn't keep avoiding my questions like a coward."

That got him. Right where it hurt. Because he was out of the corral and barely two feet in front of her within seconds. And he was angry. Well...good. She was angry, too. He stared at her. Through her. And with such blistering intensity it made her knees weak.

"So...go ahead," he said, his jaw so tight his lips barely moved. "Ask me."

She swallowed hard and ignored the rapid thump of her heart. "What happened?" When he didn't respond she pushed further. "What did Doug do?"

Tanner's expression was like granite. "There's no going back from this, Cassie."

"I don't care."

"Okay. Don't say I didn't warn you." He took a breath. Sharp. Short. And then he spoke. "He stole my inheritance."

Cassie stepped back. "What? I don't know what that means?"

"When our parents were killed he sold the farm that had been in our family for five generations and then shuffled me off to boarding school. The proceeds were split and since Doug was my legal guardian he had access to my trust fund."

"How...how much money was there?"

He named the sum. A huge amount. Hundreds and hundreds of thousands.

"And he stole it from you?" she asked, horrified. "From his only family?"

Tanner nodded. "Yes. He gambled. He wasted it on questionable investments. He bought cars, boats...anything he wanted."

"But why would he do—"

"Because he was selfish and irresponsible," he said, cutting her off. "Because he was like two different men. He was the soldier, brave and trustworthy. And he was the civilian, self-absorbed and deceitful." Tanner took a long breath. "Are you happy now, Cassie? Does knowing what Doug was capable of give you some insight you didn't previously have?"

She didn't want to believe it. Didn't want to imagine that the man she thought she loved could do something so despicable. "That's why you hated him."

He shook his head. "I didn't hate him. He was my brother and I loved him. I just didn't like him very much. And I made a promise to myself years ago that I would never act like him. Never be that kind of man."

Cassie sucked in some air. She had her answer. "That's why he left everything to you. He was ashamed."

"Probably."

"And that's also why you don't want the house and why

you're so determined not to challenge the terms of the will. And why you want to leave any money in trust for Oliver. Right?"

He nodded. "Right."

Cassie felt sick to the stomach. "I can't believe he'd do such a terrible thing."

"I've no reason to lie to you."

"I know that," she replied. "And I believe you. I just don't want to believe it."

"I told you there was no going back from this."

The sour taste in her mouth remained. It was reprehensible. The lowest of acts. And she was glad she knew.

"You know, despite what you think, I've never worn rose-colored glasses when it came to Doug."

One dark brow came up. "Really? You seemed to put up with his behavior for long enough."

"What does that mean?"

He shrugged one magnificent shoulder. "You said yourself that Doug was never around. Who puts up with that? Who values themselves so little that they would settle for a man who appeared to just want a warm body in his bed whenever he was in town?"

His words cut her to the quick, and without thinking she slapped his face. It was the first time she'd ever done anything like it.

Mortified, Cassie stumbled backward and landed against the fence. Her hand stung and she could see the growing outline of her fingertips on his cheek. Shame washed over her and she drew in a shaky breath. "I'm so... sorry... I shouldn't have—"

"No," he said with a wry half smile as he rubbed his cheek. "But I probably deserved it."

She wanted to agree, but couldn't. There was no excuse for what she'd done. "I really am sorry, Tanner. I don't know what it is about you…but you push my buttons in a way that's very confusing. One minute we're friendly and the next there's this…this unbelievable tension that I can't explain. But I am sorry I hit you. I would certainly never condone violence in any—"

He laughed loudly and she stopped speaking. "Ah, Cassie…I think we're both…*tense*. And I think we both know why."

There was an intimate, seductive tone to his voice and it wound up her spine like liquid. Cassie pushed back further against the corral and drew in a shallow breath. "I don't know what—"

"Sure you do," Tanner said as he stepped closer and rested one hand on the top fence rung. "And it certainly hasn't been easy being attracted to you and not being able to do anything about it."

Oh, sweet heaven…

Cassie's legs turned to Jell-O. She swallowed hard, watching him observe the movement of her throat with scorching intensity. He was close and she could feel the heat emanating from his body. Desire thrummed between them and she couldn't have denied it if she'd tried. It had been building all week. And longer. Since the first time he'd come to visit Doug several years earlier. Being around Tanner had made her nervous, on edge. Back then she'd put it down to him being unfriendly and distant. But now she knew the truth. He wasn't unfriendly. He was funny and charming and personable. The distance she'd felt had been of her own making. Her nerves were fueled by her awareness of him. Of her attraction. And now she had nothing to hide behind.

He wanted her.

She wanted him.

It was as simple—and as complicated—as that.

He reached up and touched her hair, twirling a few strands between his fingertips. The heat grew. Her awareness amplified by his close proximity. She could have ducked beneath his arm and ran. She could have found safety in the house with Ruthie and Oliver and defied the sudden desire racing across her skin.

It's wrong to want him...

But she didn't move. Every part of her was attuned to Tanner in that moment. Her breasts were barely inches from his chest and she fought the urge to press closer, to feel his strong body, to run her hands down his shoulders and arms and lose herself in his kiss.

"Do you think I'd do it here?" His voice was little more than a husky whisper as he looked down into her upturned face. "Do you think I'd kiss you here...out in the open? Is that what you want?"

What she wanted was to drag him into the stable and tear off his clothes and make love with him. Mindless, hot sex that would satisfy the passionate hunger thrashing through her body.

"No...no..." she said, her denials trailing off as he moved a little closer.

There was almost nothing between them now. Barely a whisper of space.

"You're sure?" he queried, his mouth against her ear.

Cassie felt his warm breath and her skin quickly turned to gooseflesh. No man had ever had such a profound sexual effect on her. Not Doug. Nor the one lover she'd had before him. This kind of thing didn't happen to her. She was an ordinary woman having an extraordinary reaction to the most beautiful man on the planet. And she couldn't control it. Couldn't contain it. Couldn't do anything other than stare into his dark brown eyes and wonder what his kiss would taste like, what his touch and complete possession would feel like.

And again, as if it had happened countless times before, she experienced a jolt of hazy recognition way down deep. As if...as if she'd known his kiss...his touch, in some long forgotten memory. In another life. Another time.

"We should get back to the house," he said softly, unmoving.

He was right. Ruthie Nevelson would have a bird's-eye view of them from her house. She was probably up there wondering what they were up to. They weren't touching. Weren't kissing. But she was pretty sure that from a distance it looked exactly as if they were.

"Yes," she said finally and ducked past him. "Good idea."

Her legs were still wobbly, but by the time she walked across the yard and reached the porch steps she'd regathered her composure and had stopped visibly shaking. She tapped on the door and waited for Ruthie's invitation to enter. She'd never been inside the Nevelson farmhouse before. But it was big and filled with beautiful antique furnishings. Cassie followed the sound of the other woman's voice and found her in the kitchen, with Oliver bouncing happily in her lap.

"He's an adorable little boy," Ruthie said when Cassie entered the room. "I can see why Tanner is so smitten."

Ruthie's brows were both up, as though there was a question in her words. Cassie did her best to ignore it. Imagining Tanner *smitten* or anything else wasn't good for her peace of mind. And it confirmed her suspicions that Ruthie had seen them by the corral.

"He's a good baby," she said as casually as she could. "I feel very blessed."

"You should," Ruthie said and sighed. "Every child is

a blessing. I never got to have any myself. But there's no point wailing about what isn't to be. Life's too short for wailing, don't you think?"

Cassie smiled. There was something incredibly likable about Ruthie Nevelson. It didn't surprise her that Tanner was so fond of the older woman.

Tanner...

In between the *almost kiss* and learning about what Doug had done, she was more confused than ever. Thinking about Doug's betrayal was mind-numbing. That he could be so callous, so inconsiderate and deceptive, chilled her to the bone. She felt deceived, too. By the man she'd believed she knew. By the man she'd believed she loved. Tanner had suggested she was simply warming Doug's bed. Was that all she was to him? Had she put her blinkers on to avoid seeing that was *all* she was?

As hard as it was to admit, Cassie knew that a man who could steal from his younger brother in such a terrible way could easily fool a gullible and trusting woman into thinking he loved her.

"Yes," she said and laughed softly. "There's no point in wailing. No point at all."

They heard a sound coming from the back and Ruthie got to her feet. "That'll be Tanner. Got him working to keep his mind off things."

"Things?" Cassie echoed.

"You know," Ruthie said and grinned. *"Things."*

You...

That's what the older woman meant. And Cassie wished she could work to take her mind off him, Doug and everything else. Not even Oliver could keep her thoughts on track.

"You know he's a good man, don't you?" Ruthie asked unexpectedly.

Cassie's skin heated. "Yes, of course I—"

"Too good to be messed with," Ruthie said and looked toward the back door. "You know what I mean. He got his heart broke a long time ago… I'd hate to see that happen again."

Cassie stilled. Obviously Ruthie was referring to what Doug had done with his inheritance. And of course Tanner was hurt by his brother's betrayal.

"I don't see how it will," she said and took Oliver into her arms. "He's leaving in a few weeks and won't be back for a while. If ever."

Ruthie looked at the baby. "Oh, he'll be back. His attachment to this little boy will keep him tied to Crystal Point."

"I'd like Oliver to know his uncle."

"Of course. You both have so little family it's important to keep in touch."

If it was a dig it was a soft one. And Cassie didn't mind. Ruthie Nevelson was like a grandmother to Tanner and she knew her motives were borne out of caring. Ruthie changed the subject and asked about her grandfather.

"He's not doing so well," she explained, remembering that Ruthie had known her granddad for many years. "I go and see him every week and sometimes he knows me and other times he doesn't."

Ruthie nodded. "It was good of Neville to take you in when your folks passed away. Especially when he was grieving the loss of his only son. I believe your grandmother had died only a year earlier."

"That's right. Gran had a seizure and died unexpectedly. Then my parents…" Her words trailed for a moment. "He was strong back then. And kind. He made a home for me and did his best. But I know the end is coming and as much as I'm prepared for it, I can't quite believe that once he's gone there'll only be Oliver and myself left in my family."

"Then you should get married and have a whole bunch of kids," Ruthie suggested. "I keep telling Tanner the same thing. Let this lonely old woman be a lesson to you." She gestured to their surroundings. "No point in having all this if you've no one to leave it to."

Marriage? More children? It was a lovely dream. "You're right. And I will." She smiled. "I promise."

"Watch making promises to Ruthie," a deep voice said from the doorway. "She'll hold you to them."

Ruthie guffawed and the sound made Cassie smile. Tanner stepped into the room and dropped his hat on the counter. Oliver squealed delightedly when he recognized him.

"Hey, little man," Tanner said and reached for him immediately. "Come here."

"See," Cassie complained lightheartedly. "I'm forgotten once he claps eyes on his favorite uncle."

Oliver was so happy to see Tanner it made her heart ache. And she was glad her son had someone else to love and protect him.

The only thing was, she wished she had someone like that, too.

"I'll make coffee and we'll go and sit in the front room."

"I really can't stay," Cassie said. "I have to—"

"Nonsense," Ruthie scolded gently. "I'd like to get to know Oliver a little better. And it's Saturday… What's more important than spending time with family on the weekend?"

She had a point. Even if thinking of Ruthie as family was a stretch. But she was family to Tanner, so Cassie wasn't about to argue the point. "Okay. I'll stay."

"Good," Ruthie said and pulled a tray down from a cupboard. "You two go on ahead and I'll bring it in."

Tanner was grinning, as if he knew exactly how it was to deny Ruthie Nevelson anything and not get your own way. He carried Oliver down the hallway and into the front living room. Cassie followed and stilled when she reached the doorway. The silky oak furniture and tapestries were magnificent and she let out a sigh.

"This is such a beautiful house."

Tanner was by the fireplace. "It became a home to me after my parents died."

Cassie crossed her arms. "We really did have similar childhoods. I mean, I know you were sent away to school, but you had a strong role model in Ruthie, like I did with my grandfather. Did you know our birthdays are only four days apart? I remember Doug telling me that a long time ago. We'll both be thirty-one next month."

He didn't say anything. He didn't move other than to gently rub the back of Oliver's head. Cassie looked at him and felt the heat in his stare.

It certainly hasn't been easy being attracted to you...

His words swirled around in her head. His confession should have sent her running. But she was inexplicably drawn to him. Like air to lungs. Like water to sand. Tanner McCord had awakened her sleeping libido with a resounding thud.

"How's your cheek?" she asked quietly.

"I'll live."

"I've never hit anyone before," she admitted. "You know, no siblings to wrestle with...no fights in the playground. That was my first slug."

"It was a good one."

She smiled and moved into the room. "Did you and Doug fight much?"

"No," he replied. "I guess the age difference made it hard to have the usual brother-on-brother wrestling matches. I did break his nose when I was eighteen, though."

Her eyes widened and she recalled Doug's slightly crooked nose. "On purpose?"

"Yeah. He hammered me afterward, but I still managed to get one good punch in."

Cassie grinned. "Well, I'm sure you had your reasons, considering the history."

He rocked Oliver gently in his arms and Cassie's heart wrenched seeing them together. He'd make such a good dad one day. She almost told him so, but stopped herself. There was enough tension between them without him mistakenly thinking she was lining him up as a candidate to be Oliver's father.

Which I'm not.

She shrugged and started looking at the rows of photographs above the fireplace and another row on the sideboard. There were pictures of Ruthie and her husband. Snapshots of horses and dogs and cattle. And there were some of Tanner, too. One from when he was at school and a few she recognized from the albums Doug had kept. A photo at the back caught her attention. It was obviously Tanner as a teenager, all rangy shoulders and long legs, wearing a plaid shirt and jeans and a cowboy hat. He stood beside a horse, a tall, pale coffee-colored animal that somehow tripped a wire in her brain. And a memory.

I know that horse...

I know that boy...

And then, like a speedy camera rolling out in reverse, realization hit.

The beach. The horse. The boy.

The kiss...

Cassie snapped her head around and stared at him. His

dark eyes narrowed just a fraction, enough for her to read the truth in them. He knew. He'd known all along.

"Oh, my God...that was you?" Her head reeled, her heart pounded. "That day on the beach...when we were young...you were the boy I..."

It made perfect, impossible sense. There had always been something familiar about Tanner. A kind of hazy awareness she couldn't decipher. Now she knew why. He *was* familiar. He was *that* boy. She looked at her son, so happy and content in Tanner's arms. Resentment flared and she quickly moved across the room and took her baby from his arms.

"I have to get out of here," she said and took a step toward the door.

He grasped her arm. "Cassie, wait—"

"Don't you get it?" she said, pulling free. "Every time I've been around you, I've always had this...feeling. This sense that I *know* you. It's twisted at my insides since that first time you came to visit Doug. I thought... I thought that I was just so attracted to you it made me imagine things. And I felt such guilt because I was with Doug and I shouldn't have been thinking that about someone else in that way...in *any* way. But it wasn't that at all. It was the memory of some silly schoolgirl infatuation when I was thirteen. It was some romantic fantasy I'd created in my head about being swept off my feet. And it stayed with me all my life. Even when I was with Doug, *especially* when I was with Doug, I was always comparing it to that feeling... that *fleeting* feeling I had when I was this lonely, love-struck thirteen-year-old crushing on the guy who kissed me for the very first time."

Within minutes she was out the room, out the door and in her car.

And driving away from the boy who'd captured her heart and the one man who had the power to break it.

Chapter Eight

Late on Sunday afternoon Lauren and Mary-Jayne arrived with pizza and sweet wine for their regular monthly get-together. Since Lauren's engagement and Oliver's birth they didn't catch up as often as they used to. However, they always made the most of their Sunday catch-up. It was over her first glass of wine and second slice of pizza that she told them about Tanner.

"That was him?" Lauren asked incredulously, eyes popping. "The boy on the beach?"

"Yeah…that was Tanner."

M.J. let out a long whistle. "What a tangled web we weave. Who would have thought that your first love would end up being *the jerk's* baby brother?"

"It wasn't love," Cassie corrected, ignoring the gibe about Doug. "We were kids and I only met him twice. And it was just a kiss."

"A kiss you've never forgotten," Lauren reminded her.

Cassie shrugged. "Every girl remembers her first kiss."

"Yeah," M.J. said and laughed. "But most of us would rather forget it. If I could erase the memory of Bobby Milton and his sweaty top lip I would do it gladly."

M.J. pretended to gag and they all giggled like teenagers. It felt so good to be with her friends. They shared a bond that had lasted decades. They'd rallied around her when Doug had been killed and then when Oliver was born. And she needed their support now, more than ever.

"So, are you going to kiss him again?" M.J. asked bluntly.

Cassie almost spat out her drink. "Of course not."

"Why not?" Lauren said. "He seems very nice and he's clearly interested in you."

"Because there's no point," she said quickly. "He's going back to South Dakota in a few weeks and the only thing I have time for is finding a new home for me and my son."

"A lot can happen in a few weeks," Lauren said and smiled. "Take it from me. It only took me that long to fall in love with Gabe."

"That was different," she said, holding on to her impatience. "Since you were looking for a relationship and I'm not. All I want is to find a home where I can live and raise my child. Do I like Tanner? Yes. Is he gorgeous and sexy and wonderful with Oliver? Yes. Do I think there's a future there? No. He's Doug's brother and that's simply too big a complication."

"Who are you trying to convince?" M.J. asked with a raised brow. "Us or yourself?"

Cassie ate some pizza and ignored her friend's gibe. They'd support her regardless. That was the way of best friends. "I know what I'm doing," she said.

But didn't believe it for a minute.

* * *

On Monday morning Tanner arrived at the house at nine o'clock with a painting contractor. The two men walked around the house discussing walls and ceilings and which rooms needed doing while Cassie remained in the kitchen with Oliver and felt like a spare part.

It's not my house... Remember that.

When the contractor left Tanner came into the kitchen and stood on the other side of the counter. "He'll be back on Wednesday morning. I thought we'd start in the bedrooms and work from the rear of the house."

"We?" she queried and sank her hands into the sinkful of soapy water. "There's not a whole lot of *we* in this, Tanner. It's your house, not mine. All I do is pay the rent and utilities. Which I'll continue to do until I find somewhere else to live. Paint whatever rooms you like, it makes no difference to me. I'll be out of here soon enough."

"You can stay until it sells."

"I'd prefer to leave as soon as I can."

"You mean you'd prefer to be stubborn and provocative."

She glared at him. "I'm not stubborn. And I'm definitely not provocative."

"Oh, yeah," he said and rested his hands on the counter. "You are."

"And you have an arrogant streak a mile wide," she yelled. "Contrary to what you might believe, you don't know what's best for me and Oliver. So back off."

He laughed loudly. "Why are you so mad at me? I'm only trying to help."

"Help someone else. I don't need or want anything from you."

"Where's all this resentment coming from, Cassie?" he

inquired, laughter still lingering in his eyes. "I thought we were friends."

Cassie pulled her hands from the sink, dried them quickly, then slammed them onto her hips. "You've got some nerve, you know that? After what happened the other day I'd think you would be—"

"So we made out when we were kids," he interrupted. "It's no big deal."

"No big deal?" she echoed. "Are you kidding? It's a huge deal. You knew. All along you knew and you didn't say anything."

He shrugged. "There was no point. And it was hardly a subject to broach when Doug was alive. We shared a kiss, Cassie. A long time ago. A lifetime ago. Forget about it."

She wished she could. "What about the other thing?"

"What other thing?"

Cassie inhaled, steadying her nerve. "You said you were attracted to me and—"

"So I'm attracted to you," he said quietly. "Stop over-thinking it."

"I can't." She crossed her arms over her chest. "And I can't believe you think it's okay and can dismiss it so easily."

"Did I say that?" he asked. "Did I once say it was okay? For the record—nothing is easy when it comes to you." He took a deep breath. "Yes, I'm attracted to you. Yes, I want to take you to bed and make love to you."

He heart stalled. "But—"

"But I know I can never do that because you love my brother."

Doug...

Had she spared him a thought since she'd seen Tanner on Saturday? Her feelings for Doug were so conflicted. And the more she knew Tanner the less she felt she knew Doug.

"I don't think… I mean, we'd be crazy to start something," she whispered. "And now that I have Oliver I can't afford to act crazy."

"I agree," he said flatly. "Forget it, like I said. I'll be gone in a few weeks and then you can get on with the rest of your life."

Sure. No problem.

And she knew he believed that about as much as she did.

Midweek Tanner took a call from the foreman at his ranch and discussed the new horses that were coming in over the next two months. His leg still hurt and he intended getting back to physical therapy when he returned home, but working with Ruthie's colt had confirmed that he was ready to get back in the saddle.

And it made him miss home. His ranch in Cedar Creek was as much a part of him as Crystal Point had been when he was young, and being in the small town had brought back a whole lot of memories. Some good. Some not. Hanging out with Ruthie was a bonus. So was spending time with his nephew. Oliver had quickly worked his way into his heart and Tanner knew he was going to miss the little guy when he returned to South Dakota.

And then there was Cassie…

She'd gotten into his heart, too, and he was trying his damnedest to get her out.

Her home was being sold and she had put on a brave face…but he wasn't fooled. And he felt a ton of guilt because of it. While the contractor worked on the house she kept insisting she was fine. While painters and yard maintenance workers came and went she was on hand making iced tea and obligingly moving belongings from one room to the next. And he still wasn't fooled. She could act as tough and indifferent as she wanted; Tanner knew that underneath she was barely hanging on.

"You know," she said on Friday afternoon as they inspected the paintwork in the third bedroom. "You're really lousy at choosing colors. What is that feature wall color... mission brown?"

"Donkey," he replied and shrugged. "And I did ask you to come with me and choose the palette."

Her mouth drew together tightly and she raised one shoulder. "Not my business."

"Well, if the house doesn't go under the hammer because I'm a little color-blind and you weren't charitable enough to help out, then it's on your head."

She sniffed. "Color-blind? You mean you have imperfections? I don't believe it."

"I'm as imperfect as the next guy."

"Nice to know." She walked around the room. "I think this needs to be done again," she said as she inspected the longest wall. "To something lighter. It's like a big brown tomb in here."

Tanner grabbed a swatch palette from a bucket near the door and pulled his wallet from his back pocket. He took out a credit card and held it toward her along with the swatches. "It's in your hands, then."

She looked at the card and frowned. "You're giving me your credit card?"

"Giving?" he echoed. "No. Loaning...sure."

She took both and looked at him oddly. "Doug never..."

"Does everything have to be about Doug?" he growled irritably.

"No, of course not," she said quickly. "It's only that he would never have trusted me to..." She stopped and looked at him. "It's nothing. Forget I said anything."

"Yeah, forget I said anything, too… I didn't mean to snap at you. Now go and spend some money."

She smiled. "I'll try not to do anything too irresponsible with it."

"I'll bet you haven't had an irresponsible moment in your life."

She laughed lightly. "Probably. However, I may be responsible, but according to some I am stubborn."

"And provocative," he reminded her.

She grinned, pushing the card into the pocket of her jeans as she clasped the swatches under one arm. "I'm sorry I haven't been much help this week. I know I'd promised I would be. It's just…"

"Too hard?" he prompted. "Too real? I get it, Cassie. I understand how difficult this must be for you."

She sucked in a breath. "Would you stop that," she snapped.

"Stop what?"

"Being so bloody understanding," she replied hotly. "About the house, about Doug…about *everything*. It drives me crazy."

"I drive you crazy?"

"It," she corrected. "*It* drives me crazy. You…well, you do…other stuff."

Tanner laughed. It was the most lighthearted conversation they'd had all week. And he'd missed it. *A little harmless flirting is okay.* "What kind of stuff?"

"Like I'd admit to anything." She tapped her back pocket. "Can you watch Oliver for an hour or so? I've got shopping to do."

"Absolutely."

"I'll grab dinner while I'm out," she said and then stilled. "I mean, if you'd like to stay."

"I would."

She nodded and quickly left the room. While she was gone he fed and bathed Oliver and had him well-settled in his crib by the time her car pulled up in the driveway. She bought paint and Chinese food. He put the paint in the spare room and they ate dinner from the cartons in the living room.

"You're something of an expert with those chopsticks," she remarked as she dipped into a carton for a chicken dumpling with a fork.

"I spent some time traveling through Vietnam and Cambodia before I went to Europe when I was young. So I picked up a few tips."

"I envy you," she said and sat back on the sofa, cross-legged. "I've never traveled. I've never been anywhere, really."

"Nothing wrong with being happy where you are."

"Happy or complacent?" She sighed. "I'm not sure I'd know the difference."

"You'd know," he assured her. "And as much as I enjoyed traveling, I was keen to put down roots when I reached South Dakota."

"Tell me about your ranch?"

"It's small by local standards," he said and drank some soda. "But the grazing is good for horses. The homestead is way too big for one, though."

"But one day you'll get married and have a family…so big will come in handy."

"I guess. One day."

"Have you ever been close?" she asked.

"To getting married? No."

She smiled a little. "Why not? You'd be something of a catch, I would think."

Tanner laughed. "I think… I think it's because I don't want to settle…if that makes sense. I remember my parents had a very strong relationship, grounded in friendship but also passionate. So I guess that's what I'm hoping for, too."

She sighed heavily. "Soul mates, you mean. Yeah, it's a nice dream."

"You don't believe in soul mates?"

"I do... I just don't know how many actually end up together. Although my friends Lauren and Gabe managed to find one another. So perhaps there's hope for us all."

"And you and Doug?"

She met his gaze. "I think you know the answer to that."

"He did love you," Tanner said quietly, absorbing her features in the lamplight. "In his own way. As much as he could love anyone."

She shrugged. "It doesn't really matter much anymore. I have Oliver and I will always be thankful to Doug for that."

Tanner heard the rawness in her voice and winced. "He was never the settle-down type, that's all. After our parents died all he wanted to do was leave Crystal Point for good."

"And that's when he sold your family farm, dumped you in boarding school and then a few years later squandered your inheritance?" Her brows came up. "What did he actually do with the money?"

"Some poor stock market decisions saw off most of it. A bit of gambling. I believe he bought a Porsche and crashed it." Tanner grinned and raised the chopsticks. "You know, the usual stuff. I was surprised when he bought this house...seemed way too sensible."

"And me?" she asked softly. "Were you surprised about me?"

Tanner dropped the chopsticks into the carton and placed it on the coffee table. Then he sat back, linked his fingers together and rested his hands on his stomach. "That he would want you? Not at all. As far as I know you're the first woman he actually attempted to settle down with. But he was a strange contradiction. In the military he was one kind of man, and out of it he was kind of lost."

"You're very forgiving."

Tanner shook his head. "I'm not forgiving at all. But if I hang on to my resentment, then he wins. Bitterness is a wasted emotion. I'd rather look for—"

"Love?" she asked, quietly cutting off his words.

Tanner stilled. The way she said it. The way the word hung in the air between them made his gut churn. He didn't want to talk to her about love. Not when his heart was in the firing line. "Aren't we all?" he queried vaguely.

"I guess. Some more than others."

He got to his feet. "I should go. I'll see you tomorrow."

And he left before he said or did something stupid.

The following week blurred into one day after another. There were more contractors. More painting. More trucks coming and going as the backyard got a serious overhaul with some new garden beds and paving. Cassie put on her brave face and helped out where she could. But inside she was churning. Tanner was mostly on hand to give orders to the contractors and she gave him the spare key so he could come and go as needed. But he never stayed longer than necessary. He spent time with Oliver. He was polite and obliging to her and that was all. They didn't talk about Doug or anything other than the house. She noticed he was unusually quiet and seemed to have a lot on his mind. She didn't ask. Didn't want to know. He was leaving in two weeks and she'd become so accustomed to having him around she knew she'd feel his departure when he went home.

Home...

Something she didn't have anymore. She'd put in a couple of rental applications during that week. Since there was nothing she could reasonably afford in Crystal Point she looked at renting in Bellandale. It wasn't optimal. In fact, it wasn't what she wanted at all. But it would be closer to the hospital when she returned to work and there were a couple of reputable day care centers close by.

It's not worth crying over...

On Saturday afternoon the last of the contractors left for the day and once Oliver was down for his nap she fed Mouse and then drew herself a long bath. By four she was in the kitchen, lazing around in her bathrobe and snacking on cheese and crackers. She was in the middle of filling the kettle when the doorbell rang. Thinking it might be Mary-Jayne stopping in for an impromptu visit, she steadied the towel she'd wrapped around her hair to keep her tresses dry, padded down the hallway on bare feet and opened the door.

And then rocked back on her heels.

It was Tanner. And he looked so gorgeous it stole her breath.

Usually he dressed in faded jeans and T-shirts. But the man who stood at her door looked as if he'd stepped out of the pages of a cowboy magazine. His jeans were dark and tailored and the white twill shirt fit across his shoulders, tapering down over his chest and washboard belly. He wore a thin leather bolo tie and a thick leather belt with a shimmering silver buckle and cowboy boots. He held a felt hat in one hand and car keys in the other.

Cassie swallowed hard. "Oh…hi."

He looked her over in a kind of slow, leisurely way that made her toes curl. The bathrobe was thin, and knowing there was only a light layer of fabric covering her nakedness quickly increased her awareness of him.

"Hello. Can I come in?"

She pulled the front of her robe secure and opened the

screen. "Of course." Once he was in the hall she asked the obvious question. "What are you doing here?"

Tanner dropped his keys and hat onto the hall stand. "I thought we could go out."

What did that mean? She tilted her head, and as the towel fell in her hands her hair cascaded around her shoulders. The movement seemed to stop him in his tracks. He watched her intently and heat quickly fanned through her blood. *One look,* she thought. *That's all it takes.* Damn Tanner McCord and his beautiful hide.

She quickly pulled herself together. "Out?"

"To the Rosemount Rodeo," he explained. "Ruthie's competing in a senior's team penning event and I thought it would be nice to cheer her on."

Which didn't explain why he was on her doorstep. "So, this would be a date?"

Color slashed his cheeks. He was embarrassed. Was she so *undatable*? "Well...no...only in the way that we'd be together."

"Like a date?" she said and smiled, and then let him off the hook. "I can't get a sitter for Oliver at this time of—"

"The baby comes, too, of course," he said. "It's something of a family event anyhow. He'll be quite safe."

Cassie shook her head. "I don't know... I've only just put him down for a nap and I'm not dressed and I probably—"

"I'll wait," he said easily.

She was about to refuse and then changed her mind. What was the harm? And it beat spending another lonely Saturday night alone. "Okay. Give me half an hour."

It took nearly forty minutes, but by then she was changed into a long denim skirt and pale blue sweater and had put on makeup, styled her hair and got Oliver ready.

"Impressive," Tanner remarked when she came into the living room. "Just over half an hour and you're done."

"Thirty-eight minutes, to be exact. So, are we taking my car or yours?"

"Mine," he replied. "I had a baby seat fitted this morning."

Cassie didn't hide her surprise. "You did? Why?"

He shrugged loosely. "For Oliver. I'll leave it with you when I go home."

Cassie tried to ignore the way her insides contracted at the idea of him returning to South Dakota. Of course she knew it was inevitable. He would leave and she and Oliver would be alone again.

Once they were outside, he lifted Oliver from her arms and gently strapped him into the baby seat she recognized as an expensive brand and one she hadn't been able to afford when she'd purchased the basic model that was buckled in the back of her old Honda.

"Incidentally," he said once the back was shut and he'd opened the passenger door, "you look lovely."

Cassie blushed. "You don't look so bad yourself, cowboy."

It was the grandest of understatements. In all her life Cassie had never found any man as attractive as she found Tanner. He was handsome, for sure, but there was something about him that appealed to her on a sensory level. While Doug had been charming and loud and always looking for attention, his brother was quieter and clearly more at home in his own skin. Gone was her idea that Tanner was some kind of disinterested loner. He was, in fact, the complete opposite. He liked company. He was funny and kind and just a little bullheaded and the more time she spent with him the more she liked him.

More than that.

Cassie knew she was in danger of falling for him…and it scared her to pieces.

By the time they reached the Rosemount Rodeo the sun was going down. There was a show ground attached to the horse arena and Cassie spotted a Ferris wheel and a few other recognizable carnival rides. A male voice was talking on the loudspeaker and there was music coming from a small stadium behind a sideshow alley. Tanner found a parking space close to the entrance gates, and once they got Oliver settled in his stroller he called Ruthie on the phone and they made their way toward the rows of stables and corrals. They stopped by the competitors' gate and waited.

"Ruthie should be along soon. She's only in one event," he explained and positioned himself in front of her and the stroller so they were out of the way of horses and riders passing by.

Cassie didn't mind. Having grown up in Crystal Point, the smell of horses and cattle was a familiar one and she liked the carnival atmosphere created by the riders, spectators and animals.

"It's fine," she said and smiled. "Thanks for getting me out of the house. I've become something of a hermit since Oliver was born."

"Managing a newborn alone couldn't have been easy."

She shrugged and glanced at Oliver gurgling happily in his stroller. "I had Lauren and M.J. on standby if I needed help. And he's such a good baby I really can't complain."

"You're an excellent mom," he said softly and touched her shoulder. "He's a lucky kid."

"Thanks," she said and felt the heat of his touch right through to her bones. "But I'm simply flying by the seat of my pants. He makes it easy. And you've made it easier, too," she said, smiling as she reached up and laid her hand on his chest. His heart pounded beneath her palm. The beat was strong and steady. Like everything about him. "So, thank you."

"Tanner!"

At the sound of someone calling his name she dropped her hand to her side like a stone. They both turned to find a middle-aged couple standing about twenty feet away, waving their arms in a way that indicated they knew him. She looked at Tanner and saw his expression harden instantly.

"Be back in a minute," he said and began to move off.

Cassie grasped his arm. "Is everything okay?"

"Fine," he assured her and gently removed her hand. "Stay here. I'll be back soon."

She stayed put and watched him stride across the gravel. The couple, a man and woman in their late fifties, greeted him with what looked like genuine joy. She watched with interest as he shook the man's hand and lightly kissed the woman's cheek. So, he did know them. And quite well by the look of things. She pushed back the tiny surge of exclusion and fiddled with the strap on her tote while keeping a discreet eye on Tanner and his friends.

"There you are!"

Ruthie Nevelson's voice quickly distracted her. The older woman was striding toward her, dressed in moleskins, a bright orange shirt and fancy vest with diamantés sewn across the lapel.

"Hi, Ruthie."

She reached them and grinned widely. "I've been looking forward to seeing this young fella again." As she peered into the stroller, Oliver gurgled. "I'm pleased Tanner talked you into coming."

"Me, too," she said and smiled.

"Where is he?"

Cassie pointed to where he stood, now deep in conversation with his friends. "There."

Ruthie frowned and her hands moved to her bony hips. "Oh…I know them. That's Malcolm and Sue Stewart."

"Who?"

"Leah's parents. Awful business, what happened to that girl. Broke poor Tanner's heart. Worse thing he did was introduce her to that no good—" Ruthie stopped and looked as though she'd said something she shouldn't have. "I better get—"

"Who's Leah?" Cassie asked quickly, figuring she must have been more than a friend and getting more curious by the second.

Ruthie waved a hand dismissively. "Oh, just an old friend of Tanner's. Well, best I get back to my horse. I'll see you later at the dance."

"Dance?"

"Sure," she said and winked. "I'm going to watch this young man," she said and pointed to Oliver. "While you dance with that young man," she added and gestured toward Tanner. "See you later."

Once she'd disappeared from view Cassie turned her attention back to Tanner and saw he was now on his way back to her. When he reached her he was smiling, but Cassie saw the tension in his jaw.

"Sorry about that."

"Who are they?"

He shrugged. "Just some people I used to know."

"People?" Her brows came up.

"Parents of an old friend," he said vaguely. "We should go and get seated before—"

"Leah's parents?"

He stilled instantly. "How do you know that? Did Doug say something to you about—"

"What's Doug got to do with it?" she asked as her skin prickled with an unexpected sense of apprehension. "Ruthie was just here and said something about it. Tanner, who's Leah?" she asked again.

"Just an old friend, like I said."

"An old girlfriend?" she corrected, oblivious to the people walking by. "Right?"

"Yes."

"*Your* old girlfriend? And something bad happened to her?"

"I'd rather not—"

"Tell me," she insisted. "What happened? What's the big secret? Why did Ruthie look like she'd said something she shouldn't?"

"I have no idea," he said flatly. "And it's not important so let's—"

"Leah was your girlfriend?" she asked, pushing relentlessly for more information. "And then?"

His eyes darkened so they were almost black and his jaw looked so tight it could have been carved from granite. "She got pregnant and lost the baby. Afterward she had a kind of breakdown and has been in and out of hospitals ever since."

Cassie gripped his forearm. "Oh, God, Tanner…I'm so sorry. I didn't know you'd lost a child. Now I understand why it's so important to you that Oliver—"

His expression was unreadable as he shook his head. "*I* didn't lose a child. She did. The baby wasn't mine."

Cassie's blood stilled in her veins. "Not yours? Then who…?"

As her words trailed the thought of the most unimaginable betrayal flashed through her mind. *No.* It couldn't be. She looked at him and shook her head, not wanting to believe it.

But saw the terrible truth in his eyes.

Chapter Nine

"It was Doug?"

Tanner flinched. "Yes."

She looked at him, her eyes huge in her face and every old hurt he'd ever felt he saw in her expression. "That's the history between you... It's not about the inheritance. It was about a girl?"

He nodded and reached down to ease Oliver from the stroller. "She fell in love with him. We were young and just out of school and I guess he was older and experienced and more exciting to her."

"Did Doug love her, too?"

"He never said," Tanner replied, hating how the lie tasted in his mouth. Doug had said he'd loved Leah. Just as he'd said he'd loved Cassie. But he wasn't about to tell her any more. Or how Doug had told Leah to terminate her pregnancy and then promptly broke off their affair when she said she wanted to keep the baby. Cassie would work out the pattern of Doug's behavior in a heartbeat.

He held Oliver close to his chest and experienced an almost painful surge of love for the little boy. He remembered how Leah's parents had remarked what a lovely family he had and Tanner hadn't corrected them.

If only it were true...

If Cassie and Oliver were his he would never let them go. But they weren't. She'd loved Doug. As Leah had.

Admit it...you'd be her consolation prize.

"He never told me any of this," she said. "Not a word. I didn't know him at all."

Tanner wasn't about to agree with her. "Come on, let's get seated. We don't want to miss Ruthie's ride."

"Tanner, I—"

"Later," he said and grabbed her hand. "This isn't the place to have this discussion. We'll talk about it later."

She nodded and they walked into the stands, finding a spot that was close to the exit in case they needed to leave in a hurry. Ruthie's event was on a few minutes later and Tanner watched with pride as his friend came out and cut the tagged beasts out of the herd, and then worked with her team to corral them well within the allocated time.

Afterward, they headed for the sideshow alley, where Tanner won a stuffed pelican for Oliver on the horseshoe toss and a pair of oversize hot-pink sunglasses for Cassie on the rifle range. They spent a leisurely hour together and it only served to amplify every buried feeling he had for her. He fought the urge to hold her hand and instead carried Oliver while she perused the craft stalls. He knew she was tense. He could see it in her walk and the tight way she held her shoulders back. And he knew she was thinking about Doug. And about Leah.

But it wasn't the time or place to have that conversation.

When she was done with the sideshow ally they made their way toward the food tent, and once they found seats he bought them burgers and fries while she gave Oliver his bottle. Ruthie turned up and when they finished eating they all moved to where the band was playing. By now Oliver was asleep and tucked in his stroller, and Ruthie waved them onto the dance floor.

"Are you sure?" Cassie asked him. "Your leg isn't—"

"It's fine," he lied, thinking his leg ached like the devil because he'd done way too much walking for one evening. But the idea of holding Cassie in his arms just once was too tempting to refuse. She didn't protest and when they reached the dance floor the song changed to a slower ballad.

"I did warn you, remember," she reminded him, "that I couldn't dance."

Tanner smiled and drew her in his arms. "And remember what I said? Just sway."

He wrapped his arms around her and could feel every lovely curve as he drew her closer. Tanner rested one hand on her hip and linked the other with hers. They danced slowly, not speaking, just moving together as if they'd danced a hundred times before. It struck him profoundly how effortless it was to be with her. How natural it was to hold her. And how easy it would be to kiss her. When the song ended she pulled back and looked up at him.

"Thank you," she said. "It's been a long time since I've done that. But I think I'd like to go now. We really need to talk and I'd like to do it at home."

Tanner nodded and they left the dance floor. It took fifteen minutes to say their goodbyes to Ruthie, collect Oliver and head back to the car. And another thirty minutes to reach Crystal Point. He pulled into the driveway and once they were out of the car she took the baby inside and put him to bed. By the time he'd fed Mouse and let the dog outside, she was in the lounge room, pacing the floor.

"Is Oliver settled?" he asked from the doorway.

"Yes." She remained standing, arms crossed, chin raised. "Did you find out about what Doug had done with Leah before or after he stole your inheritance?"

Straight to the point. A trait of hers he'd come to recognize. "After. Before. It was all around the same time."

Her gaze narrowed. "So, he stole your money and your girlfriend and got her pregnant?"

"Yes."

She dropped down onto the love seat in the corner. "I think I need to throw up."

Tanner moved into the room and stood behind the sofa. "It was a long time ago."

"Which doesn't change how utterly despicable it was."

"No," he said. "But time does alter perspective on things."

She shook her head and stared at him. "So you simply forgive and forget and move on?"

"Or get bogged down with anger and resentment," he replied. "And that's no way to live."

She twisted her hands in her lap. "I feel like... I feel like I suddenly know nothing of the man I knew, the man who fathered my son. The man you describe...he's a stranger. He's a cold, unfeeling stranger who did whatever he wanted and didn't care who got hurt in the process."

"Then don't remember him that way," Tanner said and came around the sofa. "Remember him as the man who made you laugh. The man you loved."

"How can I?" she implored. "I'd be living a lie. How could I love a man who did such things? That would make me...pathetic."

"Or human."

She jumped to her feet. "Stop that. Stop making excuses... for Doug...for me. Stop being so forgiving and get mad at him!"

The passion in her voice shifted the mood in the room on some kind of invisible axis. Tanner stared at her, wholly aware of her in a deep, soul-wrenching way. She was angry and confused and he watched as her rage gathered momentum. He knew that about her. He knew she was passionate and spirited and not the quiet wallflower his brother had often described. Around him she was fiery and full of life. She was combative and argumentative and stirred his blood and libido. And he wanted her. In his arms. In his bed. In his life.

Suddenly she was in front of him, hands on hips, her cheeks ablaze, chest heaving as she drew in large gulps of air. Heat swirled between them and without thinking he grasped her shoulders and pulled her close. Her arms dropped and then she was against him, breast to chest. And he claimed her lips. As he'd done when they were thirteen. As he'd imagined a thousand times since.

And she kissed him back. She opened her mouth and let him inside. She wound her tongue around his and groaned low in her throat when his hands moved down her arms and settled around her back, drawing her closer. There was heat and passion and urgency in the kiss. And it went on and on. He didn't stop. She didn't pull away. Her hands were on his shoulders and she sighed against his mouth in complete and utter surrender.

And in that moment Tanner knew he was done for.

He loved her.

And there was no going back. Nowhere to run. No part of his mind or body that could conceal what he'd tried so hard to deny for so long.

"Cassandra..." He whispered her full name against her

lips. "Let me stay tonight. I want to make love to you so much."

And that's when she froze.

She wrenched free and stepped back. "Why?" she asked, breathless and suspicious.

Tanner stared at her. "Why?" He repeated her question. "Why do you think?"

She took another step backward. "That's what I'm asking. Why?" She took a deep breath. "Payback maybe?"

"Payback? What does that mean?"

"You get into my bed," she shot back, eyes blazing, "like Doug got into Leah's all those years ago."

Disbelief surged through him. "That's ridiculous. You don't actually believe I would do that to you?"

"I don't know what to believe anymore," she said, shaking her head. "I didn't think Doug was the kind of man to betray his only brother in such a terrible way…but I was wrong. And I'd known him for three years. And since I've really only known you for two weeks how can I be sure of your motives?" She moved to the mantel and waved a hand past Doug's photo. "All I know is that I'm not going to make a mistake that will end up with me having all these… *feelings*…and then end up looking like a first-rate fool."

Tanner's heart thumped in his chest. "You think making love with me would be a mistake?"

"I think making love with you would be out of this world," she said quietly. "And then I'd wake up in the morning and remember you are leaving soon. And then I'd also remember that Doug treated you badly and it would make perfect sense that you'd want a little revenge."

Tanner rocked back on his boots. "I don't want revenge. I never did."

"Then what do you want?" she shot back. "A ready-made family? Because that's what you get with me, Tan-

ner. You get me and Oliver. Your brother's *leftover* family.
The family he never got to claim because he was killed.
How could you possibly want that? Not after what he did
to you. Even I'm not *that* naive."

Tanner heard the pain in her words. Felt them through
to his bones. The truth about Doug teetered on his lips.
But he could never tell her that his brother had no intention of claiming her and Oliver. Even if she suspected it,
he couldn't tell her. Hurting Cassie was the last thing he
would intentionally do. It didn't matter how he felt...Doug
would *always* be between them.

It was insurmountable. Impossible. And foolhardy to
think otherwise.

"I'll see myself out," he said flatly. "Good night."

He didn't wait for a response and it took less than a
minute to get to his car and drive off.

"So, what happened then?"

Cassie wasn't the kiss-and-tell type. But she'd needed
someone to talk to and M.J. was her friend, even though
the other woman usually dished out the kind of advice she
often didn't want to hear. The alternative was to speak to
Lauren. But she was happily wrapped up in her fairy-tale
engagement with Gabe Vitali, so Cassie figured M.J. was
the better option.

"After we kissed?"

Just thinking of the kiss they'd shared made her head
spin. It would have been so easy to let him stay.

"Yeah," M.J. said and sighed. "After the kiss, what
then?"

"We just came to our senses."

"You did or he did?"

"Both," she replied and poured a second round of coffee for them both. "The truth is I don't know how to feel about him."

"Because of Doug?"

"Because of *him*," she replied. "Because he's only here temporarily. Because he's handsome and nice and so incredible with Oliver that I could easily fall... You know what I mean."

"Fall in love?"

"Yeah," she admitted, terrified to even imagine the idea. "I was so close to saying yes when Tanner said he wanted to stay the night with me. But I was so scared about what it would mean. For him. For me. Even for Oliver. Sex would just complicate things even more than they already are."

"Sex usually does," M.J. said with a wry smile. "But if you like him..."

"I do like him. That's the trouble."

"I think the trouble is that you're scared of loving anyone again," M.J. said astutely. "Doug wasn't exactly Mr. Commitment or Mr. Reliable and you're afraid that Tanner won't be, either."

"But he is," she said and sipped her coffee. "That's the thing...I know he's different from Doug but I'm still unsure. I'm still scared."

"Well, no one ever said love was rational. Maybe you simply need to talk to him again. Have you seen him since?"

Cassie shook her head. She hadn't seen Tanner for two days. "He's probably avoiding me. The house painting and the gardens have been finished so there's no need for him to be here."

"I saw the for-sale sign out front. I'm sorry."

She sighed. "Well, I knew it was coming. The real estate people came through last week and took pictures and the sign went up early this morning. I almost wish it sells quickly so I'm forced to find somewhere straightaway. I've had no luck leasing a new house. The two I applied for that I can afford won't take a dog. So I'm back trawling the listings again."

"Something will turn up," M.J. assured her. "And I can always take Mouse if it comes to that."

"I know," Cassie said and sighed. "But I need to stand on my own two feet. And that means finding a place for myself, my son and my dog—all of whom are my responsibility. As for Tanner...he'll be gone soon. I doubt he'll stay until the house sells. He's got his ranch to get back to. And his life. And I'm just a little blip on his radar."

"Are you sure about that?"

"I'm not sure about anything," she admitted. "But I do know I'm not courageous enough to lay myself on the line. Been there, done that."

M.J. came around the counter and gave her a much-needed hug. "I still think you should talk to him. Sticking your head in the sand didn't do you any favors when it came to Doug. And it won't do you any favors with Tanner, either."

"I know. But I'm not that brave."

"Sure you are," her friend said gently. "You're as brave as they come. Make the call and talk to him. You never know what might happen."

That's the problem...

How could she explain how scared she was? Or how confused she was about Tanner? Cassie took a long breath and nodded. "Okay. I will."

But she didn't. Because late that afternoon her grandfather had a massive stroke and was rushed to intensive care. Cassie dropped Oliver at Lauren's and rushed to the hospital, where she found her grandfather fighting for his life in a hospital room, his frail body connected to tubes and monitors. The doctor saw her immediately and gave her the grim news. It didn't look good and her grandfather was critical. He probably wouldn't wake up. There wasn't anything they could do and she needed to prepare herself. She needed to say goodbye.

Then they let her see him. She touched his forehead and told him she loved him. She thanked him for being a loving, caring grandparent and hoped in some way he heard and understood her words.

After a while, with her emotions at breaking point, she got up and headed out to the waiting room. She was still sitting there at eight o'clock. Still there as other worried relatives, other families, came and went. Still there as nurses changed shifts. And still there when a tall, jeans-clad figure came into the room and sat down beside her. She didn't move. Didn't speak. But a welcome relief washed over her the moment Tanner reached out and grasped her hand, enfolding it within his.

"How did you—"

"I spoke to Lauren," he explained softly. "She told me you were here."

Cassie nodded and heat prickled behind her eyes. "I'm so sick and tired of death," she said, her throat thick. "I mean, I knew this day was coming. In my mind I've been prepared for it in a hundred ways. But right now, right here, all I can think is how I'm so tired of losing the people I love. I'm tired of loss and grief. Every time I lose someone I feel my world getting smaller…because I'm just that little bit more alone."

He squeezed her hand and she experienced a connection deep down. "You're not alone."

For now…

But she didn't say it. All she could do was remember their kiss. Remember how she'd felt in his arms.

Complete...

That's how he made her feel. In a way no man ever had before. Not even Doug. Cassie dropped her head to his shoulder and closed her eyes. He was strong, a rock, a haven for her fragile heart when she needed comfort and understanding. And he knew it. Their connection was deep, borne out of sharing a similar road in life. They could, she suspected, become the firmest of friends. And lovers. And more.

And it terrified her.

Cassie believed she'd loved Doug. He'd turned up in her life at a time she'd been vulnerable and alone, and for a while he'd made her feel as if she was part of something. A couple. A family. But deep in her heart she'd never felt truly cherished. Yet she hadn't questioned his commitment, even as he drifted back and forth into her life during the brief years they were together. She accepted it. Blindly. Foolishly. Because she'd never truly believed she deserved more from him...or from anyone.

Knowing what Doug was really like had changed that. She *did* deserve more. Only, she was too scared to trust what her heart and body yearned for.

When the doctor returned half an hour later and told them her grandfather had passed away, Cassie gripped Tanner's hand as hard as she could. He sat with her for a while and then later he drove her car back to Crystal Point and left his rental in the hospital car park. They stopped by Lauren's and Cassie remained in the car while Tanner collected her son. Lauren didn't come out and Cassie was grateful. She didn't need sympathy. She didn't want hugs and kind words. She wanted the comfort of silence. And the strength of broad shoulders that she knew instinctively would be there if she needed them.

Tanner didn't say a word on the drive home, nor when

he took a sleeping Oliver from the backseat and followed her wordlessly up the path and then inside. He put Oliver to bed and found her on the sofa in the living room, hands tucked in her lap.

"The baby's asleep," he said. "You should get some rest, too… You'll have a hard day tomorrow."

She knew that. There were plans to be made. A funeral to arrange. Her grandfather's things to collect from the nursing home. Cassie nodded and stood as a lethargic numbness crept over her skin and seeped into her blood.

"Thank you for being with me tonight."

He didn't move from his spot by the door. "Go and sleep. I'll tend to the baby when he wakes during the night."

"I can't ask you to—"

"You're not," he said, cutting her off. "Go to bed, Cassie. I'll see you in the morning."

She stood and walked toward him, all her emotional strength zapped and with no energy to disagree. "Okay. Thanks."

He reached out and held the back of her neck for a moment, rubbing her skin with his thumb. Then he softly kissed her forehead. "Good night."

Cassie walked down the hallway to her bedroom, closed the door and dropped onto the bed. She tried to cry. She tried to weep away the pain in her heart. But no tears came.

Neville Duncan's funeral was a somber affair. Around one hundred and fifty people turned up for the service and most stayed for the wake held underneath a canopy in the gardens of the chapel at the cemetery. Cassie was stoic the entire afternoon and Tanner kept a close and watchful eye over her as she politely thanked her grandfather's friends for coming.

Once the wake was over about twenty of her friends

and some colleagues from work came back to the house, where Lauren's mother had arranged for a catered meal for another, more intimate gathering. Tanner kept Oliver in his arms for most of the day and was feeding the baby in the kitchen when Ruthie spoke from the doorway.

"He's very attached to you."

Tanner looked up and smiled. "It's mutual."

Ruthie came into the room and rested her hands on the back of a chair. "You plannin' on sticking around longer than you'd thought?"

"Not at this stage. The house is on the market, so we'll see what happens."

Her gaze flicked to Oliver. "It's gonna be hard for you to leave. I mean, now you've got something to stay for."

He rocked Oliver gently. "I'll come back to see him when I can."

Ruthie cocked her head to one side. "That's not exactly what I meant. You still aiming to get your heart broken again?"

"Not a chance."

"Good," she said and smiled. "Now, get back to South Dakota, find yourself a wife and make a couple of these," Ruthie said and pointed to the baby. "Because this daddy stuff really suits you."

Tanner laughed softly. Ruthie had a way of cheering him up. And she was right. He loved hanging out with Oliver and being around him only confirmed what he'd begun to suspect—he was ready for his own family. After Ruthie left he put the baby in his crib and walked back into the front living room. There were only a few people remaining—Lauren and her fiancé, Gabe, M.J. and two older couples he remembered were Lauren's and M.J.'s parents. Cassie was by the window, sitting alone, her gaze focused on the teacup in her hand. He walked across the room and perched on the stool next to her.

"You okay?"

She looked up. "Sure."

"Oliver's in his crib, sleeping soundly."

She nodded. "Thank you for looking after him. It's been a busy day for him."

"He's handled it. He's tough…like his mom."

Her brows came up. "I'm not so tough. This is just my disguise."

Tanner glanced around the room. "Well, I don't think anyone has figured that out. And your secret is safe with me."

She leaned closer. "I wish…" Her whisper faded for a second. "I wish everyone would leave."

Tanner moved forward. "I'm not sure being alone is the—"

"I won't be alone," she said, interrupting him. "I have Oliver." She stopped and met his gaze. "And you."

Tanner's stomach clenched. All day she'd held it together, as he'd known she would. She'd spoken at the service, giving a short eulogy for her grandfather, and he'd marveled at her strength and resilience in the face of her grief. But he knew she was lost inside. He knew her heart was broken. And he wished he could fix her. He wished he could ease the pain in her heart and offer comfort. When all he could do, he knew, was simply be a friend. He couldn't hold her. He couldn't take her in his arms and stroke her skin and kiss her lips and help her forget her troubles.

It was another half an hour and nearly seven o'clock before the last guests left. By then he could see she was almost at the breaking point. Her back was ramrod straight, her arms clasped tightly around her waist and her eyes shadowed with a heavy, inconsolable pain.

Once the front door was closed and she'd waved off her friends she joined him in the kitchen, where he was stacking the dishwasher to keep his hands busy and his mind off taking her in his arms.

"Well," Cassie said with a weary sigh as she came around the counter. "I'm glad that's over."

"It's been a hard day. But I know your grandfather would have been very proud of you."

"I hope so."

He shut the dishwasher and straightened. "Do you need anything? Lauren's mother stored the leftovers in the fridge if you're hungry."

"I don't think my stomach would tolerate food at the moment."

"You should eat something."

"I can't..."

Her body shook slightly and as she gripped the back of a chair for support, Tanner raced around the counter and reached her in a few long strides.

"Cassie?"

She looked up and the tears in her eyes tore through him. "I feel so..."

"I know," he said and gathered her close. "I know, sweetheart."

She sighed heavily and pressed her face into his chest. And then she cried. Heavy, racking sobs that made him ache inside. Tanner cradled her head and held her, feeling her despair through to his bones. It was several minutes before she moved, and when he felt her resistance Tanner released her and she stepped back unsteadily.

"I'm sorry," she said with a hiccup as she wiped her cheeks. "I promised myself I wouldn't do that today."

"You're allowed to grieve, Cassie."

She shook her head. "That's just it…I'm tired of grieving. I grieved my parents and then Doug and now…this. I can't do it. I can't bear the hollow feeling and the sadness. It's too hard and it's not what I want."

"Then what do you want?"

She raised her chin. "I want to stop living my life like I'm all out of backbone."

"That's not what—"

"It is," she insisted, her voice filled with raw emotion. "It's what I've always done. I always take the safe road. I've never been anywhere. I've never been on an airplane or hiked a mountain or bungee jumped off a ledge. I never challenge anything or anyone. I never say what I really want to say. I always comply. And I never have the courage to say what, or when, or who. All my adult life I've put up with people walking over me, with being overlooked in my work, with my boyfriend taking me for granted… and I've had enough. I want more… I want…"

"You want what?"

Her blue eyes glittered brilliantly. "I want… I want you."

Chapter Ten

It wasn't what she'd expected to say. Or planned. But she was so weary from saying and doing what was expected. In that moment, while he watched her with such profound, heated intensity, Cassie knew exactly what she wanted for the first time in her life. And who. Even if it was simply for one night.

"Cassie, I—"

"Don't say no to me," she implored. "Not tonight."

He didn't move. He looked startled. "You don't know what you're saying."

"I do," she insisted. "I know exactly. Days ago you said you wanted to make love to me."

"And days ago you said it would be a mistake."

He was right. She had said that. Out of fear. And guilt. And some crazy notion that he wanted her out of some kind of cruel revenge. But Tanner wasn't that kind of man. She knew that deep in her heart. "I was wrong to say that to you. It's not what I think. What I feel."

He didn't look convinced. "Sex isn't the answer to erase the pain you're feeling, Cassie. All it will do is confuse us both."

"Maybe I want to be confused," she said and took a step closer, thinking how handsome he looked in his dark suit and tie. "Maybe I want to stop doing what I think I *should* and do what I *want* for a change. And maybe I want to feel something other than grief and sadness. I want to feel heat and sweat and pleasure and—"

"And you'll regret it in the morning," he said, cutting her off.

"So, I'll regret it," she said and shrugged. "I don't care. Isn't it obvious that's exactly my point, Tanner—I don't regret *anything*," she said hotly. "Because I've never done anything to regret. I always take the easy road. I do the right thing. I keep out of trouble. I keep myself protected from really feeling anything."

"Until Doug?"

"Including Doug," she replied. "He was no risk. Because he was never *here*. And even when he was, he always seemed far away and distracted and so completely out of reach. So that made him safe for me, don't you see? It made him easy to be with. My expectations were low and that's all I got."

"You loved him?"

"Yes," she said, and felt so much heat and tension emanating from the man in front of her it was as if a fire had been lit in the room. "Maybe I did. Or maybe I thought I did. Or maybe there's no such thing as love and there's just this…" She stopped and moved in front of him. "Just crazy chemistry and attraction. Just sex."

"Nothing's that simple," he said and swayed toward her.

"Then let's make it simple," she said and placed her palm on his chest. "Stay with me and make love to me tonight."

He moaned as if the idea gave him pain, and for a second she thought he was going to turn away. But he didn't. He reached for her and hauled her against his body, gently fisting a handful of her hair as he tilted her head back.

"And tomorrow?" he asked, his mouth hovering above hers. "What then?"

"I don't want to think about tomorrow. Only now. Only how I want to be with you tonight, without ghosts or pretense between us."

He nodded fractionally and kissed her with such intense passion she almost fainted. When he lifted his mouth from hers she was gasping for breath and so aroused her head was spinning. She pulled back and put space between them, taking in deep gulps of air, her mouth tingling from the heat and passion in his kiss.

She'd never been sexy. She'd never considered herself seductive in any shape or form. And she'd never openly offered herself to anyone in her life. But she'd never wanted a man the way she wanted Tanner, either.

"Cassie...I think—"

"Don't think," she said on a rasp of hot breath. "Don't think about anything except this moment. I don't care about tomorrow and I don't care what this means. Because maybe it doesn't mean anything...maybe it's just about two people who want each other right now." She walked toward the door and looked over her shoulder. "No ghosts," she whispered and then walked down the hallway.

Tanner had imagined and dreamed about being with Cassie more times than he dared count. And in none of those dreams had he let himself believe she'd look at him with such burning, raw desire. She was so incredibly beautiful that he was literally lost for words. Watching her hips sway and the seductive turn of her shoulder as she invited him into her bed was the sexiest thing he'd ever seen in his life.

By the time he'd forced some life into his legs she had disappeared down the hallway. When he reached her bedroom door she was standing at the end of the bed, her eyes clearly saying she was waiting for him. A couple of lit candles flicked shadows on the walls, creating a mood of tempting intimacy.

"No ghosts," she said again, as though she was confirming it one last time.

And Tanner knew there was no wall between them. In that moment, there was only the two of them, together, alone in her bedroom.

But knowing what was about to happen, he gathered his good sense for a second. "Cassie, I'm not exactly prepared for this."

She immediately understood what he meant and walked around the bed. She opened the bedside drawer and extracted a small box. "I am," she said, suddenly all brazen confidence. She dropped a condom on the pillow and moved back around the bed.

She was setting the pace and for the moment he didn't mind one bit.

One hand clasped the top of the coat-style black dress she wore and she began to unclip the buttons with excruciating, seductive slowness. Mesmerized, Tanner stayed by the door and watched, wholly aroused as she popped one button, and then the next, and the next, until the dress was opened right down the front. She shrugged and slipped the garment off her shoulders and it dropped to the floor. The smoothness of her creamy skin was highlighted by the dark contrast of the black bra and briefs she wore, and Tanner clenched his fists to pump some blood back into his hands and heart before he passed out.

The dips and curves of her body were mesmerizing. Her full breasts rounded over the low-cut bra in pure temptation. She twisted her hands behind her back and unclipped her bra. Her breasts fell forward, rosy-tipped and beautiful, and he fought the urge to race forward and take her in a rush of heat and desire. He looked at her breasts and his palms burned with an aching need to touch her. Cassie gave a little smile, as if she knew exactly how enticing she was. She hooked her thumbs into her briefs and pushed them over her hips and past her knees and feet.

There was something ethereally beautiful about her and in all his life he'd never forget how she looked standing naked in front of him—like an entrancing mix of temptation and haunting vulnerability. He wanted to say something. He wanted to tell her how lovely she was and declare every ounce of feeling he had for her. But no words came out. He could only watch, enthralled and aroused, as she met his gaze and smiled.

"Let's have a shower first," she said and backed up until she reached the door of the en suite bathroom.

A shower? Tanner wasn't sure he'd make it. He looked at her, wanting her in ways he hadn't imagined he'd ever want anyone.

But he took about two seconds to ditch his clothes and join her.

She was backed up against the wall and water sluiced over her skin. He hauled her close, kissing her hungrily. She kissed him back and clung to his shoulders. The warm water created an erotic slide between them and he wondered vaguely how he'd ever shower again without imagining, without wanting Cassie pressed against him.

She said his name low in her throat and Tanner eased back. She looked up and smiled as she grabbed the soap, put a little space between them and slowly worked the bar over his chest in small circles into a foamy lather. Tanner dropped his arms to his sides and clenched his fists. He'd let her have her way for the moment. Besides, with all the blood rushing to one part of his body he actually wondered if he might really pass out. She toyed with his nipples for a second and smiled.

"You're smiling?"

She met his gaze. "You make me smile. You make me…"

"What?" he prompted, then took the soap from her hand and dropped it back into the dish.

"Confident," she admitted huskily. "Unafraid."

"I'm glad. And you are those things, Cassie. You're strong and beautiful and smart."

She sighed, and the sound echoed through his chest. Then he kissed her, hotly, hungrily, taking her tongue in an erotic dance. She kissed him back. He kissed her again. Back and forth, taking and giving.

"Cassandra," he muttered against her lips. "Let's get out of here."

She nodded and he switched off the water. They were out of the shower in seconds and dried off just as quickly. By the time they tumbled onto the bed Tanner had captured her mouth again and kissed her long and deep. She lay down and he moved to her side. He ran his fingertips over her hip and waist before gently grazing his knuckles against one erect nipple. She moaned and raised her mouth to his again, kissing him sweetly. Tanner cupped her breasts, first one, and then the other, before he replaced his hands with his mouth. Cassie arched back on the bed as he rolled his tongue across the tender flesh.

They kissed and touched, fuelling the heat swirling between them. Each stroke was hotter than the one before, each kiss deeper. Every sigh she gave made Tanner want to love her more, need her more, as if he needed air in his lungs.

Her hands were over his chest, his ribs and his waist. There was nothing shy about her touch. When she reached lower and touched him where he ached to be touched, Tanner thought he might pass out. He ran his hands along her skin, finding the place where she was wet and ready for him, and slowly caressed her, finding a gentle rhythm that made her moan encouragingly. Tanner watched her come apart in his arms and felt her pleasure across his skin and through his blood.

"Now," she whispered breathlessly against his mouth and linked her leg through his. "Please."

Tanner speedily retrieved the condom from the pillow. She took it and sheathed him quickly. And when finally he was inside her, looking down into her beautiful face, he could think only one thing.

I'm home...

Cassie knew making love with Tanner would be extraordinary. She knew his touch would drive her wild. But she hadn't expected that his possession would consume her mind, her body and her heart. He rested his weight on his arms as they moved together and she was eased into a rhythm that created a heady sensation of narcotic pleasure that pulsed through her blood. With each smooth stroke she was drawn higher. With each kiss she was pushed toward the edge. She touched his shoulders, his arms, his back. She pressed her palms and fingers into his skin to get closer, to feel every inch of him against her. As their kisses grew more urgent, heat spread through her body like wildfire. Cassie felt Tanner tense above her and she instinctively wrapped her legs around him, drawing him closer, wanting him deeper, until they were both taken by a rush of white-hot, incandescent pleasure that left her breathless and more connected to him than she'd ever been to another person in her whole life.

When he rolled onto his back, drawing deep breaths into his lungs, Cassie felt the loss of his skin against hers as if she'd lost part of herself. He grabbed her hand and gently kissed her knuckles.

"Be back in a minute," he said. He got up and disappeared into the bathroom.

Cassie stretched and sighed. She'd never made love with such passion. Never been so in tune with a lover that it was as though they had been together in another life. Somehow, he knew her. He knew where to touch, where to stroke, where to kiss with a kind of instinctual, soul-reaching intensity.

Is this love?

It didn't feel like any kind of love she'd experienced before. Because there was a deep connection between them. They'd become friends and now lovers. And it had left her forever changed. When he returned she'd rolled onto her side and he slipped back onto the bed and lay beside her.

"Are you okay?" he asked softly.

She sighed and smiled. "Yes. I'm...good."

His eyes darkened and he traced the back of his fingers over her shoulder and waist and then laid his hand on her hip. "That was...something."

Cassie's mouth curved with delight. She'd never had such a lovely compliment. "Yes, it was." She ran her hand along his biceps and fingered the hard muscle. "You know, you have a remarkable body."

Laughter rumbled in his chest. "You, too." He moved

his hand to her cheek and kissed her tenderly. "Your lips taste so good."

She smiled against his mouth, and then trailed kisses down his neck and lingered at the base of his throat, where his pulse beat strongly. "You taste good, too," she whispered and moved lower. "Like here," she teased and moved lower again, sliding her lips down his chest. "And here."

Tanner groaned as his arms came around her and he pulled her close. He grasped her chin, tilted her face back to meet his and kissed her deeply. They made love again, this time it was slow and languorous as he trailed his mouth down her body and then back up again. He kissed her breasts, her rib cage, her belly and lower still, sending her spinning into a vortex of pleasure so intense, so agonizingly intimate, she could barely draw breath into her lungs as she came apart in his arms.

"Does it hurt?" she asked much later as she lay against his chest and trailed a finger over the long scar on his left thigh.

"Sometimes," he said as he grabbed her hand and laid it against his stomach.

"You could have been killed in that accident."

"But I wasn't," he said and caressed her back. "I'm here. With you."

She smiled against his chest. "I'm glad." She sighed. "By the way, I kind of like you calling me Cassandra."

Tanner chuckled softly. "Then I will," he said and stroked her skin. "In moments like this one."

She nodded and smiled at how intimate that sounded. "What time is it?"

He shifted a little to check the clock on the bedside table. "Just after ten."

She stirred. "Oliver will wake up in about an hour for a feed. And I'm hungry."

"Me, too," he said and rolled her onto her back effortlessly as he kissed her. "Let's go and eat some leftovers."

She nodded. Once he released her Cassie slid off the mattress and grabbed her robe from the end of the bed. Tanner was sitting up, watching her.

"What?" she asked.

He shrugged and grinned. "Nothing. I like looking at you."

Cassie smiled. "You mean you like looking at me naked?"

"Well…yeah. But I like looking at you in any way. I like watching you with Oliver. I like watching you sleep." He grinned. "Even though you snore."

She stopped tying the sash on her robe and laughed. "I do not."

"You do," he insisted, still grinning.

She popped her hands on her hips. "And when have you seen me sleep?"

"When you were sick," he replied and pointed to the chair in the corner. "I sat there for a while."

Cassie stilled. "That was you? I sensed someone was in the room. I thought it was Lauren."

He shook his head. "I didn't want to leave you alone in case you needed something."

Cassie's heart flipped over. "That was very sweet of you. You've done so much for me. I don't feel like I've done anything in return."

One dark brow came up and he glanced at the rumpled bedsheets. "No?"

Color spotted her cheeks. "Well, besides what we just did before. I'm not sure that counts."

He laughed softly and sprang off the bed, coming around to take her in his arms. "Oh, sweetheart," he said and drew her close as his hands slipped beneath the robe to caress her skin. "That counts… That definitely counts."

And for the next half hour her only thoughts were of the man who'd possessed her body and captured her heart.

When Tanner rolled out of bed the following morning it was past seven. The sheets beside him were cool, so he figured Cassie must have been awake for some time. They'd been up a couple of times during the night to tend to a restless Oliver, before heading back to bed to make lazy love again before dawn broke.

He stood, stretched and grabbed the trousers and briefs he'd dumped at the end of the bed in such a hurry the night before. His leg ached and he pressed a hand to the fracture line. He really needed to get back to physical therapy when he returned to Cedar Creek.

But the mere thought of the idea made his chest hurt.

He zipped up the trousers and stretched his shoulders out a little more. He needed coffee and food. Cassie was in the kitchen when he walked through the door, feeding Oliver and laughing with her son. She looked up and smiled.

"Good morning," she said.

It was a good morning. The best of his life. She looked so adorable in her soft pink robe with the baby in her lap, and as Tanner watched them a deep surge of unquestionable love washed over him. It was unlike any other feeling he'd ever known. And he knew he wanted them for his own. The woman he loved and the son she'd borne to another man. His brother's family. The family Doug had intended to discard.

"What are you thinking about?" she asked, still smiling.

Tanner returned the gesture. "How beautiful you look in the morning." He walked to the table and held out his hands to take the baby.

Once Oliver was settled in his arms she got up and poured coffee for them both.

"You're so good with him," she said, smiling as she brought the mugs to the table. "You really are a natural with babies. I was so unsure and awkward with him when I first brought him home. I'm a little envious."

Tanner grinned as Oliver grabbed one of his fingers and held on. "He's easy to love."

"He's going to miss you when you leave," she said on a sigh, and the mood in the room altered immediately. "So am I."

Tanner looked up and met her gaze, his insides aching. "I can't stay, Cassie."

She nodded. "I know. And I don't mean to make you feel obligated to stay or anything like that. I'm just…" She stopped and patted her heart with her palm. "I'm just saying what's in here."

Tanner pushed back the swell of emotion rising in his throat. What was she really saying? That she had feelings for him? He knew that. Two people didn't make love as they had and *not* have feelings for each other. But he wasn't about to kid himself into thinking it meant she'd fallen in love with him. She'd loved Doug. She probably still did. But last night she'd been grieving and sad and needed someone. Probably anyone. And he'd been there for her. That's all it was.

"I told you making love would complicate things."

She shrugged a little. "And I told you I didn't care. I still don't. I'm glad we had last night. It was…lovely. And I'll never regret it."

He should have been pleased. But inside, he hurt all over. If she'd had regrets it would have been a whole lot easier to leave her as he knew he had to. He needed to return to South Dakota. But the very notion of leaving her and Oliver made his bones ache.

"Neither will I," he said and knew it was a lie. Tanner did regret it. Because he knew it wouldn't happen again. She wasn't his to love. Or have.

"Would you tell me about Leah?"

Leah? He hadn't expected that. Tanner looked at her directly. "Why?"

"I'd like to know what happened...how two very different brothers could love the same woman."

Oh...God. Tanner inwardly groaned. *If she only knew.*

"We met in high school and dated for a while."

"You were serious about her?" Cassie asked. "You loved her?"

He shrugged. "I thought so at the time."

"And then Doug came along?"

"Something like that," he said, ignoring the jabs of unease crawling across his skin. "She fell for him and they had an affair."

"Behind your back?"

"I wouldn't have kept seeing her had I known," he said drily. "When she found out she was pregnant she came clean and told me Doug was the father."

Cassie's face screwed up. "You must have been devastated."

"Well, it wasn't exactly a picnic. But I could see how upset and sorry she was. And eventually I got through it."

"Is that when you started traveling? I remember Doug telling me how you took off when you were eighteen. He said you wanted to get away from Crystal Point. He said you hated the town and everything in it. But that's not true," she said, watching him over the rim of her mug. "It was him you wanted to get away from. And the memories."

"I guess," Tanner said, rocking Oliver gently. "Even

though Doug didn't live here, we'd always stay with Ruthie when we came back to town. I had plans to buy a place around here. Maybe a small cane farm or enough land to graze cattle. But the money was gone and Leah was gone, too…so I took off. I backpacked through Asia and then traveled through Europe for a while. When I was twenty Ruthie arranged for me to spend a summer on her brother-in-law's horse ranch in Cedar Creek. And I've been there ever since. I worked at a few different ranches around the county, breaking and training horses, and saved enough to finally get my own place a couple of years back."

Cassie's eyes glistened. "So had things been different, you might have stayed here. You might have bought a place close by and been a part of this town. And we might have met before I—"

"Before you met Doug, you mean?" Tanner shrugged one shoulder. "But we did meet, remember? When we were thirteen."

She nodded. "I know we did. I guess I was thinking about before Doug bought this house. When you came here that first time to visit Doug…did you remember me?"

"Yes."

"We didn't talk much that visit," she said. "At the time I'd wondered if you thought I wasn't right…you know… for your brother."

Tanner met her gaze. "I only thought, how did he get so lucky."

She smiled. "That's sweet. But now that I know you I feel very foolish for believing him so unconditionally."

"You trusted him. You had no reason not to."

"I suppose. He was a complex man and I don't think I ever really knew that until now."

Tanner could see the sadness in her expression and lifted Oliver toward her. "He's all that matters, right?"

She smiled and her eyes brightened. "Absolutely."

"Let's do something today," he suggested. "I promised Ruthie I'd work with her colt this morning, but later we could go out...maybe have lunch in town?"

She nodded and accepted Oliver in her arms. "We might even persuade Ruthie to join us," she said. "A family outing would be great."

A family outing...

Doug's family. And nothing would ever change that.

Chapter Eleven

"So, something's clearly changed between the two of you. That girl can hardly keep her eyes off you today."

Tanner strapped the girth tightly around the colt and ignored the comment. He'd made the mistake of bringing Cassie and Oliver to the Nevelson farm, allowing them to all be scrutinized by a very discerning and curious Ruthie.

"I reckon one more long reining session should do it," he said and checked the bit and bridle. "Then he should be ready to back with the saddle and ride."

Ruthie ducked through the fence. "Don't think you're getting away from me that easily."

He stilled and looked at her. "No comment."

She tutted. "Not like you to let that part of your anatomy do your thinking," she said bluntly. "Just be careful."

"I'm always careful," he said and clicked the colt to step backward. It was the truth. When it came to love and sex Tanner had been cautious and careful his whole life. He'd never let himself get too close… He'd never lasted longer than a few months in any relationship.

"You're in love with her," Ruthie said so matter-of-factly that Tanner stopped what he was doing and faced her.

"That would be foolish."

"Yes," she agreed and nodded. "It would be. And you've never been a foolish man. Until now." She crossed her bony arms and frowned. "Next thing I know you'll be asking her to go back to South Dakota and marry you."

Tanner's body turned rigid. "No one's business," he said and quickly got back to the task. He wasn't about to admit that the thought had crossed his mind more than once that morning. Being with Cassie and Oliver was like nothing he'd ever experienced before. For the first time in his life he was exactly where he wanted to be. And with whom he wanted. And as much as he knew the whole situation was a complicated mess, he didn't want that to end.

"I like Cassie. She's a sweet girl and was always too good for your brother. But he'll always be between you," Ruthie said, the ever frank voice of reason. "As much as you don't want him to be. As much as you try to ignore it."

Doug…

Most of his life Tanner had gone from loving, to hating, to resenting his brother. But he'd never envied Doug or wanted anything his brother had. Until the day he was introduced to Cassie. It had taken about two seconds to realize she was the same girl he'd kissed on the beach all those years before. Doug had told him she was compliant and uncomplicated and undemanding—exactly the kind of woman his brother was attracted to—one who wouldn't challenge him or ask anything of Doug he wasn't prepared to give. And Cassie, with her sweet demeanor and haunting vulnerability, was an easy target for his charming, often misguided brother.

But when she told Doug she was pregnant and wanted a commitment his brother had done exactly what Tanner would have expected…he'd retreated into his soldier shell and told her they'd discuss it when he returned from tour. All the while planning on abandoning her and the baby if she chose to continue with her pregnancy. Just as he had with Leah.

"I know what I'm doing," he said and led the colt around the corral.

Ruthie followed, unperturbed by his brush-off. "I hope so. And remember, once you tell her how you feel there's no taking it back."

He was still thinking about Ruthie's words half an hour later as he dumped the long-reining gear back to the small tack room at the end of the stables. Ruthie was right. There was no taking it back. Which was exactly why he hadn't said it. He *was* in love with Cassie. He loved Cassie *and* Oliver and ached to make them his own. But he wasn't in the market for a rejection. And while Cassie had hinted that she had feelings for him other than the attraction that had landed them in bed together, he couldn't be sure.

"You know, there's something sexy about watching a man work with a horse."

He turned. Cassie stood in the narrow doorway. In jeans and a bright red shirt she looked so dazzling it stole his breath. "Have you been watching from the house?"

"I may have admired you from the kitchen window once or twice." She stepped into the small room. "What were you and Ruthie talking about?" she asked and grinned. "Me?" She chuckled and the lovely sound hit him directly behind the ribs. "I think she's onto us."

"Yeah," Tanner said and managed a tight smile as he shifted a couple of saddles onto a rack. "She doesn't miss much."

Cassie came closer and sat on a hay bale. "Everything okay?"

"Sure. Is Oliver asleep?"

"Yes. Ruthie's watching him." Her mouth curved. "So I thought I'd come and keep you company for a while. I was also thinking of turning over a new leaf...you know, like start trying new things."

Tanner's hands stilled on a saddle. "New things?" he queried.

"Well, I've never been on an airplane, so that's something I'd like to do at some point. And I thought I might like to learn how to ride a horse," she said and smiled suggestively. "If I can find someone to teach me."

Tanner's stomach was in knots. They both knew there wasn't time for that. He was leaving in a week or so. But he smiled agreeably. "Ruthie's got an old gelding down the back pasture that would do well enough."

"Great," she said and got to her feet. She came close and touched his arm. "We should probably get going if we're to have our outing this afternoon."

"Sure," he said and grasped her hand. "I need to clean up first. Let me finish up here and I'll meet you in the house."

"Okay," she said and stretched on her toes to kiss him.

Tanner wrapped his arms around her and returned the kiss. They remained in the tack room for a few minutes, making out, kissing and touching as if they hadn't a care in the world. When they finally pulled apart he was aroused and unable to hide the fact.

"Ah—Cassie, we'd better stop."

She smiled, as though she knew exactly what she'd done to him. "See you soon," she said and walked off.

By the time he returned to the house, showered and changed it was past one o'clock. Ruthie declined their invitation to join them and waved them off as they headed off down the driveway. Oliver was gurgling happily in his baby seat. Cassie was humming to an old song on the radio. In that moment he had everything he wanted.

The Mount Merry Animal Haven was half an hour outside of Bellandale and had always been one of Cassie's favorite places as a child. She was delighted when Tanner suggested they visit. It had been a home and sanctuary for animals in need for decades and while the proprietors had changed hands, the peacefulness and serenity of the place had remained unchanged. With Oliver in his stroller and Tanner by her side, they walked around the farm in the afternoon sunshine and Cassie experienced something she'd long forgotten but always longed for.

Family...

As she had when her parents were alive. Or when her grandfather had taken her in and made a home for her. She'd buried her grandfather the day before and today could have been a sad, terrible day. But Tanner had made sure she wasn't alone. He'd taken her to Ruthie's and included her in his day. Being with him and Oliver took her mind off losing her grandfather and even if it was just for that moment, she'd treasure the memory forever.

After they visited the baby animal yard and patted an ornery mule whose name was Duke, they had lunch in the small teahouse on the property. For the next hour they chatted to the owners about the animals and laughed when they shared stories about the two ill-mannered llamas that had recently been re-homed with them.

Tanner was attentive and charming and so easy to be around that with each passing hour, she fell for him just that little bit more. Had she ever been so comfortable around anyone before? Had anyone ever made her feel so at ease and so happy in her own skin?

No. It was a startling realization. For the past few years she'd believed Doug was the kind of man she wanted. But she'd been so wrong. Even though Tanner was a little bossy and sometimes showed an arrogant streak, he possessed such elemental goodness that it was impossible to *not* be drawn toward him.

But he's leaving...remember?

The idea of losing him from her life was heart-wrenching. He hadn't spoken about his impending departure and she hadn't raised the subject, either. Because her heart didn't want to hear it. She didn't want to lose him. Even though she knew it was inevitable. The house was for sale, she needed to find a new home and Tanner was going back to South Dakota.

Accept it...there's no changing the inevitable.

Or was there?

All her life she'd accepted things. Without argument. Without resistance. Hadn't she blindly accepted her mediocre relationship with Doug? As if it was all she deserved? His brief visits and lack of commitment should have sent warning bells screaming off in her head. But instead she'd simply acquiesced and accepted it. When she'd told him she was pregnant he'd fobbed her off and said they'd talk soon. On his terms. Not hers. Even when she knew she deserved better. But she wasn't that woman anymore. Tanner had shown her that. He'd somehow given her the gumption she'd been lacking most of her life.

After lunch they had photographs taken with a bald parrot named George who wore a tiny crocheted jacket and nibbled on Cassie's earlobe. Tanner bought Oliver a T-shirt from the gift shop and chatted to the elderly sales assistant behind the counter, who they quickly discovered was the aunt of the owner and volunteered in the shop on the weekends.

The older woman came around the counter and peered into the stroller. "He's such a beautiful baby, such gorgeous big brown eyes," she remarked and smiled. "You must feel very blessed." She looked at Oliver again, then Tanner, and met Cassie's gaze. "And goodness, doesn't he look the spitting image of his daddy."

For a second the silence was deafening. Cassie knew she should have corrected the other woman. But nothing came out. Tanner remained standing by the stroller, silent and unmoving. Of course it was a natural assumption. They were together. They had a baby with them. Anyone who didn't know them would come to the same conclusion and think the baby was theirs. It shouldn't have made her feel uncomfortable. But it did. She looked at Tanner and tried to read his expression. But his face was a handsome, impassive mask. Of course he wouldn't want people to assume that another man's child was his. Oliver was Doug's son. One day, Tanner would have his own family. His own child. And Oliver would be the nephew he saw occasionally.

And I'll be forgotten.

It hurt to think it. But she had to stop silly dreams from taking over. Tanner wanted his own family. Not his brother's leftovers. They'd had the discussion a week earlier and he hadn't denied it. And she didn't blame him. She couldn't. He probably regretted last night, too. He'd warned her how sex would complicate things and he was right on the money. She'd allowed her loneliness and her libido to take control.

They left around four o'clock and headed back to Crystal Point. Tanner was quiet on the drive home and with

Oliver sleeping soundly in the backseat and the radio off, the only sound was the gentle hum of the engine.

"Everything okay?" she asked.

"Of course."

She wasn't entirely convinced. "It was a nice afternoon."

"Yes," he said and glanced over his shoulder to Oliver. "But I think we wore him out."

"He'll sleep well tonight," she said and fought the urge to lay a hand on Tanner's jeans-clad thigh. His touch was like tonic and she wanted to feel it again. She wanted to be swept away by his kiss and feel the ecstasy of his complete possession. She wanted him in her bed. She just wasn't sure if that's what he wanted, too. "So...are you staying for dinner tonight?"

"Am I invited?" he asked, looking at the road ahead.

"Of course."

He looked sideways for a moment. "Okay."

There was an elephant in the room. Or more to the point, in the car. And Cassie figured out what it was quick smart.

"You don't have to stay the night, Tanner," she said and crossed her hands tightly in her lap. "I'm not going to jump you like I did last night, if that's what's on your mind."

She saw a smile crease his mouth.

"You're not?" he queried. "Too bad for me, then."

He was impossible to read and Cassie's temperature rose a little. "So, you want to stay?" she asked, suddenly annoyed. "Is that what you're saying?"

"Of course I want to stay," he replied tensely.

"Could have fooled me," she muttered and looked out the side window.

"What?"

She shook her head. "Nothing."

He was staying. *Great.* She should have been happy. It's what she wanted. Another night in his arms. Another night tasting his kisses and feeling the tenderness of his touch. But she was angry instead.

By the time he pulled the car into the driveway she was so annoyed her skin was hot all over. She grabbed Oliver's bag and her tote and waited for Tanner to get the stroller from the car before she hiked up the path to the door and unlocked the house. Tanner followed behind her and met her in the nursery. She held out her arms and took the baby.

"Thank you. I'm going to get him bathed and fed."

Mouse barked and Tanner nodded. "I'll feed the dog."

"Okay," she said stiffly and waited for him to leave the room before she took another breath. She hugged Oliver close and felt some of her rage disappear. She loved her son with all her heart. And he was her only priority.

She bathed him, dressed him in his pajamas, then went to the kitchen and made up his bottle. Determined to avoid Tanner for the moment, she returned to the nursery to feed her son and stayed another half an hour until he drifted off to sleep.

By the time she was back in the kitchen it was nearly six o'clock. She grabbed the kettle to make tea and only stopped when she heard Tanner moving in the doorway.

"Is he asleep?" he asked.

"Yes," she replied, not looking at him. "Do you want tea? Coffee?"

"Coffee," he said and came behind the counter. "But I'll do it. You make lousy coffee."

Cassie turned and glared at him. "I do not."

"Oh, yeah, you do."

She popped a tea bag in her mug and slid another mug along the counter. "Fine. Suit yourself."

Since she was trapped in the kitchen and couldn't get

past without pressing close to him, Cassie stayed where she was. He made coffee as effortlessly as he did most things, which only amplified her irritation. She crossed her arms, raised her chin and stared at the ceiling.

"You're not going to slug me again, are you?" he asked, resting back on the countertop, coffee in hand.

Her eyes flashed in his direction. "You're such a jerk."

"And you've got a bad temper."

"Around you?" she countered. "Yeah. And while we're on the subject of my faults, I'm sorry about what the lady said in the shop. I should have corrected her."

He straightened and placed the mug on the counter with deliberate emphasis. "Why?" he asked quietly. "Because you can't bear the thought of Oliver being anyone else's but Doug's?"

He sounded offended. And mad. Cassie looked at him. "No, I just didn't think you'd want—"

"If you must know, I wish he *was* mine," he said, harsher than she'd ever heard.

Did she just hear him right? *Oh, God...I wish that, too...*

"You...you do?" she stammered.

He nodded and she saw the pulse in his cheek throb. "It sure would make this mess a hell of a lot less complicated."

"Mess?" she echoed. "That's what we are to you?"

He sighed impatiently. "Don't play with my words. That's not what I meant and you know it."

Cassie flapped her hands. "I don't know anything when it comes to you. You're...you're...impossible to read. Impossible to get close to." When his brows came up she planted her hands on her hips. "And I don't mean in bed. If communicating with you was as simple as sex, then we'd obviously be fine."

"Then perhaps that's what we should do?" he suggested and placed an arm either side of her as he leaned closer.

"Forget the arguing. Forget the talking. Forget everything but this."

She looked up, mesmerized by the dark passion in his eyes and the intent in his expression. And she wanted him. She wanted him so much she ached.

He kissed her, long and hard and so intense it had possession stamped all over it.

And of course she kissed him back. It was pure instinct. Pure longing. Pure, unadulterated desire for his touch that drove her beyond coherent thought. His tongue found hers as his hands roamed down her back and he lifted her up, holding her against him intimately as their mouths melded together. Cassie gripped his shoulders and wrapped her legs around his waist as he walked backward.

They made it to her bedroom in record time and their clothes came off just as quickly.

It was hot and quick and explosive. There was no finesse this time, no tender touch. Cassie came apart in his arms, begging for him to possess her and he took her on a wild, heavenly ride that she never wanted to end. She told him what she wanted and he did the same. She said words she'd never spoken to another person. She demanded. She complied. She gave herself up and offered all she could give in return. There was no going back. No way to retreat. They were in that one perfect moment, completely in tune. As the pleasure built she gripped him hard, holding on, feeling every ounce of his need for her and hers for him. Until finally they were thrown over the edge and rode the waves of an earth-shattering climax.

When it was over they both dropped back onto the bed, breathless and stunned by the intensity of what they'd just shared. She'd never behaved like that before. Never begged. Never moaned and writhed and been so completely out of control. Her entire body pulsed in the aftermath. And all she could think was how she wanted to make love with him again. And again. He was her lover. The only one who mattered. The only one she wanted.

And then Tanner said four words that brought her back to reality with a thud.

"We didn't use protection."

Cassie stilled. No. They hadn't. She did the math in her head and figured there was very little risk. "I'm sure it's fine."

"That was irresponsible of me. I'm sorry."

"My fault, too," she said a little irritably, thinking he had no right to shoulder all the responsibility.

He was still breathing hard and Cassie watched his chest rise up and down. She wanted to touch him again. She wanted to feel him over her and inside her. She didn't want to talk about what might be. Although the notion of having his baby filled her entire body with a heady warmth.

"You'd tell me, wouldn't you?"

She ignored her breathlessness and sat up. "What?"

"If something happened...you'd tell me?"

"Do you mean would I tell you if I were pregnant?" She twisted around to face him. "Of course I would. But there's not much chance."

"Would you mind?" he asked. "I mean, if it did happen?"

"Would I mind having two kids under two years of age?" She laughed lightly. "Piece of cake. But since there's little chance it will happen, I'm not going to get worked up about it." She reached out and traced her fingertips along his rib cage and he quickly grabbed her hand. "You really do want children, though? I mean, one day?"

He entwined their fingers. "Definitely."

"You'll make a good dad," she said, ignoring the twinges inside. He would make a great dad. The best.

And she wished…she wished that Oliver would one day have a father like him.

I wish Oliver had Tanner for a father.

And there it was. Exactly what she wanted. She wanted Tanner. Because…because she was in love with him. Wholly and completely. He'd captured her heart with his kindness and goodness. He was what she'd secretly dreamed of all her life.

"I wish… I wish he was your son, too," she said, so quietly she wondered if he'd heard.

Tanner didn't move. Didn't say anything. An uneasy silence filled the room. Something was wrong.

Finally he released her hand and sat up, swinging his legs off the bed. And still he stayed silent. He grabbed his jeans from the floor and stood as he slipped them back on. Cassie watched, fascinated and confused, motionless as he left the room without looking at her. Or saying a word.

I said the wrong thing…

She pulled her knees up and hugged them.

What do I do now?

Hadn't she just bared herself to him? Didn't he know what her words meant?

She shimmied off the bed and looked for her clothes. She found some gray sweats in a pile of freshly washed and folded clothes she'd laid on the chair in the corner and snatched them up quickly. Once she was dressed she walked down the hallway. She checked on Oliver and then headed for the living room.

Tanner was standing by the window, his jeans low on his hips, his chest bare. Looking at him made her breath catch in her throat and he turned at the sound.

"Are you okay?"

He nodded, but he looked tense, as if he had a heavy weight pressing down on his shoulders.

"I'm sorry if I said something I shouldn't have," she said and stepped into the room. "I'm so confused at the moment all I can do is—"

"I could be."

Cassie stilled as the air caught in her lungs. "What?"

"I could be Oliver's father."

She shuddered. What was he saying? "I don't understand what you mean."

But with his next words she understood. And it rocked her to the core.

"Marry me."

Chapter Twelve

She looked stunned. And she looked as though she thought he'd lost his mind. Which, considering he'd just proposed marriage to the woman who had loved his brother and probably still did, he clearly had.

"You're not serious?"

"Perfectly."

"But we hardly..." Her words trailed off. "That's crazy."

"Not really," he said and sat down on the sofa. "Oliver needs a father. He's my nephew and I love him. And you and I are... We're good together."

"Good in bed, you mean?"

"I mean good together," he said again. "We work. We have a lot in common. We get along. And yeah, we're great in bed together. It's a starting point, Cassie. And more than what some people ever get."

And I love you...

But he didn't say it. The words stuck on the edge of his

tongue and if he thought he had a hope that she loved him, too, he would have said them. Maybe over time. Maybe once they were married and had more children together. Maybe she'd forget she'd loved Doug before him.

She moved farther into the room and sank into a chair. "But marriage? I mean, there's so much to consider. For starters, where would we live?"

"South Dakota."

Her eyes grew wide. "You're asking me to move to South Dakota? With Oliver? Just like that?"

"What's keeping you here?" he asked. "This house? It's being sold. Family? Oliver is your family. There's nothing really keeping you here now, is there? Your grandfather's gone. Doug's gone. And I don't mean to hurt you by saying that."

"But I have friends who—"

"I'm your friend, Cassie," he said quietly. "And I'm asking you to be more than that. I'm asking to be your husband."

She was visibly shaking. Shocked. Maybe appalled. He couldn't tell. He wanted to rush over and take her in his arms and tell her everything would be okay. He wanted to assure her that he'd care for her and Oliver forever. That she could rely on him. Trust him.

He waited, hoping she'd come to see it was the most sensible option. The best thing for Oliver. And them. But she didn't say a word. She stared into her lap, hands linked.

"Cassie?"

She took a breath and looked up. The emotion in her eyes couldn't be disguised. "I don't know... I feel a little overwhelmed by this. It's all happened so fast."

"And you need time to think it over?" he suggested.

She nodded. "Yes. For Oliver's sake."

"Then I'll stay as long as you need." He came across the

room and sat beside her, taking her hands gently within his. "I know you're scared, Cassie. I know this might seem like it's come way out of left field. But think about it sensibly... We both want what's best for Oliver. And I..." He stopped, squeezing her hands. "I care about you both. And I want him to know family and to have what we both missed out on. And we can give him that...you and me. We can make the kind of life together that was taken from us when we were kids."

Tears glittered in her blue eyes. "But if we got married you'd be stuck with us and—"

"That's the whole point, Cassie," he said and drew her hands toward his chest. "I want to be stuck with you. To you. I want to be the person you rely on. I want to be there for you, Cassie. I know this is the right thing to do," he said and tapped his chest with their linked hands. "I feel it in here."

She shuddered and exhaled heavily. "I need... I need some time to think about it."

"Of course," he said and stroked her hair. "I'll give you all the time you need."

She met his gaze and smiled tremulously. "The thing is...I don't want to take advantage of you. I couldn't live with myself if I thought I was doing that. I know you're doing this for Oliver and—"

"I'm doing this for me," he assured her and smiled. "Selfishly, I might add."

She shook her head. "You're the most *unselfish* person I've ever met, Tanner. And I know logic is on your side and I'm probably being typically overcautious and afraid...but this is a huge step and one neither of us can take lightly."

"We won't," he said firmly. "Take some time to think it over. Take a few days. I'll still be here. Call me when you've made a decision." He dropped her hands and got to his feet. "This is the right thing to do, Cassie. For all of us."

He stared down at her, hating to leave, but knowing she needed some time alone.

And then he left.

"Are you considering it?"

Cassie looked across the table at her friends. Lauren and M.J. had arrived an hour earlier for an emergency Monday-night meeting. She'd had thirty-six hours to think about Tanner's proposal and was as confused as ever.

Lauren's question hung in the air. Was she? She said yes a hundred times in her mind. Until a tiny voice of reason had talked her out of it again and again.

"I don't know."

M.J. got more to the point. "But you're sleeping with him, right?"

"Well…we've been together…yes."

"And you're in love with him?"

Her skin heated. "I…I think so…"

M.J.'s dramatic brows came up high. "So, you're lovers and you *think* you love him and he's great with Oliver and he wants to marry you and take you to live on his ranch in South Dakota. What's the problem?"

"Me," she replied with a sob. "*I'm* the problem."

"Is this about Doug?" Lauren asked gently.

Doug? Had she spared the other man a thought for the past two days? Not exactly. His memory had faded in and out. Her head was filled with Tanner and little else. But maybe, in her deepest heart, it was about Doug. Maybe all her reluctance stemmed from the man she'd once thought she'd loved.

"I'm not sure," she said and sighed as she pointed to her temple. "I know in here that marrying Tanner makes perfect sense. But in my heart I feel as though I'm cheating. I know Tanner adores Oliver and wants to do what's best for him. And what he said about us both losing our families when we were young and how now we can make sure that doesn't happen to my son...that makes sense, too. But, is it selfish of me to take that dream? Being with Tanner is easy. Oh, don't get me wrong, he makes me mad and drives me crazy at times...but we have this incredible connection that I've never felt before. But I know Tanner's feelings aren't the same. He loves Oliver and for the moment he wants me...because I'm here and I'm Oliver's mother and it's logical for him to take us both. But he also wants to find that one great love and I know that couldn't possibly be me...not with our history...not with Doug's memory in the background. So I'm scared. I'm scared of letting him go and not ever feeling this again. I'm also scared that one day in the future Tanner will wake up and realize he's made a huge mistake."

"I get what you're saying," M.J. offered a little more gently than usual. "But I don't think it's up to you to stop Tanner from making a mistake."

Her friend was right and Cassie knew one thing. She had a decision to make.

And fast.

On Tuesday morning Cassie was getting Oliver dressed when her phone rang. It was Doug's lawyer. She'd spoken to him a couple of times over the past few months when she'd made tentative inquiries about Doug's estate. But this was the first time he'd called her. She gripped the handset, took a breath and listened to the deep voice on the other end of the phone.

And by the time the call ended Cassie felt as if her heart was suddenly wrapped in stone.

She'd called. And Tanner was foolishly hopeful she'd come to a decision. He hadn't seen Cassie or Oliver for days and he was eager to spend time with them both. He pulled the car into her driveway around seven, got out and walked to her porch.

She met him at the door and opened the screen. She looked tired, he noticed, and a little pale. And then he figured she'd probably gotten as much sleep as he had during the past few days. He moved to kiss her but she ducked away and headed for the living room.

Okay...not exactly the greeting he'd hoped for. He'd been walking around on autopilot for days, wondering, hoping...but never letting himself get accustomed to the idea that she would accept his marriage proposal.

"Is Oliver asleep?" he asked when they reached the front room.

She was by the window, arms crossed and her expression distant. "Yes."

"I've missed him," he said and smiled. "I've missed you."

"Really?"

Tanner stepped around the sofa. Something was wrong. "Cassie, I—"

"Where's my letter?"

He came to an abrupt halt about five feet from her. "What?"

"My letter," she said again, unmoving. "From Doug."

Tanner's blood ran cold. "How did you—"

"The lawyer rang me today. I guess he wanted to dot the *i*'s and cross the *t*'s before the file is closed. And he asked if I'd received the letter from Doug. The one that was in the safety deposit box. The safety deposit box you said was empty. You know, *my letter*."

"Cassie," he said quietly. "I can explain."

"Explain?" she echoed. "Are you serious? I don't want an explanation, Tanner. I just want the letter."

His chest tightened. "No, you don't.'

She crossed the floor in a couple of strides and stood in front of him. "I want it. I want to read it. I want to know what's in it. I want to know what Doug had to say to me before he headed into some covert, secret military operation that ended up killing him. I want to know what his last thoughts to me were."

"No," he said again, firmer this time. "You don't."

Her eyes were huge in her face. "Why are you being like this? You've obviously read it... What's in it that makes you think I wouldn't want to read it, too?"

"You need to trust me."

She shook her head. "I don't *need* to do any such thing. And right in this moment, trusting you is the last thing on my mind."

He didn't move. "This is for the best, Cassie."

She glared at him. "You arrogant jerk! You had no right to keep something like this from me."

"I know you're upset," he said, refusing to comply. "But I did it *for* you, Cassie...not to distress you."

"I don't care," she said angrily. "You don't get to decide what's best for me." She sucked in a long breath. "Where is it?" she demanded.

"I destroyed it."

She shuddered visibly. "How could you do that? You had no right."

Tanner braced his hands on his hips and exhaled heavily. "I did what I had to do."

"It wasn't your decision to—"

"Actually," he said, cutting her off, "it was. Doug left the contents of the safety deposit box to me, and that gave me the right to do whatever I thought was best with what was inside."

Her expression was as cold as granite. "And that makes

you what? My *keeper*? Well, think again. I'm not some naive wallflower that you can manipulate however you see fit. Doug wrote that letter to me, and he obviously wanted me to—"

"Doug left it in that box because he knew I wouldn't give it to you," Tanner argued. "He wrote it for some reason of his own. But he knew me, Cassie. He knew I'd never let you be hurt like that."

"Hurt?" She shook her head. "That doesn't make sense. What's in it that's so terrible?"

"Nothing," Tanner said quietly. "Forget I said—"

"Damn you, Tanner, what did it say?"

The pain and frustration in her voice was unbearable and Tanner fought the urge to take her in his arms. She was breathing hard and her eyes were all fire and rage. But he didn't budge. "I can't tell you."

She stepped closer, toe to toe, her chest heaving. "Oh, yes, you can. And you will. I want to know. *I have a right to know.* I loved him. I had his child. I cried and grieved when he died. So how dare you stand there all arrogant and condescending and with the audacity to tell me that I—"

She loved Doug. That was all he heard.

"Okay," he said, exasperated and frustrated. "Are you sure you want the truth? Because there's no going back once you know. Do you want to know every ugly word?"

"Yes," she said, eyes blazing and defiant.

Tanner drew in a sharp breath. "Okay, Cassie. He wasn't coming back!"

She frowned. "I don't—"

"Even if he'd survived that mission. He had no intention of returning. He didn't want you," Tanner said flatly. "He didn't want the baby. And he wasn't coming back to Crystal Point."

She rocked back on her heels. "I don't believe it," she whispered.

"I'm not lying to you," he said wearily.

Her head shook. "But how could it be true? He never said anything like that to me. He only said we'd talk when he got back." She stopped and looked at him. "He *was* intending to come home. I know it. Perhaps you misunderstood what he—"

"I didn't misunderstand," Tanner said quickly. "When it came to Doug I could guess exactly how he was going to react even before he said or did anything."

Cassie's arms dropped to her sides. "Perhaps he was under pressure and feeling stressed when he wrote it? If he'd talked about it and discussed things…it would have been different. He would have…" She stopped speaking and met his gaze. There was pain and disbelief, and then a sharp realization in her expression. She sighed. "Oh, of course. He did talk, didn't he? He talked to *you*. You've known all along…before you read the letter?"

"I knew," Tanner said softly and nodded. "Doug called me one morning just after you told him you were pregnant."

"But he didn't want to talk to me? He didn't want to discuss it?"

"I don't think so."

She sighed heavily and moved to the sofa. "He didn't want me?" Her words were hollow. "He really didn't want me? He didn't want our baby?"

Tanner knew she was hurting. "I'm sorry…no."

"Who does that?" she asked, looking broken and hopeless. "What kind of man behaves that way…"

"A selfish one," he said and swallowed hard. "But you knew that, Cassie. You dated him for three years. You knew Doug was self-absorbed. You just chose not to see it."

She looked down into her lap for a moment, hands twisted, heart clearly broken. Then she took a deep breath and met his gaze. "You told me the safety deposit box was empty. You lied to me. And you knew this all along and yet you didn't tell me?"

"I couldn't."

She shook her head. "You knew when you arrived here weeks ago and you didn't say anything to me. You let me think he'd had every intention of coming back and that he wanted us. You simply let me believe it and didn't say a word. Not even after we…" Her words trailed and she blinked, batting moisture from her eyes. "We made love and you didn't say a word. Even after that you're still protecting him."

Tanner's chest heaved. She was so wrong. "No, Cassie… I was protecting you."

Cassie was numb all over. She couldn't think or see anything other than Tanner's deliberate intentions to keep the truth from her. Doug wasn't coming back to Crystal Point. He was going to do exactly what he'd done before…bail.

It should have crushed her. But it didn't.

Tanner's lies did.

He might have it all tied up in some neat little package of wanting to spare her feelings, but all he'd done was prove he couldn't be relied upon. He couldn't be trusted.

"I don't need protecting," she said coldly. "All I ever wanted or needed from you was the truth."

"I'm sorry, Cassie. I knew Doug—"

"This isn't about Doug!" she snapped and got to her feet. "Don't you get it? This is about you. Me. *Us.* This is about you making the decision to lie to me, to treat me like I'm some kind of weakling who can't handle real life. Well, I'm not," she said, getting madder with each passing second. "I'm not weak. I'm not emotionally frail. And I'm not a pushover. And right now all I feel like is the world's most gullible fool for believing that you could be trusted. When clearly, you can't."

Every ounce of rage and disappointment in her heart rose to the surface. All her life she'd felt as if she wasn't quite equal to the task of standing on her own two feet. After her parents died her grandfather and her friends had lovingly wrapped her in cotton wool and tried to keep her from enduring more loss and hurt. But in doing that she'd become dependent, avoided making any major decisions and constantly ducked confrontation. Through school. In work. In life. When her grandfather went into the home and the house sold she had stayed on, avoiding change and disruption, accepting the easy road. And she'd become involved with Doug for the same reason. He didn't demand anything. He didn't treat her like a partner. He kept her locked in her gilded cage. Just as her grandfather had. And that's why she'd blindly accepted his continued lack of commitment to their relationship. It was easy. Uncomplicated. *Safe.*

When all she'd really done, over and over, was settle for the easy road.

Even when Oliver came along she hadn't truly grown up to take responsibility for herself and her son. She'd stayed in the house, hoping and avoiding the inevitable. It was a sobering realization and not one she was proud of.

But over the past few weeks things had changed. She'd changed. Because of Tanner.

For the first time in her life someone challenged her. Defied her. Made her feel up to the task and treated her like an equal.

Except it was all a lie.

He'd done the same as everyone else. And worse. Because she'd trusted him.

"I want you to go."

"Cassie, I think we should talk. I know—"

"No," she said angrily. "I don't want to hear it. I don't want to hear about how you didn't tell me for my own good, or how you didn't want me to get hurt, or how you think lying to me is acceptable. It's not. We made love," she said, her voice breaking. "You asked me to marry you. You said you cared about me and Oliver. Those things override anything else. And I don't want to be with someone who thinks it's okay to lie to me about something so important. I'll get over Doug not wanting me or Oliver," she said, her throat so tight it was almost closed. "But I can't get over—"

"So, Doug gets a free pass," he said harshly, interrupting her. "And I don't."

She nodded. "That's right."

He laughed then. Not with humor, but with a kind of weary, resigned acceptance. "Then I guess that tells me everything I need to know."

"I guess it does."

He stared at her, into her, through her. "Goodbye, Cassie."

Then he left. And she dropped onto the sofa and sobbed.

Cassie was thankful she had Oliver and the task of packing up her belongings to keep her mind off her troubles. She hadn't seen or heard from Tanner in six days. She didn't even know if he was still in town. The Realtor had brought a few prospective buyers through the house and each time she'd died a tiny death. Afterward, she'd quickly picked herself up and got back to the job of being strong and resilient and determined to stand on her own.

But she missed him. She missed him so much she ached inside.

And then she remembered that he'd lied to her and betrayed her and the anger returned. Not even Lauren and M.J. could budge her from her feelings. Both women made it clear they thought she was being unforgiving and stubborn. But she would not be swayed. It was over. And it was time she acted like a responsible thirty-one-year-old single mother and stopped whining. It was time to grow up.

But he came by early on Monday morning. She was in the front room and she saw his car pull up outside. She watched as he got out and walked across the lawn. He looked so good. Her heart raced at the sight of him. And then broke just a little bit more. He wore jeans, a dark shirt and leather jacket. He looked handsome and familiar and the memory of every kiss, every touch, came rushing back. He stood at the edge of the garden for a moment and stared out along the street before he pulled the for-sale sign out of the ground. She knew immediately what it meant.

It's done... It's sold...

It's over...

He laid the sign flat in the garden bed and then walked up the path. Cassie pushed some blood into her legs and met him at the front door. She didn't say a word. Neither did he. She headed back into the lounge and waited.

He looked tired. He looked as if he'd been through hell and back. She fought every impulse she possessed to keep herself from rushing into his arms. Too much had been said. There was too much regret and recrimination. He'd go back to South Dakota and forget all about her. And she'd forget him. Someday.

"You sold the house?"

"Not in the way you might think. I have something for you," he said as he pulled an envelope from his jacket pocket and dropped it onto the coffee table. It was a large manila envelope that looked official and had Oliver's name on the front.

"What is it?"

He didn't move. "As it turns out there was some money from Doug's estate. More than we'd first thought. From a new insurance policy Doug had taken out just before he was killed," he said. "Once all the debtors had been paid there was enough left."

Cassie frowned. "Enough for what?"

He waved a hand vaguely. "Enough for this. The deeds for the house are in there, put in trust for Oliver until he's twenty-one. As his mother and legal guardian you now decide what is to be done with the house. So you can stay, or sell...or do whatever you want to."

Cassie's legs were numb. He had to be joking. "I don't understand. How can that be? There was nothing left. Doug hadn't—"

"It was a new policy," he replied flatly. "Like I said. The lawyers missed it at first because it wasn't in the original will. Anyway, it means you can stay here. You can raise Oliver in this house. Which is what you wanted, right?"

The old Cassie had wanted that. But now she couldn't be certain of anything. It was tempting, that's for sure. The house had been her home for such a long time and was filled with memories. It was a safe harbor. Like an old glove that fit her hand perfectly. But she'd also promised herself she'd stand on her own feet.

It was too much to take in and she sat down heavily. "I never thought something like this would happen."

"A lot of things happen we don't expect," he said, still not flinching.

The meaning of his words burned through her entire body. She hadn't expected to fall in love with Tanner Mc-Cord. But she had. She hadn't expected to become his lover and long for him in ways she'd never wanted anyone before. But it was for nothing. They were a pipe dream. There were too many obstacles. She knew that Tanner would always feel Doug between them. He'd drawn the line in the sand when he'd decided to deceive her. There was no going back from that.

"I think I'm in shock," she said softly. "Don't get me wrong, I'm happy that my son will be looked after. And I guess this means that if it was a new policy, then maybe Doug did plan to..." She stopped and shrugged. "I don't know what it means or why he did it, but perhaps he wasn't only always thinking of himself. Maybe he did think about us and the baby I was carrying."

"That's probably it," Tanner said and shrugged. "Anyway, I just wanted to let you know."

She tried to smile and failed. Her bottom lip trembled. "So...what now?"

He shrugged again. "I'm flying out on Wednesday."

He was leaving. Going home. Ending things in the most final way possible.

"I see. Well, have a safe trip."

He nodded fractionally. "I'd like to say goodbye to Oliver."

"Sure."

Once he'd left the room Cassie let out a long breath. Her hands shook and she clutched them tightly together. Nothing had ever hurt so much.

Several minutes later he reappeared in the doorway. His back was straight. His face a stony mask. There was such finality in his demeanor. She knew they were over.

"Goodbye, Cassandra."

She didn't move. "Goodbye, Tanner."

And then he was gone. Out of her house. Out of her life. For good.

Chapter Thirteen

Cassie fell back into a post-Tanner rhythm way too easily. But she knew she was behaving like a complete fraud. Of course, she wasn't about to admit it to anyone. Not even her friends. They seemed to believe her happy smiles well enough and no one appeared to guess that she was broken inside.

The house deeds still remained on the coffee table, where Tanner had left them. The soft cotton T-shirt he'd left by the bed was unmoved. Oliver seemed a little quieter than usual and even Mouse acted as though he missed him.

She was, in a word, miserable.

He'd breezed into her life, made her fall in love with him and then breezed out again.

If she wasn't so brokenhearted she'd be madder than hell at him.

Then she got her period and discovering she wasn't

pregnant had her crying for two days. It was silly. She'd never believed she might be. But still...the idea of having Tanner's baby made her remember what she'd had at her fingertips and then lost.

M.J. had unexpectedly gone north to help a friend who needed a hand running her boutique for a few weeks, but Lauren came and went at regular intervals, checking up, making sure she wasn't becoming a boring recluse with only her baby for company. She assured her friend she wasn't, but doubted Lauren believed her. She should have been happy. She had her son and her home. She had what she thought she wanted. But she was unhappier than she'd ever been in her life. The house gave her no comfort. Of course she was happy that Oliver had his legacy and his future was secure. But it was a hollow victory.

Lauren and Gabe helped celebrate her birthday and she put on her bravest face, even though her heart was broken.

And then five weeks after he left Crystal Point she had an unexpected visitor.

Ruthie Nevelson.

"We need to talk" was all she said, and Cassie quickly ushered her inside.

Once they reached the living room Ruthie spoke again.

"This is a nice home," she said and crossed her thin arms. "I can see why it means so much to you."

"It used to belong to my grandfather," she explained, feeling the other woman's scrutiny down to her toes. "When he was ailing we had to sell it so that he could afford full-time care."

"And that's when Doug bought the place, isn't it?"

She nodded. "That's right."

"I'm not sure why he wanted to do that," Ruthie said and shrugged. "It's not like he ever wanted to put down roots.

Maybe it was guilt. Maybe it was a way to stay connected to this town. I guess we'll never know."

Cassie tried to be casual, tried not to let Ruthie see that she was so wound up she could barely string words together. The older woman was Tanner's greatest ally and she had come for a reason. Only, Cassie had no idea what that was. But she got the sense she was about to find out.

"Ruthie, is there something that—"

"I have something for you," she said and pulled a narrow envelope from her small handbag. "Actually, it's for your son. It's a letter from Tanner."

Cassie took the envelope with shaking fingers. "What does it say?"

Ruthie shrugged. "I don't know. But knowing Tanner, I would guess that it's from the heart."

Cassie swallowed hard. "What should I do with it?"

"Read it yourself. Or give it to him when he's old enough to understand," Ruthie said and paced the room. When she reached the mantel she looked at the photographs. Then she turned and made an impatient sound. "I encouraged Tanner to go home, you know. I saw how deeply he was getting involved with you and tried to stay impartial. But I couldn't. And I can't understand why you would want to waste time hanging on to the ghost of a man who wasn't worthy of either of you."

Cassie's shoulders dropped. "It isn't about Doug."

"Of course it is," Ruthie said and tutted. "You and Tanner have been on a collision course since the day his brother bought this house."

"What did Tanner tell you?"

"Enough," she replied. "That he asked you to marry him. That you turned him down."

"I didn't," Cassie said quickly. "I mean, not exactly. We

had an argument and in the heat of everything that was said it was all kind of forgotten."

"Well, I'm pretty sure he didn't do any forgetting," Ruthie said and frowned. "Do you have any idea of what that boy has done for you? What he's sacrificed so that you and your son can have a safe home?"

Cassie stared at Ruthie. "What? I don't understand what you—"

The older woman sighed crossly. "No, I guess you don't. Well, it's high time you learned exactly what kind of man Tanner McCord is."

"I know what he is," she said dully. "But I also know he kept the truth from me. He lied by omission."

"Yes," Ruthie said tersely. "He did. And he shouldn't have. He should have told you what a no-good lout Doug McCord was from the very beginning. But he's too decent, too honorable to *dishonor* his brother that way."

"That's no excuse. He was wrong. And he wouldn't admit it. He wouldn't stop being arrogant and bullheaded and thinking he knew what was best for me. And in the end it didn't matter what was in the letter Doug wrote because there was an insurance policy that—"

"Nonsense," Ruthie said and waved her hands. "There was no insurance. No anything. Doug made sure of that. All he left was a pile of debt and a child he had no intention of claiming." The older woman sat down. "You're not that naive. In your heart you know everything you found out about Doug is true. The lies, the betrayal and the way he stole Tanner's inheritance and frittered it away. And then the terrible way he treated Leah."

Cassie clutched her sides. "I know that. I know Doug wasn't perfect. But what does that have to do with this house. Tanner said there was an insurance policy and I—"

"He took out a second mortgage on his ranch," Ruthie

said, cutting her off. "And that's how you got to keep this house."

Silence consumed the room. Cassie dropped into the chair by the window. It couldn't be true. He wouldn't do that. It was impossible. Tears grew hot behind her eyes and she met the other woman's gaze. "But...I don't understand. Why would he do that?"

Ruthie shook her head with clear exasperation. "Because, you foolish girl, *he loves you*."

Cassie swallowed the lump in her throat. It was too much. Too hard to grasp.

He loves you...

"I don't think—"

"And he loves your baby," Ruthie added. "Frankly, I don't think I've ever seen a man as much in love as Tanner is with both of you."

Cassie was too stunned to move as she tried to absorb what she'd just learned. "But...he never said... He never said he felt that way. When he proposed he talked about Oliver and how we were good together, how we made sense. But there was no mention of him being...of feeling...of loving me. Why wouldn't he—"

"Lay his heart on the line?" Ruthie inquired, eyes wide. "Oh, I don't know. Perhaps it had something to do with you being in love with his brother?"

"But I'm not," she insisted hotly and got to her feet. "I don't feel that way about Doug...not anymore. And I don't think I ever really did. I cared about him and loved him in a way. But not like I love..."

She stopped, feeling Ruthie's questioning glance down to the soles of her feet.

"Go on," Ruthie prompted. "Say it."

Cassie took a deep breath and sighed. "Not like I love Tanner."

Ruthie smiled. "Well, good for you. And now that's out in the open, what are you going to do about it?"

Cassie was still thinking about the other woman's words long after she'd left.

He loves you...

Did he? Had she been so foolish? So blind? He'd never mentioned love. He cared, that's what he said. They were good together, in bed and out of it. They could give Oliver a home...a family.

Love hadn't rated a mention.

If it had...

Would she have responded differently? Would she have found it in her heart to forgive him?

So, Doug gets a free pass and I don't...

There was anger in his voice when he'd said the words. And regret. And pain.

And still she hadn't budged. She'd remained stubborn and resolute. Determined to think the worst. To blame him. To make him suffer. For what? Doug's sins? If so, what did that make her? A scared, confused little girl who'd been duped and wanted to lash out at the one person she'd subconsciously believed would take it and not bail on her? Would not leave her? Would not abandon her?

The realization hit home with the force of a sledgehammer.

Doug's letter was exactly the excuse she'd needed to push Tanner away.

The intensity of her feelings for him had terrified her and once she'd been dealt an out clause she'd grabbed it with both hands. Like a coward. Like the girl who'd never had to stand on her own two feet.

But she wasn't that girl anymore. She was a woman. And it was about time she started acting like one. She took a breath, grabbed the letter Ruthie had given her and opened it. Tanner's neat handwriting jumped out and she shuddered with emotion as she started reading.

Dear Oliver,

I'm not sure how old you'll be when you read this. Hopefully old enough to understand what I'm saying. I just wanted you to know about your dad. He was a lot older than me so we didn't spend much time together when I was young. But he was always there, always happy to play games and be a great big brother. He had his faults but he was a brave soldier and gave his life for his country. I want you to know that if he were here he'd teach you all the things our father taught us…like how to ride a horse and fix a fence. And how to be honest and honorable and try to always do what's right, even if you know someone might get hurt.

It's not easy growing up without your dad around. I know because I lost my dad, too, when I was young. But just know that if your dad had been here he would be very proud that you're his son. I can't promise I'll always be around for you, but if you ever need me you can trust that I will be there. I'll be here for you to talk to, to ask questions or simply to listen.

Being around you and your mom reminded me what it was like to be part of a family and I love you both more than I can say.
Tanner

Cassie clutched the letter, tears streaming down her face. And she knew, for the first time in her life, what she wanted. And who. She grabbed the telephone and called Ruthie. A few minutes later she had the details she needed.

She checked the clock. It was late in South Dakota. But not too late. Once she dialed it took several seconds and then a deep, unfamiliar voice answered.

"Hi," she said and drew in a breath, feeling stronger than she had in a long time. In forever. "My name is Cassie Duncan. And I need your help."

Tanner stretched out his shoulders and gripped the saddle in his hands. He was tired. He couldn't remember the last time he'd slept through the night.

Liar...

The last time he'd slept more than four hours had been when he'd had Cassie's arms wrapped around him. They'd made love and afterward he'd fallen asleep with her curled up against his chest. He missed making love with her. He missed her so much he ached all over. And he missed Oliver.

But he was right to leave.

He wasn't going to beg for her and act like a fool any more than he already had. He had his fair share of pride and she'd battered his ego with a shovel. She couldn't forgive him. And she didn't care enough to try. Besides, she'd made it abundantly clear that her feelings were still with his brother.

I loved him. I had his child. I cried and grieved when he died.

"Everything all right?"

Grady Parker's voice thrust him back into the present. His best friend was looking at him, one brow up. "Sure," he said and rested the saddle. "Fine."

He'd been at his friend's ranch most of the morning, cutting out the older calves from a large herd of Charolais cattle while Grady and his foreman took some of the steers to market.

"Any chance you can ride down to the pasture behind Flat Rock and check out the mustangs? They've been down by the watering hole most of the week, but I'm pretty sure there's a roan filly that's lame. Might be worth you looking at her before I call the vet out."

Flat Rock was a thirty-minute ride, but still part of Grady's land. The Parker ranch was one of the biggest and oldest in the county and butted his place along the edge of the creek. Tanner didn't really feel like a one-hour round-trip but knew his friend was right. And the filly needed to be looked at.

"Yeah, no problem."

Grady nodded. "Great. I gotta head into town for an errand so if I'm not back just leave Solo in the corral."

Solo was Grady's mild-tempered paint gelding. A horse that Tanner had broken in a few years earlier and had been riding that morning. "Okay."

His friend moved to leave, then hesitated for a moment. "You sure you're okay? You've only been riding again for a couple of weeks. If it's too much I can—"

"Stop worrying like an old woman, will you?" he said and tucked the saddle on his hip. "I'm fine. The leg's not giving me much trouble and I'm good to ride."

Grady lingered for a second and then shrugged. "Okay. I'm taking the girls with me," he said about his three young daughters. "And thanks for your help today."

Tanner waved the other man off and grabbed Solo's gear. Once he was tacked up he swung into the saddle and headed off. The trail to Flat Rock was well-worn and he eased the gelding into a steady trot for most of the way. Ten minutes in and he knew a solitary ride was exactly what he needed to clear his mind.

If that were possible. He spent most of his days and nights thinking about Cassie. Wondering how he'd made such a mess of it all. He loved her…but he hadn't the courage to say the words. He wanted her, but he'd been unwilling to stay around and play second fiddle to his brother.

He had to get her out of his head. And his heart.

Once he reached Flat Rock and the mustangs, he singled out the filly and took a short video on his cell. She did appear to be slightly lame and he texted Grady to get the vet out when he had the chance.

By the time he got back to the ranch it was past two o'clock. Grady hadn't returned from his trip to town, so Tanner unsaddled Solo and left him in the corral and headed for his truck. It was a short trip back to his ranch and he slowed as he drove beneath the wide white gates. Two *M*'s entwined on the logo and he let out a long breath. He'd called the ranch The Double M, hoping that one day he'd have someone to share it with. For the briefest moment he'd thought that someone was Cassie.

But he was wrong.

The gravel driveway was long and straight and he spotted a vehicle parked out front of the house. As he got closer he realized it was Grady's dual-cab truck. And his friend was resting against the back, arms crossed, hat slung low over his forehead.

Tanner pulled the truck to a halt and got out.

"What are you doing here?" he asked and noticed that his friend's daughters were in the backseat.

Grady jerked his head to one side in the direction of the house. "See for yourself."

Tanner turned his gaze to the farmhouse and stood motionless. A dog sat on the porch. A huge black-and-white dog he'd recognize anywhere. Mouse.

It's not possible…

The door opened and a figure emerged.

Cassie.

His heart thundered in his chest. His legs wouldn't move. His skin felt as if it was on fire. He saw her walk onto the porch and still he didn't want to allow himself to believe it.

He glanced toward Grady, who had now pushed himself off the rear of the truck and was grinning.

Grady tapped him on the shoulder. "Go get your family."

Tanner stood motionless, unable to move his legs. She was near the porch step, her beautiful hair flowing around her shoulders. He tried to move and failed. It was only when he heard Grady's truck pulling away that he gathered the strength to shift his limbs. He walked across the yard, his chest so tight he felt as though his heart might burst through his rib cage.

When he reached the bottom step he stopped. Mouse, who was tethered to a railing, whined and wagged his long tail. Tanner heard a baby laugh from inside the front door. Oliver. His heart rolled over.

"Hi," she said softly.

Tanner met her gaze. "Hello."

She took a deep breath. "You left something behind."

Tanner's insides jumped. "I did? What?"

She exhaled heavily. "Me. Us."

"Cassie, I…" His words trailed. He wanted to take her in his arms. He wanted to feel her kiss and her sweet touch. But first, he had to be sure. "Why are you here?"

She stared at him, her eyes glistening. "Your friend Grady is a nice man. He picked us up from the airport yesterday and we stayed at a motel in town."

His brows came up. Grady had some explaining to do. "You got on an airplane?"

She nodded. "My first. I've been doing a lot of things

for the first time lately. I started taking real responsibility for myself and my son. And I got a backbone, too."

He smiled a little. "And what do you intend to do with it?"

Her shoulders pushed back. "Fight for what I want."

"And what's that?"

Her mouth curved and she moved closer to the edge of the step. "You."

Tanner sucked in a breath. He wanted to believe her. He wanted it more than he'd wanted anything in his life. But resistance lingered. He didn't want to get his hopes up. Didn't want to have her for a moment only to lose her again.

"That's not how you felt a month ago."

"I'm not the same woman I was a month ago," she said quietly, moving onto the lower step. "I've changed. Knowing you has changed me." She paused and took a steadying breath. "I know about the house. I know what you did." She dropped onto the next step down. "But I would never have stood for it."

She was closer. Almost touching distance. "It's what you wanted. What you'd hoped for. You love that house. You grew up there. Why does it matter how it came about?"

"Because it does matter." She swept her gaze around the yard. "What if something happened and you lost all of this, because of me? I couldn't bear it."

"Money and possessions have never been important to me, Cassie. You should know that by now."

"I do know," she said and took another step closer. "It's one of the reasons why I…why I feel the way I do about you."

His heart stopped beating. Was that her roundabout way of saying she loved him? "You love Doug."

She shook her head. "I *loved* Doug. Once…a lifetime

ago. Before I knew you. Before I realized what it was to be with someone who is my friend…and my lover…and my truest soul mate."

"Cassie, I can't—"

"Don't say no to me," she implored, her face all emotion, her blue eyes glittering brightly. "Not when I came all this way to tell you how I feel about you."

Tanner's throat closed over. "Then tell me."

Her breath caught. "I'm in love with you."

And there it was. All he needed to hear. All he wanted. Her heart. Her love. "You're sure?"

She nodded. "Never surer. I love that you make me smile in one moment and make me mad the next. I love that you make love to me so passionately that I feel like the most desirable woman in the world. And I love how you love Oliver, and I want to make him all over again with you."

Tanner quickly took the two last steps and met her halfway. "I love you, too," he whispered against her mouth before he kissed her. "So very much."

She kissed him back and Tanner wrapped his arms around her. Feeling her close as if she was the air in his lungs.

Finally she pulled back a little and placed her hands on his shoulders. "I read the letter you wrote to Oliver. I knew as I read the words that you would always be there for him. That you would always love him and protect him. And I couldn't ask for a better father for my son. And the children I'm going to have with you in the future."

"And Doug?" he asked quietly.

"A memory," she replied. "And the person who brought us together, even if that was never his intention."

Tanner touched her face. "I will love you all the days of

my life, Cassie. You were the first girl I kissed." He smiled, cradling her cheek. "And you'll be the last."

She smiled. "You can bet your boots on that score, cowboy."

Oliver made a sound and Tanner tensed. "Where is he?"

"In the hall, in his stroller. He's missed you so much."

"I've missed him, too. And you." He linked an arm around her waist and they walked up the steps. "I've even missed this goofy dog of yours."

"Our dog now," she said and smiled.

"And our son," he said as they moved into the hall and noticed Oliver waving his hands excitedly from his stroller. A minute later they were in the living room, side by side on the dark leather sofa, and Tanner had Oliver in his arms. "He's grown so much," he said, bouncing him gently.

Cassie curled against him. "You really are remarkable with him. He sleeps and eats much better for you than me." She smiled and her eyes lit up. "I can't wait to have more children. The ranch and this house are so big and roomy, it should be filled with half a dozen kids."

Tanner laughed. "Six kids? I better get a second job."

She stroked his arm and smiled. "No need. The house in Crystal Point has just gone under contract. It's sold and the money will pay off the second mortgage you foolishly but adorably took out on the ranch." He went to protest but she placed her fingertips against his mouth. "I won't negotiate on this, Tanner. It's done."

"You took something of a risk, selling the house and coming here."

She shrugged. "I've turned over a new leaf. I needed to go after what I wanted. I've never done that before." She squeezed his thigh. "But it feels good. And I think I'm going to want to get my own way a whole lot more in the future."

He laughed. It was the first time he'd done that in weeks. "I think I like this new leaf of yours. It's very…sexy."

"Good, get used to it. I'm not a pushover anymore."

Tanner raised a skeptical brow. "Since when were you ever a pushover?"

"Well, not with you," she said. "But with other people. With Doug…I'm ashamed to say I put up with things. It was easy. No pressure. No risk. When we first met I was at a genuinely low ebb. My grandfather had gone into full-time care and I'd recently been overlooked for a promotion in my job. And then he showed up, all smiles and charm. And we sort of fell into it. He only came around to check out the house he'd bought and to meet the tenant. He certainly didn't intend on staying. I don't think he intended having a girlfriend, either."

Tanner nodded. "He was always more at home with his military colleagues than he was with his civilian life."

She smiled agreeably and without any lingering look of heartache. "I know. And when we were together there weren't any fireworks or bells and banjos or that kind of thing. It wasn't particularly passionate, either, if you get my meaning. It was simply…easy. And when he came home every now and then, I had a boyfriend and he had someone to look after his needs."

Tanner swallowed hard. "You don't have to justify your relationship with him to me."

"I know. But I think that's why I found it so confusing to be around you," she admitted. "When you came to visit that first time I was surprised by how aware of you I was. Doug had told me you were this moody and disinterested loner who liked horses better than people, and when I met you all I felt was this intense attraction. I couldn't get a handle on it. And I felt guilty. I knew I shouldn't have been secretly lusting after you when I considered myself to be in a relationship with your brother."

He chuckled. "Ah—that's why you ignored me?"

She nodded. "You did a fair amount of ignoring yourself."

"I know. I remembered who you were straightaway and I was knocked for a loop. And then I got to know you a little and all I could think was that my brother had somehow got the woman *I* was meant to be with to love him."

"So you stayed away?"

"Yes," he said.

"Until Doug was killed?"

Tanner sighed heavily. "I knew what he'd planned. I knew he hadn't the intention or foresight to make things right. And I was tired of being angry at him. I wanted it over. I wanted to make sure Oliver had what was rightfully his so I could move on." He met her gaze. "Except after two days with you I realized I was kidding myself."

"Two days?" Her eyes glittered. "You knew you loved me after two days?"

"Absolutely."

"I had no idea," she said.

"I did ask you to marry me, remember?"

She grimaced. "I know. But I thought you asked me because of Oliver and because we're…you know…good in bed together."

He grinned. "Well, that was certainly part of it. But I asked you to marry me because I love you. I was just too afraid to say it."

She pressed against him. "I wasn't much better. I'm so happy it's all out in the open now. There's nothing between us now."

"Cassie, about Doug's letter," he said, a little more soberly. "Have you forgiven me for keeping it from you?"

She nodded. "There was nothing to forgive. I know you only wanted to protect me and in some way protect Doug, too. Once I got over my stubborn childishness I understood."

Tanner sighed and grasped her hand, linking their fingers. "He wasn't all bad, you know. While he did some questionable things, like all of us he had his own demons to deal with. He was never the same after our parents died."

"He gave me Oliver," she said and sighed.

"He gave me my family," Tanner said and marveled at the woman and child he was holding in his arms. "And I'll always be grateful for that."

She pressed even closer and kissed him. "Does that mean you're going to ask me to marry you again?"

Tanner smiled. "Pushy, eh?"

"Just curious," she replied and grinned. "And I am up for trying new things these days."

Tanner moved, placed Oliver in his stroller, and then he dropped to his knees in front of her.

"Marry me, Cassandra?" he asked quietly. "Marry me and let me love you for the rest of our days," he said, proposing for a second time to the woman he loved.

And this time she said yes.

Epilogue

Cassie was sure she'd forgotten something. She had her something old—a pendant that had been her mother's—and her something blue was an exquisite lace handkerchief that Ruthie had gifted her.

I'm getting married today...

Their wedding was to be a simple ceremony at the courthouse with a justice of the peace and then dinner at the O'Sullivan pub down on Dryer Street. She was getting married, four weeks and one day after she'd arrived in Cedar Creek. She'd fallen in love with the small town, with its wide streets and unique mix of old and new storefronts. And she'd fallen in love with Tanner a little bit more every day.

And although they were doing everything fast, Lauren, Gabe and M.J. had flown in for the wedding. As had Ruthie.

"You look so beautiful."

Cassie turned from her spot near the bedroom window and saw Tanner in the doorway. "And you're not supposed to see the bride before the wedding."

He put a hand to his heart. "I promise it'll be our little secret."

Cassie smiled lovingly. He looked so handsome in his dark suit. She never tired of admiring him. And she knew it was mutual. "If M.J. catches you in here you'll be in big trouble."

"She's on the phone in the kitchen yelling at her boyfriend, so I'm off the hook."

Cassie laughed. "She doesn't have a boyfriend."

"So you say," he said and stepped into the room. "She's down there calling some poor guy an arrogant jerk and telling him she never wants to see him again." His eyes darkened with delight. "Sounds like love to me."

"Poor M.J.," Cassie said and grabbed her small rose bouquet. "Well, since you've seen me there's no backing out now."

"No chance," he said and looked her over. "You look amazing."

Cassie had chosen a knee-length ivory chiffon dress with a beautiful beaded bodice and pearl-colored heels. Her hair was down, her makeup minimal and the ring on her finger felt as though it had been there forever. They'd chosen it together from a small jewelry store in town. It was an antique setting with perfect white stones set in platinum. It wasn't huge or ostentatious. It was elegant and understated and exactly what she'd dreamed of.

"You know, you could have had a big fancy wedding with all the trappings," he said, and not for the first time since he'd proposed.

"I know," she replied. "But this is what I wanted. Just you and me and Oliver surrounded by the people we really care about. And you know how I love the steaks at the O'Sullivan pub," she said and laughed.

"Even without the finest Parker Charolais beef on the table," he said, grinning. "Who doesn't?"

Grady's brother-in-law owned the pub and it was no secret the two men barely tolerated one another. "So, how about you go and grab our little angel and we'll get going."

"He's with Ruthie. So, for the next—" he checked his watch "—ten minutes, you're all mine, Miss Duncan."

She smiled lovingly. "Soon-to-be Mrs. McCord."

He moved closer and reached for her hand, and then kissed her knuckles softly. "I can't wait."

"Me, either," she said with complete love in her heart. "I love you."

He grinned, but Cassie wasn't fooled. He was as moved by emotion as she was.

"I love you, too."

And an hour later they were in front of the justice of the peace, declaring their love and devotion to one another. Cassie cried a little during the ceremony as Tanner spoke of loving and honoring her for all his life. Once their vows were made and their marriage officiated, Tanner gripped her hand, took Oliver in the crook of one arm and led them out of the courthouse and onto the front steps.

And into the rest of their lives.

* * * * *

THE ONE MAN
TO HEAL HER

MEREDITH WEBBER

For all the Maytoners, who keep me going.

PROLOGUE

ALEX SAT HUDDLED on a red plastic chair against the wall of the ER room. A woman doctor she vaguely recognised had come towards her earlier but had whisked away when a rush of ambulance cases had been brought in, and now, two hours later, Alex still sat, a little more hunched over, exhaustion having caused her to nod off so several times she'd nearly fallen off the chair.

Twice a male nurse had approached, but, unable to stand the thought of a man touching her, she'd shrunk back and lied, saying she was waiting for someone.

Then the woman doctor she'd seen earlier must have cleared the urgent patients and approached once again.

'Are you here for treatment?' she asked gently.

Alex nodded, not sure she would be able to speak, let alone move, so thick was the cloud of despair and un-happiness that enveloped her.

The doctor knelt and reached out to touch Alex's cheek, brushing at the tears that kept dripping out of her eyes no matter how hard she tried to stop them.

She wondered what the doctor would make of her pathetic behaviour. Probably assume she was a street kid, although would a street kid be wearing clean clothes?

'Can you tell me what's wrong?'

The question focussed Alex's mind.

'I'm bleeding.'

She whispered the words, and heard the huskiness of fear and shame in them—saw the doctor's look of shock—wondered what the doctor would think...

'I'm Dr Isobel Armitage,' the woman said gently. 'Come with me and I'll see what I can do to help you.'

She took Alex's hand, pressed her fingers reassuringly, and led her to a cubicle, pausing only to draw the curtains around it.

The male nurse who'd offered assistance earlier eased through the gap in the curtains. The doctor must have felt Alex cringe and try to hide behind her because she turned and hugged her tightly, asking the nurse to leave them.

'She wouldn't talk to me earlier,' he complained, but the woman called Isobel just shooed him away.

'Are you feeling well enough to tell me who you are? Answer a few questions?'

Alex nodded, and somehow managed to supply her name, Alexandra Hudson, and age, sixteen, but when she came to an address the courage that had shored her up to actually get to the hospital deserted her and she burst into tears.

Once again the doctor held her while she cried, then poked her head outside the door to ask some unseen person to bring in tea with plenty of sugar.

'A hot drink will do you good,' Isobel said, passing the box of tissues to Alex before wrapping a blood-pressure cuff around her arm. Isobel talked as she worked, making notes on a chart that still had no address on it.

The talking helped so by the time the tea arrived the tears had stopped, although the doctor—Isobel—waited until Alex finished her tea before asking quietly, 'Can you tell me what happened?'

Alex lifted her head, knowing she had to be looking

at Isobel as she spoke although cringingly aware of how rough she must look with a tear-streaked face and tangled hair, her clothes thrown on any old how.

Deep breath!

You can do this!

And she did—or she began…

'It was Mr Spencer—Dad's friend. He—he…'

'He raped you?'

Alex nodded.

'I need to examine you,' Isobel told her.

The words were gentle but Alex could see the woman's anger flashing in her eyes. How much of this kind of thing—of men's violence towards woman—had she seen in her job?

'Did you tell your parents?'

Alex knew the question was the obvious one and the doctor had to ask it, but—

The pain of their reaction speared through her yet again, but she had to tell—to explain…

The words came tumbling out in a shivery kind of whisper, forced past the hurt—the rejection…

'They called me a liar and a slut and told me I was no longer their daughter. They're religious, you see. Mr Spencer, he preaches in the church sometimes and I told Mum weeks ago that he kept touching me and she sent me to my room for talking filth.'

Now she was crying again—tears rolling down her cheeks—like a big sook.

She had no idea what the doctor was thinking until she took both of Alex's hands in hers, gently squeezed her fingers once again, and said quietly, 'We should report it to the police.'

Alex nodded. She'd already thought about this and

knew the doctor was right, although the woman looked very surprised by her agreement.

'There's other kids there, at the church, younger than me,' she explained, 'and he touches them too. He shouldn't be allowed—someone has to stop him.'

'You're something special,' Isobel said, smiling at Alex, 'but there's your family to consider as well. There'll be publicity, a court case—how will they handle it?'

Alex shrugged.

'They've kicked me out, what more can they do to me?'

And something in her determination must have come through in the words—the hint of the growing strength that she knew lay beneath her unhappiness—because Isobel reached around her and gave her another a warm hug.

'We'll look after you,' she promised. 'And I'll stand by you all through it. But first...'

She stopped, obviously thinking of the next step.

'I have to phone someone from the police. A woman called Marcie Clarke. She's kind and understanding and has done this kind of police business before,' Isobel told Alex. 'When she gets here we can examine you and take samples.'

'Samples?'

The word fluttered from Alex's lips and Isobel frowned.

'It hasn't just happened? You've been home?'

'I *had* to go home,' Alex told her, the experience coming back to her in all its horror. 'I had to clean myself up and scrub away what that man had done to me, but it was two days ago and there's still blood and I don't know what to do.'

She broke down completely, crying giving way to desolate sobs, then the doctor's arms were around her again, comforting and soothing, shushing and promising that everything would be all right.

Three hours later, the rape reported, Alex comforted by the information that a torn hymen could bleed for a couple of days, and Marcie in charge of what little, probably useless, evidence Isobel had managed to retrieve, the kind doctor who'd got her through the ordeal disappeared to take a phone call.

Alex was exhausted, too tired to even care about what would happen next—where she'd find a bed, how she'd live. Did Heritage Port have places for homeless teenagers?

It was all too much, so she curled up on the narrow bed in the cubicle and fell asleep.

At some time someone must have come in and put a light cover over her because when Isobel woke her gently, she was clutching it tightly around her body like the ultimate security blanket.

'Do you have somewhere to go?' Isobel asked, handing Alex another cup of tea and a healthy-looking muffin.

Alex shook her head.

'Would you know of someplace?' she asked, and heard her voice crack as the reality of the situation nearly overwhelmed her again.

'Well, I've one idea,' Isobel told her. 'Do you like kids?'

'Love them,' Alex replied, and to her surprise she even found a smile. 'I've done a lot of babysitting. I started when I was fourteen because I've been saving money to get a car—a red car! And I volunteer at a pre-school play group at the community centre on Saturday mornings.'

'I thought you looked familiar!' said Isobel. 'I sometimes take my twins to that play group.' She thought for a moment. 'I know this sounds daft and it's a bit sudden, but would you like to come home with me? I've got two monsters so I can promise they'll take your mind off your troubles for a while. I'll be in the house but I'll need to sleep at some time, so if you're there I can. My husband's also a doctor and he's due at work any minute and one of the twins has a cold so they can't go to kindy. Dave, that's my husband, and I have been talking about getting an au pair for some time, but neither of us has ever had time to do anything about it. You need a home—and ours might not be it—but just for today at least, would you like a job?'

This time it was Alex who hugged her!

CHAPTER ONE

SHE'D COME HOME to Heritage Port with plenty of misgivings, but within hours of her arrival Alex had known she'd done the right thing. Although her childhood had been happy, her best memories of the place were of the three and a half years she'd spent with the Armitage family, minding the rambunctious twins, finishing school and even starting her pre-med studies at university, she and the twins' parents juggling their timetables so everything ran smoothly.

Well, as smoothly as could be expected with two little mischief-makers in the house!

It wasn't that the horror of the rape and the humiliation of the trial that had followed it didn't occasionally still disturb her dreams—her ex-fiancé had blamed it for what he'd termed her inability to respond to his kisses, let alone anything more intimate—but she found herself pleased to be home in one of the most beautiful places in the world.

As the taxi carried her from the airport, bright sun shone on the rolling ocean, white-fringed waves crashed on the rocks at the headland, and shushed up the beach. The river was as green and peaceful as she remembered it, and, best of all, somehow, in the intervening years, the hard knot in her heart had loosened.

Now, sitting beside the hospital bed, she was able to look at her father and remember the man who'd first taught her to bait her fishing hook—the father she'd loved...

'So, where have you come from?' one of the nurses in the ICU asked as Alex, her luggage stacked in a corner of the room, held her father's hand, and talked to the sleeping man about fishing in the dark shadows of the mangroves that arched over the little inlets off the river.

'Here,' she told him. 'I've just been away for a while.'

Away when the girls she'd been at school with had been marrying and having babies...

Away when her mother had died without forgiving her for 'making a fuss'...

Away, but always waiting for a letter that said two simple words, 'Come home.'

'How long's a while?' the nurse asked, making conversation, Alex knew, but welcoming it in the sterile room, the silence broken only by her voice and the machines.

'Sixteen years.'

'Long time!'

And it had been.

When the Armitage family, with their darling twins, had shifted to Melbourne so Isobel and Dave could continue specialist careers, Alex had chosen to go north to Brisbane to finish her medical training.

From there, on Isobel's advice, she'd contacted her parents, writing to them to tell them where she was and what she was doing. Although she'd received no response, she'd continued writing—birthdays and Christmas—always somehow hoping...

Then, three weeks ago, in far-off Glasgow, she'd received a letter from her father. Her mother was dead, Rusty, the dog, was dead, Mr Spencer had died, and he, her father, was going into hospital for open-heart surgery to replace a wonky valve.

The letter hadn't asked her to come home, but here she was, sitting in the intensive care unit in the new modern hospital at Heritage Port, talking quietly to her heavily sedated father, and remembering happy times.

Will Kent, head intensivist, doing a round of the ICU, was surprised to see the woman there, her arms cradling her head on the bottom of the bed, apparently deeply asleep. Mr Hudson might be his patient in this unit, Will's fiefdom, but the man had been unconscious since he'd arrived.

'Who's the woman in with Mr Hudson?' he asked one of the nurses.

'His daughter—Alexandra, I think she's called—just arrived from Scotland. Apparently hasn't been home for years. Some daughter!'

Alexandra Hudson—Alex!

Of course she hadn't been home for years—banished as she'd been at sixteen. Ending up with his next-door neighbours, Isobel and Dave Armitage, as a nanny for their twins.

He peered more closely at the patient.

There didn't seem to be anything familiar about the man—old now, and grey with illness—but he *did* remember the day Isobel had asked him to accompany her and Alex back to the Hudson home so Alex could get some clothes. Dave had been working, and Will had felt enormously proud that Isobel had chosen him to go along. He'd seen himself as the protector of the two women—a tall, lanky, bespectacled, twenty-two-year-old protector!

Mrs Hudson had thrown Alex's clothes from an upstairs window, ranting all the time about 'whores' and 'sluts', while Mr Hudson had barred the door, standing there like an ancient biblical prophet, his only prophecy doom.

Poor Alex had been scarlet with humiliation and hurt, tears leaking from behind the big dark glasses she'd worn even inside in those days. He'd wanted to put his arm around her—to give her a hug—but he'd known she'd shy away, as she had from all but the twins' hugs and kisses.

Not that he'd have kissed her—she'd been, what? Fifteen? Sixteen?

He couldn't remember—remembered only the deep pity he'd felt for the so obviously damaged teenager.

Was this patient, here in the ICU, recovering from an operation for a heart valve replacement, *that* Mr Hudson?

Was the sleeping woman really Alex?

And had his thoughts disturbed her that she stirred and lifted her head?

Huge blue eyes she'd hidden behind darkened glasses for all the years she'd lived next door stared unseeingly at him.

Huge blue eyes framed by golden blonde hair tipped with silver here and there and softly tousled by sleep. The early beauty she'd tried to hide with shorn hair and the glasses had come to fruition. Even sleep-tousled, she was stunning.

'Alex?'

She straightened up from the bed and frowned at him.

'I'm Will, Will Kent—from next door to the Armitages, remember?'

The frown deepened and she shook her head, so obviously puzzled he had to smile.

'You pinched my job,' he added, remembering how he'd pretended to complain about losing the occasional babysitting he'd done for the Armitages.

'Superman?' she whispered, disbelief filling the words.

He flourished a pretend cloak and bowed low.

'At your service, ma'am! But also head intensivist at the hospital. Your father's in my care until he's well enough to be transferred to the coronary care unit.'

He saw her face light up as things fell into place and she shot to her feet and advanced to give him an all-enveloping hug.

'Oh, Will,' she murmured, 'it's so good to see a familiar face.'

She eased back, looking at him, then laughed.

'Not so familiar—you've grown up!'

'Not even Superman can stay twenty-two for ever,' Will said gloomily, and she laughed again, her face lighting up with delight—so gloriously beautiful Will felt his lungs seize.

Breathe, he told himself, and tried to remember how.

Fortunately, as his brain seemed to be similarly paralysed, instinct took over and his lungs filled with air while he tried to catch up with Alex's conversation.

'Intensivist? Weren't you heading towards O and G when you left Port? What made you change your mind? It can't have been the late night callouts, you'd get more of them in this job.'

'Whoa!'

Will held up his hand, pleased to see his limb was obeying messages, although other parts of his body were obviously still in shock.

'I'm on a ward round and really need to check your dad and the other patients.'

'Can we catch up later?' Alex asked. 'I couldn't get home before the op, but I've spoken to the surgeon who did the operation. He gave me the impression he wasn't too positive about the outcome.'

As Will was still feeling startling and unfamiliar re-actions to Alex's hug, he wondered if this was wise, but she was entitled to ask questions about her father's health.

But beyond that, he was intrigued. The damaged teenager who, in the beginning, would duck away if she saw him over the fence, and who'd shrunk back from any physical contact—even a simple handshake—had emerged, like a caterpillar from a cocoon, as this beautiful butterfly.

He wanted to know just how she'd managed the trans-formation—*and* how deep it went. He knew Isobel in par-ticular had worked hard to restore Alex's self-esteem, but there'd been a fragility about the teenager that couldn't be hidden behind dark glasses and a dreadful haircut.

'As far as your father's concerned, the operation went well, but he wasn't in the best of health before it. Other heart problems apparently. I only know this stuff from his chart but I gather that if it hadn't been a necessity...'

He paused, wondering how to tell this woman he knew but didn't know just how precarious her father's health was.

'Look, I should be through by eight and your father will still be sleeping off the anaesthetic until morning at least, so you might as well get out of here for a while,' he said. 'We *could* eat in the canteen but the food's ap-palling. There's a nice new bar and restaurant at the top of the old Royal Motel. It has a fancier name now—the motel, that is—which I can never remember. And it's in walking distance. We could have a meal—give us time to catch up.'

She nodded her agreement as a nurse came into the room. Will's attention, or ninety-five per cent of it, re-turned to his patient as he discussed Mr Hudson's prog-

ress and checked the results the monitor was revealing
by the second.

Alex had slipped away, for which he was truly grateful, although he felt a momentary regret he hadn't looked
at her more closely, if only to confirm his impression
she'd blossomed into a startlingly beautiful woman.

Will Kent!

Alex stood in the little bathroom off the family waiting room of the ICU and smiled as she ran the name
through her head.

But had the Will Kent she'd known had laughing
brown eyes that crinkled with smile lines at the corners, and lips that seemed to be on the verge of a smile
all the time? Of course, eighteen years ago, when he'd
left Port to finish his studies, his eyes probably hadn't
been crinkled, *and* they'd been hidden behind the dark-
framed glasses, and, anyway, in the state she'd been in
back then she wouldn't have noticed anything about any
man. Certainly not his lips…

And she'd better not notice them now, she reminded
herself. As she'd pointed out, Will was all grown up now,
and undoubtedly married with children. In fact, throwing herself at him, hugging him, had undoubtedly embarrassed him no end, rendering him practically speechless.

Back then he'd been the Armitages' next-door neighbour christened Superman by the twins—or probably
their parents, given his surname. Self-effacing—that was
how she'd have described him—but somehow he'd always
been around in that first year she'd been with the Armitages. In and out of the house, borrowing textbooks from
Dave or Isobel, seemingly always there if she'd needed
him. She tried to remember.

He'd certainly helped her rescue Riain out of the tree

one day, and had carried Rosi down to the doctor's the day she'd fallen off the swing.

Superman!

She smiled at the memories and told herself that today, with all the emotions of her return home churning inside her, she'd probably have hugged any familiar face.

An image of Will as he was now, dark hair touched with silver, lips stretched in a surprised smile, continued to linger in Alex's head, making her feel hot and embarrassed and somehow ashamed all at the same time.

Why had he suggested dinner?

He could have talked to Alex in the visitors' room, or his office, but a bar?

Had a beautiful woman giving him a hug gone straight to his head?

Or had his mother's gentle nagging—you've got to start going out again some time, Will—prompted the choice?

His mother was probably right!

He *did* have to start going out again.

Three years now—three years, eight months and five days, if he was counting—since Elise's death, and Charlotte deserved to have a mother...

He stared out at the lights sparkling in the darkened town beneath him and gave a huff of laughter.

'That would be ironic laughter,' he muttered to himself, remembering trying to explain irony to Alex, she pushing the twins on the swings while he'd leaned over the fence. Later, that was, after she'd got used to him being around and had actually asked him for some help with some assignment she was doing.

'Definitely ironic!'

'Are you talking to yourself?'

He turned to see her, and all the physical reactions he'd had at the hospital happened again.

'Never!' he lied. 'That would really label me a nut job.'

Alex smiled, intensifying all the stuff going on inside his body.

'You might think back to when I met you,' she teased. 'You were hanging upside down on the side fence, so the nut-job label was firmly in place from the beginning.'

Will gathered the tattered remnants of his dignity.

'I was being a bat!' he reminded her. 'Showing the twins how they hung in their trees.'

She laughed with such frank and open delight his insides melted.

But along with all the physical confusion came the clang of warning bells.

They were both damaged people, besides which she was probably married, or engaged, or partnered—too beautiful to still be single—while he was no catch—single father still hurting from the loss of his wife, shying away from the very thought of love. Not that this was a date...

'Are you okay?'

'I guess,' he answered the still smiling woman, although okay was a long way off.

He was sitting at a table that had a view over the mouth of the river and up along the coast as far as a distant headland.

The view provided the distraction he needed.

'Can we see your house from here?' he asked, looking not out to sea but up the river.

Alex looked too, checking the scattering of houses on the far side of the river from the town—reached by ferry during its operating hours or by a long detour back around via the highway when the ferry stopped at midnight.

'I think so,' she said. 'You see the ferry down by the wharf and the fishermen's co-op on it—the shed-looking thing? Beyond that there's the bit of waste land and the huge old fig tree—well, we're two houses down from the tree, although you probably can't see the house because they seem to have built an enormous place beside it.'

She smiled and shrugged her shoulders.

'*We're* two houses down,' she repeated. 'It's funny talking about "my house" when I haven't been there for so long. Although I didn't make it back in time to see Dad before the operation, we'd spoken on the phone a couple of times, and he'd been so upset about what had happened in the past that I promised when I came I'd stay with him, at least until he's over the op.'

Will smiled, brown eyes twinkling in his tanned face, and Alex immediately regretted this reunion.

It was because he was a familiar face that she was noticing little things about him—like the twinkling eyes.

And she certainly shouldn't be noticing twinkling eyes when he was wearing a wedding ring.

She touched his finger.

'You're married, that's nice. Kids?'

The twinkle disappeared and Will's open, friendly face went completely blank.

'Let's get you a drink first.'

He was on his feet, waiting for her order.

On his feet too quickly?

Far too quickly!

Get with it, Alex!

'G and T in a long glass, please.'

That's better. Or it would have been if she hadn't watched him walk towards the bar, seeing the breadth of his shoulders and how his back sloped down to slim hips and—

You will *not* look at his butt! The man is married, he is off limits, he's nothing more than an old—not exactly friend but someone she *had* known quite well.

It's just that he's the first familiar face you've seen that you're reacting this way.

He brought her drink and a small bowl of cashews for them to share, then settled back down at the table, this time looking out at the stretch of beach.

Do I ask again? Alex wondered, as an uneasy silence hovered around them.

'I'm a single father,' he began, still staring out along the beach. 'My wife died when Charlotte was born—cancer—Charlotte's three and a half.'

Will turned back to his companion as he spoke, aware of how stiff and remote he must have sounded as he'd blurted out his story.

Lack of practice in telling it—he knew that. Telling it was one of the reasons he'd avoided going out—telling it hurt...

Had she felt that pain—heard it in his voice—that her fingers, cold and slightly damp from the glass, reached out and took his hand, giving it a squeeze?

'Oh, Will,' she said softly. 'I cannot imagine what pain that must have caused you—and what a loss it must have been. We see awful things every day in our work, yet we somehow think we're immune to it.'

She hesitated, her fingers tightening on his hand.

'Do you want to talk about it—to tell me?'

And suddenly he did. It was almost as if he'd been waiting for Alex to return—or someone like Alex to come along—so he could put it all together and let it all out, releasing some of the terrible tension he'd carried inside his body for so long.

'We met as students, married after graduation then waited a while to have kids—an intern's life is appalling so we were hardly ever together. Then, when we decided to have a family, Elise, her name was Elise, was diagnosed with breast cancer when she was three months pregnant. It was a very aggressive strain and the specialists wanted her to abort the baby and get immediate treatment. She refused, knowing the treatment would leave her sterile.'

He paused but Alex kept quiet, perhaps sensing there was more.

'We fought about it, Alex,' he finally added, looking into the blue eyes across the table from him, seeing her understanding and concern. "That's what hurts so much now, that I fought her over this, said terrible things.'

'But only out of love,' Alex said quietly, and he knew she understood.

'She wouldn't accept any treatment or even pain relief that would have crossed the placenta and harmed the baby, and by the last month of the pregnancy she was in a coma—treatment was too late.'

Alex sipped her drink, knocked flat by the deep pain behind Will's simple tale. To her, in that first year at the Armitages', Will had always seemed like part of the family. And, perhaps because of the family link, he'd been totally unthreatening, unlike the youths and young men she'd see on the street or in the park—males who'd make some casual remark, not really even aimed at her, but enough to make her cringe and scurry back home with the twins.

Will had just been Will, studying medicine because, she suspected, he'd idolised Dave and Isobel.

Now the pain he'd had in his life made her heart ache for him.

No wonder he'd grown up...

'So, your daughter?'

His smile lit up his face.

It did weird things to her insides too, but she could ignore them.

'Charlotte,' he said simply. 'She's the greatest—a precious gift—she's why we came back here to Port. Look, here's a photo.'

Alex waited while he pulled out his wallet and dug in the folds, and she wondered if he was giving himself time to get over the memories of his wife's death.

The small, wallet-sized photo, showed a little girl with a mop of brown curls and a smile that could melt stone. Alex's breathing faltered as she looked at the beautiful child. Mr Spencer had stolen more than her innocence, he'd stolen her ability to get close enough to a man to want a sexual relationship, let alone a child.

But Will was speaking again and she switched off the futile regrets to listen.

'Mum minds her when I'm at work, although I've built a separate flat in Mum's house so we're independent a lot of the time.'

The happiness faded from his face.

'It worries me, though, that I rely so much on Mum. Now she's retired she should be out doing things, not minding a nearly four-year-old.'

'I bet she's fine with that,' Alex told him, and touched the hand that still held the photo, just gently...

'She says so and it will be easier when Charlotte goes to kindy next year, then school—'

'And then, whoosh—they're gone from your life.'

His smile wasn't the worst one she'd ever seen, but it was close, yet even the weak effort affected Alex.

Jet-lag—it had to be!

Jet-lag and seeing a familiar face, that's all that was going on.

She let go of his hand and concentrated on her drink.

'So, tell me about you,' he said, and she knew her own smile would be even weaker than his had been.

In so many ways it was a success story, yet—

'Perhaps we should eat,' she suggested, hoping a move from this table—any kind of movement—might…

What? Make him forget he'd asked?

Or break the sense of intimacy—it had to be a false intimacy because of the past—that seemed to be enclosing them.

'We can talk over food,' she added, because she knew she'd been far too abrupt.

Will stood up with such alacrity she had to believe he'd felt it too. He led her into another part of the room where most of the diners already finishing their meals, lingering over dessert or last drinks.

'Tell me about Charlotte—favourite games, toys, books,' she said, when a waiter had ushered them to a table and slid serviettes onto their laps.

Will grinned at her, which kind of undid a lot of what the move had accomplished, in that a different kind of tension had appeared, tightening her skin and skidding along her nerves.

'You're supposed to be telling me about you,' he reminded her.

Alex waved away his objection but he ignored the gesture.

'No way, you tell first,' he ordered, waggling his finger at her, like a teacher with a reluctant pupil.

'Here's the short version,' Alex said. 'You'd gone south

to finish your degree before I left the Armitages', but I got that scholarship Isobel made me work so hard for, went to Brisbane, got my degree, got engaged—church upbringing still strong, so marriage seemed a logical step. I'd wanted to specialise in cardiology, Dave's influence, I suppose, although I couldn't handle the surgery. I was offered a terrific training job in London, qualified, got unengaged, moved from London to Glasgow, and now I'm home.'

Given that Will was still smiling at her, she thought she'd done rather well.

'That's it?' he asked. 'What happened to the fiancé? And you're a beautiful woman, why only one?'

She'd been pretending to study the menu while she'd talked but now she looked directly at Will.

'I was so sure I'd recovered from the rape—been to counsellors, talked and talked,' she said, pleased to hear how calmly she could say the word, even back here where it had happened.

She paused then admitted something she'd never before put into words.

'But relationships—they just don't seem to work. Not that I've had that many, but I've tried, Will, I really have, but when it comes to taking the next step—the intimacy thing—I pull back. It's unfair to the men, apart from anything else, so in the end I stopped dating and, really, my life is simpler and I'm happy with it. There's something missing in me, Will, and that's all I can put it down to.'

Had she sounded depressed that Will reached out and covered her hand with his?

Nothing more than a sympathetic touch, but it fired Alex's slowly settling nerves again. She removed her hand to close her menu.

'I think I'll have the rack of lamb,' she said, far too brightly.

* * *

Will waved the waiter over, gave their order, talked to him about a good red wine to have with the lamb. They would sell it by the glass, which was all he wanted.

The waiter returned with a bottle of red, showed it to Will, offered him a taste, then poured them both a glass.

Will lifted his to toast Alex, who clinked her glass with his and kind of smiled. Maybe it would have worked if sadness hadn't still been lingering in her eyes...

Not that he'd meant to notice her eyes—

'So, Glasgow? What on earth were you doing there?'

This time Alex's smile was better, and he heard an echo of laughter in her voice.

'It's actually a very lively city, and I had a dream job. Then Dad got in touch and—well, here I am. As I said, I'm a cardiologist and although I hope I won't get a lot of intensive-care patients, I imagine we'll see a bit of each other around the hospital. I've joined a practice here.'

'Brian Lane's?'

Alex nodded.

'But that's great, he's a good friend of mine,' Will said, smiling enthusiastically. 'I have a room in the same building—we'll be running into each other all the time.'

Before Alex could reply—well, what *was* there to reply—the smile faded from Will's face and he asked, rather uncertainly, 'It *is* good, isn't it?'

His sudden uncertainty told Alex that he was as un-practised in the relationship game as she was. Not that this was a relationship. Will was still obviously getting over Elise, while she, Alex, could make an epic disaster of even a casual date.

'I think it's good,' she said quietly. 'You've already made my homecoming so much easier, Will, so having you around as I learn my way around the hospital will be fantastic.'

His face lit up as his luminous smile returned, and Alex was swamped by a shivery sensation of...

What?

Happiness?

No, that would be ridiculous.

Fortunately, the waiter returned with their dinners, and operating on her rack of lamb, separating out the cutlets, gave Alex time to recover from whatever it might have been.

Will was talking about Charlotte now, apparently answering the questions Alex had asked earlier in the conversation.

And in every word Alex heard the love this grown-up Will had for his little daughter, while the happiness she'd brought him shone in his eyes.

'She sounds great,' Alex said, and to her surprise Will blushed, much as he had as a young man when she'd caught him hanging on the fence.

'I talk too much about her when I do go out. Mum says I need to do some speed dating to get back into the way of speaking to women. She says Charlotte needs a mother and she's probably right.'

Serious brown eyes met Alex's across the table.

'But I've got out of the dating habit,' he admitted, before adding ruefully, 'Not that I was ever that good at it. Do you remember Isobel telling me—some time that year—that I should write out a list of things to talk about before going to a party? Questions, she said, ask women questions about themselves and actually listen to their answers—that's very flattering.'

Alex smiled.

'I suspected at the time she was talking to me as well.

She kept encouraging me to go out and meet young people. As I remember, you were all of a dither because you thought this girl you liked would be there, right?'

She studied Will, whose entire attention now appeared to be on his meal.

'Did it work for you?' she asked.

He looked up and smiled, and although the now-familiar reactions to his smile tumbled through her body, they stilled when he answered.

'It did,' he said quietly. 'The girl was Elise.'

Which killed that conversation dead, Will realised as the words landed between them with an almost audible thump.

He had to think, to say something—anything—because talking to Alex was making him feel good inside, while looking at Alex—well, best he didn't consider how *that* was making him feel!

But where was his list?

Ask questions, Isobel had told him way back then.

He stopped pretending to be eating and looked up at the woman across the table from him, delicately cutting morsels of lamb from her cutlets.

'How did you feel about coming back to Port?'

She met his eyes, and smiled.

'Ask questions, huh?' she teased, then looked thoughtful, as if actually considering her reply.

'Hearing from my father—that was a shock. After so many years, it took a while to take it in, but then I reread his letter, saw the bit about his health, and coming back seemed the only possible thing to do—the natural thing. As if it was time…'

How could he not reach out to rest his hand on hers?

How could he not squeeze her slim, warm fingers?

'It must be hard,' he said, and her smile brightened.

'I don't really know yet,' she said. 'In the taxi, coming from the airport, seeing the river and the sea, well, it *felt* right. In fact, I felt a surge of excitement, as if this was where I should be. But since then I've been at the hospital and then here—not really home at all.'

'But you'll go home—to your old house—stay there?'

She nodded.

'I think so—for a while at least, while Dad convalesces, then we'll see how it works out. It's been nearly twenty years since I left home, Will, and I don't really know him any more.'

Her smile this time was less joyous, nothing more than a slight curl of her lips, and her eyes held Will's as she added, 'It might sound strange but up to that time I was happy here, you see. I had a wonderful childhood with the river right beside us. I think I've let what happened to me affect my life for far too long. I want to start again, back in the place where I belong.'

He wanted to kiss her, in praise of her courage, nothing more—well, almost nothing more.

'If anyone can do it, you can,' he said.

'Thanks,' she said softly, lifting her hand from under his and replacing it on top, where it sat, warm and comforting, although wasn't he supposed to be comforting her?

She really should stop holding his hand. This was just a dinner between colleagues—old friends—not a date.

But holding Will's hand felt...*nice*. Pathetic word but it covered the situation.

Very nice would be even better—

A low ping of a message arriving on Will's mobile broke into her thoughts, and the gravity on his face as he read the message told her it wasn't good news.

'I'm sorry, Alex, but your father's had a setback—

heart attack or stroke. His surgeon is on his way, but I'll have to go.'

'I'll come with you,' Alex said.

Will was on his feet, asking the waiter to put the dinner on his account, shrugging into the jacket he'd hung on the back of his chair.

'I'm so sorry,' he said to Alex as he walked her to the door, slipping a comforting arm around her shoulders and giving her a hug. 'His surgeon was worried about him undergoing the operation when he'd had a heart attack three years ago but the leaking heart valve was restricting his life and eventually would have killed him. Now this!'

Will insisted on driving her to the hospital.

'I can drop you back at your car later,' he said.

'No car. I got a cab from the airport earlier and walked from the hospital this evening,' Alex whispered, while all the 'what ifs' clamoured in her head. She should have come sooner, tried harder to heal the wound between herself and her parents, at the very least thanked Dad for getting in touch with her in the end.

Now it might be too late. A post-surgical patient was too fragile to have heroic lifesaving measures practised on him.

'He'd signed a health directive stating he didn't want to be resuscitated,' Will said quietly as he opened the door of his car for her.

Alex found a wan smile.

'I was just thinking he was hardly a candidate for the more heroic revival techniques.'

Will patted her hand. 'Let's wait and see.' He closed the car door and walked around the hood to get in beside her.

They arrived at the ICU to find a flurry of activity as they prepared to take the patient to Radiography for a CT scan of his brain, a stroke now seeming the most likely cause of his deep unconsciousness.

Alex stood beside her father's bed, with Will on the other side.

'If it's a stroke it would have to be haemorrhagic, rather than a clot—he'd be on blood thinners post-op,' Alex said, trying to think professionally so she could block out the emotion and nerves.

Will nodded glumly. 'Any bleed with already thinned blood could be catastrophic.'

Alex watched helplessly as gentle hands stripped away the tubes and monitors before lifting her father onto the scanner's stretcher and sliding his head into the machine.

In ten minutes they had the answer, a subarachnoid haemorrhage where an unsuspected aneurysm had burst.

Her father was returned to his bed and reattached to monitors and breathing apparatus, but Alex knew it was too late. Such a catastrophic bleed had only one outcome, especially in her father's weakened post-op state.

And heroics, had any been available, weren't an option. Within an hour of them returning to the hospital her father was dead. Alex looked down at the man who, in her childhood, had been so good to her. It had been a strict upbringing, but Dad had been patient, and caring, and always kind.

Until the end...

She looked across the bed at Will, who'd stayed quietly there to support her.

'I suppose I'll have to organise a funeral in that damn church!' she muttered, again using practicalities to keep the fear and pain at bay. 'And face those women who spat at me when I took their precious Mr Spencer to court.'

'I don't think so,' Will said, something in his voice making her look up from the figure on the bed. 'I get to see the health directives of all patients coming into the ICU, and also any personal requests in the event of a patient's death. Your father left very specific instructions. There were to be no services at all, from memory.'

'Poor Dad,' Alex whispered, then she turned away from the bed, aware that tears were close to falling and not wanting to give in to the mix of rage and grief inside her until she was on her own. 'I'd better get home and go through his papers and just hope he left some instructions.'

Will could hear the tears thick in her voice, and knew instinctively she wouldn't want to cry in front of him. The teenager who'd lived next door was all grown up now, and he had to respect her adulthood for all he wanted to take her in his arms and comfort her.

He insisted on driving her home, aware that if he missed the last ferry he'd have a long drive out to the highway and back into town, but he knew she'd been tired and jet-lagged before her father's death had hit her, and he didn't want her returning to that house of hurt on her own.

He kept the headlights shining on the front of the house, while she dug around under pot plants for a spare key.

'It's always here,' she muttered when he joined the search, and it was he who found the hollow rock among the pebbles on the path.

He unlocked the door for her and pushed it open, wondering just how hard this would be for her. She was standing back, just a little, and he sensed she was gathering the nerve to walk into the place that had once been her home.

He was about to suggest she stay somewhere else—at his mother's place or a hotel in town—just for tonight when an unnerving voice yelled from the darkness.

'That you, Bruce?'

To Will's surprise, Alex laughed and laughed, stepping past him and reaching out to switch on a light, calling, 'Buddy, where are you? It's Alex, Buddy.'

The pink and grey galah shot like an arrow down the hall, landing on Alex's head and dancing a little jig there before settling on her shoulder, turning his head a little to one side as he studied her, then letting loose with a loud 'Who's a pretty girl, then?' as he nuzzled his head against her cheek.

Now the tears she'd held in check spilled from her eyes, although through the dampness she was smiling.

'Silly bird,' she said, turning back to Will. 'We've had him since he was a fledgling and we have no idea where he got the name Bruce, but no amount of patience on Dad's part ever got him to say another name. He talks a lot of other rot, but he always comes back to Bruce.'

The galah was brushing his feathers against the tears as if to dry them up, and seeing the love between the pair made Will's heart twist, but at least the bird had made it easier for Alex to step back into her childhood home.

She had found a tissue and finished the mopping up operations.

'Thanks, Will, for everything,' she said quietly. 'Not only for now but for before, because that first year with the Armitages you were always around and so—so *normal* you helped me be normal too. I'll be okay now I'm home—home with Buddy. I've left my luggage in the visitors' room of the CCU, but I can collect it tomorrow. I imagine there'll be a ton of forms to fill out and arrangements to be made.'

He was being dismissed in the nicest possible way and although he'd have liked to help her—to save her the pain of making arrangements for her father whatever they might be—he knew he had to go.

He touched her shoulder and, daring the bird to object, kissed her lightly on the cheek.

'You thought he'd take your eyes out, didn't you?' Alex teased, smiling now, then she reached out and gave him a hug. 'Thanks again!'

He walked away, aware of the woman in the lighted doorway, blue eyes watching his departure, a pink and grey bird dancing on her shoulder, still enquiring about the whereabouts of Bruce.

CHAPTER TWO

THE RAUCOUS CRIES of 'Where's Bruce?' woke Alex long before she'd have liked to awaken, but as the bird was sitting on the pillow beside her head and tugging at her hair, she gave in and clambered out of bed.

Blearily making her way to the kitchen, surprised by how automatic her movements through the house were, she made a coffee and took it out onto the big deck that looked over the river, suddenly glad to be awake as the rising sun turned the placid waters pink and mauve and gold in turn. She breathed deeply, taking in the eucalypt-scented air, watching an osprey swirl across the sky in search of breakfast, hearing the putt-putt of dinghy engines as fisherman set out up the river to set their crab pots or try their luck with lines.

Another breath...

Yes, she was home.

All the pain of long ago hadn't damaged the sense that this was where she belonged—maybe not for ever, or even for very long—heaven knew what the future held—but for now it was enough.

Not quite enough to heal the pain of the past or the loss of the man she'd come home to make peace with—only time would do that—but here she could handle it, cope with it, do whatever had to be done.

Finishing her coffee, she walked back into the kitchen, surprised to find a note she hadn't noticed earlier, although it was propped in a prominent spot on the sill of the window looking out over the deck.

Thank you for coming, Alexandra. I hope with all my heart you will stay here at the house. Bacon and eggs in fridge, fruit and veg in the bottom drawers, and meat in the freezer.

Later we'll talk but for now it is enough to know that you are here.

Please forgive me.

Love, Dad.

Alex smoothed the paper, willing away the tears, then held it to her cheek as if she could feel her father's touch in it.

A noise out the front—on the road side of the house— turned her in that direction. Buddy was still on the veranda railing, giving cheek to the gulls and oystercatchers on the mudflats of the river.

The noise was barely there—someone trying to be quiet—but surely not a burglar at this time of the morning.

She made her way to the front room and peered through the curtains. A dark maroon SUV was parked outside, the driver's side door open. Had Will's car been maroon?

But why would he be sneaking around outside her house at the crack of dawn?

One way to find out. She walked down the hall and opened the door, and there he was, as large as life.

'You shouldn't open a door like that—you should have a locked screen or a spyhole in the door.'

Alex laughed, and hoped it was because of his lecturing tone, not because she was glad to see him.

'I brought your luggage from the hospital and the forms you'll need to fill in. Apparently your father had left instructions for his body to go to the university. It was with his health directive and a note from the university telling you whom to contact. I was going to leave the papers with the baggage—I thought you'd still be sleeping.'

'When I've got a bird who's better than any alarm clock?' Alex complained, as Buddy swooped back from the deck to inspect the visitor.

'He's obviously disappointed I'm not Bruce,' Will said, holding out his hand towards the bird, who eyed him cautiously for a moment before condescending to jump onto Will's forearm.

Alex watched the little scene, curiously unsettled by it, not just Buddy on Will's arm, but Will being here at all. But she could hardly leave him standing on the doorstep with her luggage.

Yet asking him in seemed...not dangerous—it couldn't possibly be dangerous as this was Will...

'He must be missing Dad,' she said, mainly to avoid a decision. Buddy had walked up Will's arm and was perched on his shoulder, nibbling gently at his earlobe. 'He's usually very shy with strangers.'

Two o'clock in the morning—that's when Will had reached the decision to collect Alex's luggage from the hospital and see what he could do as far as the paperwork was concerned. If he went early, he'd decided, she would probably still be asleep and he could leave the lot in the front porch.

That way he'd avoid seeing Alex, and as images of her and replays of their evening had already kept him awake for hours, he'd come to the realisation that the less he saw of her the better.

At least until he'd sorted out a few things in his mind and body. His body's reaction to her was understandable enough, she was a beautiful woman, but the voice in his head that kept whispering 'hurt' and 'vulnerable' and other warning words was a different matter.

He'd already worked out, at least a year ago, that when he did find a mother for Charlotte, it would be a different kind of marriage. Two mature people finding companionship and sexual satisfaction and, yes, love of a kind, but not *love* love.

Love love hurt too much when you lost it—devastated and destroyed you. There was no way he could go through that again—and Alex, with the pain of her past, deserved better than some lukewarm version of the real thing.

So now he was standing at her front door, a galah on his head, feeling like an absolute galoot.

'Thank you so much,' Alex said, and he felt a stab of disappointment, sure he was about to be dismissed. Not that he'd expected to be invited in—hadn't expected her to be up—but, seeing her in too-small, pink, floral pyjamas, he really didn't want to go.

'Have you had breakfast?' she asked.

Hope rose again.

'No, Charlotte's stayed over with Mum because I'm on call this weekend so I thought I'd drop this stuff off early so you'd have it when you woke up. Thought it would save you dashing over to the hospital to get some clothes to wear.'

She smiled and the day seemed brighter, and while his head might be calling him all kinds of a fool, his heart swelled just a little in his chest and beat a little faster.

Attraction, that's all it was—physical attraction after too long a celibacy. But knowing that didn't stop him carrying her suitcases inside, the bird now flying in front of him as if to show him the way.

Alex led the way up to her bedroom, then, aware of how girlish it still looked—her bedroom at sixteen—she hesitated.

'Just leave them here in the hall, I'll sort them out from there. Dad left a note about food in the fridge and I was about to cook a hearty breakfast before facing whatever lay ahead.'

She turned towards him.

'Now it seems you've handled most of what lay immediately ahead, so the least I can do is feed you.'

She looked worried, puzzled, uncertain—exactly the way Will felt—but she recovered first, offering a rueful smile as she said, 'It's weird, isn't it, meeting again like this?'

Weird didn't begin to sum it up! Although why, he couldn't fathom...

'Go and sit on the deck,' she told him when they reached the kitchen, and he saw the majestic sweep of the river through the windows. 'Bacon and eggs okay? And I've coffee made if you'd like a cup while you wait.'

To Alex's relief, Will accepted a cup of coffee and headed out onto the deck, lessening, though not by much, the tension in her nerves. She was reasonably certain the attraction she was feeling towards him was nothing more than his familiarity. Coming home had been like landing in another life, and he was a familiar figure to cling to while she found her way around.

Not that she could cling to Will.

It had been more than three years since his wife had died and even though he'd said he'd got out of the dating

habit, there had to have been other women in his life—
or another special woman.

And, anyway, it felt wrong, this attraction to him. If
he was looking for a woman he'd be thinking in terms of
a mother for Charlotte—someone stable and committed
to both him and his daughter.

And given the mess she'd made of relationships in the
past, she'd hardly qualify for either role.

The bacon was sizzling and she pushed it to one side
of the pan and added eggs.

'How do you like your eggs?' she called through the
window.

'Sunny side up,' he replied, and the fact that she liked
hers that way as well did not mean one damn thing!

She made toast, set it, butter, salt and pepper, honey
and marmalade on a tray with their cutlery and carried
the lot out to the table, then hurried back in for the plates
before Will could offer to help her.

Distance, that's all she needed. A bit of distance between them and all the unwanted and inexplicable physical reactions in her body would eventually disappear.

Will watched the river come to life, fishing boats mo-
toring towards the mouth, kayakers paddling furiously
past, one lone windsurfer trying desperately to stay upright in the lightest of breezes.

He'd have breakfast then leave and, really, was there
any reason he'd have to see Alex again?

No reason at all, and it was definitely best that he
didn't—

Though why?

He tried to work out why the instant attraction he'd
felt towards her seemed so wrong. Almost dangerous.

How could it be?

Because instant attraction didn't work?

Because she'd admitted being bad at relationships and he didn't want to upset Charlotte by bringing a woman who might not stick with them into her life?

Or because such a strong attraction could lead to love? Wasn't that the crux of it?

Seventeen years ago she'd been, to him, the kid who'd shifted in next door. A kid in all kinds of pain—that had been obvious.

He realised, as the word 'kid' came into his thoughts again, that that was how he'd always seen her. The kid who'd minded the twins, a quiet shadow in the house next door.

Although he'd realised just how much inner strength she'd had when her rape case had come to court, one long year after the complaint. The Armitages—either Dave or Isobel—had always gone with her when she'd had to appear right up until the day of the judgment. Dave had been down south at a conference and Isobel had asked Will to accompany her and Alex, somehow guessing the verdict wasn't going to be the one they wanted.

He'd been there on one side of her, Isobel on the other, and her hand had gripped his as the jury pronounced the rapist not guilty.

He'd been so proud to have known her as she'd stood up, head high, fixed Mr Spencer with a withering look and marched out of the court.

'At least,' she'd said to her two supporters, 'other people will be suspicious of him now and he'll be too scared to touch another child.'

He glanced up as the woman who'd been the 'kid next door' slid a tray onto the table. 'I'd forgotten just how wonderful it was to sit out here.'

'It's fantastic,' he agreed, taking in the too-small floral

pyjamas again and wondering if it was possible to keep thinking of her in that 'kid next door' way.

She passed him his plate, refilled his coffee cup, and settled beside him so they could both look out at the river.

No, came the answer to his wondering. If anything, the pyjamas accentuated her womanliness, somehow emphasising the softness of the body inside them, straining buttons suggesting how much she'd filled out.

'I think I've figured out that it's Saturday,' she said, pausing in her obvious enjoyment of breakfast. 'Does that mean you have the day off?'

Ordinary question—work question really. Talking of work would be good. But before he could reply she was talking again.

'I was only asking, and I know it's a cheek when you've done so much already, bringing my stuff and Dad's papers from the hospital, but if you don't have to rush off, and don't have anything planned with your daughter, I wondered...'

Her voice trailed off and, instead of watching the river, she was studying her bacon and eggs as if they were some rare anatomical discovery.

'I'm on call, which means Charlotte is with Mum. I don't have to rush off unless I'm paged,' he said. 'So out with it.'

She looked up, her face turned to his, serious, worried, a shade embarrassed.

'I know I've been in the house since late last night, but really only in my old bedroom and the kitchen and I kind of went to both of those automatically, if you know what I mean. It's not that I'm scared—but—'

An abrupt break this time, but he thought he'd caught on. He shooed Buddy away before the bird stole a second piece of bacon, and touched Alex lightly on the shoulder.

'You want me to go through the house with you, just be there while you do it the first time?'

She nodded, her embarrassment obvious now as colour rose in her cheeks.

'I know it's stupid,' she said, straightening in her chair and taking a deep breath, 'but it's been so long, nearly twenty years, and walking into their bedroom, the living room, downstairs into Dad's workshop—'

'Will be traumatic enough even with company,' Will finished for her.

She smiled her agreement, just a wan little smile, but Will's body responded to it as automatically as she'd gone to her bedroom the previous night. He leaned forward and kissed her, just a quick gentle kiss, on lips that tasted of bacon and coffee and something indefinable, which he had to assume was just Alex.

'It'll be okay,' he assured her. 'Everything will work out.'

Heaven help me, Alex thought. She was having enough trouble coping with her return to this house, her father's death and Will's presence, without him kissing her. Not that it had been a kiss kiss, just a comfort kiss, but her body hadn't seemed to recognise the difference and her nerves were twittering with excitement.

And she'd asked him to walk through the house with her, so he wasn't leaving any time soon!

He was focussed on his breakfast—or possibly on keeping Buddy from eating it—so she could sneak a look at him. Maybe if she looked enough, she could work out why he was affecting her the way he was.

Lovely profile—maybe not such a good idea, the looking—straight nose, just enough chin, and a forehead that was broad and smooth, the dark hair just a little long so a bit flopped across it in a rather endearing way.

Endearing way? Are you out of your mind, woman?

But her looking had fixed on the lips that had just kissed her—well, touched hers in a sympathetic-friend kind of way.

They were pale, and delineated by an even paler line around them, not that they needed the delineation because they were very nicely made, not too full or fleshy but not mean and straight. Without doubt, the man had great lips.

Which, of course, led to her wayward mind wondering what a real kiss from those lips would feel like.

'Gone to sleep sitting up?' Will asked, fortunately *after* she'd taken her eyes off his lips and was gazing sightlessly out over the river.

'Just about,' she answered, smiling at him to show how awake she was and how unaffected she'd been by his presence, and the kiss, and her perusal of his profile.

Liar!

'So, we'll be off on our expedition?' he asked, and she forgot her confusion over Will as all the anxiety about really seeing the house—her home?—returned.

'Best we do,' she managed, stacking their plates on the tray and standing up to take it back to the kitchen.

'Let me,' he said, his eyes meeting hers, his fingers brushing lightly against her hands as he removed the tray from her weakening grasp.

With the dirty dishes deposited safely in the kitchen, Alex led the way first to the living room.

'I don't know why I've felt so—so reluctant to do this,' she said, aware she was standing far too close to Will but too disturbed by the past for it to bother her body.

Much!

'Too much pain in the past,' Will said, putting his arm around her shoulders and drawing her even closer. 'No matter how convinced we are that we've got over it, any trauma in childhood or adolescence must leave an emotional...' He hesitated, then said, 'I suppose "bruise" is as good a word as any. It's there but you don't realise it still hurts until you touch it.'

'You're right,' she agreed, leaving the comfort of that arm and stepping into the room, looking around at the bare mantelpiece above the fireplace where once pictures of her, from babyhood to teenage years, had been arrayed. Now a forlorn vase of plastic—or maybe silk—irises made an attempt to brighten up the room.

And failed dismally.

The furniture was new, which was good, but the little nest of tables that had been her grandmother's was still tucked to one side of the three-seater, and her mother's magazine stand was beside the chair in the place that had always been designated as her father's—fishing magazines in place of the gossip magazines her mother, for all her religious beliefs, had loved.

Wandering around the room, she touched the mantelpiece, the old brass screen that stood in front of the fireplace, the little nest of tables.

'Ghosts?' Will asked, and she was surprised by her reply.

'No, not at all! It's different, but that's about it. And it's still a comfortable room. I think fireplaces do that, don't you?'

Before he could reply she was leading the way upstairs. Bathrooms were bathrooms and the downstairs one held no memories—bad or good—but her parents' bedroom—who knew?

But when she walked into it she stopped, looking all around, unable to believe her mother's once frilly, pale blue and green bedroom had been transformed into what looked more like a monastic cell than a frequently slept-in space.

Gone was the big bed that had dominated the room, replaced by a large single pressed up against a wall, made up with military precision, not a wrinkle to be seen. Next to it her father had set one of the pair of old bedside tables, and on it he'd had a lamp, a picture of his bride and himself on their wedding day, and as many of the photos off the mantelpiece as he could fit. Photos of Alex from babyhood to her last school photo, the plain navy uniform of the church-based school, also wrinkle-free—obviously in honour of the photo day.

'I can't believe it,' she whispered, touching the photos then turning to cross the room to the cupboards built into one wall. Her father's suits were neatly hung in about a tenth of the wardrobe space, while his shorts and polo shirts, his underwear and socks were all set out on the shelves, aligned to meet and pass any inspection.

'It's as if he tried to get rid of all traces of her,' she murmured, more to herself than to Will. 'Do you suppose he did it when she died, or when he knew I was coming home?'

It wasn't a question anyone could answer, so Will didn't try, but he was concerned by how the changes in the room had affected Alex, and couldn't help but wonder just how much of the past might come back to haunt her in this place that had been her home.

'Are you sure you're okay, living here, even for a while?' he asked, as she turned in the centre of the room, taking in the bareness yet again. His heart ached to help her, but who could help someone suffer pain?

'Mum's got a spare bedroom if you'd like to camp there until you make a decision about where you'd like to live,' he heard himself say, though common sense had been relentless in telling him the less he saw of Alex the better.

After all, what could he offer her, still grieving himself over the loss of Elise?

To his relief—at least, he thought it was relief—she smiled and shook her head.

'Leave my river view? I might have been away from it for a long time, but it's always been there in my head, and no matter how unhappy my leaving here was, nothing could take away the pleasure I will get from just being by the river—*my* river!'

The smile brightened, and she added, 'Do you really not have to go to work?'

'As long as I'm not paged and I pop in to show my face later today, I'm covered,' he said, and her smile grew mischievous.

'Then let's go down and see if Dad's tinnie is still under the house. Knowing him, the boat should be in top condition. We can go out on the river and down some of the offshoots where I used to take the twins fishing.' She paused before adding, 'Didn't you come with us once because Isobel was worried I couldn't handle the twins in the boat on my own?'

Her vague memory of the outing confirmed what Will already knew—that he'd played a very insignificant part of her life with the family next door.

She was already heading down the stairs, and he followed, out the front door and around to the river side of the house, where the slope of the ground meant there was plenty of room under the wide deck for a workshop and an aluminium dinghy on a small trailer. The ubiquitous Aussie tinnie!

Slightly bemused, he watched as Alex lifted a petrol container and placed it in the boat, close to the outboard engine, then hooked up the fuel line, pumped it a couple of times, and pulled the rope start on the engine.

It roared to life and, satisfied, she turned it off, and walked to the prow to pull the trailer down to the water.

'Are you going like that?' Will asked, and she looked down at herself in surprise.

'Good grief, you might have told me I was still in my pyjamas, and very old pyjamas at that! What if you take off your shoes and get the boat into the water while I duck upstairs and change?'

She'd walked away but spun back to add, 'Probably into something as old and ill-fitting as these pyjamas. I doubt any of my Glasgow clothes will cope with going out in the tinnie, but as all my old clothes—well, the ones Mum didn't throw at me that day—are still in my bedroom, I'm sure I'll be able to find something.'

She reappeared in shorts, her long legs pale from a Scottish winter, and a T-shirt that definitely was a little too small.

Not that he should be noticing the way her breasts pushed against it!

He was ordered into the middle seat, and those long, pale legs pushed the little boat out into deeper water, Alex swinging into it as soon as they were far enough out to lower the motor, then they were chugging away, the light breeze from their movement pushing her hair back from her face as she lifted it to the sun and smiled with what looked like sheer joy.

'How could I have stayed away from this for so long?' she asked, expertly avoiding a youth on a jet ski and taking them closer to shore, to where a gap suddenly appeared in the mangroves.

She moved the tiller gently and they eased into a deep

green cave, sunlight filtering through the mangrove branches meeting over their heads.

'It's like another world,' she whispered, and he had to agree. Beneath the boat the water was dark green and very mysterious, while the weird shapes and tangles of mangrove roots suggested hiding places or homes for elves and fairies.

'Dad bought me a little tinnie when I was five. It had a very simple motor, only one half horsepower so I could use it without a licence, and this was my very favourite place.'

Will felt a now familiar squelch of his heart. How was it that this particular woman could touch him as she did? It wasn't part of the attraction business, strong though that was. It was different, strange but wonderful at the same time.

He gave up on the puzzle and simply enjoyed the beauty and the solitude, the quiet broken only by the humming of bees and the twitter of an occasional bird...

CHAPTER THREE

'BEST WE GET back,' Alex said, when they'd drifted across the shadowy water to the end of the inlet. She glanced over at him. 'I've been meaning to ask, why Intensive Care?'

Will turned from his fascination with the mangroves and smiled at her. 'Too stupid to decide which specialty?'

'I doubt that very much,' Alex replied, although she wondered if it had been a stupid question. His wife had been in a coma—he'd have spent a lot of time in Intensive Care...

Hoping to cover her insensitivity, she rushed into speech.

'Have you any of Brian Lane's patients in there? I could shower and change into respectable clothes and come with you.'

Shower with Will in the house?

'Or better still meet you at the hospital. Dad's car will be in the garage.'

He didn't reply, though frown lines appeared on his forehead as he studied her.

'You don't have to do that,' he said. 'Even if you intended starting with Brian immediately, you wouldn't be expected in before Monday. Have a rest, relax, enjoy being close to your river again.'

Alex turned the boat back into the main river, heading for home. She could hardly tell Will that she didn't want to be alone in the house, because it was more than that. For some reason, although for years she'd not only enjoyed but had treasured her own company, right now she was—

Afraid of it?

Not exactly.

More afraid of how she'd react to it in these totally different circumstances and without the father she'd come home to get to know.

You've already proved to him what a wimp you are, asking him to walk through the rooms with you, so don't make it worse. You're better than that! Stronger! she told herself.

'You're right,' she said out loud, 'especially as there's so much to do here. And I don't officially start with Brian's group for another fortnight. I thought I'd need that long at home with Dad while he got over the op.'

Did her voice quaver that Will reached out and touched her knee?

Whatever! The touch reminded her of all the reasons she *shouldn't* be spending more time with Will. A man with a child needed stability in his life—or in the child's life at least. How could she, with her record of broken relationships, provide that?

'I'm only a phone call away,' he was saying. 'If you need anything, anything at all, give me a call. My home and mobile numbers are with the papers I left in your living room. Seriously, Alex, I want you to know I'm here for you if ever you need a hand.'

Did that sound pathetic? Will wondered, sitting back and studying the woman who was steering the little tinnie up onto the beach outside her father's house.

He helped her slide the boat onto the trailer and wheel it back up into place beneath the house.

No excuse now for lingering, although every cell in his body was suggesting lingering wasn't all it wanted from this woman.

'Well, I'll be off, but do yell if you need me,' he said, as Alex busied herself taking the fuel tank out of the boat and storing it away.

She finished the task and came to stand beside him.

'You could live to regret that offer,' she said, a smile lighting up her eyes, although her face seemed sombre. 'You're probably the only person in town willing to talk to me.'

'You can't mean that!' he said. 'All that business was fifteen years ago—more like twenty, in fact—who'd remember?'

Now the smile touched her lips but not convincingly.

'Only all my parents' friends. It's worse now Dad has died. The talk will be I came home to grab whatever he's left behind.'

'But your own friends, surely there'd be someone—'

'Who didn't blame me for the sainted Mr Spencer being exposed for what he was? I was at a church school—all my friends were from the school. Once the jury said not guilty I was branded as a whore who slept around and used Mr Spencer as a scapegoat when things got difficult.'

'But—'

The smile had gone, replaced by a look of such weariness he wanted to hold her in his arms and comfort her as he would have one of the twins.

'Even my friends who believed it was Mr Spencer thought it was my fault—I must have led him on, that kind of thing. To most of them, to a lot of people, the man was a saint.'

She gave a tiny shrug—a bare lift of the shoulders— and tried another smile, this one so pathetic he did take her in his arms and hold her close, a hug, nothing more...

Although—

'So why stay here, now your father's gone?'

She eased out of his arms and looked, not at him but out across the river.

'It is my home,' she whispered, 'and the river is in my heart. I did no wrong, so why should I be driven away from what I love?'

Will heard the strength back in her voice, saw it in the now upright stance, and felt like clapping. She had guts, the kid he'd known all that time ago—the kid who had grown into this beautiful woman and brought such confusion into his life the instant he'd set eyes on her again.

'I'll talk to you later,' he said, knowing he had to get away and sort out the confusion. He'd go home—where he should be—and play with Charlotte.

Now!

He was surprised by how early it was when he arrived home. Charlotte was up but still in her pyjamas, the cereal she'd had for breakfast sprinkled liberally down her top.

'She's all yours,' his mother said, but when she held out her arms to give Charlotte a hug, although the little girl was only going through an ever-open door to another part of the house, Will saw the love between the two of them and was reassured that his mother wasn't regretting her offer.

'I can't stay long, Daddy,' Charlotte told him as he peeled off her pyjamas. 'Nani and I are going to a party later.'

'A party?'

Vague memories stirred in his head but so much had happened since late yesterday afternoon he couldn't catch the right one.

'It's on the fridge,' Charlotte told him, dashing naked to the refrigerator to pull off a garish party invitation. 'Chloe's party!'

Answers clicked into place. Chloe was the granddaughter of his mother's best friend and the two children played together often.

'Nani and me bought her a present—we bought her a fairy doll that flies. Can I have one too, Daddy?'

He lifted his daughter, tucked her under one arm and carried her shrieking to the bathroom for a quick wash and a good teeth clean.

'Maybe for your birthday,' he said, wondering just what kind of toy a fairy that flew might be. He'd have to check it out.

She ran ahead of him into her bedroom, and, watching the small, naked form, he felt a heart-crunching sense of love mingled with the fear that he knew all parents must feel—fear that something bad might happen to her.

'Are we going to the park?' she asked, sitting on the floor pulling on her undies. 'Or the beach?'

'Which would you like?' he asked, although he knew the answer. She'd just discovered she could swing on the monkey bars at the park, although he held a little of her weight as she shifted from hand to hand, and was ready to catch her at any moment.

'Okay, park,' he agreed, when she gave the expected answer, 'but do you need two skirts?'

It was an argument he wasn't going to win. The daughter he'd thought of as a tomboy for her first three years had suddenly gone girly and now wore frilly skirts, the frillier the better, one on top of another.

Then came the serious business of choosing a top. She delved through her drawers in search of the one with the most spangles on it.

He said a silent prayer of thanks that his mother kept Charlotte's 'good' clothes in her unit, so would be able to sort an outfit for the party.

But pushing her on the swing, altering the words of a monkey song *he'd* learned at kindergarten to 'when Charlotte Ke-ent has a swing' with her pointing her toes to the air instead of a monkey tail around a branch, he usually felt a sense of contentment.

Charlotte loved the swing and insisted on the song, but, unfortunately, pushing a swing, even while singing, was a mindless operation, and his mind drifted to Alex's return into the ambit of his life.

Common sense said back away, he had Charlotte to consider, but Alex was already so isolated he couldn't do that.

He could be there for her while she settled in and made new friends, then ease away.

Ease away—that was a laugh.

'Daddy, it's a magpie.'

He realised from Charlotte's tone it wasn't the first time she'd pointed the bird out to him, so he shut the door on the part of his brain already too overloaded with Alex and concentrated on his daughter, moving from swings to the slippery slide and finally the monkey bars.

Will had hurried away, striding up the side of the house as if all the furies in hell had been chasing him. Alex had watched him go, bemused by his sudden departure, but at the same time glad he'd gone so she could sit down somewhere quiet and try to work out exactly what emotion Will Kent had awoken in her body.

And now she thought about it, *that* was something she *had* to do alone.

The phone was ringing as she walked back into the house, and her immediate reaction was to ignore it, but she'd been a doctor too long to ignore a ringing phone, so she lifted the receiver and said her name, hoping she sounded more positive than she felt.

'Anthony Mitchell here…' The caller hesitated and Alex realised he wasn't sure how to address her. 'I'm the dean of medicine at Heritage University. I want to offer my sincere condolences on your father's death.'

Slightly surprised, Alex thanked him, and was wondering just why he might be phoning when he continued.

'I'm not sure if you've been told but he donated his body to the university. I'd like to call in and see you some time to discuss your father's generous gift and to explain how we go about things. I realise this is a very tough time for you, but—'

Alex could hear the embarrassment in the man's voice and guessed he wanted to see her as soon as possible.

'I could see you today,' she said, to save him further discomfort. 'Do you want me to come to you, or what?'

'No, no, I wouldn't ask that of you. I'll come to you. Say half an hour?'

Half an hour to find some respectable clothes, have a shower—

'That would be fine,' she heard herself say.

A few polite farewells, and the conversation was done.

Alex closed her eyes and breathed deeply. This was good, it's getting back to normal, she told herself, heading up the stairs to rifle through her suitcases for something suitable for entertaining the dean!

* * *

Her first impression was that deans hadn't looked like that when she'd been at university. Or maybe her being younger had made them look older.

Walking up the path was a tall, fair-haired, fortyish man in pale chinos, a dark blue T-shirt and sandals.

Closer up he was definitely unlike any dean she'd ever seen. Alex had a quiet bet with herself that more young women than young men would enrol in medicine simply to be taught by him.

'Anthony Mitchell,' the dean with a distinct resemblance to a Greek god said, offering his hand. 'Actually, it's Tony—much easier.'

Alex took the offered hand and introduced herself, also using the shortened version of *her* name.

'Come through, I've tea or coffee, or a cold drink if you'd prefer. We'll sit out on the deck, if that's okay with you.'

'More than okay,' Tony replied. 'I live in an apartment overlooking the ocean but I've often wondered about these houses along the river. Wow!'

They'd reached the deck, and his exclamation of appreciation made Alex warm to him.

'The view's so peaceful in spite of all the activity on the river,' he said. 'I bet you used to sit out here for hours as a kid.'

Alex smiled at his enthusiasm.

'More like out there, looking back,' she said. 'I had a tinnie from the time I was five. I grew up on the river.'

She was about to ask what she could get him when Buddy joined the party, his shrieking 'Where's Bruce' startling the visitor, who stepped back in surprise.

'Sorry,' Alex said. 'That's Buddy. He's a little uncontrolled and before you ask, no, we never knew where he got the name Bruce or who Bruce might have been, let alone where he is at any given time.'

Tony laughed and held out his hand to the bird, who studied it for a while, before choosing to perch on the railing.

At least Buddy had broken any awkwardness, and now, when Alex offered a drink, Tony settled on coffee, also offering to help.

'No, sit and admire the view,' Alex told him, mostly because she didn't want a stranger in the kitchen when she was still, in some ways, trying to find her own way around it.

The coffee was easy and instinct took her to the big pantry and the pile of cake tins always kept on the middle shelf.

Only one remained, but when Alex lifted it she felt the weight.

Could it be?

She opened the tin to find, as she'd half expected, the treacly aroma of Anzac biscuits wafting out at her.

Swallowing hard, she put some biscuits on a plate, put milk and sugar, small plates and napkins on a tray, and carried it out to set it on the table in front of the dean.

Tony!

Returning with the coffeepot, she found him munching on a biscuit.

'Home-made Anzacs, I thought you'd just got back from overseas.'

Another swallow, and a quick sniff back of tears, hopefully unnoticed as Buddy swooped to take a biscuit from the plate.

'My mother was the baker in the family—cakes, slices, biscuits—but my dad always made the Anzacs. He said because his father was a dinkum Anzac who had landed at Gallipoli, he was the only one entitled to make the biscuits. He must have made these before he went into hospital.'

Sniffing and swallowing was no longer enough and Alex excused herself, heading for the house so she could wipe away the evidence of the completely unexpected emotion she was feeling.

But Tony was up before her, sliding an arm around her shoulders.

'I'm sorry—it's far too soon to be having to tackle stuff like this. Some guy at the hospital told me the sooner I got it over and done with the better, but I can go away and come back another day. Have you someone to stay with you? A friend?'

A friend?

It was a logical question for how could someone who'd grown up in this town come home to no one?

Although there *was* Caitlin...

If she was still around...

'I'll be fine,' Alex assured her visitor, easing away from his solid, comforting body. 'It's silly because I've been, well, separated, I suppose you'd say, from my family for nearly twenty years, then something like my dad's Anzac biscuits make me cry. But I'm okay now. Sit down and have your coffee and another biscuit, and tell me what I need to do to finalise things for the university.'

She'd thought she'd sounded very together, but Tony was eyeing her somewhat dubiously, although he did sit and sip at his coffee.

'If you're sure you're up to it,' he said.

'I am,' Alex said firmly, but was nearly overwhelmed again when Buddy flew to sit on her shoulder.

She had *one* friend.

Two, if she could find Caitlin, her childhood best friend.

Three, if she counted Will.

But maybe she shouldn't count Will.

Tony was talking about the river and a group at the university—mainly medical-school staff—who'd formed a kayaking club and had fortnightly outings on the river, and once a month a trip away to some other river to try the rapids or paddle across estuaries.

'You'd be more than welcome to join,' he said, and as Alex was about to reply that she didn't have a kayak—and didn't have very good balance in the ones she'd tried— she realised it was a good way to meet people socially.

'That sounds fun,' she said. 'Perhaps you could give me details.'

'Better than that,' Tony told her. 'Our monthly meeting is next Thursday evening. I could pick you up and take you, maybe have dinner later—a group of us often go on.'

Had his original invitation sounded too much like a date? Alex wondered, but, group or not, she needed to be doing something with her spare time, and maybe meeting other men—other than Will, that was—because the Will thing was just too confusing...

'I'd love it,' she said, and realised she meant it. It was just the thing she needed to help her settle back into the town, and doing anything on the river would be fun.

They finally got down to the paperwork, Tony explaining that her father had expressed his wish that no memorial service be held.

'He wanted a minimum of fuss,' Tony told her, 'although that wouldn't stop you having a few of his friends and relations around if you wished. He made all the arrangements himself, and it really only needs one signature from you, acknowledging that we're taking the body. Virtually signing him over to us.'

Alex signed, although she couldn't help but wonder what had prompted her father to do this. She was a listed organ donor herself, and later intended willing her body to a university, but it seemed such an alien thing for her father to have done.

'Did he ever say why?' she asked Tony, who looked slightly startled by the question.

'I never asked him,' he said. 'I suppose I just assumed it was because you'd studied medicine and he felt he was doing his bit. He talked about you a lot. I know he was very proud of you.'

Hmm!

Alex tucked that thought away to consider some other time, and agreed she'd be ready for the Thursday meeting if Tony collected her at six.

'Though it's probably better if I take my car—that way, if we're late you won't get stuck here when the ferry stops.'

He shrugged. 'I can always get home around by the highway. It's a bit further but not a worry. And the place where we meet is tricky to find the first time. I'll see you at six.'

With which he walked through the house with her, shook her hand, and departed.

CHAPTER FOUR

ALEX WALKED BACK into the house, aware her clothes were
scattered in the upstairs hall, knowing she had to un-
pack—to sort things out—but totally lost as to where
to start.

Presumably the house was now her house. In fact, it
wasn't a presumption, her father had told her the details
of his will—'everything to my daughter Alexandra', as
simple as that. So it *was* her house, although it felt very
alien right now. Apart from the kitchen and the deck,
which definitely felt like home.

But her old bedroom?

Her father's room?

Could she live in either?

The sewing room!

For some reason, when she'd walked through the house
with Will she hadn't thought to enter the sewing room.

Because it had been so much her mother's domain?

Because she'd feared it would be as much changed as
her parents' bedroom?

Well, no time like the present…

She stepped over clothes and suitcases to open the
door at the end of the hall—the door to the room that
looked out over the roof of the deck to the river. Here

her mother's long sewing desk had been built in so she could sew and see the river at the same time.

Alex's hand hesitated on the doorknob as she wondered, for the first time, why her parents hadn't made this room—the room with the view—their bedroom?

She opened the door and almost closed it again, the transformation was so startling. Gone was the long bench and the cabinets that had held cloth and cotton; gone was the serviceable felt carpet that had covered the floor; gone were the shutters her mother would lower over the windows when the setting sun peeked in.

In their place were a brand-new bedroom suite, the bed clothed in the softest of grey linens, a polished timber floor, sleek blinds that rolled down to keep out the glare but not hide the view, and sitting in the middle of the bed the threadbare galah that had been Alex's favourite toy even before the advent of Buddy.

Down the far end was a door and, opening it, Alex found a tiny en suite bathroom, grey with touches of pink, just like the bedroom colours.

Tears streamed down her face as she considered the amount of work her father must have done to transform this room for her. And regret that it had been so long, that she'd not come home sooner, that they'd lost so many years together, all gathered in her chest like a physical pain.

She sank down on the bed, hugging her misery to herself, rocking as she cried out the pain of the lost years.

Will hadn't intended visiting. In fact, his intention had been to see as little as possible of Alex until he'd sorted out how he felt about her. But after Brian's phone call he knew it would be better to talk to her in person. That way, he could, hopefully, gauge if she was ready to start work earlier than planned—emotionally, and also physically, given the long plane trip—or if he should advise Brian to get a locum.

So, with his mother and Charlotte off at their party, he drove to the house and rang the bell.

No reply.

He checked the car was in the garage, and the boat in the shed beneath the house.

He rang the bell again, called her name, then began to get anxious about her.

She'd been through so much emotional turmoil in such a short time...

Buddy's arrival from the back of the house—an agitated Buddy—tightened Will's tension and banished any doubts about entering the house.

He found the rock that hid the key and opened the door, Buddy bouncing on his shoulder, enquiring about Bruce.

'Forget Bruce, where's Alex?' Will muttered at the bird, who cocked his head as if considering the question, then flew off through the house, swooping back to land on the banister at the top of the stairs.

'I'm not stupid enough to follow you without at least looking down here,' Will told him, walking swiftly through the lower rooms and checking the deck.

Buddy had moved and was lifting pieces of Alex's clothing in his beak, making more of a mess of the upstairs hall than had probably been there in the beginning. Although the chaos of half-unpacked suitcases made Will's heart beat faster.

He checked the first room—the monastic room of her father—empty.

Checked the next, the Alex schoolgirl room—also empty.

It was only as he shut the door he noticed another door at the end of the hall—a room they hadn't entered earlier.

Why? he wondered, but as Buddy was now jumping up and down on the doorknob, Will approached it, calling to Alex, although softly this time.

She was asleep on the bed, her arms wrapped around her body and something that looked like a very dead bird. Tearstains on her cheeks tugged at Will's heart as he stood looking down at her.

She was breathing, she was okay, he should let her sleep, and although he knew he couldn't stand there, looking at her, he was reluctant to leave.

Buddy solved the problem, bouncing up and down on Alex's head with his raucous cry of 'Who's a pretty girl, then?'

Her eyes opened slowly—blue as the late afternoon sky beyond the windows.

'I'm sorry for intruding, I had a message for you and you didn't answer the door and—'

'It's okay,' she said sleepily. 'I don't know why I fell asleep. I should be up—there's stuff to do.'

She sat up on the bed, looking around in unmistakeable wonder.

'My father did this for me,' she whispered to him. 'He did all this and I didn't know. I didn't look in here this morning—too many memories, I suppose—but he's transformed it, made this beautiful room with the river right there...'

And the tears came again.

He'd have had to be made of marble to have not reacted, Will realised as he sat beside her on the bed and put his arm around her, drawing her close to offer comfort.

'You've had a rough homecoming,' he said quietly. 'You're entitled to a good cry.'

'Not really,' she protested, easing a little apart but remaining in the circle of his arm. 'I don't know why I'm being such a wuss.'

'Such a wuss, such a wuss!' the bird shrieked, and Alex recovered completely.

'Buddy, you've learned new words!' She stared at the bird in amazement, truly surprised but very thankful for the diversion, because being held by Will was far too enticing and she'd been battling an urge to snuggle closer.

'Give me a minute, I'll meet you out on the deck,' she said.

She'd been about to add that they could watch the sunset when she realised that might not be a good idea. Too much romance in joint sunset watching...

He walked away and she eased herself off the bed, hurried into the little bathroom and splashed water on her face, brushed her tousled hair.

Will had said something about a message.

Presumably for her.

Get downstairs and ask him, she told herself, for all she'd have preferred not to have seen Will quite so soon.

Not until she'd sorted out a few things in her head—and body—and preferably not until she'd gone to the kayaking meeting and met people and had at least the beginnings of a normal social life.

As if that would help! the cynic in her head whispered.

Ignoring it, she headed downstairs, joining her visitor on the deck as the setting sun painted the western sky with extravagantly brilliant red and purple and orange streaks.

She shook her head at the beauty of it and refused to give way to tears again. Instead, she plonked down in a chair out of touching distance from Will and said brightly, 'A message?'

He studied her for a moment, as if assessing her current emotional state—or perhaps her ability to understand a message.

'Brian Lane phoned. He'd heard about your father's death and someone had told him I'd seen you at the hospital so I think he wanted me to suss out how you were—how your father's death had affected you.'

'Because?' Alex asked, aware she was frowning but unable to guess where this conversation was going.

Did the man she was going to work with think she might be too emotionally fragile to handle the work?

'Because he'd like you to start earlier if you could,' Will told her. 'He's in Melbourne, where he's trying to arrange care for his mother, who has dementia, and he's having a tough time finding somewhere suitable. His wife's got three children under four so she stayed at home, but Brian really needs more time down there.'

'And the other partner? Mal Parker?'

'Is booked to fly to the US on Tuesday for a conference. He could cancel, but Brian phoned me to ask what I thought. It's not a frantically busy practice—two practitioners can handle it easily. I don't know if Brian told you, but apparently his aim in taking you on was so he could return to Melbourne, where both his and his wife's families live.'

'So it normally has two doctors, but one can manage?' Alex asked, as she took in what Will was telling her and realised that starting work would be the best possible thing for her in the circumstances. Especially if she was busy!

'That's right. The practice manager will sort out the appointments so you're not overwhelmed but they had already planned to have only one doctor there for the next fortnight so it shouldn't take too much fiddling.'

Will stopped and looked at her expectantly.

'What do you think?'

What did she think, apart from how his eyes seemed to be saying things that weren't coming out in his words?

Worrying about her?

Forget the man's eyes!

'I'm happy to do it. It will be good to have something to do—something to keep me busy while I settle back into the town. But I need to speak to Brian myself, and maybe arrange to go into the rooms tomorrow. I wonder if I could get the practice manager to meet me there to show me around and explain how they do things.'

'I'm sure Brian can arrange it, and I have his number here if you want to phone him now.'

Will pulled out his mobile and scrolled through it, finally coming up with what he was looking for. He passed her the phone, their fingers touching, electricity jolting through Alex for all the transaction was purely business.

She carried the phone inside to write down the number—*and* to get away from the distraction that was Will. Her reactions to him were nothing more than by-products of the emotional storm she'd come home to, she told herself as she jotted down the number.

They had to be because they were like nothing she'd ever felt before.

Will had joined her in the kitchen.

'Mum and Charlotte are eating out so what if I go down to the co-op while you're talking to Brian and get us fish and chips for tea? I'm sure it's the proper homecoming dinner to eat on your deck.'

Fish and chips on the deck!

Twenty years ago it had been a Sunday evening treat because her mother had never cooked on a Sunday. Sunday had been a day for church in the morning, and reading or playing quietly in her room in the afternoon. Her parents, with their strong beliefs, had spent Sunday afternoons studying their Bibles. As an adult, Alex had often wondered why they had found it so hard to apply its teachings about love and forgiveness to their own daughter.

But fish and chips on the deck would be a true homecoming. They had always been the best part of long, slow Sundays.

'Sounds lovely,' she said, ignoring all the alarm bells about Will and proximity that were going off in her head. After all, she'd need someone to talk to about the job she was to start on Monday, and Will would probably know something of the set-up in the practice.

Business, purely business, she reminded herself.

Brian was delighted to hear from her, offered his sympathies, thanked her effusively and promised to get Marilyn, the practice manager, to phone as soon as possible.

'I'm sure she'll be only too happy to spend time with you tomorrow, because we all owe you a huge debt for this.'

Strangely at ease now that decision had been made, Alex returned to the deck, where the more muted colours of the dying sunset were just as beautiful a sight.

Tomorrow, learning about the practice, then on Monday the excitement of starting a new job would banish all the other strange emotional stuff that had been going on in her head since her father's death and the weird physical stuff going on in her body since meeting Will again, and soon she'd have a whole new life in the town she'd once called home.

She'd brought the handset of the phone out onto the deck with her, and the ringtone startled her out of her dreams of a new life.

Sure it would be Marilyn, she answered with her name, then listened in shock as a woman's voice screamed into her ear.

'You ruined my life, you slut!' the voice said, then the caller slammed the phone down.

Alex stared at the slim piece of plastic that had delivered the message—stared warily as one would at a snake or perhaps a poisonous spider.

It had to be a wrong number, and the woman hadn't listened when she'd said her name.

That would explain it.

But the venom in the voice had unsettled her.

Fortunately, the next phone call—and, yes, she was a doctor, she'd *had* to answer it—was Marilyn, so a sensible conversation about where and when to meet the following day pushed the ugly words to the back of Alex's mind.

Will's return was another diversion—a confusing diversion but right now confusion was better than mulling over the phone call.

Seeing her there, with the river behind her reflecting the fading colours of the sunset, Will wondered how he could not fall in love with her.

If only love wasn't off limits—too hard, too hurtful—and then there was Charlotte...

'Fish and chips for two,' he said, far too brightly, 'and a bottle of a nice sav blanc to go with them. I should have asked what you'd like. I just thought...'

He was behaving like a schoolboy with his first crush on a girl, except this girl was a woman, and a beautiful one at that, and he wasn't sure...

Well, in truth, he wasn't sure what he wasn't sure about, although deep down he knew it was to do with

Charlotte and her well-being, and love, love lost, and pain...

'Sounds great. I'll get us glasses—and do you want plates or will we eat them out of the paper?'

Ah, something he *was* sure about.

'I think they taste best out of the paper.'

She grinned at him.

'Me, too!'

Yet for all the light-hearted chat, he sensed a tension in the air.

Sexual tension?

Yes, some of that! Inevitable from his point of view whenever he was near Alex.

But something else as well.

She returned with not only glasses but an ice bucket as well, set them on the table, then poured the wine before propping the bottle in the bucket amidst the ice.

She smiled again.

'You know, I imagine this is the very first time that the ice bucket has held anything alcoholic. My parents got it for a wedding present, and I remember at Christmas they'd get a bottle of non-alcoholic wine from the supermarket and the ice bucket would be set in pride of place in the middle of the table.'

Maybe he was imagining her tension, he decided as he smiled at her little tale and carefully unwrapped enough of the parcel of food for them to begin eating.

'Did you speak to Marilyn?'

Alex nodded around the end of a very long chip.

'She can't do tomorrow morning so I'm meeting her at two in the afternoon. She sounds very nice.'

'She is,' Will replied, 'and one of the most efficient practice managers I've ever met. She runs those rooms like a military operation yet everyone loves her and is happy to have her yell at them when things don't go according to plan.'

'Does she yell very often?' Alex asked.

'Only at the doctors,' Will assured her. 'They *will* run over their appointment times and ruin her timetables!'

Alex laughed.

'Every practice needs a Marilyn,' she said, seemingly at ease, yet again Will sensed there was something bothering her.

Was the attraction he was feeling not one-sided? Was Alex feeling something towards him but conflicted over it because he knew her from the past?

Or *his* past?

Heaven knew, he felt weirdly disloyal towards Elise for the way he was feeling, so perhaps—

'Grave thoughts?' she said, startling him out of his meandering imaginings.

'Stupid thoughts,' he countered, determined to put all the attraction stuff aside. 'Brian said one of the reasons he was pleased to appoint you to the team was that you were happy to assist in operations.'

It wasn't quite a question but she took it as one.

'I love being involved when my patients go to Theatre. I worked in a private hospital in Glasgow so often worked on the surgeon's team. I tossed up doing surgery, but I like patient contact and felt I wouldn't get enough as a surgeon.'

Nice, easy, medical conversation, and he had to be imagining the thread of tension in her voice.

Most likely tiredness, exhaustion even, given her recent arrival and the stress that had followed it.

Alex wasn't sure how long she could sit there, eating chips and chatting away to Will when the echoes of the phone call were still ringing in her head.

But much as she longed to tell him, she knew she couldn't keep leaning on him for support, especially when the attraction she was feeling towards him showed no sign of abating.

So they talked of work, of patients they'd had, and finally of a young lad who would be her patient.

'He's seventeen, with congenital heart problems that have got beyond salvage, so he's waiting for a donor heart.'

'Would someone do it here?' Alex asked, surprised, although organ transplant techniques were now so advanced most major hospitals could cope with them.

'If a suitable donor turned up, yes. Ideally, he should be in a capital city while he waits, but it could be months.'

'Or even longer, and he'd be away from his friends and family and in the end it could all be for nothing,' Alex finished, and Will nodded.

'Brian and the cardiovascular surgeon have both backed him wanting to stay here, sure it's better for him to grab whatever happiness he can, but I worry sometimes that it was the right decision.'

'You've got the facilities and personnel?'

'To do either a harvest operation or the transplant, yes, but if the heart was here, we'd have to bring in a team of surgeons to do the harvest. That's already been set up, with cardiovascular people prepared to fly in, but it's more likely the heart would be somewhere else, and it would be harvested where the donor is and then flown here.'

The idea that she might be involved in a transplant sent a different kind of thrill through Alex's body.

Good, this was good. Getting excited about work would soon stop her getting excited about Will.

Perhaps, she added ruefully to herself as he smiled at her and it was obvious the other thrill was still there.

But it *had* diverted her from the phone call, which she was now prepared to put down to a wrong number.

So they talked of work, sipped wine, and ate their fish and chips. The talking of work part was okay, but watching Will take a sip of wine—he took very few sips, his glass still half-full—or his lips close around a morsel of fish was flustering, to say the least.

Darkness had fallen on the river, so it had taken on a silver sheen, and occasional soft shushing sounds as ripples from a passing craft washed ashore somehow made the scene even more peaceful.

He should go!

Will knew that as well as he knew his name.

But sitting here with Alex was as close to total relaxation as he'd felt in a long time.

Almost total relaxation.

She was taking a sip of wine, and even in the gloom he could make out her lips closing on the glass—full, sensual lips…

He imagined them closing on his mouth, sipping—

Body hardening, he pushed away his glass, stood, and gathered up the paper wrappings, tipping out one last, cold chip.

'Want it?' he said, holding it out to Alex, aware he was using it as an excuse to touch her fingers, equally aware he had to sort out his feelings before this went any further.

Buddy saved the day, swooping from his perch on the railing, where he'd been quietly scolding some errant seagulls.

'Too late,' Alex said, laughing at the antics of the bird as she too rose to her feet.

Close enough to touch, to reach out and draw her into his arms.

She was close enough to touch him and a treacherous voice in her head suggested if she told him of the phone call he'd do the touching—he'd hold her to comfort her—but this whole situation was too...false? Artificial? Too *something*.

She'd come home to her father's death and Will had been there for her—Will was the only familiar person in the town she once had known, but wasn't it too easy to confuse comfort for something more personal?

But she *did* take the wrappings from him, aware it was probably an excuse to touch his fingers!

Leading the way back through the house, she thanked him for bringing Brian's message and explaining so much of the set-up she'd be going into.

Did she sound as stilted and formal to him as she did to herself?

Maybe, for he grinned and gave a little bow.

'My pleasure, Dr Hudson,' he said.

She smiled.

'You can call me Alex,' she replied teasingly.

And was startled when he said, in a surprisingly deep and serious tone, 'I would like that very much, Alex.'

Upon which he kissed her cheek and was gone.

'I will not press my hand to where he kissed me,' Alex muttered to herself, scrunching the chip wrapping tighter so her fingers wouldn't stray.

But as she went upstairs, stepping over the chaos of clothes still littering the hall, to go into the new bedroom, she couldn't help but wonder if she'd ever get to share the beauty of this special room with someone special.

Special like Will?

She thrust away the thought and busied herself putting

clothes from the hall and her second suitcase into her new wardrobes, setting out her toiletries in her new bathroom.

It's the beginning of a whole new life, she reminded herself, and it's up to you to make the most of it.

But not alone, her heart protested, not alone…

CHAPTER FIVE

SUNDAY MORNING AND Alex luxuriated in the comfortable new bed, lying there, looking out at her beloved river. She thought of the past, the life she'd once had, here by the river—of her mother, who'd been unable to comfort her when she'd needed it and had died without forgiving her for a sin she hadn't committed.

Long ago, with help from counsellors, she'd forgiven her mother's behaviour, aware that if she hadn't taken that step it would have poisoned her life.

But her father?

What had *he* been thinking when he'd made this room for her?

Regret?

He'd asked for forgiveness and she'd given it whole-heartedly, but this gift spoke of love.

'Love' hadn't been a word much used in her home—apart from love for God. Although Alex had felt loved when she and her father had been out in the tinnie, when he'd held her hand to steady it while she'd baited a hook…

Was that what love was?

A steadying hand?

Now she grieved for the man who'd held it out to her, setting aside the pain of his later rejection.

And sorrow that she hadn't had more time to spend

with him—time to tell him all was well—almost swamped her.

It's hunger, she told herself, and left the warm nest of her bed.

Her father had stocked up on basics but it was obvious she'd have to shop, especially as she was starting work the next day, and shopping time in future might be severely restricted.

Time to take her father's car out of the garage.

Wondering why she hadn't even bothered to check what kind of vehicle it was, she found the keys hanging where they had always hung, used the automatic door-opener to open the garage then went out and blinked in surprise at her father's choice of vehicle—a fairly new, bright red, small SUV.

Red! Like the car she'd been saving up for all those years ago, although back then all she'd wanted had been something small and cheap!

But what fun to have this to run around in, was her next thought, then guilt that she wasn't feeling worse about her father's death damped down the pleasure.

Although, she thought, she now understood enough of her father's thinking not to get too depressed.

The bedroom, this smart new *red* car—these were his way of saying he was sorry—of making restitution for the lost years, which made it okay to take pleasure in his unexpected gifts.

Didn't it?

She shook her head, nearly as confused over her father renewing contact as she was over Will.

Think shopping, not Will!

Marilyn proved every bit as pleasant and efficient as Will had said, and Alex knew she'd soon settle into the routine of the practice. She'd been there for two hours and was going through the patient list for the week when the pager Marilyn had presented to Alex buzzed.

'It's the hospital,' Marilyn told her, as Alex lifted the phone to make the call.

She listened as a nurse explained the problem then hung up and turned to Marilyn.

'Do you know a Mr Miller—Peter Miller?'

'Unstable AF,' Marilyn said succinctly. 'Brian had been hoping his heart had settled down but if he's in hospital it's playing up again. He knows to take his pulse every day and to head straight for the hospital if he goes into fibrillation so I guess your welcome to Port will be a cardioversion.'

'Can you get his file for me, please?' Alex asked, wanting to know as much about the patient as she could before she met him.

Marilyn returned, handing it to Alex and adding, 'Do you want me to let the ICU know we'll need someone to do the anaesthetic for you?'

'I suppose so, if that's the procedure, although perhaps we should call Mal Parker.'

Marilyn shook her head.

'He'd be happy to come—Mr Easygoing, that's Mal— but I think you should do it—plunge right in—then nothing will seem as strange later. You'll meet some of the hospital staff and begin to know your way around and it'll give you confidence in starting the new job.'

Alex nodded, but she wasn't quite sure about Marilyn's theory. In fact, she was beginning to feel a little over-whelmed—too big an information dump in too short a time, and now this...

The procedure itself was simple and usually a nurse with cardiac training would set it all up—could probably do it—so all the doctor had to do was wait until the patient was anaesthetised then turn the switch to deliver an electric charge to shock the heart back into normal rhythm.

But in a strange hospital, with a new anaesthetist—and she didn't even know where the patient would be.

Not that she wouldn't manage.

'Will Kent is on call at the hospital this weekend,' Marilyn said. 'I've phoned him to come in.'

'Will Kent? But he's an intensivist,' Alex protested, not at all sure she was ready to see Will again.

'Well,' Marilyn replied, 'that's who does all the small anaesthesia jobs at the hospital. Intensivists are trained in practically everything.'

'Of course!' Alex said, still trying to get to grips with the fact she'd be working with Will on her first job in the hospital. 'Well, I'll go and see Mr Miller, find out when he first noticed it. We've got twenty-four hours, thirty at a pinch, to safely do the shock treatment, and if there's any doubt he can go onto drugs for a month and have it then.'

Marilyn nodded approvingly, and Alex headed for the hospital, Mr Miller's file tucked under her arm.

At least, she thought as she crossed the road to the hospital building, she knew the way to the coronary care ward as it was on the same floor as the ICU where her father had been.

Atrial fibrillation—the offset beat of the patient's atrium—could cause blood clots to come loose from the wall of the heart, blocking arteries, leading to strokes—

The information buzzed in her head.

But every hospital was different, so—

Thud!

Of course it had to be Will she'd run into—Will who

held her shoulders to steady her, Will who smiled down into her eyes.

'Going somewhere?' he asked, the twinkle in his eyes sending tremors through her body.

'First patient.'

She blurted out the words, her thoughts swooping between the procedure and how solid Will's chest had felt when she'd hit it.

'Then we'll go together,' he said, the hint of laughter in his voice echoing that twinkle. 'Did Marilyn tell you I'm doing the anaesthetic?'

She looked directly at him now, and sighed.

'Is that so bad?' he asked, the laughter still there.

'No,' she muttered at him, not wanting to reveal that she'd been kind of hoping for a few Will-free hours so she could try to sort out her reactions to him.

Had he sensed her reluctance that he said, 'We could get Mal in to do it.'

She glared at the man who had brought unnecessary complications into her life. 'I haven't spoken to the patient but it sounds like a straightforward cardioversion. A monkey with a bit of training could do it so I really think I can manage.'

'Ah, but as well as the monkey?' Will teased, falling into step beside her. 'Anyway, at least I can introduce you to some of the staff, and tell you all the gossip about them, and help you fit right in.'

Alex sighed.

She wasn't exactly flustered but Will's presence was having its usual unsettling effect and the one thing she didn't need when she was working was any kind of distraction.

But it was impossible to argue. She needed an anaesthetist and he was, apparently, it.

They were already at the nurses' station in the coronary care ward and he was introducing her as Brian's new recruit.

'He's been held up in Melbourne so Alex will be taking over his patients, who include...'

He finally stopped talking and turned to Alex.

'Peter Miller,' she said.

'Oh, good,' the nurse answered. 'Can you do him now? It's just that he managed to get through this afternoon's milking and if you can zap him tonight he can stay a few hours then get back home in time for morning milking.'

'Not a problem I encountered in Glasgow,' Alex said, smiling at the thought of a procedure needing to be scheduled around milking time, but the hinterland of this town was famous dairy country.

A nurse led her into a large private room, where her patient was lying on the bed, chatting to another nurse, who was checking the monitor leads taped to his body. Alex introduced herself to Peter and asked him about his symptoms, at the same time reading the information the monitor was providing. His pulse was running at just over a hundred and twenty—jumping between that and a low of ninety, and the hospital information board told her he'd had drugs to slow it and also an injection to thin his blood.

In the corner of the room was a bulky but efficient shock-treatment machine, with leads set out ready to be attached to pads on Peter's skin.

'Two years since last time,' Peter was telling her. 'The nurse says it's good to have gone that long.'

'It is indeed,' Alex told him.

She flicked through his file to the last cardioversion to check if he'd had any adverse reactions but, no, he'd been fine.

By the time she looked up a small crowd had gathered at the door.

'Not much happens around here,' Will said, 'so they're curious about the new doctor.'

'Well, that's a pity because the show's over for them. We need to shut the door.'

The small crowd at the door melted away as the CCU nurse went towards them.

Concentrating now on her work, Alex checked Peter's weight so she could set the correct charge, watched as the nurse stuck the rectangular pads into place, one onto his chest close to his left nipple and the other opposite it on his back. Once Peter was settled, Will put an oxygen mask over his nose and mouth, asked the nurse to hold it, and slid a catheter into the back of their patient's hand.

It was a swift procedure, a small amount of drug, the nod from Will, a single charge—Peter's body lifting slightly off the bed—then all eyes went to the monitor to see if the heart had reverted to a normal beat.

'Well done,' Will said to her, and although it could have sounded patronising, Alex took it as the praise it was.

'It was a fairly simple start to my Heritage Port career,' Alex told him.

'But good to get it over with?'

He smiled as she spoke and the smile did things to her insides that it really shouldn't be doing in a clinical situation—a work situation.

But Alex knew that what he'd said was true, not solely because of the medical procedure, but here she was in the hospital, with people she'd be working with for a long time to come—or so she hoped—and tiny seeds of friendship were being scattered around.

Will had disappeared but Alex waited with the nurse until Peter was fully awake.

The nurse wheeled in a smaller machine and attached new leads for an ECG to ensure the heart was stable while Alex spoke to her patient.

'I've had some drugs sent up from the pharmacy for you—I see you've been on them before—a blood thinner and a drug that slows the heart rate—instructions are on the boxes. You probably know the shock treatment could last a day, a week or six years, so I'd like you to stay on them for a month. See your own GP next week so he can check on you, then come and see me. Phone for an appointment in four weeks.'

Peter nodded, and thanked her, and she finally departed, leaving him eating cold hospital sandwiches and drinking a cup of tea.

'Want a cuppa yourself?' a nurse called as she came out.

'Yes, that sounds good,' Alex told her, as tiredness from what now seemed like another never-ending day swamped her.

Had it really only been this morning she'd driven into town to shop?

Had it only been three days since she'd arrived in Australia?

A cuppa was exactly what she needed, and she sank down onto the couch in a small tearoom behind the nurses' station and gratefully accepted one.

The woman who'd offered the tea had made herself a cup as well, and she settled herself on a chair opposite Alex.

'I remember you, you know,' she said. 'I was only a kid, but my family went to the same church and that bastard was always touching us kids. I feel ashamed now I didn't say something but at least my parents shifted us away from there. I remember Mum saying they treated you something cruel, those church people and your family.'

Alex shook her head, exhaustion hanging heavily in her body, but the woman's words had struck home.

'I hadn't even thought about people remembering,' she said. 'It was so long ago and so much must have happened since.'

Yet the woman on the phone had remembered...

'I don't think it'll bother you. I think these days people are far more aware of sexual abuse, and I bet a lot of the folk who thought him innocent changed their minds over time. You did right and I remember my mum saying how brave you were to stand up to him and all those others that reckoned he was God.'

Even in her tiredness, Alex found a smile.

'Thank you,' she said. 'That really makes me feel good, but right now I need to finish this cuppa and get home before I fall asleep. I start work in the morning, so I might pop in before I go to the rooms, if that's okay, and check on any patients I've got here.'

The nurse, whose name, belatedly, Alex read was Robyn, took her teacup, assured her she'd be welcome any time, and Alex found her way out of the hospital, across the road to the car park, then drove home very slowly, catching the last ferry and realising, as she spoke to the ferryman, that she'd have to find a bed somewhere in town for nights when she'd missed this last one. She wouldn't have liked to drive the long way round as tired as she was tonight.

And there'd be plenty of nights like this...

The chug of the ferry was soothing, and she drove off the ramp and along the river road.

It had been nearly twenty years but tonight it really felt as if she was coming home.

Until she saw the shattered window!

She couldn't help but notice it as she swung the car into the drive and the headlights shone straight onto the front of the house.

A bird, she decided, although coldness in her chest suggested that was wishful thinking.

Parking the car, she locked it and then the garage door, before walking along the front path, taking in the damage more closely.

The slope of the land, down towards the river, put this part of the house only a few feet above the ground, so by standing on tiptoe she could peer through the hole in the window and see the glass, glinting in the light from the streetlight outside, scattered over the floor and furniture in the living room.

She didn't see the rock until she went inside, or the note wrapped around it.

WHORE!

In blood-red letters!

She'd have to report it but right now she was just too tired, though finding a room in town was becoming a better and better idea.

Angry that the home she'd been so looking forward to had been rudely assaulted, she stomped through the rest of the place, checking there was no further damage.

Remembering Will coming in with the key from outside, she went back out and found the hollow rock, brought it and key inside.

Did people who made anonymous threats and threw rocks escalate to personal violence? She was sure she'd learnt something about these things in psychology lectures many years ago, but right now she couldn't think.

Glad she'd shopped, she checked the doors were locked, heated a ready meal in the microwave, ate most of it, and went straight up to her new bedroom.

Things would look better in the morning.

They didn't!

In fact, the broken window looked more menacing somehow.

She'd woken at six and after surveying the damage had phoned the police.

'I know you probably can't come out now,' she said, 'but I'm starting work and will be out all day and I want to get a glazier to fix the window as soon as possible.'

'Where do you work?' the policeman asked, and Alex explained.

'What if you could take a photo then put the rock and the note in a plastic bag and take them both to work? We'll send someone round to collect them and take a formal statement. Perhaps you could get your secretary or someone to phone and tell us a suitable time.'

Impressed by how obliging he was, Alex agreed, then she did an internet search and found a twenty-four-hour glass replacement firm. They could come in the early evening when she hoped she'd be home from work. It was the best she could do and, to her surprise, the positive actions she'd taken made her feel a whole lot better about the attack.

She fixed herself a simple fruit and cereal breakfast and took it out on the deck, sharing it with Buddy, who seemed to have forgotten about Bruce in his delight with being able to say, 'Such a wuss.'

'That could get old very quickly,' Alex told him—not that it made the slightest difference to his performance.

The nurse on duty in the coronary ward was as welcoming as Robyn had been the evening before. She found a space for Alex at the desk in the nurses' station so she could read the computerised records of the patients before she met them, then led Alex around the rooms, introducing the patients.

To her, they were a typical mix—a woman with congestive heart failure, a youngish man who'd just had a pacemaker implanted and should be discharged later in the day, another man undergoing tests, which would include an angiogram later that morning.

'Am I doing that?' Alex asked, as she hadn't seen any mention of it in the diary Marilyn had emailed to her.

'No, he's Mal Parker's patient and he'll do it today before he goes away. The doctors usually like to keep patients overnight before and after an angiogram.'

Alex nodded. If beds were available it was a wise move, as there could be complications after the procedure, including bleeding from the site through which the instruments had been threaded—in this case his groin—or reactions to the dye used to highlight problems.

'So I'll be discharging him tomorrow,' Alex said, and the nurse nodded.

'Unless he's asked Will Kent to see to it,' the nurse said. 'Will will be doing the anaesthetic,' she said, and Alex knew from the tingle in her nerve endings that Will was close.

'Mal has asked me to discharge him,' Will said cheerfully, 'so don't try to pinch my patients, Dr Hudson. You can have him back for his next appointment.'

Alex turned to face him.

He was in doctor gear—casual doctor gear, as befitted a hospital in a large coastal town. Under his unbuttoned white coat she could see a dark grey polo shirt and paler grey slacks.

With his stethoscope hanging out of his coat pocket and a wide grin in place, to Alex he was sex on legs.

Blimey! Was she *really* thinking things like that while she was at work?

'And good morning to you,' she said, hoping she sounded far cooler than she felt.

'Cardioversion was good, wasn't it?'

He sounded cool!

She nodded. It was easier than speaking, but she knew she had to get over this Will thing—and soon—because she was going to be seeing him around the hospital all the time.

But right now escape was the best option.

'I've got to fly. First patient due and you've already told me how fierce Marilyn can be if we run late.'

She whisked away, hoping it looked like professional haste, not a desperate escape bid.

Will watched her go, aware there was something bothering her.

Him?

Hardly!

'So, are you going to talk to your patient about his anaesthetic or just stand there, mooning over the pretty new doctor?' the nurse asked.

'I do not moon!' he said gruffly, although that probably *was* what he had been doing.

'She's really beautiful,' the nurse said in a kindly voice—perhaps excusing the mooning.

'I knew her way back when,' Will said firmly. 'She lived next door for a few years.'

'Oh, yeah,' the nurse teased as they went in together to see the patient. But he was also worried about the mooning. It was happening too fast, this attraction to Alex. And although he'd known her 'way back when', the attraction hadn't been there so he couldn't blame that for the way this had hit him.

He saw his patient, chatted to him about the upcoming operation and the light anaesthetic that he would be given, checked for allergies, discussed the weekend surf, and headed back to the ICU.

But the nurse's silly tease stayed with him, bringing this time a sense of foreboding.

He had Charlotte to consider, and an ill-conceived relationship could affect her, while an ill-fated one—which surely this would be—could be even more disastrous.

His ICU patients were all behaving themselves, more's the pity, because there wasn't an urgent problem to distract him from his thoughts.

Although there was always paperwork. He'd get on to that—letters to the general practice men and women whose patients he was tending.

He'd just have to try and keep images of Alex from flashing through his mind. Had he ever mooned over Elise? He'd loved her, he knew that, but early on in their relationship, had images of Elise flashed through his mind at inappropriate times?

The policeman came at five-thirty—Marilyn deciding it was too risky to try to schedule him between appointments. Her curiosity about the visit was evident but Alex was reluctant to explain, mumbling something about official stuff that had to be done and hoping Marilyn would assume it was to do with her father's death.

When he did come, a young constable, he was very sympathetic about the broken window, and he took the note and a copy of the photo but doubted it would be much help. Reluctantly, Alex told him of the phone call.

'But you've just arrived in town. Who could you possibly have upset?'

Alex shrugged. She looked into his pale blue eyes and realised, if he was a local, he could have been at kindergarten with the twins. The past would be unknown to him.

Did she have to tell him?

Not really, but now she'd reported it, and if the aggravation continued, wouldn't the police start looking for a reason?

Taking a deep breath, she said quietly, 'Before I left town more than fifteen years ago I upset a lot of people, including my parents. I can only think that there's someone out there who thinks I deliberately harmed them. I really, really do not want the whole situation stirred up again, but if this escalates then I suppose you'd have to look for someone from back then.'

The policeman looked puzzled and Alex regretted, more than anything, getting officials involved.

'I see,' he finally said, although it was obvious he didn't have a clue. 'We don't normally do patrols out on that side of the river, but I'm sure we can arrange for a car to drive that way from time to time. Maybe its presence might put a stop to this.'

Or not, Alex thought.

But the young man departed with her statement and the note, and finally she could go home—go home and get the window fixed.

Driving home wasn't quite the pleasure it had been the previous evening, but the trip across on the ferry soothed her, allowing her to slough off the tiredness of the day and feel renewed. It was dusk as she drew into the drive and as far as she could see there was no further damage.

Maybe it was over—whoever it was had got their anger off their chest and she'd been foolish bringing the police into it.

Maybe!

By Thursday she was certain the harassment had stopped. She'd settled in at work, was enjoying meeting her new patients, was getting to know the nurses at the hospital, and had been spared contact with Will, who was apparently in Sydney at a two-day seminar.

The patients behaved themselves so she was able to leave work early on Thursday, getting home in time to shower and change into casual clothes before Tony arrived.

She had a snack in case the meeting went for longer than her stomach could handle, and considered having a glass of wine to steel herself for the effort of her first social outing.

Best not, she'd decided.

Tony arrived on the dot of six.

'Were you waiting up the road until it was time?' she teased, and he smiled, and took her arm to lead her out to his robust four-wheel-drive, complete with not one but two kayaks on the top.

'Do you paddle one and lead the other, like people did with horses in the old days?'

He chuckled, a nice warm sound, and explained one was an old one a friend had given him, too small for him but he'd thought it might suit her.

'You're being very kind,' she said.

'Well, people were very kind to me when I first arrived in town. It's paying it forward, isn't it?'

So they chatted all the way to town, easy talk, very little of it personal, although they did establish that although he'd been married in the past, neither had children, and both were currently unattached.

It felt strange, getting back into the swing of social life. Strange to realise that this was the beginning of a friendship that could lead anywhere.

Perhaps not anywhere, Alex admitted to herself, given the spark of attraction was missing—at least on her part.

But friendship would be good. That's what she'd need as she settled back into her old home town.

And friendship she'd have, she decided later, if she joined the kayak club, for it was an extremely pleasant evening, listening to the club's plans for the next month, hearing the stories and feeling the camaraderie amongst the members, most of whom had gone on for a very noisy meal later.

'So, what do you think? Can you see yourself joining that crew?' Tony asked, as he drove her home after dinner.

'I can,' Alex admitted, for there'd been a warmth among the members and a feeling of welcome. 'But first I'll have to see if I can stay upright in a kayak.'

'I'm sure you'll manage,' Tony told her, 'and once you do you'll never give it up. Gliding silently through the backwaters of the river, or riding rapids, there's so much pleasure to be had.'

Alex could understand that, especially the silent gliding part for she usually switched off the tinnie's engine to glide among the mangroves.

They were nearly home and although Tony had shown

no indication he was interested in a more personal relationship, she did wonder if he'd try a kiss. And, pondering this, she was the last to see the desecration—the word 'Bitch' spray-painted in two-foot-high letters across the front of her house.

'Good grief!' Tony growled. 'Who on earth would do something like that?'

Alex felt sick, almost too sick to get out of the car.

'You can't stay here,' Tony said as she shrank against the door. 'I've a spare bedroom. Let's get you whatever you need and you can stay with me.'

It was a wonderful idea, and for a moment Alex was tempted, then anger came to her rescue.

'No way,' she said, finding some of the fight that had carried her through the court case all those years ago. 'I will *not* let someone chase me out of my home.'

Especially not out of my beautiful new bedroom!

'Then I'll stay here,' Tony offered.

Suddenly exhausted, Alex shook her head.

'No, I'll be all right. I'm sure whoever did this is long gone, and there are good locks on the doors, although if you wouldn't mind just walking through the house with me...'

The anger hadn't lasted long, that she'd made this pathetic plea to this man she barely knew.

He came, and together, turning on lights and checking each room, they walked through the house and out onto the deck, where the moonlight turned the river to a sheet of silver.

'I'm happy to stay,' he said, 'at least until the police come. You *will* phone the police.'

'I'll ring them in the morning,' Alex promised. 'There's nothing can be done now.'

He gave her a hug, and when she walked him to the

door he dropped a swift kiss on her cheek—a kiss of comfort, nothing more.

A good friend in the making, she decided as she watched him drive away. But who was behind the harassment? Who could she possibly have hurt so much that nearly twenty years later they still held such bitter hatred towards her.

Saddened by this person's pain, and apprehensive now about her decision to return home, she took herself to bed, taking comfort from the river and from Buddy bouncing on her pillow.

'If only you could really talk, you could probably tell me who did this,' she told him, but all he did was ask who the pretty girl was.

At least that meant, worried as she was, that she drifted off to sleep with a smile on her lips.

CHAPTER SIX

THIS TIME THE noises outside her front door woke her—at the unearthly hour of five-thirty.

Fear gripped her for a moment, and then rational thought told her the harasser wouldn't be doing anything in broad daylight.

So who was doing what?

She walked through to her father's room and peered out the front window. Tony's big vehicle was pulled up on the kerb, and three, or maybe four, young men were scouring the front of her house with brooms and something that smelled like turpentine.

Tony was apparently supervising, and must have sensed her presence for he looked up and waved.

'I took plenty of photos for the police but thought you'd rather have it removed before the entire neighbourhood saw it. These lads are students of mine who think they might get extra credits for their good deed.'

'Well, I certainly hope they do,' Alex replied. 'Just give me ten minutes, I'll get some clothes on and organise coffee and toast for all of you. I think I might even have some croissants in the freezer.'

Tony smiled at her, and Alex felt a twinge of regret that the smile didn't provoke even a small tingle in her nerves.

It was a very nice smile, he was a very good-looking

man, he was kind and thoughtful and obviously clever—
his list of good attributes could probably go on for ever.

So why—?

She knew why, although she'd managed to put Will
out of her mind for the past few days.

Or almost out of her mind...

Tony and his crew finished their job and settled on
the deck, first helping her carry out all they would need
for their breakfast. They chatted easily, confident young
men, remarking on the beauty of the river, then moving
on to medical talk, telling her they'd probably see her
around the hospital before too long.

She thanked them for their help and was surprised
when, as they were leaving, one of them hung back.

'You know,' he said, 'we could easily make up a roster for someone to sleep out here with you until this is
sorted.'

The others jeered.

'In a spare bedroom or on your couch,' he growled.
'Just till they catch whoever did it.'

'Thank you,' Alex said, touched by their concern. 'But
Tony's already offered and I've assured him I'll be fine.'

More jeering and hooting but this time directed at
Tony. Would she, as a student, have treated the dean with
as much levity? Definitely not, but perhaps this was to
do with this being a smaller, more intimate university.
For whatever reason, it seemed healthier than the awe in
which she, as a student, had held the professors.

They departed, Tony telling her he'd left the kayak in
the shed beneath the house, beside the tinnie.

'And you should shift the key to the shed from above
the door—it's the first place a burglar looks.'

Alex laughed, but she would shift the key, and check
all the locks before she went to work. Tony would email

the photos to her to show the police and had even offered to go to the police station with her, but she was feeling stronger again, and ready now to fight this person or at least find out who it was and why they felt she had ruined their life.

By lunchtime she was glad it was Friday, with two free days ahead of her—well, free except for a ward round.

Getting back into the routine of work had taken more out of her than she'd expected it would, so a relaxing weekend—lazing on the deck with a good book, perhaps trying out the kayak—was looking very appealing.

Her phone line flashed.

Marilyn, to tell her Dr Kent wanted to see her after her last patient at four.

'Thanks, Marilyn,' Alex responded, hopefully calmly, although her heart was giving jittery little bumps. 'He's probably picked up something that might interest me from the seminar.'

Which made sense!

In fact, she hoped that was why he wanted to see her.

Or perhaps he just wanted to check out how her first week had gone.

Another buzz on her phone told her the next patient was waiting while she sat here thinking up excuses for Will's visit so she wouldn't start thinking it was personal and getting all excited!

You are thirty-six years old and should be over this excited stuff, she told herself firmly. Besides, it would never work.

She went out to meet her next patient.

But the Will who entered her office at four-thirty and loomed over her desk certainly didn't look as if he'd come for any social reason, neither, given the scowl on his face, did she think it was to pass on newly learned knowledge.

'Just what is going on in your life that I've had police questioning me about my actions?' he demanded, and Alex learned the meaning of dumbfounded.

'The police *what*?' she managed when she'd finally found her voice.

'Visited me at work, asking why my vehicle had been seen parked outside your house last night.'

His anger was hot enough for her to feel the sizzle of it across the desk. But when she'd made sense of what he'd said she found anger of her own.

'And what *was* your vehicle doing outside my house last night?'

He slumped into a chair.

'Foolish as it now seems, I got back from Sydney and thought I'd call in and see how your first week at work was going,' he muttered.

Not to see me—the thought breezed through her head, silly disappointment in its wake.

'I went out to a kayaking meeting—there's a group at the university—'

'I know all about the kayaking group at the uni—Tony Mitchell's lot.'

Uh-oh—so Will and Tony Mitchell didn't get on! That much was evident from the way he'd said the name.

'Ah, I get it!' Will continued, in a voice that could have frozen fire. 'He came to see you about your father—thought, gorgeous new woman in town, I must get to know her, and already you're in the kayaking group.'

'I am *not* in the kayaking group.' Alex spat the words at him. 'Yet!' she added, mostly out of spite. 'And Tony Mitchell asked me to the meeting as a kind gesture to a new person in town. I've only met him three times but he seems a thoroughly nice man and very helpful as well.'

'Three times?'

Alex sighed. She wasn't sure why but suddenly they were arguing about something that didn't really matter—except that it obviously did to Will.

Not that she had to explain anything to Will.

Of course she did—not only had he been incredibly kind since her arrival but he'd been there for her that last dreadful day in court.

'Tony brought some students around this morning to clean some offensive writing off the front of the house. I assume, as the police have spoken to you, you know about it.'

Will studied the weary-looking woman across the desk from him and wondered how the situation had developed into a heated argument.

Because he'd been shocked and concerned by the police visit?

Or because he was jealous of Alex's association with Tony Mitchell?

Deeply, gut-churningly jealous!

Which, given his ambivalence over the rights or wrongs of having a relationship other than friendship with Alex, was ridiculous.

He shrugged his shoulders and leaned across the desk to touch her hands, lightly clasped in front of her on the polished wood.

'I'm sorry, Alex. Charging in here and roaring at you. But when the police told me what had been happening, I couldn't believe you hadn't told me—talked to me about it.'

He saw shadows chase across her face but she didn't move her hands.

'At first it was just a phone call, and—you'd been so good, done so much already—I didn't want to seem a complete wimp by telling you about it. Then there was the rock and I did tell the police about that. It was only when Tony drove me home after the meeting and saw the writing on the wall that he became involved.'

She smiled, as if at some memory, and it took all Will's self-control not to tighten his grip on her hands at the mention of Tony Mitchell.

'Tony brought students out this morning to clean it up and they were so sweet, offering to set up a roster to sleep over each night so I wouldn't be alone.'

'I bet they did,' Will said, and Alex laughed.

'No, the young man who suggested it was very proper, offered to sleep on the couch. The others carried on but it was all good-natured and I know they'd have done it if I'd wanted it. I imagine to them I'm like an elderly aunt.'

'I doubt it,' Will said, 'but the boy was right, you shouldn't be in that house on your own.'

She moved her hands and stood up.

'Will, I haven't come home after all this time to that beautiful room my father made for me to be chased away by someone with a grudge.'

Will stood too, moving to the side of the desk, closer—wanting to touch her but still conflicted about it all.

'I can understand that,' he said gently, his anger forgotten in his concern for Alex. 'But if someone's nursed that grudge for twenty years, who knows what direction it might take next.'

She moved now, closing the distance between them, putting her hand on his arm and looking up into his face.

'I know, it worries me too, but I *won't* be hounded out of my home.'

How could he not kiss her?

He was thinking of a cheek kiss but somehow her lips were right there, and once his mouth had touched them he was lost, especially as she was making breathy little sounds that seemed to indicate she didn't mind the kiss at all.

Soft, pliant lips, tasting new and fresh, tasting of the river, and sunlight, and beginnings and maybe endings...

His mind buzzed with sensations he couldn't possibly be feeling, yet kissing Alex was like nothing else he'd ever done before. Kissing Alex was a journey and a revelation, and he gathered her closer, nestled her in his arms, fingers wanting to explore, but his mind insisting he concentrate—for now—on the kiss...

Alex knew her bones were melting. Bone-melt from a kiss was something she'd heard of but had never experienced so right now, given she had Will to lean on, she was going to explore it fully.

His skin was just a little rough—as if he hadn't shaved since early morning—but the roughness, when it caught her skin, was tantalising in some way.

His lips demanded and she gave, his tongue invaded, and she welcomed it, tasting, testing, right where she'd wanted to be since first meeting Will again, for all she still felt, deep down somewhere she couldn't find right now, that it couldn't work.

She'd failed other relationships but to get into one where there was a young vulnerable child and fail that?

Unthinkable!

She was easing away from his body when an angry buzzing from the desk broke them fully apart, and, seeing the time, Alex realised Marilyn must still be in the outer room, perhaps waiting for Alex to leave so she could lock up.

And here she'd been kissing Will with such abandon when anyone could have walked in!

Alex pressed the key and spoke to her office manager.

'I'll lock up,' she said to the unseen Marilyn. 'Will's got some stuff to pass on from the seminar, so you go on home.'

Would Marilyn go without poking her head in to say goodbye? Alex hoped not because she knew her lips would be swollen, her cheeks reddened from the kiss, and her clothes probably not as neat as they might be.

'Just don't forget to lock the inner doors as well,' Marilyn reminded her, before adding, 'Goodnight, Dr Kent,' in a voice that suggested she knew full well why the pair of them had forgotten the time.

Alex looked at the man she'd been kissing.

'I don't know, Will,' she said, sighing wearily to underline the futility of the words. 'I'm afraid to get into a relationship with you—afraid I'd let you down.'

'I doubt you could ever do that,' he said, yet she heard a shadow of doubt in his words.

Unfortunately, he smiled and spoiled all the determination she'd been mustering.

'But I do know I'm hungry,' he announced, 'and no matter what rubbish we've got in our heads about this attraction between us, we do still have to eat.'

'Fish and chips on my deck?'

Alex regretted the words before they were fully out of her mouth.

Will grinned.

'Or fish and chips at the beach, so you could look at the ocean for a change, but perhaps, until we're a bit surer about where this is going—how we feel about a relationship between us—I think we should stick to restaurants. There's a great Indonesian place in town, or Greek, if you fancy throwing plates.'

'Indonesian,' Alex said. 'I feel like spicy but not too hot.'

'Do you now?' he whispered, and kissed her again, but briefly this time, finishing the kiss with a brush of his fingers down her cheek.

'I'd have said very hot,' he teased, and she knew she'd reacted with a blush.

Alex waited until they'd ordered and were sipping a pleasant fruit cocktail before she asked the question that had been burning in her brain.

'Why aren't *you* sure where this is going or how you feel about a relationship between us?'

He took her hand. 'Are you?'

She shook her head but persisted. 'No, but don't answer a question with a question. Why?'

He smiled and the way his eyes crinkled at the corners almost halted her breathing.

They're wrinkles, for heaven's sake, a voice in her head scolded, but she'd already moved on to study his lips as he spoke, and the way he ran his fingers through his hair when he was...

Frustrated?

Well, so was she but he *was* trying to explain so at least she should listen.

She was a woman, she could do two things at once, so look and listen.

But, even listening, he didn't seem to be making much sense.

'Excuse me,' she said, aware she should have been listening more closely, 'but are you saying the attraction is nothing more than frustration because neither of us has been in a relationship for a while?'

He gave a huff of laughter that suggested more despair than humour.

'That's what I don't know. It's just I've never felt like this before—never experienced almost instant attraction, not with Elise, not with any woman—so I have to think it must just be frustration.'

Hand in the hair again, long, slim fingers—clever fingers—

'Then there's love!' He blurted out the word as if it was anathema to him. 'What if we get into a relationship and it leads to love? And then there's Charlotte...'

He took her hands and squeezed her fingers. 'See, I'm a mess.'

Ah, that made sense—the falling in love thing, not the mess. He'd lost the woman he'd loved—been so hurt by it he didn't want to risk it ever again. She wanted to get up and go around and hug him, tell him it was okay.

Not that her own situation was much better.

'I agree with you about Charlotte,' she said, hoping to get his mind off lost love. 'Not that I don't love children but the fact I haven't been able to make a relationship work before worries me. I don't want to get involved with you to the extent I get to know her, too, then it all falls apart. I don't think that would be fair to her.'

'So you're a mess as well,' Will said, almost cheerfully, 'and the whole thing's a mess and perhaps it's better if we just hope it all goes away.'

'Do you think it will?' Alex asked him, and when he smiled this time, she knew the answer, at least from her side of things.

The shake of Will's head confirmed his thoughts and

fortunately their meal arrived or they'd probably have kissed again, right there in the restaurant, then left without eating if the urgency Alex was feeling was any guide.

'Saved by the rijsttafel,' Will joked.

'And *my* gado gado!'

They shared the meals, and ate, and talked of Alex's first week at work, and the seminar Will had attended in Sydney, but the thread of desire had thickened to a rope and it tightened between them until words became impossible.

'I'll follow you home,' Will said as they left the restaurant, and although Alex protested, she knew she'd feel safer if he was there....

But the reminder of the harassment broke the spell between them and she realised she couldn't go on needing the support of someone every time she drove home after dark.

'How did the police get on to you?' she asked, as he held the car door open for her.

'Apparently they questioned everyone in the street, and a neighbour had seen my car. I stopped it and phoned you because the house was in darkness.'

'Was it late?'

'Eightish, I suppose,' he said, bending down so he could hold her hand as he spoke. 'I guess the neighbours went to bed before the real culprit turned up with the paint. Look, are you sure you won't stay with me—well, not me but with Mum? Or get a hotel room in town?'

Alex reached up so she could kiss his cheek.

'While we're both so confused?' she teased. 'You know full well we'd end up in bed in that hotel room, and right now I think that would make things worse instead of better. Besides, there's Buddy, and I really love my house, Will, and I *won't* be hounded out of it.'

* * *

The courage of her statement shook him. She was something special, this woman...

But hadn't they just agreed the attraction between them couldn't go anywhere?

His churning thoughts made it impossible to speak so he nodded, kissed her cheek, shut the door and went to his own car. At least she hadn't protested about him following her home.

He pulled into the drive behind her and waited while she came out, lowering the garage door with the remote.

'No graffiti tonight,' she said, but a quaver in her voice suggested she wasn't feeling nearly as brave as she made out.

He grew angry again that someone had targeted her like this—as if she hadn't been through enough—and the dark outline of a car parked on the verge about four houses up disturbed him as well. He'd check it out before he went home.

'You're looking at that car up there,' Alex said, and Will remembered just how observant she was. 'It's probably a neighbour's visitor, or one of my student fans taking on the job of guardian.'

'I'll check it anyway,' Will promised, although now he thought he recognised the shape of it—a shape very like the big four-wheel-drive Tony Mitchell drove.

He took her key and opened the door for her, ducked as Buddy swooped out the door then back in again to land on Alex's shoulder.

'He doesn't seem upset,' Alex said, but Will was more concerned about the futility of having a bird as one's only protection.

'You should get a dog,' he told Alex, who laughed.

'And leave the poor thing on its own all day? I'd have

to get a dog-walker and a vet and Buddy mightn't take to him and then where would I be?'

'Safer, if it was a big dog,' Will growled, but he knew it was a losing battle and changed tack—thinking of the weekend ahead of them.

'Can I see you tomorrow?' he asked. 'I'm on call again so Mum's taken Charlotte up the coast to my sister's place. She has three little ones and Charlotte adores them. We could have an early surf, the tide would be in, and the waves are forecast to be small but curlers. Then we could finish with breakfast at the surf club.'

'You and Dave were always surfing. You still surf?' Will met her eyes.

'It's the one thing that kept me sane after Elise died,' he said, and Alex understood.

How often, way back then, had she taken the children to the beach to explore the rock pools while Dave and Will had surfed and Isobel had sat on the veranda of the surf club, reading, until it had been time for them to join her for breakfast.

Thinking back to that time, she realised that playing with the children and their innocent, non-judgemental love for her had been a huge part of her recovery from the trauma and torment of that time. As surfing had obviously been for Will...

Lecca, the twins had called her, and rarely had ten minutes gone by without one or other of them, often both, flinging themselves into her arms for a hug.

'Lecca, we love you,' they would say, and slowly their love had made her whole again.

Could she revisit that time again?

With another child?

Not yet!

Not until she was really sure she could handle a relationship—not make a botch of it, ruin it, possibly hurt the child...

But she *could* go to the beach! *Could* explore the rock pools and remember more good things of the past.

'I'd love it. I'll meet you there. What time?'

CHAPTER SEVEN

MEETING HIM THERE meant he wouldn't have to drive her home, come back into the house and thus put them together in close proximity of a bed. Will saw that immediately and supposed it was wise.

Not that he felt very wise, mostly frustrated, not sexually frustrated—well, that too—but frustrated that his usually intelligent brain couldn't seem to work out how to handle his attraction to Alex.

'Six-thirty too early? You'll surf?'

She laughed.

'Will, don't you remember when you and Dave tried to teach me to surf? Didn't I tell you then that the river was my watery habitat, like the surf was yours? But I love the rock pools, the sea anemones and little, brilliantly coloured crabs. I'll be very happy there while you brave the waves.'

He smiled and pulled her close, intending just a brief, goodbye kiss, but she kind of melted against him and he was lost, claiming her mouth again, seeking to know her through the touch of lips and tongue.

They were both flushed—he could feel the heat in his cheeks—and breathless when she eased away from him.

'Doesn't seem to be going away, this attraction, does

it?' she said, trying for casual, but her voice too huskily intense to carry it off.

'We'll work it out,' he assured her, pulling her back to where he was beginning to feel she belonged—right there in his arms.

She nestled there and he held her, breathing in a faint lemon scent from her shampoo, and woman smell, the scent of Alex.

Once again it was she who broke the embrace.

'Six-thirty in the morning,' she said, and kissed him lightly on the cheek.

She stood in the doorway as he left, and he couldn't help glancing up the road, pleased to see the big four-wheel-drive had departed.

Although now he remembered what had brought him to follow Alex home this evening, he began to wonder if perhaps she did need someone to keep an eye on her—or at least her house—overnight. She'd waved as he'd got into his car, then disappeared inside, shutting the door behind her. He knew she'd lock it, but the thought of someone attacking her house while she was in it made him feel extremely uneasy.

Feeling foolish, he turned his car and drove up the road, as if he was driving away, then turned around and passed the house again, now only lit on the river side— Alex had obviously gone up to her bedroom. He parked where the man he'd thought might be Tony had been parked, and sat for a while, contemplating what he knew was foolishness.

The buzz of his pager stopped further speculation, and lights going on at the front of Alex's house suggested she, too, had received a message.

Rather than use his mobile he returned to Alex's house and knocked on the door. He could hear her voice so she must be just inside. The door opened, the phone still in her hand. Not wanting to interrupt her call, he listened as she spoke, although the words '...if you get an anaesthetist there to do a TOE. I'm on my way' weren't very revealing.

Finishing the phone conversation, she turned to him.

'Patient I haven't seen yet, Paul Wilcox, fifty-nine, apparently phoned the ambulance with ripping, tearing pains in his chest, going through to his back. He's one of Mal's patients and I glanced through his file—suffers from hypertension and Mal suspected an aortic aneurysm but the bloke hadn't got around to having the tests Mal ordered—or he's had them and there were no results in the file. Ambos report shortness of breath, sweating, weaker pulse in one side and some paralysis. They gave him morphine for the pain and beta blockers to slow his heart rate, and he's due at the hospital about now.'

'I'll drive,' Will said. 'If there was an aneurysm and it's ruptured, he'll have bled out before we get there.'

It sounded harsh but the empathy in Will's voice told Alex he was simply stating an unnerving fact.

'Or it's an aortic dissection and, depending where it is, we'll need someone to operate,' Alex guessed. 'You were paged?'

She knew it was an unnecessary question, but she was trying to switch fully to medical mode, something that used to be so easy back when Will hadn't been around.

Will nodded, but he was either concentrating on getting them to the hospital in the shortest possible time or he, too, was switching to his medical persona.

'What will you do?' he asked.

'They'll do a CT scan as soon as the ambulance unloads him. If something shows up on the scan—a problem in the ascending aorta—we'll do a TOE when we get there to get a clearer picture of just where it is and how bad it is, always given the first scan shows dissection. I've asked for an anaesthetist to be on standby for the TOE—oh, I suppose that's why they paged you.'

'The transoesophageal echocardiogram, that magic invention,' Will said. 'You know the Americans call it a TEE, like the thing you put under a golf ball, because they spell oesophagus with an "e". I'm always amazed how close we can get the probe to the heart.'

It was conversation, and Alex, focussed on her patient, didn't reply, too busy wondering just what facilities the hospital had and how easy or otherwise it would be for them to operate on the patient tonight.

They'd paged Will, so presumably—

She *had* to ask!

'If it's a type-A dissection in the ascending aorta, is the hospital equipped for an emergency op? For cardiopulmonary bypass? Do they have a cardiovascular surgical team? Would they have a synthetic graft, say, to help with the repairs? Could they rally enough people in to manage the whole complex procedure?'

Will didn't answer immediately, too busy driving carefully onto the ferry, but once he'd switched off the engine he turned to her.

'Hey, they didn't open a cardiovascular surgical unit to play around with angiograms and cardioversions that even docs like you can do,' he teased. 'We've got the lot and an absolutely fantastic staff who all know they are permanently on call—mainly because of the young lad who needs the new heart. It's a regional centre of excellence, so the hospitals in nearby coastal and inland towns send their patients here.'

'Patients who would previously have gone to Sydney,'

Alex mused, still considering the complexity of the operation that might lie ahead for Mr Wilcox.

She could understand Will's pride in the service the hospital offered when they arrived to see the efficient machine already gathering pace. The patient was in Theatre, the CT scan up on a screen, a radiologist ready to do the TOE, which, once done, clearly showed where the aorta had formed into two channels.

Will introduced her to Norm Wright, the cardiovascular surgeon.

'You'll assist?' Norm asked, before heading off to change and scrub.

'Love to,' Alex assured him.

'And, Will, you'll play number two to the anaesthetist?'

'When don't I?' grumbled Will, then he turned and smiled at Alex. 'The hospital board's been advertising for a new anaesthetist, and, though we've a couple of trainees, for jobs like this they hook me in.'

He smiled as he finished the explanation and Alex's heart skipped a beat.

You can't go into Theatre with heart skips, she told herself firmly, and by the time she was gowned, masked and scrubbed, she actually believed it.

The team was just as efficient as Will had said it would be. Once in Theatre, he introduced her to the perfusionist, who would run the heart-lung machine, monitor the patient's blood, and administer the drug to stop the heart while the actual operation took place.

The anaesthetist, a woman, was at the head of the table, Will beside her, their eyes already trained on the monitor, trays of equipment were in place, and the assisting doctors and nurses were talking quietly as they waited for orders.

A younger surgeon opened the patient's chest, Alex falling easily into place in the team, responding to requests to cauterise small vessels, twisting clamps to hold the chest open.

The perfusionist worked neatly and swiftly to connect the patient to the bypass machine, and on Norm's nodded command injected the cardioplaegic solution that slowed down the heart to near stopping but kept it alive with rich nutrients.

The bulge where the dissection had taken place was clearly visible, but Norm checked all around it, making sure no other vessels were affected. Alex watched the way his gloved fingers moved, so deftly, so surely, and listened as he talked the team around him through the whole procedure.

With the tear repaired, Norm slipped a polyester sleeve around the damaged part of the big blood vessel, checked there was no more obvious damage anywhere, and nodded to the perfusionist to stop the cardioplaegia. It was always a 'hold the breath' moment. If the heart didn't start on its own, it would need a shock to get it going, but, to everyone's relief, it began a steady beat.

Next step in the procedure was to check for blood leaking from the damaged artery, but the repair was secure and the job of closing the patient's chest began.

Norm left the theatre as his assistant was closing, and the anaesthetist handed the patient over to Will.

Alex, too, stayed, assisting with the closure, waiting until the patient, accompanied by Will, was wheeled into Recovery.

Knowing he would stay there until the patient regained consciousness, Alex made her way to the locker rooms, where she showered and changed back into civilian clothes.

Felt in the pockets of her slacks for her car keys then remembered she'd driven in with Will.

She poked her head into the recovery room, and was surprised to see Will handing over to a younger man.

'Saved by the wonderful Dr Turner,' Will said. 'A very virtuous young intensivist who's early for his shift.'

Relief and tiredness mingled in his smile, and Alex was surprised to see it was after five o'clock. It had been late when they'd started, probably close to midnight, so it had been a five-hour op—tiring for anyone.

'You're *not* tired?' he demanded, apparently disconcerted that she was still on her feet.

She smiled at him. 'I will be now I know how long I've been standing up in there,' she told him. 'What next? Do you stay?'

He shook his head. 'No, it's over to Dr Turner now. I'll look in on him again before I leave the hospital, and then he'll be my patient once he's in the ICU, but I wouldn't think they'll move him there for some hours yet.'

Another smile, this one a better effort.

'Breakfast at the surf club?'

'They wouldn't be open,' Alex protested, although the mention of breakfast had made her realise she was hungry and if she wanted to sleep she'd need to eat first.

'They will by the time I've showered and dressed again,' Will said, standing up and touching her lightly on the arm. 'Do you mind waiting?'

She shook her head, even so light a touch rendering her momentarily mute.

'So I'll see you down at the car in half an hour, okay?'

Was it the smile or the light touch on her arm that had ignited her nerves again?

Or just plain tiredness?

Alex sighed. She knew it wasn't tiredness…

But was it love?

How could she tell?

She'd thought she'd been in love when she'd got engaged. It had only been later she'd realised that love hadn't really come into it. A certain amount of attraction, for sure, and liking, and friendship, and all kinds of good things, but love?

Love felt like a foreign country and right now, if what she was feeling for Will was love, it was a very confusing country where she knew neither the language nor the customs.

CHAPTER EIGHT

THE SUN WAS coming up over the ocean, colouring the world with a golden sheen. The low waves Will had forecast curled onto the beach in a froth of whiteness then receded, leaving shining wet sand behind. A few surfers were out on boards, but for once Will didn't envy them. Sitting here with Alex had filled him with a sense of peace he hadn't felt for a long time.

The operation had gone well, which added to his feeling of well-being, but it was the woman opposite him, the sun glinting off the gold of her hair, her blue eyes shining as she took in the scene and breathed in the air, that made him feel…complete?

It was okay! It would work. He'd *make* it work.

'You look very serious.'

Her teasing smile filled him with warmth the sun itself couldn't match.

'Very,' he said, with an answering smile. 'I was deciding that we've got to stop dithering about the past and look to the future—see where whatever it is between us takes us, with no hang-ups, no doubts, no looking back.'

She reached out and took his hand, her face aglow with what he'd like to think was love but which was probably just the morning sunlight.

'Yes, let's,' she said, and, for the moment, that was

enough, until she added, 'But cautiously—there's Charlotte, remember, and she shouldn't be hurt.'

A shadow crossed his contentment because he knew Alex was right. If they got too close and things didn't work out, his daughter *would* be hurt. It was a thought not very far from his mind at all times.

But that was for tomorrow—for now, surely, they could explore today!

He tackled the breakfast the waitress had placed in front of him—the surf club's renowned 'big' breakfast.

'Can you eat all that?' Alex asked, looking up from her tasty-looking scrambled eggs.

'Just watch me,' Will challenged. He began on the sausages—small sausages—pushing Alex's fork away when she sneaked it over to pinch a slice, although he did—later—drop a slice on her plate.

Silly stuff, but the tension, not only of the operation but of the last, well, four years really drained out of him and he relaxed, listening to Alex talk about her work in Glasgow—where the sun never came up over the ocean for breakfast—and telling her a little of his own life since he'd moved back to Heritage Port.

Getting-to-know-you stuff, but here, on his favourite beach at sunrise, it took on a special significance, as did the woman with whom he was sharing the experience.

Will was in an odd mood, Alex decided, but obviously a happy one. Every now and then he smiled for no apparent reason. She sneaked glances at him as he ate— almost total concentration on his breakfast at first—and it seemed as if the faint lines in his face had smoothed out, and a tension she'd sensed since first meeting him again had eased from his body.

Because he'd put the past behind him?

Because he was coming to the end of his grieving?

Hadn't he said something? Something about how surfing had helped him heal after his wife had died?

But he'd also said he was afraid of love...

Could anything less than love work?

And what did *she* know of love?

Vague uneasiness stirred inside her, but she pushed it aside, ate her eggs, and decided Will was right—she would look to the future.

Just because her past relationships had failed, it didn't mean...

He looked up and caught her watching him. He smiled and blew a kiss, and this time the stirring was completely different, and, tired as she was after a night without sleep, she began to hope he'd stay when he'd driven her home.

Although—

'I came back to town with you but I can get a cab home,' she told him. 'That way we can both have a sleep and maybe get together later.'

'Or better yet, we both go to my place for a sleep and I'll drive you home later?'

The roguish gleam in his eyes told her exactly how much sleep he expected they'd have.

'We go to your place for a *sleep*?' she repeated, and he laughed and squeezed her hand.

'We could have a sleep later,' he suggested, but whether it was tiredness or the doubts that had sneaked in about grieving and love Alex suddenly felt it was all going too fast.

'Much more sensible that I get a cab home and see you later,' she said firmly, although she softened the words with a smile and a return squeeze of his fingers.

'Do we want sensible?' he grouched, and now she saw the tiredness in his face.

'Today we do,' she said. 'Well, for this morning at least! We're both too tired for much else.'

'It's age, isn't it?' he grumbled, but Alex knew he'd agreed. 'But no cabs,' he added. 'I'll drive you home. It's only another half-hour there and back.'

They left the surf club hand in hand, and she rested her fingers on his thigh as he drove her home.

'Just drop me off, no need to get out,' she said, as he opened his door.

'No?' he said, climbing out of the car and reminding her of the problems she'd had during the week.

'Is that why you insisted on driving me home?' she asked, as they walked together to the front door, but Will didn't answer, turning her instead and attempting to walk her, none too gently, back towards his vehicle.

But Alex glanced over her shoulder and saw the tiny pink and grey bundle outside the door.

'Buddy!' she cried, breaking away from Will and racing forward.

The galah was definitely dead, but as Alex lifted the bird's stiff body she heard the raucous cry from inside.

'It's not Buddy,' she said, thrusting the bird at Will so she could open the door. 'It's just a stuffed bird. A piece of taxidermy.'

She opened the door and the grey and pink bullet sped towards her, landing on her shoulder and scolding her loudly for being out all night.

Tears of relief she couldn't hold back were running down her cheeks, and Buddy, sensing her distress, brushed his head against them, quieter now, but still scolding his 'pretty girl'.

'That settles it,' Will said, passing her in the hall and heading for the kitchen. 'I'm staying while you sleep, then you can pack a bag and come to my place—stay in

Mum's flat. I'll put the bird into a bag and take it into the police station this afternoon.'

With Buddy still on her shoulder, Alex sank down into a lounge chair.

'Who could hate me so much?' she whispered, when Will returned.

Will had no answer except to ease her out of the chair and take her in his arms, holding her close until the tears were spent, then guiding her feet upstairs to the big bedroom with its view out to the river she loved.

Later, when they'd both caught up on some sleep, they'd have to talk—to go back to the time they'd first met and try to work out who she might have upset so much that the anger still burned.

'I upset everyone I knew,' she murmured, as if she was following his thoughts, but when he began to ease the tunic she'd been wearing off over her head she didn't protest, simply helped him, then pulled off her leggings herself.

'Let's just go to bed,' she said, and Will knew it wasn't an invitation to do any more than be together—to share the bed—and hopefully sleep, although now his mind was churning with ways and means to track down whoever was tormenting Alex.

Preferably before the attacks escalated to violence against Alex herself...

Alex turned in her sleep, or half turned as she met a warm body. Memories of the long night, breakfast at the beach then returning home.

Will...

He must have stirred for now his arm came around her, drawing her close, so she was spooned against his body, and, secure in his arms—secure in a way she hadn't felt for so long—she slept again.

Until, slowly, an awareness grew—awareness of his body, of his body's reaction to hers—and still half-asleep she moved so the arm that held her close shifted and his hand rested on her breast, caressed it gently—awakening *her* body as his was awakening.

'You're still asleep,' Will murmured, his lips warm against her shoulder. 'Bad time to make decisions.'

But his hand had left her breast and was trailing across her stomach. Her nerves were alert to every touch while her body ached for more.

Ached for more?

When had her body ever ached for anything, let alone more?

She must have stiffened for his hand stilled, lay flat on her stomach, warm and kind of heavy.

And the breasts he'd touched felt heavy too—sensitised and...

His lips pressed against her shoulder, against the base of her neck—surely that couldn't be an erogenous zone—but now they'd slid to kiss the sensitive hollow below her ear, firing such erotic responses she felt breathless.

Certain she'd end up pulling away, disappointing him, she turned and traced her fingers across his face, kissed his lips then drew back to look at him.

Or could it work?

Sleepy brown eyes, unshaven chin, lips that asked to be kissed.

She kissed them again and sighed.

Looked into those now serious brown eyes.

'This is where things usually break down in my relationships,' she whispered, touching his face again, tracing the laugh lines near his eyes. 'I *have* tried before, but I go all stiff and cold and somehow the few men I've known found that off-putting.'

'But you've never tried with Superman!' he teased, and she smiled and let him draw her close, let him wrap his arms around her and hold her against his warm body.

'If this is all you want, Alex, that's okay. Just lie there, let me hold you, let's just be together in a nice warm bed while the rest of the world goes by.'

She snuggled closer, confused now, the ache for more still there. Will's hands caressed her back, her neck, fingers kneading her scalp, and she moved her hands against *his* back, feeling the muscles over the bone, then higher, feeling the shape of his head, the tension in his neck...

'It isn't really okay, is it,' she said, as she, in turn, kneaded, but his neck muscles, not his scalp.

He drew back so this time he could look at her, and the hint of laughter was back in his eyes.

'We'll work it out,' he promised. 'I can understand physical intimacy being hard for you, but it's not a walk in the park for me either, and this instant attraction thing— well, that's just plain scary.'

'Superman scared?'

'Very,' he said, serious again, although when he kissed her it didn't feel like a scared kiss.

Maybe a little tentative, but only until she kissed him back, opened her mouth to his tongue, and pressed close to his body again.

How long they kissed for she had no idea, but when Will eased away, sat up in bed and announced that was enough for one day, she felt devastated.

Or her body felt devastated...

He *had* to go!

He had to go right now, or things would escalate and

he'd lose this woman altogether, and although he couldn't really understand it, he knew he couldn't let that happen.

Will was trying to untangle himself not only from Alex but from the sheets yet still retain enough covering to hide his burgeoning erection.

Her hand touched his hip.

'Stay?'

Nothing more than a sibilant whisper but it tightened his groin even more.

Now Alex was sitting up, sitting behind him, her arms around his chest, her fingers brushing against his nipples in such a way he almost groaned with agony.

'Help me?'

The words were pressed against his shoulder and, given his condition, there was no way he should have agreed.

But somehow they were lying down again, well, Alex lying down, he resting his head on his elbow, lying on his side so his reaction would be less obvious.

He looked into the beseeching blue eyes and knew he was lost.

'Are you sure?' he asked.

She nodded then reached up to trace his lips with a fingertip.

'Just show me how, Superman, show me how it could be,' she whispered.

Will took a long, deep breath. A cold shower would have been better but hardly appropriate at this time.

'So, first we kiss,' he said, determined not to rush her, wanting desperately to show her how enjoyable consensual sex could be. 'But while we kiss we can explore each other—that's what hands are for. Are you okay with that?'

She nodded again but this time he detected the hint of a smile on her so-delectable lips.

So, lying side by side, they kissed, and while his hands stroked and teased her back and breasts and belly, hers, more tentative, sent fire flashing through his body.

He slipped his mouth away from hers, kissing her ear, nibbling at the lobe, kissed his way down her neck while she pressed kisses against his head.

She stiffened when his mouth closed very gently around a nipple, but before he could pull away she'd relaxed and her hands were holding his head to her breasts.

Urgent sensations speared from Alex's breast to her sensitive core, and her body shuddered with something she supposed must be desire. Will's attentions to her breast immediately stopped and she had to hold his head to show she wanted more.

Well, she thought she wanted more...

And now it all became a little confusing, sensations she'd never known swamping her body and anaesthetising her brain.

Will's teeth were teasing at her nipples, first one then the other, while his hand was sliding down her body, finger tickling at her navel, hand sliding lower, fingers gently brushing against the lips, touching and retreating, each retreat a tease that notched her tension higher.

She was mindless now, beyond thought, giving in to the sensual eroticism of Will's touch, so when his fingers slid into her she shuddered, but it was a shudder of a different kind. And now those clever fingers were touching her inside and out, moving slowly then swiftly, then slowing again—teasing. She knew he was teasing because the tension building inside her was close to an eruption of some kind, but not, she knew, even in her dazed state, a frightening eruption.

So when it came, the explosive release, she thrashed

on the bed, shuddering again, pins and needles racing from her toes up to her scalp, her body so light only Will's arms anchored her to earth.

She snuggled against him, spent but confused, aware this was a two-way thing and now it would—or should—be her turn to pleasure Will.

But Will seemed unfazed, his hand, still now, between her legs, his other arm holding her close.

As sense returned, with it came sensation and she knew she wanted more—possibly needed more.

So it was up to her.

She slid back enough to run her hands across his chest, and kissed him as her thumbs brushed his nipples. Kept kissing him, feeling his response, not only in the kiss but in the tightening of his body.

'Be very sure,' he whispered against her lips, and as she swallowed the breath of the words she felt for him, guiding him into her wetness, letting him fill her as tremors from her orgasm still lingered.

Moving with him now, feeling his body heavy on hers, feeling *his* desire rising in the urgency of his movements, her own building again until an even stronger release matched his, her cry echoing in his groan.

They lay, still joined, entwined, replete for now, the sun on the river throwing shadows on the ceiling, then Will slid to one side and leaned again on his elbow, looking down at her.

'Okay?' he asked huskily.

'Very okay,' she replied, then smiled at him. 'Maybe you really are Superman.'

He was about to protest but she stilled him with a finger to his lips.

'I need to talk,' she said, 'to tell you—to explain.'

He nodded, but wrapped his arm around her so she was close as she poured out all the pain and hurt of her old relationships—all two of them.

'I'm not an idiot, Will, I knew I needed help. I went to psychologists, counsellors, even, one time in Glasgow, to a sex clinic. I learnt how to give myself an orgasm, but it seemed an empty and not particularly pleasurable exercise so when that didn't help I decided to forget about both sex and intimate relationships. Plenty of people live without both, why couldn't I?'

Will had to smile. 'Perhaps because you're a beautiful, vibrant, sensual woman, and deep down you knew it wasn't enough?'

She gave a light laugh that had more than a touch of cynicism in it, and he knew immediately that the shadows of her past still hung darkly over her life.

Life!

What was he doing, lolling around in bed with her, when right now the priority had to be keeping her safe?

'I could stay here like this for ever,' the woman he was worrying about murmured, eyes slumberous again, body stretching lazily.

Temptingly!

His response was to tighten his arms around her, but only for a moment.

'Tempting though it is, my love,' he answered, 'there's stuff to do. Shall we save water and shower together?'

Alex's mind spun—he'd called her his love—stuff to do, like dead birds—and showering together, being naked together. Hadn't they skipped a big part of the getting-to-know-you thing?

Uncertainty gripped her, the 'my love' endearment forgotten as all the early awkwardness of an intimate relationship hit home. It had been so long since she'd been this close to anyone, and never really successfully.

Part of the prudery her fiancé had accused her of, she knew, but now?

With Will?

'I'll start the shower,' he said, as if sensing her confusion, 'and then I'm going to come back and take you by the hand and lead you in there, where I'm going to soap you all over and sluice it off you and not do one thing you would not like me doing, okay?'

But before he could put his words into actions she turned towards him and put her arms around him, burying her face in his shoulder.

'I might not be very good at all this.'

She blurted out the words, wanting them said, willing him to understand, but feeling incredibly foolish and naïve.

His arms locked around her.

'You are a beautiful, sexy, glorious woman who has been treated very badly in the past, not only by that rat Spencer but, I suspect, also by other men in your life. But your body's response to mine was unbelievable so do not, ever, doubt your sexuality.'

He kissed her lips, a long, seductive kiss that had the nerves she'd never felt before responding once again.

'We don't have to shower together,' he said, when he finally moved his lips from hers. 'In fact, I'll shower very quickly and go pick up dinner because we need to eat, while you can have the shower all to yourself and think about the times we *will* share it, okay?'

His eyes were wary, as if he feared he'd upset her in some way, so this time *she* kissed *him*, whispering as she drew back, 'So much more than okay,' although all kinds of doubts still lingered in her head.

She showered quickly herself, phoned the hospital—patient doing well—then made a salad to go with whatever he brought back from the co-op, keeping busy to keep her mind off what had happened, although that was impossible because her body had such vivid recollections of it that just remembering made her want to be back in Will's arms again.

Was this lust?

She had no idea, although she now knew, in her body as well as in her head, that sex was meant to be enjoyed, and, even more importantly, that she had the ability to enjoy it.

Had it happened too quickly?

The question nagged at Will as he drove to the co-op, but the pleasure that still lingered in his body told him the answer was a definite no.

Alex's response to his foreplay had been so volcanic it had electrified his own desire, and even thinking about it now made him hard.

But he guessed she'd never experienced a shared orgasm before and the intensity of it had shaken her, and had probably brought back all the restrictive teachings of her church school and prudish parents.

He muttered curses to himself as he thought of what she'd been through then the reality of what was happening to her now hit him like a cold shower.

The thought of her in danger—physical or emotional danger—was like an arrow pricking at his heart, arousing the strong protective feelings he hadn't felt since Charlotte's birth.

He'd take her home, he'd keep her safe—

Imprison her? a snide voice in his head whispered.

No, that wasn't love.

Now, where the hell had love come into it?

Wasn't he the man who'd sworn off love?

He pulled into the co-op car park, pleased that thoughts of food could push the other confusing issues to the back of his head.

They ate on the deck, Buddy, who'd been imprisoned in his cage while they'd slept, taking great delight in hopping between them.

'Who knew you had a galah?'

Will's question brought Alex out of her pleasant daze and she frowned at him.

'Why?'

He answered her frown with a smile that made her nerves twitch—again!

'Because whoever left the bird outside knew,' he said, serious now, the words squelching twitching nerves very effectively.

She tried to think—think back.

'Friends from school?' Will prompted, but Alex shook her head.

'Some, maybe,' she said. 'Caitlin Kerr was my best friend, so I'd have told her when I got him, and if you think about it, she could have told anyone. So could Mum and Dad. But only Caitlin ever stayed over. Her family went to the same church as mine, so my parents liked her.'

Had her voice quavered that Will reached out and took her hand?

'I know you don't want it to be this Caitlin—that would be too much of a betrayal—but can you think of any reason why all that happened would have hurt her?'

'No, and no, and no! Caitlin was the only person from the school who ever got in touch with me. She was at the trial one day—not inside but waiting outside the court— and she pressed a letter into my hand then rushed away.

She said she believed me and how sorry she was, but she couldn't risk her parents' anger by seeing me again.'

'She believed you?'

Alex found a rueful smile, although memories of that time still caused deep pain.

'At least someone did—apart from Dave and Isobel, of course.'

'And me, I never doubted you,' Will assured her, before moving on.

'So Caitlin has to be a starting point. She believed you so if we find her, maybe she'd be willing to talk to us about what happened after you left town—or after the court case. She might even know who would have been most upset.'

'Mrs Spencer, I would say to that,' Alex offered, 'but I can't see her even thinking a swear word, let alone spray-painting it on someone's house. She was very godly and so shadowy she was barely there. And anyway, the Spencers left town.'

'How do you know that?'

Alex had to think, then it came back to her.

'Would you believe one of the nurses at the hospital? Apparently, there were more people than I realised who thought I'd told the truth, and her family was one of them.'

'So, we'll talk to her as well. Can you remember her name?'

Alex shook her head.

'I should be able to, but it's gone. Anyway, she's in the CCU so I'll be able to find her. Maybe Robyn.'

'Robyn Alcorn, she's a wonderful person—I'm sure she'd be happy to talk to us. What time is it?'

Alex glanced at her watch, surprised to find it was mid-afternoon.

'You're not going looking for her now, are you?' she asked.

'The sooner the better,' Will declared. 'Although I want you to pack up some clothes. You can stay with me—well, in Mum's flat—until it's sorted.'

Alex shook her head.

'I'm sorry, Will, but I won't do that. Everything is moving just too fast. I need some time to come to terms not just with the stalking but with...'

She balked, and Will squeezed her fingers and smiled the smile that made her heart ache.

'With you and me?'

'Especially with you and me, because it isn't just you and me, is it? It's you and Charlotte as well, and if I mess this up, and I could, then I wouldn't want her getting—I don't know, perhaps confused about the situation.'

The words hit Will like a slap across the head with a wet fish! What on earth was he thinking—where was his brain?—that he'd completely left Charlotte out of the equation when he'd suggested Alex move in with his mother?

Then there was the fact that maybe Alex didn't want a stepdaughter and her talk of messing things up was a way of telling him that...

She reached out and took his hand.

'It can't possibly be as bad as whatever you're thinking,' she said gently. 'All I'm saying is that this is very new and we don't want to rush things.'

He took a deep breath to allay the panic that had been fluttering in his head and in his heart—and obviously on his face!

'Okay,' he said. 'But as Mum and Charlotte are away until Tuesday, I'll stay tonight and first thing tomorrow we get a security firm here and have alarms installed—

alarms and sensor lights and whatever else the experts recommend.'

He stood up and pulled her to him, holding her loosely in the cradle of his arms.

'I can understand your need to be here—to let the house become your home again—but *I* need you to be safe.'

A different warmth flooded Alex now and she kissed this man who'd brought such unexpected pleasure into her life. Not that his next suggestion was all pleasure.

'We have to do it, Alex,' he said gently, when she protested about sitting down to write a list of all her parents' friends, her friends, and even neighbours they'd had in the past.

'It's been twenty years,' she reminded him.

'Which only makes it worse,' he said, with a gravity she'd not heard before. 'Someone who has nurtured such hatred for twenty years is not entirely sane.'

Alex shivered at the thought, but found a pad and pen and sat down, putting Caitlin at the top of the list.

'I'll get my tablet from the car,' Will suggested. 'We can check if any of the people you remember are still at their old addresses and get phone numbers.'

'Wouldn't a phone book be just as easy?' Alex smiled as she said it, and smiled even more widely when he admitted it probably would work well.

The Kerrs were listed at their old address, which immediately presented a new dilemma.

'Do I ring and ask for a number for Caitlin?' Alex said, dread at the thought gripping at her stomach.

'Better I do it. Let's think of a reasonable excuse.'

But in the end Will didn't have to use any excuse.

'We no longer speak her name in this house,' the man who answered the phone said, and hung up.

'Well, that went well!' Will said. 'Perhaps we stick to lists and then we track down Robyn and get her to tell us what she can about the people on it.'

Alex tried, but after jotting down some names of her parents' friends then girls she'd been close to at school, she pushed the pad away.

'You know,' she muttered, 'writing out a list of people who might hate you is not the most cheerful thing to be doing on a Sunday afternoon. Let's take the bird to the police station then you can show me where you live while you get a few things for the night.'

She must have sounded even more depressed than she felt for he agreed immediately, once again hauling her out of her chair and holding her in his arms.

Which, inevitably perhaps, led to other things, and it was much later that she locked a loudly protesting Buddy in his cage and they left the house.

First stop the hospital, to check on their joint patient, only semi-conscious as yet, but the monitors showed he was doing well.

'This wasn't where you used to live,' she said, when Will pulled up in front of a modern-looking house that was tucked against the cliff and looked out over the ocean.

'No, Mum moved after Elise and I were married,' he explained. 'That's what made this so convenient. I don't know if you remember the old house, but it would have been impossible to convert it to two flats. Whereas here we not only had the land, but the beach is right there for Charlotte.'

Charlotte!

Definitely the pivotal point in Will's life!

And suddenly something about entering his flat—seeing toys and other evidence of Charlotte—held Alex back.

Failure at relationships with men was one thing, but if she failed in a relationship with a child?

'No, I'll wait in the car. The view is lovely.'

Extremely weak, but he didn't argue so maybe he'd realised it was too early to get too involved.

'I'll just grab some clean clothes and a toothbrush,' he said, although he did kiss her swiftly on the cheek before he got out of the car.

She was asleep when Will returned, and he stood and looked at the miracle that had come into his life—the miracle that was Alex.

He didn't want to think too far into the future, something about this relationship was too fragile for that, but just seeing her there, relaxed in sleep, filled him with inexplicable joy.

Could they make this work?

Could *he* make it work?

He'd loved Elise deeply and completely, to the extent that her death had nearly destroyed him. It had been only the little scrap of humanity that was Charlotte that had kept him going—her and surfing, because out there on the ocean he could cry...

But what he felt for Alex was different—it had an element of physical passion he'd never known before.

Could such passion last?

And if it didn't, wasn't Alex right about not wanting Charlotte hurt in the fallout?

And what of hurting Alex?

If the relationship failed, she'd blame herself!

He looked through the window at the beautiful woman sleeping in his car, doubts and memories jumbling in his head.

The one thing he *did* know was that Alex had been hurt enough in the past and, whatever the future held, there was no way he could hurt her again.

Should he walk away now?

He shook his head as he went to get behind the wheel.

No way could he walk away now—not when she was still under threat.

Not when he loved her?

He frowned at the random question thrown up by his brain.

Love?

So quickly?

No way!

His love for Elise had grown like a seedling, spindly and unsure at first but strengthening over time as they'd grown to know each other.

This was different—so different…

Enough!

He stood by the car door to phone the hospital, hoping to track down Robyn Alcorn and enlist her help in finding out who might want to harm Alex.

Alex opened her eyes and gazed around her. She was in a car with the sea beyond the windows.

Outside Will's house.

She could hear his voice—muffled, outside the car—talking on the phone?

She sat up, suddenly very awake and smiling at her memories of the day.

'Robyn's on days off,' Will announced, opening the car door and slinging an overnight bag into the back seat.

'She'll be on duty on Wednesday, so we'll stick to making the list and have it ready when we talk to her then.'

Alex wanted to protest—that making the list was too hard, too hurtful—but she knew he was right.

'Are you always this masterful?' she asked, smiling at him as he reminded her to fasten her seat belt.

'Always,' he said firmly, leaning across to give her a kiss. 'Police station next, then home to your place. Do you need to do any shopping on the way?'

Not only masterful but domesticated.

Domesticated by his mother or Elise?

The reality of his first wife struck her suddenly, and she wondered how much of a factor a dead wife could be in a relationship. She'd been too caught up in thinking about the effect of the relationship on a child—

If there *was* a relationship!

Maybe it was all too complicated, right from the beginning, and now was the time to back away.

The thoughts were only tiny darts pricking at her senses, but they were still there.

Except when she looked at Will, saw the little smile hovering on his lips, the gleam in his eyes when he glanced towards her...

No, she had to find out what lay ahead—be it good or bad.

She had to give her all to this relationship, if only to prove that she *could* make one work!

She reached out and rested her hand on Will's thigh, and smiled back when he turned to smile at her.

CHAPTER NINE

WAKING IN THE morning with a man in her bed felt strange to Alex, strange but wonderful. But Will was obviously a morning person—no doubt because of Charlotte—soon up and about, making cups of tea, bringing them, with the phone, back to bed with him.

A little lost in the newness of it all—the unfamiliarity—Alex looked out at the river, sipping her tea, doubts about the rightness of the situation still niggling at her. The sex was new and wonderful, but was that casting a rosy glow over everything else?

Making her think love?

Making her think it could make a difference in a relationship—maybe make it work?

'Ha, just what we want—a twenty-four seven security service. I'll phone them now.'

Will's small cry of triumph made her forget her doubts and concentrate on the present.

His phone was by his wallet—the wallet from which he'd extracted a couple of condoms—and within seconds he was arranging for someone to be at the house as soon as possible.

'So, you'll have to get up and put some clothes on,' he told Alex, smiling down at her. 'Not that I don't like you exactly the way you are.'

The smile, his cheeriness should have reassured her, but a feeling that things had moved too fast still clung to the edges of her mind. He was out of the room before she could put it into words—although she probably couldn't anyway. It was nothing more than a slight uneasiness...

Thoroughly pleased with his efforts so far this morning, Will explored the refrigerator.

'How about an omelette?' he called up to Alex, needing to keep busy because he was still uneasy about the situation. Nothing he could put his finger on—Alex was wonderful, beautiful and sexy and great company, and he suspected he was already in love with her.

He who hadn't wanted love...

But the suddenness, and Charlotte, and losing Elise the way he had, threw shadows on his happiness.

'So keep busy,' he told himself, shooing Buddy away from the eggs he was beating. 'We'll have breakfast then do the list, whether Alex wants to or not, and later maybe go out on the river again—go further up, explore...'

Alex—even thinking her name brought a surge of desire.

Maybe they wouldn't go up the river later...

She wandered into the kitchen, wrapped in a purple kimono, hair tousled and face slightly flushed.

'Are you really this domesticated?' she asked, as he grated cheese then chopped some tomatoes.

'Well trained,' he said. 'Four years of bachelorhood, remember, and a child to feed. I had to learn to feed the pair of us, although I've always cooked. Elise would have fed us on lamb chops, mashed potato and peas every night of the week—cooking was never her thing.'

His gut clenched as soon as the words were out. Was mentioning Elise a good or bad thing?

But she'd existed—she was Charlotte's birth mother—

so surely if she came into the conversation naturally, some of the awkwardness he guessed Alex was feeling might dissipate.

'Well, I'm glad you cook, for whatever reason,' Alex told him, coming closer to kiss his cheek. 'Because most Sunday mornings I just laze around and probably don't eat at all until lunchtime. You'd have been starving by then.'

She started the coffee-machine while he cooked the omelette, dividing it onto two plates, adding a little of the chilli sauce he'd found in the pantry.

They ate on the deck, and the strain he'd felt earlier seemed to drift off in the soft spring air, Alex smiling as he fed Buddy a very small piece of his breakfast.

'He'll drive you mad now, begging at every meal,' Alex teased, and a certainty that this was right for him—for both of them—banished the rest of his doubts.

He took Alex's hand in his.

'I hope there will be many meals for him to drive me mad at,' he said quietly, and knew she understood when colour rose in her cheeks and she squeezed his fingers in hers.

'I hope so too,' she whispered. 'I really do!'

And she was pretty sure she meant it.

Loud knocking at the door finished the conversation.

'Security man!' Will said.

Alex leapt to her feet, gathering up their plates and mugs.

'I'll have to put some clothes on. I didn't think he'd be this quick!'

She took the dirty dishes to the kitchen and dashed upstairs, leaving Will to open the door.

Security, she discovered, wasn't a simple matter of putting in an alarm. Once told of the problems she'd been having, the specialist insisted on CCTV cameras outside the house, one covering both street approaches and one at the side of the house where the power box was.

'We can take that one away later,' he said, 'after the perpetrator has been caught. But it will be handy to have it there for now because most people believe if you turn off the power then the alarms won't work so we would get a close-up of whoever it is who is pestering you. We'll conceal them as best we can and do as much as we can today when a stalker is less likely to be around.'

Bemused by all the technological marvels he was suggesting and his obvious knowledge of problem situations, Alex just nodded, going along with what he was suggesting because not taking notice of an expert would be stupid.

'It'll be costly,' the man said, and she shook her head.

'Doesn't matter,' she told him at the same time as Will offered to pay. 'Nonsense, it's my house and my security, and as I'll have to have a base in town for nights when I'm working late, it will be good to have the place secure.'

With a promise that work would begin within an hour, and a substantial deposit, the man departed.

'Back to the list,' Will said, and something in his voice told her he meant it.

But the list was impossible! The three couples she'd considered closest to her parents no longer had addresses in the phone book, neither could they be found on Will's tablet—well, not with any certainty.

'They all had children so I suppose if the children moved away the parents might have followed once grandchildren came along.'

'We'll put them on the list anyway,' Will insisted. 'Robyn might know something about them.'

So Alex obediently wrote them down.

'Now, schoolfriends other than Caitlin,' he said, and Alex listed the names of classmates with whom she'd been close—and others she only vaguely remembered.

'Other people at the church—the hierarchy who stood by Spencer at the time?' Will persisted.

Alex shook her head.

'It's all a blur, that time, Will. I don't know if I've deliberately deleted it all from my memory or if I was just so stressed back then that nothing stuck.'

'That's okay. I'm sure the police can search out the files and see if there was anyone who stood out as particularly hurt by the business.'

'Apart from poor Mrs Spencer,' Alex muttered.

Will pushed the list away, took her hand, and said, 'How about that boat ride?'

As Alex opened the door to the boatshed beneath the house she saw the kayak.

'Better still, let's try the kayak. Can you paddle one?'

Kayak!

Tony Mitchell!

Will felt a faint uneasiness in his stomach that he was pretty sure wasn't the omelette.

'I've been in one,' he said carefully, hoping his uneasiness wasn't jealousy.

'Then show me how,' Alex demanded, and although he'd have liked to say that surely she wouldn't still be joining the kayak club, he knew that was nothing more than selfishness. Alex needed to build a life back in her home town—a life for herself, not just a life with him, and that was if the 'life with him' thing worked out.

But he still felt majorly grouchy as he carried the kayak down to the water, holding it carefully while he stepped precariously into it.

'Shouldn't you have a life-jacket on?' Alex asked.

'Of course I should, but all I'm doing is a little "here's how to do it" paddle right in close to the shore. I can stand up in the water here.'

Why was she doing this? Alex wondered, as she watched Will settle into a rhythm with the single oar, digging it in one side then the other.

Because you need a life apart from Will, the sensible part of her brain reminded her.

However you might feel about him, there's still a lot of uncertainty there, and, given your propensity to muck up relationships, you have to make friends to fall back on.

She knew the sensible voice in her head was spot on, but seeing Will smiling as the art of kayaking came back to him she knew that this time she would do her darnedest to make the relationship work!

'We can both join the kayak club,' she told him, as he held the little craft steady for her to climb in.

'We'll see,' was all he replied, and although she'd have liked to analyse the tone of the words, she was too busy trying to stay out of the river, the kayak seeming to tip dangerously every time she moved.

'It won't tip,' Will assured her. 'Just get comfortable and then try the paddle.'

'Get comfortable when it's going to buck me into the water any minute?' Alex shrieked.

'It won't, I'm still holding it.'

She glanced around and Will was still there, waist deep in water now but still holding the flimsy craft as steady as he could.

'You really didn't have to get wet,' she protested, and he smiled and what she could only assume was love surged through her.

'I wanted to be sure you were safe,' he said simply, then the smile slid away and he added, 'Always.'

Her heart stopped beating—only for a moment—but something about that simple declaration had touched her as nothing else ever had.

It *had* to be love!

But how to handle it, how to nurture it and help it grow...

She lifted the paddle and imitated Will's movements earlier.

'Let go,' she said. 'I have to do this on my own!'

A bit like love, the doing-it-on-your-own thing.

Sure, you could share it with the loved one and that shared love needed care and attention too—but the love in your heart?

How did you protect that?

And if you couldn't, just how badly would it hurt?

But somehow she was paddling, still in the shallows at the river edge. The thoughts of love racing through her head must have helped the rhythm, and the feeling was great.

Until she tried to turn to go back to where Will waited. The disaster she was coming to expect from all her personal endeavours came as the kayak tipped her unceremoniously into the river and she emerged, dripping, the paddle clutched in one hand, the kayak in the other.

'You did well to grab them both. Most first-timers lose one or the other,' Will said, mostly, Alex suspected, to cover the fact that he was laughing at her.

Or with her?

Because now she was laughing too, both of them saturated, Will towing the kayak back to her beach while she slogged through the water in her sodden clothes.

'Now we'll *have* to shower together,' Will told her, as

seeing her body through the wet material sent a surge of desire through his.

'I guess so,' Alex replied, and together they returned the kayak and its paddle to the shed, but when they entered the house, intending to strip off their wet clothing before going further, they realised three men from the security firm were there, and even if they showered together, they could hardly make love while the men were prowling around.

'Another time,' Will whispered in her ear, and they squelched upstairs, Alex directing Will to the main bathroom while she sought refuge in her new en suite.

The phone was ringing as she came out—the hospital, to say Adam Hawkins had been admitted.

Not wanting to leave before speaking to Will, she waited until he returned from his shower.

'Adam Hawkins,' she said. 'He's been admitted to hospital.'

'He's the lad I was telling you about earlier—the one waiting for a new heart. You've met him?'

'Thursday. I'd been reading his file and wanted to see how he was doing on the portable IV infusions, and check he was getting enough support from the community nurses. I know his GP monitors him, but, well, I suppose I wanted to meet him.'

Will checked his pager.

'He'll have been admitted to the ICU but no one's paged me so I assume Josh Turner's coping with the situation.'

'He's not in the ICU, he's in Theatre—they've found a heart and it's being flown in as we speak.'

Alex's own heart was racing. She'd stood in as an extra surgeon once in Glasgow but somehow here, with Adam her patient, it was different.

'I've got to go,' she told Will, aware there'd be a full anaesthetic team in Theatre and Will wouldn't be needed until after the op.

'I know,' he said, and he took her face in her hands. 'You'll do brilliantly, the lot of you, and know I'll be thinking of you all the time.'

He dropped a kiss on her lips, a kiss of such sweetness her mind, as she drove, kept drifting back to it when she should have been concentrating on what lay ahead for Adam and how much the cardiovascular surgeons would call on her to help.

Making her way swiftly to the ICU when she arrived at the hospital, Alex realised just how quickly she'd settled in, and how easily she'd been accepted by the staff.

She headed straight for the main theatre, to find Adam already on the table. Well, she assumed it was Adam as he was totally covered except for his bony chest, which had already been cut open, and held agape by clamps. The diseased heart flopped about in his chest like a deflated balloon, moving a little as it tried to keep working.

She watched as Norm Wright, who apparently had the lead role in the procedure, attached a cannula to the vena cava, slid a tube into place in the cannula, turned on a switch on the bypass machine and watched as Adam's blood drained into it. The return cannula had already been inserted into the patient's aorta so blood was now flowing through Adam's body but completely bypassing his heart.

The donor heart had been removed from its cooler bag and the vessels to be attached to Adam's vessels neatly trimmed. The surgeons swiftly severed Adam's heart and carefully, with minute stitches, attached Adam's veins and arteries to the new ones.

Finally, the job was done and the moment of truth had

arrived. Norm detached the tube from the cannula and unclamped the aorta. Now warm blood from the heart-lung machine began to flow into the new heart—the icy-cold organ not long emerged from the cooler.

The strain in the room was palpable, Alex as stiff and silent as the rest. Norm's assistant reached into Adam's chest and gave the new heart a couple of gentle squeezes.

Nothing.

He repeated the procedure and this time it worked. The shiny new undamaged heart remembered its job and began to beat. Relief flowed through the team but the job wasn't done. Now Norm inserted a tiny electrode that would keep the new heart beating at ninety-nine beats a minute for a few days until it picked up the rhythm on its own.

Norm and his assistant stepped back.

'Dr Hudson, would you like to close?'

Pleased to be part of something so wonderful—apart from passing a clamp or two—Alex moved forward eagerly. Drawing the sides of the sternum back together, she fixed them with wire, then began the tedious stitching up of the skin, layer by layer, until Adam's chest looked as if it had been zipped back together.

Having been part of the final surgery, she accompanied her patient back to the recovery room, although he was now in the care of the anaesthetists until he regained consciousness.

The anaesthetists and Will, who was waiting in Recovery, anxious to know how the operation had gone and to check Adam's status, for he'd be Will's patient in Intensive Care for the next little while.

Alex's heart warmed at the sight of him, and she answered his raised eyebrows with a broad smile and a thumbs-up.

But exhaustion was creeping in and as Will spoke to the anaesthetists she slipped away, past Norm Wright, who was talking to Adam's anxious but cautiously optimistic parents, and into the locker room to shower and change.

Change!

Taking it literally, she couldn't but think how much change there'd been in her life in the last few weeks.

Coming home, her father's death—and Will!

Standing under the shower, she tried to sort through her thoughts. Coming home had been the right thing to do—she knew that now and not only because of Will. Her father's death—that was strange. She felt she should be grieving more for the man who'd done so much to make up for the past, but as she pondered her reactions she realised the tears she'd shed had been over little things—kindnesses she hadn't hoped for.

And, gradually, she realised that she'd grieved for her lost parents a long time ago—and probably for too long—although time was really the only healer for grief.

Her father's gifts—especially the Anzac biscuits—made her feel he was still around, the kindly man she'd known as a child, and somehow she knew that now he'd always be with her...

She went into the small office beside the theatres and wrote up her notes of the operation. The surgeons' notes would be more comprehensive, but Adam was Brian's patient—her patient now—and needed the record.

Will appeared when she was closing down the computer.

'I need to get out of here for a while,' she said to him. 'The ferry starts at dawn so I'll go home, check on Buddy then come back to check on Adam before I go to the rooms.'

'Good idea, but you'll need to take these.'

Will handed her a couple of keys and a card with numbers written on it.

'These are the keys for the new deadbolt the security people put on the front door and the card has the numbers for the security system. The keypad for it is in the hall, and you just key in the numbers to deactivate the alarm.'

'Oh, great!' Alex muttered. 'I put in the wrong numbers and wake the entire neighbourhood at five in the morning.'

Will closed her fingers around the keys and squeezed her hand.

'You won't key in the wrong numbers,' he told her, his dark eyes serious for once. 'Just drive carefully. I mean it, Alex, because I'd hate anything to happen to you.'

It wasn't exactly a declaration of love but, standing at the desk in the ICU when a young patient had been given a new chance at life, it sounded like one, and it was only with the greatest difficulty that Alex refrained from kissing him there and then.

She made do with a husky, 'I'll be fine. I'll come back here—see you—before I go to work, okay?'

He nodded and gave her fingers a final squeeze. She was walking away when he called quietly, 'Go out the main entrance not the one near the car park.'

She turned back, aware that she was frowning at the suggestion.

'Why?'

'Media! They hear stuff by osmosis and Adam's fight and his wait on the list for a new heart has been widely publicised. They'll be looking for someone to comment at the staff entrance.'

Now he smiled at her as he added, 'Port is still a small town at heart.'

The smile filled her with warmth and she walked away with a lighter step.

Will watched her disappear from the unit and shook his head at the speed with which his life had turned around. For all his doubts about allowing any woman, let alone Alex, into his life, somehow it had happened.

Yes, it had been sudden, and the suddenness had made him wary at first, worried that it might be nothing more than a physical attraction. But the more time he'd spent with her the more certain he'd become that he wanted her in his life for ever.

But his life included Charlotte's life.

Was Alex ready to meet her?

Was *he* ready to introduce her to Charlotte?

He saw Adam Hawkins's parents perched outside the ICU.

'You know when he gets in there, it's only one at a time, and then only for a few minutes. The operation was a major stress on his body and he needs to recover from it.'

They nodded, understanding, but needing to be near, even if it was only outside in the corridor.

'You know Adam's courage and his personality while he waited for a heart has made him a local hero, which means the press will be after you for stories.'

'Of course they will,' Mrs Hawkins answered for Will. 'After all, it was the press and their stories that helped raise the money we've needed for him over the years, and made people aware of the importance of organ donation. But...'

She looked beseechingly at Will.

'Could the hospital do it for us? Have a press conference? Just tell them Adam's got his new heart and now we can only wait and see.'

She paused, then added, 'We'll be able to talk about it in a little while, but just now...'

She broke off with a tremulous smile and Will understood that she didn't want to hope too much—didn't want to believe in a miracle until she saw her son's recovery with her own eyes.

'But we really don't want to talk to anyone right now,' Mr Hawkins added, his voice breaking with loss and strain.

'I'll sort it all out,' Will promised, although he did wish Brian Lane could be here to take the conference with the hospital media boss and Norm Wright, the cardiovascular surgeon. In Brian's absence, Alex would have to do it. It wasn't that he doubted she'd manage—she'd probably done dozens of similar conferences in the past.

But back in the town where the media had crucified her?

Although that was so long ago, did it matter?

He assured himself it didn't but the assurance failed to settle a knot of tension in his gut.

She'll be fine, he assured himself, and, later on, as he stood at the back of the room and watched, he found she was, answering the questions put to her with a poise and confidence that replaced the tension he'd been feeling with enormous pride.

One more night together then, Will had decided, he'd spend his spare time for the rest of the week with Charlotte, making up for time they'd missed.

But also mentioning Alex?

He wasn't sure.

He'd talk to his mother.

Talk to Alex first to be certain she'd agree to meet his daughter the following weekend.

CHAPTER TEN

OFFICIALLY ON A day off after a week on call, Will finished early and went home to have a sleep. Guilt that he was sleeping while Alex worked didn't last long and he woke refreshed and full of plans.

He'd collect her from her work and drive her home, organise a meal delivery so they could eat and go to bed early.

His body stirred at the 'go to bed early' idea but he dismissed it. They needed to talk, if only while they ate their dinner, and Alex would be tired.

He phoned her rooms to ask Marilyn to pass on this plan, no longer caring who knew about him and Alex. Not that Marilyn seemed at all surprised.

Hospitals! Word spread like wildfire through them.

Alex smiled as she looked at the message slip Marilyn had passed her.

'Lover-boy will collect you after work, and organise dinner,' it read, and she knew the cheeky note showed that the office manager had accepted her.

And Will!

As a couple?

Wasn't it too soon?

'Just go with the flow,' she said to herself, speaking out loud to give the words emphasis.

'What flow?' the patient who'd followed her into the room asked, and Alex smiled.

'Any old flow, I suppose,' she said, smiling at the man who'd already taken a seat.

'The nurse checked my heart—does she send the printout from the machine to you on your computer?' he asked.

'She does indeed,' Alex told him, bringing up his file. 'And your heart is looking very healthy. The stents Dr Lane arranged to have put in are working well, and, from your blood-test results, your blood pressure and this ECG, I would say you're fine.'

She'd stood up and approached her patient as she was speaking, wanting to listen to his chest. He knew the routine well enough to pull up his shirt, and when she was done he thanked her, pulled down his shirt, then said, 'You don't remember me, do you?'

Alex shook her head. Wainwright, the patient's name was Wainwright.

'I remember you as a little kid, always out in that tinnie you had,' he said. 'I had a trawler down at the co-op docks and you once asked me if I'd pay you for yabbies.'

Alex smiled, although his earlier mention of the past had sent an icy shiver down her spine.

Now the smile was genuine as she remembered happy times.

'You told me you used nets and didn't need bait,' she said, and Mr Wainwright laughed.

'You must have been all of seven and you told me you were saving up for a car—a red car. Did you ever get it?'

'I did eventually,' Alex told him, the smile slipping off her face as she thought of how she'd come by her red car.

'Well, it's good to see you,' Mr Wainwright said, pushing himself to his feet. 'Do I still have to come back for a check-up in three months?'

'I think for a fellow fisherman I could make it six, unless your GP decides to send you back to me.'

They shook hands and Alex walked out with her patient, and was surprised to see the waiting room empty.

'What's happened?' she asked the receptionist at the desk. 'Did you spray some kind of patient repellent around?'

The young woman laughed. 'No, but Dr Kent told Marilyn how you'd been up all night with Adam, so she contacted your last two patients and also let Dr Kent know you'd be finishing early.'

So now everyone knows about us, Alex thought, seeing the knowing smile on the receptionist's face.

As Will had said, Port still had the heart of a small town.

Will!

They talked very little on the drive home, Alex content just to be near him. But once on the ferry she turned to him and smiled.

'Thank you for doing this—I *was* too tired to drive, and probably too tired to get the numbers right on my new security system.'

'Worry not, for Superman is here,' he said, leaning across to kiss her cheek before putting the vehicle into gear to drive off.

It made her laugh but as he drove the short distance to her home she studied the man who'd not only brought laughter into her life but had also taught her how to love.

Because it had to be love, the warmth inside her, the slightly dizzy way she felt when she was with him, and the way her nerves tightened and her toes curled when he smiled at her...

So she stood close to him as he disarmed the alarm and sat close to him on the deck as they had a drink and ate the dinner he'd ordered.

They talked about her day, about Adam and his parents, about everything and nothing, although Alex knew it was chat.

'So, what is it you want to say?' she finally asked, and her heart squeezed tight when Will hesitated.

'It's about Charlotte,' he admitted. 'I need to spend any spare time I have with her this week, but I'm off duty next weekend and I wondered...'

He stared out across the river at the lights of the houses opposite then looked towards the centre of the town—towards his house and his family.

'Wondered?' Alex prompted, although she was sure she knew what was coming.

'Wondered if you'd like to do something with us. Go to the beach or the park or just have breakfast at the surf club, or maybe I could make dinner at my place, or—'

Alex pressed her fingers to his lips.

'I do get it,' she told him. 'You want me to meet Charlotte and, more importantly, her to meet me.'

She hoped she sounded more composed than she felt, because this was it, the test.

It wouldn't be about Charlotte liking her—that wouldn't happen until they knew each other better and Charlotte was assured Alex wouldn't steal her father.

No, it was about commitment, and whether the feelings she had for Will were real enough to be a strong foundation for a family—Will, Charlotte and herself.

And later...

The thought of having Will's baby spread sheer happiness through her body, but she'd leapt too far ahead.

And Will was talking again, his nerves obvious as he

practically babbled about it being up to her, and how he didn't want to foist Charlotte on her, and—

This time she stopped him with a kiss.

'It's okay,' she said, when they broke apart. 'You decide how best you want to do it and I'll fit in. Perhaps you'd like to bring her here, we could go out in the tinnie. Dad always kept a couple of little life-jackets for the neighbours' kids or grandkids, and Buddy's good with kids—he seems to like them, lets them pat him and sits on their shoulders.'

'Oh, Alex,' he said, and he put his arms around her, hauling her to her feet so he could kiss her properly. 'That would be wonderful!'

The kiss deepened, which led to moving like some clumsy four-legged animal up the stairs and into the room by the river.

Alex pushed herself away, excitement overcoming her tiredness.

'I need to shower,' she said. 'I won't be long.'

She saw Will's face and saw some of the uncertainty that had been in his words earlier.

Very carefully, she took his hand and led him into the bathroom, slowly stripping off his clothes, letting him remove hers, hoping he'd understand this act of showering together was her commitment to him.

Understand that she loved him!

There, it was out, no more dithering. What she felt for Will couldn't be anything but love, although in a shower with him, spreading soap across his body, enjoying the sensations when he returned the favour—well, some of that was lust...

To Will, her unspoken invitation to join him in the shower was a gift—the gift of trust, something he was certain Alex had never been able to give another man.

Will touched her gently, reverently, and when they made love beneath the water, he was speechless with an emotion he'd never felt before, yet wary that such happiness had come his way, aware how quickly happiness could be stripped away...

She fell asleep before him, curled into his body, and although he knew it would take time for Alex and Charlotte to get to know each other, he let himself dare to dream about the future—about family...

Alex woke, kissed the cheek of her still-sleeping lover, pulled on a robe and went downstairs to get the paper that her father must have organised to have delivered every day. Although at first she'd thought she'd cancel it, this morning she was glad she hadn't because today it would hold the end of Adam's story.

Disarming the alarm before she opened the door, pleased with herself for remembering the numbers, she slipped out, picked it up, then unfolded it as she walked back inside, wanting to see what was said.

'Oh!'

'What is it? What's wrong?'

Will was coming down the stairs and must have heard her involuntary exclamation.

'Nothing, it's just... I didn't think...'

Her voice trailed off when she couldn't find the words she needed, so she handed the paper to Will, pointing at the picture that topped the lead story—a picture of her, Norm and the hospital's media expert.

'It should have been a picture of Adam, not us,' she finally managed, disturbed by the exposure, though unable to explain why.

'You can never tell what the press will do,' Will said. 'And, anyway, it's a great picture of you. Norm, they've made to look like a mad scientist—they took it when he put on his glasses to read the official statement.'

Alex had another look and had to smile—Norm did look like a mad scientist—but her uneasiness remained, staying with her all day, while patients praised the picture or talked about Adam, intensifying as she drove home.

She sat in her car on the ferry, wanting to phone Will but not wanting to break into his time with Charlotte.

She could text him—just say Miss U. That wouldn't interrupt too much—

Her phone buzzed—a text, the message she'd been sending in her head there on her phone.

She stared at it, then, with total inanity, kissed the plastic screen, although she didn't tell him that when he phoned later, after Charlotte was in bed, to tell her the same thing but in a lot more words.

For some reason she slept late. Dressing quickly, she skipped breakfast—one of the nurses would get her a coffee and muffin from the shop downstairs. She set the security alarm then raced out the door, grabbing the paper from her front lawn on her way to her car. She'd have a quick look at it on the ferry.

But Will phoned while she sat in the queue of vehicles, waiting to board, and the paper was forgotten.

Until he said, 'Have you seen the paper?'

'No, I'm going to read it on the ferry. Hang on a sec while I get the car on board.'

She negotiated her vehicle into the tight spot the ferry lad was showing her, morning traffic making the trip more difficult, then got back to the phone.

'Don't open the paper,' Will said. 'I'll meet you at your rooms. Come straight here, you can do a ward round later.'

'Don't open the paper?'

'Please, Alex, I'm asking this of you—just do it for me, okay?'

Totally bemused, she agreed, but as she drove off the ferry she glanced at the paper lying next to her handbag on the seat beside her and wondered what it could possibly contain that had Will so excited.

Or upset?

Yes, he'd sounded more upset than excited.

The drive to work was agonising, and several times she reached out to just sneak a look, but she'd promised—or kind of promised.

Missing her ward round meant she was now early to work, but Marilyn was already there, her face set in an expression Alex couldn't read, so when the efficient, unflappable woman burst into tears, Alex was at a total loss.

She stepped swiftly towards her and put her arms around Marilyn's shoulders.

'Whatever it is, it can't be *that* bad,' she said, but shook her head.

'It is, it is, and Will's told me all about it and it's so unfair but it will hurt the practice, I know it will.'

Someone's died and the relatives are blaming Brian or Mal, Alex guessed, so she gave Marilyn's shoulders an extra squeeze then said, 'You look like you could do with a decent coffee and I missed breakfast. Let's pop down to the canteen together for a muffin and a coffee. Do you want to freshen up first?'

Marilyn straightened up, sniffed back her tears and trotted off to the washroom to obliterate any sign of them, calling over her shoulder, 'Will's in your office.'

Great!

Now perhaps she'd learn what on earth was going on.

She headed down the passage that led to her office, surprised to hear Will's voice. He must have been speaking very loudly—yelling?—because the rooms, with thick walls and heavy doors, were fairly soundproof.

He stopped his conversation as Alex walked in so the last words she heard were, 'My lawyer will be in touch with you.'

His face was pale but bright spots of anger burned on his cheeks.

'What's wrong? Is it Charlotte? What's happened?' Alex asked, coming towards him, her arms out to hold him.

He stood up from her chair and pulled her close.

She could feel his chest rising and falling as if he was taking deep breaths to steady himself.

'Not Charlotte, but you, my darling,' he said, his lips in her hair, his hands pressing her to him. 'Obviously thwarted by the security measures at your house, your stalker has taken to the media.'

Alex pushed away from him.

'What on earth do you mean?'

As Will seemed to be unable to say whatever words were needed, Alex snatched the paper from the bag she'd dropped on a visitor's chair and opened it.

There, across the top of two columns on the front page, was the picture that had appeared the day before, with Will and the media rep blotted out, only her face remaining.

And under it the headline: *'Woman who ruined the life of a good man returns to Port.'*

The story recounted the tale of the trial and Mr Spencer's acquittal—the headlines from the following day—the huge *'ACQUITTED!'* headline that had haunted Alex for years inserted into the text. It told of her family's shame, hinted that her mother had died of humiliation and a broken heart, and went on to insinuate that she'd only returned to get what she could after her father's death.

Somehow, as she'd read, Alex had sunk down into her chair, and now, hands trembling, she put the paper on her desk and looked up at Will.

'Poor Brian,' she whispered. 'He'll have to come back and start his search for a replacement all over again.'

'Don't be ridiculous,' Will growled. 'We'll fight this, it's slander, or libel, whatever they call the one that's printed. And we'll find out now who did it, because there couldn't be two people in town who hate you this much. We have to fight, you can't just run away.'

Alex reached out and touched his arm.

'Will,' she said, her voice catching on the simple syllable, 'if it was only me I'd do as you say, get myself a lawyer and fight to the death, but it isn't only me. It's the practice and don't say it won't suffer because people tend to believe just about everything they read. And a fair number of the practice's patients are older people who will remember the fuss at the time. Once that man was acquitted, I was branded a liar as well as a slut. I'll contact Brian, get him to find a locum, and get out as quickly as I can.'

'And me?' Will said, and Alex dredged up a smile from the black, anguished turmoil inside her.

'Do you really think I could taint Charlotte and your mother with this nonsense? It doesn't matter what we do, how we fight—and, yes, I'll get around to fighting—mud sticks, Will, you know that. And I can't have it sticking to an innocent little girl—have parents of the other kids pointing at her at kindy next year, people avoiding your mother. I won't do it but this is home for you and your family. You'll stay here, find a mother for Charlotte, and live happily ever after.'

So far, she told herself, she'd managed okay, but when she added, 'I told you my relationships didn't last,' the enormity of the loss she was facing—the loss of love—hit her like a fist slamming into her stomach, and she doubled over, resting her head on the desk, glad she hadn't eaten breakfast as bile rose in her throat.

A soft tap at the door and Marilyn entered, bearing coffee and a muffin.

'I know how busy you are, so I popped down on my own. It might be a bit cold now,' she said, speaking as if she hadn't been in floods of tears a little earlier, 'because Robyn Alcorn—the nurse from the cardiac unit—phoned to tell me it was all lies in the paper. She's said she's already rung the paper and wants someone to interview her for the other side of the story.'

That tiny scrap of unexpected kindness was the last straw.

As Alex lifted her head to thank Marilyn, the tears she'd been holding back overflowed.

Grabbing for a tissue from the box on her desk, she wiped them away.

'See, one kind word and I burst into tears,' she said. 'Of course I can't keep working here.'

'But we need you,' Marilyn said. 'With Brian and Mal away, and, what's more, all the patients you've already seen are singing your praises, talking about how they looked you up online and saw the work you'd done in Glasgow and they all think they're lucky to have you here in Port.'

'But will they think that now?' Alex asked, pushing the coffee and muffin to the side of her desk as the smell of the offering was making her feel ill.

Or more ill!

Will had been standing by the desk, statue still since Alex had pointed out the repercussions for their relationship.

His body screamed denial even as a small, still-functioning part of his brain suggested she might be right—at least about the slur on Charlotte.

But he looked at the woman at the desk and knew he couldn't let her out of his life. They could move away—all of them—he thought with a burst of optimism, but immediately discounted the solution. Alex would always be aware of the dark shadow hovering over her.

It would taint their life—their happiness.

No, there was only one way to do this and that was to fight.

'I'll see you later,' he said, and walked away, wondering what they'd done with the list, pathetic though it was.

They'd left it on the bench in the kitchen, he realised, feeling in his pocket where the key Alex had insisted he take hadn't yet been slipped onto his keyring.

He'd done a ward round and Josh was on duty so he phoned the ward and told them he'd be away from the hospital for an hour and to page him if he was needed.

Once on the ferry he phoned Robyn Alcorn's mobile number, which Marilyn had given him. She agreed only too happily to meet him at the hospital.

'I mightn't be able to help much,' she said, 'but I'll do whatever I can. It's cruel and scandalous what they've done to that woman, and she's a really good doctor too—the town needs people like her. People with roots here so they won't always be wanting to move somewhere else.'

Satisfied he'd done what he could for the moment, Will concentrated on getting safely to Alex's house, battling the hot anger churning through his body.

* * *

'Can you get Brian on the phone for me?' Alex asked
Marilyn when Will had left the room. 'I need to find out
what he'd want me to do.'

'He'll want you to stay,' Marilyn said stoutly, although
Alex suspected there was a shade of uncertainty in her
voice.

And that uncertainty raised another question.

'Have any patients cancelled?'

Marilyn looked embarrassed. She shrugged her shoulders, but as Alex held her eyes she finally admitted, 'A
couple said they'd rather see Brian or Mal and made new
appointments in a couple of weeks. No one knew Brian
might not have been back, you see.'

Alex sighed.

'So, do I have any patients? Perhaps not everyone gets
the paper.'

'Of course you've got patients,' Marilyn said. 'Don't
worry, we'll keep you busy, and being busy you won't
have time to think about all this rubbish.'

Although 'this rubbish' is what I'll have to think
about, Alex thought, but there was no point in saying
it out loud.

She made it through the day, most of her patients not
mentioning the newspaper article, and the ones who did
were angry about newspapers dredging up old scandals.

'As if it matters what happened twenty years ago,' one
elderly woman said, 'and from what I heard, acquitted or
not, that man was no good!'

Brian, when contacted, had said he'd return within
a few days, but for support, nothing else—he wanted
her to stay.

By the end of the day she was so physically and emotionally wrung out that even the ferry crossing failed to soothe her.

Arriving home, she looked in surprise at the huge bunch of bright flowers on her kitchen bench, and the note, a simple 'I love you', sitting beside it.

So Will had been here...

Just to leave flowers?

Alex looked around and realised the list was missing.

She had to smile—Superman springing into action on her behalf?—but she knew it was all too late. Whatever happened, some mud would stick and he and his daughter deserved better than that.

She opened the refrigerator and looked at the contents, Buddy perched on her shoulder, expecting a treat. It had been more than a week since she'd shopped and most things in there were looking a little tired and definitely uninspiring.

The freezer offered some ready-made meals that only needed a quick zap in the microwave but none of them appealed.

The phone rang as she was still peering into the freezer, hoping for inspiration.

A reporter, asking if she'd like to comment on the article.

'Wouldn't my comment have been more appropriate before you printed it rather than after?' she snapped, and slammed the phone back down.

At least in a town this size, with only one newspaper and no local television, she wouldn't be hounded by the press.

Deciding she wasn't hungry, she sank down onto one of the kitchen stools, rested her chin on her hand and gazed at her flowers, uncertain whether to smile or weep.

CHAPTER ELEVEN

Noises outside—a car pulling up.

Deciding there wasn't anyone in the world she wanted to see—well, apart from Will but it wouldn't be him—she had every intention of ignoring the expected ring on the doorbell.

But there was no ring, just the sound of a key in the lock, and although she knew, really, really knew she shouldn't get excited about Will being here, her heart leapt in her chest then hammered like a wild thing.

'Anyone home?' he called. 'You on the deck, Alex? You've got visitors.'

Visitors?

Plural?

She turned to see Will striding into the kitchen, a curly-headed moppet perched on one arm, and what looked like half a dozen shopping bags dangling from his other hand.

'I'd told Charlotte all about Buddy and she wanted to meet him,' he said brightly. 'And I've brought takeaway.'

Again! Alex thought, but that was only because she didn't want to think about the ramifications of this visit.

Buddy, meanwhile, was showing obvious delight to have a small person visiting him, bouncing up and down on the bench and going through his entire vocabulary, starting with the inevitable question about Bruce, telling Charlotte what a pretty girl she was, and finally finishing with such a wuss.

Charlotte was clearly delighted, looking at Alex with her father's sparkling brown eyes.

'Daddy said he could talk,' she said, kicking herself free of her father's arms and standing next to the bench, holding out a tentative hand towards the still-talking bird.

'Sometimes he talks too much,' Alex responded, her heart aching as she saw just what she'd be losing—this beautiful, trusting child, as well as Will.

'Look, Daddy, he's hopping up my arm.'

Her delight was so obvious Alex had to smile, although she wasn't so sure about Will moving to stand beside her and rest his hand on her shoulder.

She should be angry at being ambushed this way, but how could she be?

So she told herself it might be the last time they were together and allowed herself to indulge in all the wonderful feelings a simple touch on her shoulder could produce.

Charlotte was obviously entranced by the bird, who was tugging at her hair and hopping on her head.

'Look, Daddy, look at him.'

'Let's go outside and watch the river,' Will suggested, and Alex recovered enough from the unexpectedness of the visit to find some biscuits in the pantry and cheese from the fridge.

Will produced a couple of bottles of light beer from the bag he'd carried in.

'You did say you liked beer, didn't you?' he checked, and Alex could only smile.

She took the measly plate of snacks out onto the deck then squatted down to talk to Charlotte.

'I'm Alex,' she said.

'I know, Daddy told me,' the very confident young lady said. 'And he told me about the river and that you've got a boat. Can we go out on the boat?'

'It's getting a bit late for boating,' Alex said, wishing she could add that they'd go another day but not wanting to make false promises to a child.

Particularly this child!

Buddy had fluttered onto the railing and Charlotte, done with her conversation with her hostess, followed.

'Oh, you've got a beach. I like beaches. Can I play on your beach?'

This time Will came to Alex's rescue.

'I think it's a bit late and getting a bit cold for playing on the beach, poppet,' he said, 'but I brought the bag of toys you take when you go visiting. Perhaps you'd like to show them to Buddy.'

Overcome by the unexpectedness of it all, Alex sank down into a chair, watching the little girl pull a zoo of soft stuffed animals out of a bag, holding each one up for Buddy's inspection before placing it carefully in a row on the edge of the deck.

The simple scene made Alex's heart ache for what might have been—the family she'd been foolish enough to allow herself to dream of.

'Okay, here's the beer, and here's the list.'

Will sat beside her, setting her beer on the table and pulling out the list.

'The ones marked with an R are people Robyn knows and she's going to contact them. You and I are going to search out the rest. We'll start with the ones at the bottom. These are people Robyn remembered from school—older sisters of her friends. She says she knew about the touching and, because she was younger, she must have heard it from someone.'

There were six names and someone, possibly Robyn, had added phone numbers of the ex-students' parents.

Alex looked at the man who was doing all this for her—looked at the man she loved—but the despair she'd been feeling all day had only intensified.

'What good would it do?' she asked. 'It's too late now—the story is out there.'

'That's why we have to get every bit of evidence we can to refute it, and once that's done, the paper will print a retraction,' Will growled. 'And soon!'

Alex shook her head, but he wasn't having any of it, reaching out to put his arm around her shoulders, pulling her towards him as he said quietly, 'Alex, you gave me the greatest gift of all, the strength to love again. So now, my love, I'm asking you—begging you—to take some of my strength, and fight this with me.'

She looked into his eyes, intense with feeling, and the 'love' word hung between them.

He was right!

It was time to fight back.

'I'll just get my mobile,' she said, and slipped into the kitchen, returning with a smile as she watched Buddy dancing around the stuffed toys, Charlotte clapping her hands in delight.

Moving a little away from the child, she phoned the first number on the list. Wilson, she remembered the name.

Her heart jittered around in her chest as she considered the reaction of whoever answered when she said *her* name, but her voice only quivered slightly when she responded to a 'Hello'.

'Mrs Wilson, this is Alex Hudson, and I was trying to get in touch with…' she glanced at the list '…Barbara.'

'Oh, Alex, how good to hear your voice. I wanted to

phone to say I knew it was a lie. He didn't rape Barbara but he did touch her a lot. She didn't tell me until after the Spencers had left town, so I couldn't help you at the trial, but I've talked to other people and the man was a monster.'

Alex tried to speak but couldn't, the lump in her throat too big to let air through. Seeing her predicament—and probably the tears streaming down her cheeks—Will took the phone and introduced himself. Yes, he was the doctor from the ICU, yes, he remembered Mr Wilson being in. How was he?

But eventually he got the conversation back on track.

'I knew Alex back then, Mrs Wilson. She lived next door with two doctors from the hospital who believed her story completely, as my family did. But ever since she came home to see her father again, she's been a target of a stalker—phone calls, a rock through her window, nasty things spray-painted on her house. This is obviously the work of the same person and we're trying to find out anything we can about what was going on at the school and church at that time.'

Silence on this end of the phone as Mrs Wilson poured out all she knew to Will, Alex having recovered now and wondering what on earth could be taking so long.

Then Will talking again.

'Thank you, Mrs Wilson, that would be a great help. The more people who are willing to write to the paper, telling what they knew of the man, the better. Alex is a wonderful doctor and it's wrong that she should be driven out of town like this.'

More silence then, 'No, you're right, we won't let it happen.'

He put down the phone, and put out his hand for a high five.

Alex responded although it seemed a little premature to be high-fiving.

'Well?'

Will settled back beside her and took her hand, cold and slightly damp from the beer glass.

'Mrs Wilson says that her daughter told her there was a rumour he was having an affair with one of the students. If that was the case, maybe he'd told the girl he'd marry her. Given that he left town almost straight after the trial, it might have given that girl—or woman now—reason to think you'd ruined her life.'

'Oh, dear, how desperately sad,' Alex said.

Will frowned at her.

'For who?' he asked.

Alex turned towards him. 'For the girl, of course. You can bet if he didn't rape her to begin the affair, he seduced her into sex, then just used her. Maybe she was getting older than he liked and he turned to me.'

She shuddered and Will put his arm around her again.

'Let's eat before we do any more. Charlotte will have some food then promptly fall asleep. I assume you don't mind if we put her on the couch until we're finished here and I can take her home.'

'Of course not,' Alex told him, turning to watch his daughter still entertaining the bird. 'She is such a sweetie!'

The sadness in Alex's voice meant Will had to give her another hug, before getting up to heat and serve the takeaway he'd brought.

They ate at the table, Buddy behaving himself for once, and when the meal was over, Charlotte yawned.

'Are we going home, Daddy?'

Will picked her up.

'How about we stay a little longer?' he said. 'I'll take

you upstairs to have a wash and then you can have a sleep on Alex's couch while Daddy finishes some business.'

'Okay,' his daughter said sleepily, and Will blessed the fact that she'd always been a good sleeper. Playing flat out one minute then asleep the next.

'But I'll want my animals, and can Buddy come in while I sleep?

'I'm sure he can, but he mightn't stay there. Although maybe he's ready for a sleep too, and we can put his cage in near you.'

Alex was happy to put Buddy to bed in his cage, and Will moved the cage into the living room so Charlotte could turn her sleepy eyes towards her new friend.

Will put his arm around Alex's shoulder and together they watched the child fall asleep, Buddy obviously realising he had a serious job and refraining from comment.

They were walking back to the deck when Will's phone rang. Praying he wasn't needed at work, he checked the screen—not work—and answered.

And listened.

And listened.

Alex returned to the deck and waited. She'd failed in her first attempt at a phone call, so what else was there to do?

Think about the situation, that's what, her head suggested, but Will and Charlotte's visit had brought her such happiness she couldn't be angry about it.

He finally joined her, a huge smile on his face.

'Well, Mrs Wilson's story is borne out. That last call was Robyn who's heard it from three different sources—this talk of a secret affair.'

Alex shook her head in disbelief.

'And no one knew?'

'Someone must have,' Will said. 'Or at least suspected.'

Another phone ringing, this time the landline. Fortunately, Alex had carried the handset out onto the deck so that if anyone did ring, it wouldn't wake Charlotte.

Lifting it, she said a very tentative hello, then heard the familiar voice on the other end, a voice that had changed very little in twenty years.

'Caitlin, I can't believe this. How are you? Where are you?'

She listened as her old best friend explained she was living in Sydney, then added, 'But for some mad reason, I always check out the local paper on the internet.'

There was a pause before she added, 'Well, it isn't an unknown reason at all, Chrissie is a reporter for it.'

Alex remembered Caitlin's older sister. She'd been pretty and very popular at the church.

And? Alex wanted to add, but something held her back, some instinct that said Caitlin had more to say.

'I'm so sorry, Alex,' she finally continued. 'I know I should have said something at the time but my parents—well, they don't speak to me any more because I even suggested such a thing—but Chrissie was having an affair with Spencer. It had been going on for a couple of years—from when she was sixteen, like you were. I didn't know for sure until after he left town and Chrissie turned on me because my friend had ruined her life for ever. She ranted on like a madwoman, going on about how he had promised to divorce his wife and marry her and how she wanted to have his babies—awful stuff!'

'Oh, Caitlin, I'm so sorry,' was all Alex could manage.

'You're sorry?' Caitlin all but shouted the words. 'How do you think I feel that my sister has done this to you? She's probably sleeping with the newspaper editor now to get him to print such scurrilous stuff. I'm going to get a retraction, make her tell the whole story.'

'Calm down,' Alex said, smiling as she remembered the young Caitlin firing up over injustices. 'I know what she's done was unforgiveable, but if you think back to how young she was and how much it must have scarred her—let's see if we can sort it out without hurting her even more. She's a victim too.'

'Well, you're a nicer person than I am,' Caitlin said, 'but keep in touch and let me know what I *can* do.'

Alex wrote down the phone number Caitlin gave her, and promised to keep in touch.

'Found your old friend?' Will said, smiling at her as she looked up from the phone.

'Yes,' she said soberly, 'and my stalker.' She explained about Caitlin's sister, and her job as a reporter on the local paper.

Will reached out and touched her shoulder, kneading at it and running his fingers along her neck.

'But you're not going to use that, are you?' he said, and Alex smiled up at him.

'How could I?' she said. 'Do you really think a six-teen-year-old schoolgirl would have seduced him? Do you think he didn't pick her out and groom her until he knew she was ready? What he did to her has already cast a huge shadow over her life. I can't hurt her any more.'

'So,' said Will, 'we go back to the lists and get as many people as possible to write letters to the paper, naming Spencer, the women telling of the times he touched them when they were young, others explaining how their strict church upbringing meant they couldn't come forward at the trial.'

He pulled her to her feet and held her in his arms.

'We'll beat this,' he said. 'Just you wait and see!'

* * *

The media storm that followed the newspaper article was beyond anything Alex could ever have imagined. Somehow, in far-off America, the Armitages had heard of it, and a letter signed by both of them appeared in the paper.

But what affected Alex most was the number of women who came forward to say he'd behaved improperly towards them, one even admitting he'd raped her but she'd been too afraid to come forward.

They all praised Alex for speaking out when she had and so warning him against trying it again on other teenage girls.

And all sent regrets that not only had the wrong verdict been reached but that the case had once again become public.

'Which still leaves us with Chrissie,' Will said to her one evening, some weeks later, when, as had become a custom, Charlotte was asleep on the couch and they were sitting on the deck.

'I think I need to speak to her myself,' Alex said. 'I don't want to hand her in to the police, but I do want her to know that I know it was her.'

'I'll come with you—you have no idea what she could do. She could be more incensed than ever.'

Alex smiled at her protector.

'No, Will, it's something I have to do alone. I'll meet her in a public place—a coffee shop. Nothing can happen there.'

And nothing did, apart from tears and apologies and the outpouring of a grief that had been so deep for Chrissie it had escalated to a kind of madness.

'I hadn't thought about Mr Spencer for years. I'd buried all thoughts of that time,' Chrissie said through her tears. 'But when I found out that you were back in town all my anger came flooding back. Something inside me just…snapped.'

'Have you thought about getting counselling?' Alex suggested gently. 'I could get some referrals from the hospital for you.'

'Caitlin's been on to me about counselling,' Chrissie said.

'It can be very helpful,' Alex said softly. 'I should know—I saw a counsellor for years.'

Her tears spent, Chrissie managed a watery smile. 'It's a bit late, but I know I need it.'

'It's never too late,' Alex said. 'I'm only just beginning to realise that myself.' She reached across the table and took Chrissie's hand, prompting another flood of tears.

'I'm so sorry for what I did to you, Alex.' Chrissie sobbed. 'I know you could have exposed me as the girl who had the affair with him. I've been disciplined at work, even though the editor has been delighted with the controversy. Distribution numbers are way up as everyone reads the salacious gossip about a man they once thought was wonderful. I was such a fool.'

She sighed, and more tears slid down her cheeks.

Alex squeezed her fingers.

'It wasn't your fault,' she assured Chrissie. 'It was *never* your fault.'

Promising to get professional help, Chrissie said goodbye.

Emotionally drained, Alex struggled back to the rooms, where Brian Lane insisted he'd take the afternoon patients and do the ward round.

'After all,' he said, 'I'll be gone for good in a couple of weeks. My wife will take that long to pack up the kids and the house, and I want to see each and every one of our patients so they know you have my full support.'

He smiled at Alex, then added, 'Not that most of them need it. The way the phone's been ringing, I might regret leaving the practice.'

Alex thanked him and departed, driving slowly home, enjoying the ferry journey.

Friday, and Will was off duty so he and Charlotte were coming to stay over so they could go out on the river early in the morning, before it got too hot.

Alex had been very uncertain about this arrangement, but when they'd talked to Charlotte about it and showed her Alex's old room, where she would sleep, she'd asked, 'But where will you sleep, Daddy? Will Alex let you sleep in her bed? Because that room's nicer than the other room.'

'It's as if she's blessed us,' Will had said, and Alex knew he was probably right.

They came at dusk, Will laden down as ever with bags of toys and clothing.

But this time Alex had cooked dinner for them, spaghetti and meatballs at Charlotte's request.

With Buddy on her shoulder and tweaking at her hair, the little girl played happily on the deck while Alex finished the dinner and Will made a salad to go with it.

Charlotte ate and immediately asked to go to bed.

'But with Buddy in his cage as well,' she insisted.

Finally alone, they stood on the deck, looking at the river, silvered by the light of the moon.

'Have I ever mentioned that I love you?' Will murmured, kissing Alex on the temple.

'Not often enough,' Alex whispered, leaning into him and turning so his lips could meet her mouth.

The kiss was different, not a prelude to passion, as so many of their kisses had become, but more a declaration of the love they shared and a promise of what was to come.

Together they had faced the pain of the accusations against Alex and come through it, their love stronger for being forged in devastation.

Slowly, they made their way upstairs, opening the gate at the top that Will had installed to keep Charlotte safe. They stopped at the door of Alex's old room and looked at the sleeping child, Buddy in his cage on the desk at the end of the bed and Alex's old toy galah clasped in her hands.

'She's a precious gift,' Alex whispered. 'Thank you for sharing her with me.'

'You're the gift, to both of us,' he countered. 'You gave me back the gift of love.'

They made love quietly, ever aware of the sleeping child just down the hall, and Alex fell asleep with her hand on Will's shoulder, secure, for the first time, in a relationship.

A relationship that exceeded all her dreams.

EPILOGUE

ALEX COLLECTED CHARLOTTE from kindergarten, laughing as the little girl hugged her around the legs.

'That baby's taking up too much room and I can't hug you properly,' Charlotte complained.

'But not for much longer,' Alex promised her. 'One more week, that's all you have to wait.'

The dark eyes, so like Will's, looked up at her.

'And you really will let me help look after him?'

'Or her,' Alex reminded Charlotte. They'd decided not to know the sex of the child she carried for all Charlotte was convinced it would be a boy.

'And, yes,' Alex added, 'we'll need you to help. When the baby's out on the deck in his pram, you'll have to keep Buddy from bouncing on him and waking him up.'

'I can do that easily. Buddy loves me,' Charlotte declared, as Alex fastened her into her car seat.

And Buddy did indeed love the little girl who'd come to live with them. He was her constant companion when she was at home, and even greeted her before he greeted Alex when the pair of them came in together.

'And we'll call him Bob.' Charlotte wasn't finished with the baby conversation and her favourite television character was named Bob.

'We'll see,' Alex responded, glad Charlotte wasn't

old enough to understand a parental 'We'll see' often meant no.

Or even 'No way'.

'So how's my family?' Will asked, coming out of the house to greet the pair.

'What are you doing home?'

Alex's question was lost in Charlotte's cries of delight as she flung herself into his arms.

'I thought my wife stopping work, even if it's only for a few months, was a special enough occasion to deserve a celebration so I skived off, leaving Josh in charge, and cooked our dinner. You sit out on the deck and put your feet up, and I'll bring you a small libation of French champagne.'

'French yet!' Alex teased, finally getting her turn in her husband's arms.

But she was happy to sit on the deck and put her feet up. There'd be little time to rest after the baby arrived. She'd taken three months' maternity leave then Will would take the next three months off work, so the baby would have a parent at home all the time.

After that a nanny would come two days a week, with both Alex and Will working alternate short weeks.

Alex looked out at the river and sighed.

In theory it sounded good, but would it work?

'You're worrying again,' Will scolded, as he brought out their drinks, the champagne cooling in her parents' ice bucket.

She touched the side of it, thinking back, remembering her parents in happier times, aware that all the pain and bitterness she'd felt had vanished through the power of love.

Will's love!

And the smile of a little girl who already called her Mummy...

'Happy?' Will asked, as he sat down beside her and took her hand.

'There should be a better word,' Alex said, smiling as Charlotte and Buddy joined them, both having sensed there might be biscuits on the table.

'We're calling the baby Bob,' Charlotte announced to her father.

Will raised one quizzical eyebrow at Alex.

'This too shall pass,' she said. 'We know that now. With the love we share we're strong enough to cope with anything. Even a little girl called Bob...'

* * * * *

MILLS & BOON
True Love
Romance from the Heart

Celebrate true love with tender stories of heartfelt romance, from the rush of falling in love to the joy a new baby can bring, and a focus on the emotional heart of a relationship.

LET'S TALK
Romance

For exclusive extracts, competitions
and special offers, find us online:

- facebook.com/millsandboon
- @MillsandBoon
- @MillsandBoonUK

Get in touch on 01413 063232

MILLS & BOON

THE HEART OF ROMANCE

A ROMANCE FOR EVERY READER

MODERN

Prepare to be swept off your feet by sophisticated, sexy and seductive heroes, in some of the world's most glamourous and romantic locations, where power and passion collide.

HISTORICAL

Escape with historical heroes from time gone by. Whether your passion is for wicked Regency Rakes, muscled Vikings or rugged Highlanders, awaken the romance of the past.

MEDICAL

Set your pulse racing with dedicated, delectable doctors in the high-pressure world of medicine, where emotions run high and passion, comfort and love are the best medicine.

True Love

Celebrate true love with tender stories of heartfelt romance, from the rush of falling in love to the joy a new baby can bring, and a focus on the emotional heart of a relationship.

Desire

Indulge in secrets and scandal, intense drama and plenty of sizzling hot action with powerful and passionate heroes who have it all: wealth, status, good looks…everything but the right woman.

HEROES

Experience all the excitement of a gripping thriller, with an intense romance at its heart. Resourceful, true-to-life women and strong, fearless men face danger and desire - a killer combination!

To see which titles are coming soon, please visit

millsandboon.co.uk/nextmonth